Alphonse Du Breuil

Vineyard Culture Improved and Cheapened

Alphonse Du Breuil

Vineyard Culture Improved and Cheapened

ISBN/EAN: 9783337423070

Printed in Europe, USA, Canada, Australia, Japan

Cover: Foto ©Andreas Hilbeck / pixelio.de

More available books at **www.hansebooks.com**

VINEYARD CULTURE

IMPROVED AND CHEAPENED

BY

A. DU BREUIL

Professor of Viticulture and Arboriculture in the Royal School of Arts and Trades

PARIS

TRANSLATED BY E. AND C. PARKER

Of Longworth's Wine House

With Notes and Adaptations to American Culture

BY

JOHN A. WARDER

Author of "American Pomology"

144 ILLUSTRATIONS

CINCINNATI, OHIO

ROBERT CLARKE & CO. PUBLISHERS, 65 WEST FOURTH STREET

1867

EDITOR'S PREFACE.

IN attempting to adapt this manual to the wants of
American vine planters, the Editor has been actuated by
a desire to add something to the usefulness of the work when
it is presented to his countrymen, in its new form.

Prof. Du Breuil is one who deservedly stands high in the
horticultural world, and he has been honored with the post
of teacher of vine and tree culture in the Imperial School of
Arts and Trades of France, and has traveled in the provinces
as a lecturer employed by the Government. His published
works are standard.

The vastness of the interest arising from the cultivation of
the vine in France can only be judged by the immense returns
of the products made to the Government. This is also shown
by the production of such magnificent works as the large folio
of VICTOR RENDU, or the *Ampelographie Universelle* of COUNT
ODART The former volume, which may be seen in the Agricultural Library at Columbus, Ohio, has a map of France,
showing the portions devoted to viticulture, and a list of the
regions in which the vine is cultivated, from which it appears
that only eleven of the eighty-six provinces have no vineyards.
Twenty-seven produce common wine, and forty yield a
superior article. In the south, between latitude 43 and 44

degrees, are produced the Roussillon, the Languedoc, and the heavy wines of Provence. As we proceed northward, the vineyards produce a lighter wine, but possessed of great delicacy.

To give an idea of the extent of this culture and its amounts, the following statement is made on the authority of Victor Rendu:

In 1857 there were 2,000,000 hectares occupied as vine-yards; nearly 5,000,000 acres. The produce amounted to 30,783,223 hectolitres, over 813,000,000 gallons of wine, and 1,085,802 hectrolitres, nearly 29,000,000 gallons of brandy. The annual value being 478,088,302 francs, or nearly 91,000-000 dollars.

In this country vine culture is yet in its infancy, but our people have made rapid strides, *now that they have started in the right direction,* and there is no calculating the extent which our vineyards may attain within a few years. The character-istic energy and intelligence, with abundant wealth, have been embarked in the business, and the efforts must be crowned with successful results. Still we have much to learn, and for want of proper information and attention to the pointings of experience guided by common sense, many will fail.

When I say we have at length started in the right direction I mean to refer to the errors of the early vine planters, who attempted to naturalize and acclimatize the foreign grapes, and who signally failed. Now, we are producing new varieties by crossing and selecting the species and varieties indigenous to the country, which are better adapted to our soils and climate, and among the numbers that are annually presented to the public, there will, no doubt, be some that are eminently fitted for our cultivation.   The great difficulty will soon be to make a judicious selection of those we wish to plant.

In reference to this subject, Mr. T. S. KENNEDY, President of the Kentucky Horticultural Society remarks: " Grape culture in this country is infinitely more profitable than it is in Europe, where from a single species more than two thousand good varieties have been produced, and upwards of four hundred of them are now cultivated in France and Spain exclusively for wine."* He supports his statement by the following statistics, taken from Harasthy's work.

THE AVERAGE WINE PRODUCTION OF EUROPE REDUCED TO AMERICAN ACRES AND GALLONS.

	Acres.	Millions gallons.	Gallons per acre
Austria, and her provinces	2,685,950	714†	265
Greece, and her islands	41,781	8	195
Italy	2,887,970	1,275	441
France	5,013,774	884	176
Spain	955,004	144	152
Portugal	238,751	26	107
Belgium, Switzerland, Ionian Islands . .	112,212	4	33
German States	358,338	52	149

The aggregate number of acres under vine culture in Europe is 12,285,780.

The total average yield of wine per year is 3,107,039,000 gallons.

The wines, at twenty-five cents per gallon, are worth, total annual value, $776,759,750.

---

* " Western Ruralist," Louisville, Ky., Vol. 1, No. 1.   April, 1867.
† Of these 714,000,000 gallons, Hungary produces some 450,000,000.

In Germany, the average income per acre, at twenty-five cents per gallon, amounts to $37 18.

In the other countries, the average per acre, $63 98.

But taking each country separately, their annual average production of wines amounts, at twenty-five cents per gallon, as follows:

	Total Amount.	Per Acre.
Austria, and her provinces	$178,500,000	$ 66 46
Greece, and Grecian Islands.	2,040,000	48 82
Italy	318,750,000	110 37
France	221,000,000	44 07
Spain	36,125,000	37 92
Portugal	6,375,000	26 70
Belgium, Switzerland, Ionian Islands . .	942,500	8 50
German States	13,026,250	37 18

As yet the high prices of grapes and of wines in this country, and the large yield per acre, have been such that the gross earnings of the land appear to sustain the assertion of Mr. Kennedy, though when our gross product approximates that of older wine countries, it can not be doubted that the returns to the farmer will be greatly diminished; at the same time the cheaper production will be greeted as a boon to the consumer, and this is a consummation which is much to be desired.

Two hundred and fifty gallons per acre has been considered a very moderate estimate of the average crops of our vineyards, four times that amount having been produced, and one dollar a gallon is certainly a very low figure for the product. But the true friends of the vineyard interest look forward to the time of much cheaper production.

The careful attention of the reader is asked to the teachings of Prof. Du Breuil, from whom we may learn much that is useful, though we may not be inclined to adopt literally all of his suggestions. The American workman is not a machine, blindly to follow in the ruts that have been worn for him by his predecessors, nor hastily to adopt suggestions: it is our boast that we have intelligent labor, which ever becomes skilled labor—the thinking laborer has greatly the advantage over the mere routinist, and though he may not be a good subject, the American workman makes a capital sovereign, who always prefers to direct his own efforts, and will often improve upon the teachings of his professor.

To distinguish the Editorial matter from the text it is set in smaller type, and within brackets.

JNO. A. WARDER.

North Bend, O., April, 1867.

AUTHOR'S PREFACE.

THE culture of the vine, as now practiced, exists under circumstances which have necessarily influenced the various processes of which it is composed. In those regions which are at a distance from the great centers of consumption, such as at Languedoc, l'Aunis, Saintonge, the want of a market and the difficulty of transportation have reduced the price of wine to the minimum. Hence it has become necessary to reduce the expenses of cultivation as much as possible. The vines are not staked, but cover the ground with their shoots; to diminish the expense of transportation to market, the wines are distilled into brandy.

Burgundy, Bordelais, Champaign, Maconnais, Beaujolais, etc., are more favorably situated as to outlets for their products; they have a denser population, and their climate is more favorable for the production of wines of high quality, commanding a better price. Here it is justifiable to expend more capital in the culture and management of the vineyard, the vines are set more closely, and are trained upon stakes.

However, within a few years, the circumstances that existed at the introduction of vine planting, and which then modified its arrangements, have been materially changed in several respects. The price of labor is not only exorbitant, but in many localities hands can scarcely be obtained. Hence the absolute necessity of substituting the plow for the hoe, wherever that implement can be used. Then, again, the constantly increasing price of stakes must require the adoption of some cheaper mode of support. Railroads, which penetrate every portion of the empire, have opened markets to the most remote parts, and have thus enhanced the value of the products; this, in the south, will tend greatly to diminish the production of brandies, because of the greater value of the wine.

These increased facilities of transportation have induced great changes in the culture of some vineyards. Thus the cheap wines of Languedoc are now easily carried to Switzerland, and come into competition with those of the Jura, which are thus almost driven from the market. It will therefore be necessary to cheapen the production in the vineyards of that region. Elsewhere, as in l'Aunis and Saintonge, one half of the northern wines are mixed with a small proportion of brandy, flooding the market under the name of "Cognac,"* very sensibly lowering the price of brandy wines. In those regions it will be necessary to substitute, to a large extent, vines that will produce good table wines, in place of those choice varieties now grown.

The increasing value of choice wines should direct our attention to the inquiry whether it would not be profitable to endeavor to shelter the vines that produce them, and thus to protect them from sudden changes of temperature, which so often diminish the vintage.

The various modes of cultivating a vineyard in different places are no doubt the result of long-continued observation

---

*Not Cognac *Brandy* but Cognac *Wines.*

and experience, and should therefore be regarded with consideration, but it can not be claimed that the management has reached its highest degree of perfection, nor that it may not be much benefited by the sciences which have made such valuable advances during the last half century.

These considerations have induced me to believe that the time has arrived when we should bring to the vineyard all the improvements that are adapted to its management. These are the objects that we have endeavored to attain in the book we now offer to the public; which is, indeed, simply the reproduction of the lessons upon this important subject which have been presented at the School of Arts and Trades, and in the several Departments of France where the lectures were repeated.

We shall successively examine the various operations of vine culture, and shall endeavor to modify them in the following particulars:

1st.   The substitution of the plow for manual labor.

2d.   The use of wire trellises instead of stakes.

3d.   Shelter from inclement weather.

The various processes of cultivation being modified as much as possible, we shall make the application to each of our principal vineyards in the different regions into which we have been called during the ten years of our traveling instruction.

CONTENTS

VARIOUS MODES OF SUPPORTING GRAPE-VINES—*Continued.*

IX. OPERATIONS OTHER THAN PRUNING.

X. ANNUAL CULTIVATION OF THE SOIL.

XI. MANURES AND CHEMICAL APPLICATIONS FOR VINE-YARDS.

MANURES AND CHEMICAL APPLICATIONS FOR VINEYARDS
—Continued. PAGE

XII. MAINTENANCE AND RENEWAL OF THE PLANTS.

XIII. INCLEMENT WEATHER, DISEASES, HURTFUL INSECTS.

VINEYARD CULTURE

IMPROVED AND CHEAPENED.

LIKE most of our most useful food plants, the vine, *Vitis vinifera* of the botanists, appears to have come originally from Asia. From the time of Homer it was found in a wild state in Sicily and Italy; but prior to this the Phœnicians had introduced it into cultivation, first in the Islands of the Archipelago, in Greece, then in Sicily and Italy, and finally in Marseilles. As it progressed into more temperate regions the products of the vine became successively meliorated. The mild climate of France is the most favorable for the production of good wines; and so this branch of culture has extended so greatly that in 1815 it occupied a surface of two millions hectares, producing nearly forty millions of hectolitres of wine, valued at a billion, paying to the State and to the communes, more than two hundred millions, and furnishing occupation to more than eight millions inhabitants. This has, therefore, been placed in the second rank in the scale of the land interest of the country.

M. de Gasparin has well remarked that in the center, and especially in the south of France, the vine yields a harvest, the product of which is almost certain, whereas other crops are not always to be depended on; that it was one that needed the least labor relatively to the net profit received, that it banished fallows, and continuously occupied the whole extent of country that had a suitable climate; that it is adapted to all kinds of soils, and occupied those which produced nothing but useless thorns and briers; that it furnishes labor at all seasons, to all ages and to both sexes; that it yields several important products, and valuable merchandise; finally, that it requires little manure, allowing this to be applied to other crops.

I.

CHOICE OF SITE FOR A VINEYARD.

CLIMATE.—The vine grows vigorously in all parts of France, and its berries will ripen at almost any point; still its pulp does not acquire in all parts those qualities which render it fit for the mannufacture of wine. The saccharine properties indispensable to vinous fermentation are not formed in sufficient quantities in the pulp of the grape, except under influence of a bright sun and pretty high temperature. Beyond the 50th degree of latitude, the vine no longer meets with the necessary degree of heat, and the sugar of its grapes yields nothing by fermentation but an acid liquor.

But though an insufficient degree of heat injures the quality of the grape, a too high temperature is not less hurtful. The saccharine principle, in that case, is developed in such abundance that the grapes yield a thick liquid, rich in alcohol, but of very inferior quality.—

This is what occurs in vines cultivated below the 35th degree of latitude.

As we approach too near the equator this cultivation often meets with another difficulty, namely : the uninterrupted growth of the vine, which produces on the same stock blossoms, green fruits, and ripe fruits ; each bunch displaying the same phenomenon ; wine making is therefore impracticable.

It is, then, between the 35th and 50th degrees of latitude that the vine can be cultivated to advantage. It is also between these two limits that we find the richest wine countries, such as Spain, Portugal, Italy, Austria, Styria, Carinthia, Hungary, Transylvania, and especially France, which is celebrated for the variety and quality of its vines.

Latitude, however, is not the only condition on which success depends ; we must also take into account the elevation of the soil above the level of the sea, for that circumstance exercises no small influence on the climate of a country. This explains why certain localities in France, otherwise situated in a latitude favorable to the vine, but too elevated above the level of the sea, do not admit of this cultivation. In Hungary, the cultivation of the vine ceases at an elevation of about 980 feet ; in the north of Switzerland at 180 feet, while it reaches to 2,130 feet on the southern slope of the Alps, and may reach 3,150 feet in the southern Apennines. Thus we see that this limit of elevation varies as we approach or recede from the equator.

The exposure of the land, and its natural shelter, also modify the condition of climate : the southern exposure being warmer than the northern, the limit of elevation toward the south will be higher than toward the north. Certain deep valleys, sheltered from the cold winds, will admit of the cultivation of the vine, although situated beyond the degree of latitude to which it can usually be grown. Other regions, although situated within this limit, exposed to the cold and damp winds of the north-west and west, will not admit of the production of wine. The deep and sheltered valleys of the Moselle and Lower Rhine, on the 51st degree of latitude, produce excellent wines; while in the provinces of ancient Normandy, and the largest portion of Brittany, much further south, the culture of the vine had to be abandoned.

[In applying these data as a guide to the selection of a site for grape culture, in this country, we must bear in mind the fact that equal latitudes are not blessed with a similar mean temperature. Humboldt long ago observed a very great difference in the climates of countries that were equidistant from the equator. His observations, and those of other students of physical geography, have resulted in the establishment of lines of equal temperature. These are called the *isothermal lines;* they are very curiously curved, and do not at all coincide with the parallels of latitude. This is very manifest in the maps that have been prepared, upon which the lines are laid down. It will be observed that a given line reaches much farther to the north on the Pacific than on the Atlantic coast of this Continent, while in South America the reverse is the case. In the interior of our Continent the lines are deflected northward on account of the effects of the interior basin, in which we reside, which is about one thousand feet above the level of the sea. The line which passes through Savannah, Ga.,—(N. Lat. 32°), dips southward in its westward course, skirting along the coast of Texas, and from the point of its crossing the Rio Grande at its mouth—Lat. 26°—it is deflected southward in its passage over the high lands of Mexico, to Lat. 20°, turning again to the north as it descends the coast, and meeting the peninsular of Lower California near the tropic of Cancer. Here we have, in crossing the Continent, an extreme variation of 12 degrees of latitude. If we trace these lines upon a map of the world, we shall see that as they leave our Continent eastward they all turn decidedly to the northward, on account of the influence of the gulf-stream, which carries the temperature from the tropical seas toward the arctic region, and striking the west coast of Europe, modifies the climate there, even in high latitudes. Let us now follow the line that passes through Cincinnati, in its eastward course; it is but slightly turned to the north until it reaches the Atlantic, when it is deflected northward, and crossing this ocean is projected upon the west coast of France, in latitude 49, and reaches the banks of the Rhine, in the wine region, latitude 48 degrees. We are in the habit of·considering France a warm country; and so it is, as shown by these lines, though nearly the whole of its territory lies north of latitude 43, which is near the north line of Iowa, passes through Milwaukie and Madison, Wisconsin, Grand Haven on the west and Fort Gratiot on the east of Michigan, by the mouth of Lake Huron, through Canada, to Niagara Falls, north of Albany, and almost touches Maine as it reaches the ocean. The latitude of the wine region of the Rhine, in France and Germany—49 north—is found in the inhospitable region of British North America, a whole degree beyond Lake Superior.

This difference in the temperature of the two Continents is attributed in great part to the different distribution of land and water under the equator in each. Europe feels the influence produced by the broad extent of burning sands exposed to a tropical sun in Africa, while in the Western Hemisphere the space between the equator and the tropic of Cancer is chiefly water, which reflects the rays and does not heat the air to the same extent as the sands of the desert.

Certain data have been reached which are of great importance. We can not depend entirely upon a given mean temperature of the whole year, for this may be accompanied by great extremes, on the one hand, from which the resultant mean has been derived; or, on the other hand, there are regions, like some of the uplands of South America, where the mean temperature is as high as that required by the grape, but the heat is at no time great enough to induce the proper ripening of the fruit—the change to sugar.

The summer mean temperature, or that of the season of growth, is considered the safer criterion, and it is stated that 65° is the lowest at which grapes will ripen. Baussingault, the distinguished French Philosopher, who has bestowed much careful study and observation upon the influence of meteorology upon vine-growing, has left us the following conclusion: "in addition to a summer and an autumn sufficiently hot, it is indispensable that at a given period—that which follows the appearance of the seeds—there should be a month, the mean temperature of which does not fall below 66.2° Fahrenheit."

Mr. James S. Lippincott, of New Jersey, has contributed some very valuable papers upon the philosophical bearing of climate upon the culture of the grape. These appeared in the Reports of the Agricultural Department at Washington, for 1862 and 1863, and they should be carefully studied by all who are intending to plant vineyards.]

Soil.—Clayey, compact, impervious soils are not adapted to vine culture; the superabundance of moisture which they contain, causes the root to rot, and the stocks to languish and droop. Silico-argillaceous, and rich, deep soils, do not suit the vine any better. It will grow in them with great vigor, but that very vigor in-jures the quality of the grapes, which then contain an insufficient proportion of the saccharine principle, and consequently yield but a light wine, without aroma.—Nevertheless, while taking into account all these objections, it may be said that all soils, suitably exposed and in a favorable climate, are adapted to this cultivation, whatever their composition may be in other respects. A glance at the different soils which produce the best wines of France will prove this.

Silico-argillaceous soils mixed with a considerable portion of gravel and silicious stones: such as the vineyards on the banks of the Rhine, the hills of Reims, of Romanée-Conti (Burgundy).

Sand, more or less pure, mixed with round stones of various sizes, so much so as even at times to give the ground the appearance of the dried-up bed of a torrent: vineyards of Bordeaux and Médoc.

Limestone soils: vineyards of Champagne, Pierry, Ay, Èpernay, Avize and Grammont; vineyards of Xérès in Andalusia.

Clay-slate soils: vineyards of Malaga, Granada, Aragon and Anjou.

Other celebrated vineyards are located upon granitic lands, such as those of Mas, of Condrieu, of l'Ermitage, of Saint Peray, as also a few of the vineyards of Burgundy.

Although volcanic lands are rarely used as vineyards, they nevertheless deserve to be mentioned. The vineyard of Roquemaure in Vivarais, some of those on the banks of the Rhine, those of Vesuvius and Ætna, are located on soils of this description.

[Our experience in this country has led us to similar conclusions, though the most intelligent grape growers express themselves very much at fault, when asked to describe the best *"grape lands."* We find the vine cultivated with success and profit in the sands of New Jersey; indeed, some varieties appear to escape the mildew, in such soil, that suffer from the malady elsewhere.

On the pebbly drift of the Hudson, some vines have been remarkably successful. On a similar, but more fertile soil, in western New York, and in Pennsylvania, on Lake Erie, the grape-culture has been very successful, and along the same shore we find the vine yielding most satisfactory results on the light, sandy soils, on the rich limestone clays, and even in the close, heavy, whitish clays of the shales, some of which look cold and repulsive enough to the farmer. All of these are respectively called *"grape-soils,"* and are claimed to possess peculiar advantages.

In the blue-grass region were planted some of the first vineyards of the West. The French in Kentucky, and the Swiss at Vevay, Indiana, selected the rich, heavy clays of this limestone region, which occupies a circle around Cincinnati that would be described by a radius of fifty miles. Within this magic ring the first—and the first successful—efforts at grape-culture were made. The soils here are sufficiently heavy, and by some are considered too rich for the profitable culture of the vine.

The limey clays, tempered with the detritus of sandstones, as found in the coal-measures, have also been very successfully planted with the grape, about Pittsburgh and Wheeling, and at some other points. In the prairies of Illinois, the grape has been grown on black soils, but it can hardly be said with success, except upon the borders of the Mississippi, where it is chiefly planted on the loess deposit, which also prevails to some extent in the lands of Missouri that are devoted to the vine.

With all these facts before us, can we say with confidence that this or that is essentially a *grape-soil*, to the exclusion of other lands with very different characters and constituents?

This subject has been repeatedly brought before the members of the *Ohio Pomological Society*, and of the *Lake Shore Grape Growers' Association*, and the reader is referred to the papers and discussions printed in their Reports. It would, indeed, appear that any and all soils may prove to be adapted to the culture of some variety af the grape.]

Thus we see that the vine can give good results in soils of various composition, but those soils are better adapted to this cultivation if they contain a certain quantity of pebbly stones, which appear to act favorably on the fertility of the soil, by rendering it more accessible to air and water, and assisting it to draw the heat from the sun's rays. Therefore, care must be had not to clear the soil of pebbles, if appropriated to vine-culture, but only to remove such large stones as may impede cultivation.

[The radiating power of stones upon the surface of the soil, has been suggested as a valuable means of aiding the maturing of the grape, and has been applied to practice in New England, where this material often abounds. The stones were all taken out of the soil in its preparation, the vines were well cultivated until they were established, and then a complete covering of stones was replaced upon the surface. These served the purpose of a mulch, and kept down the weeds, but allowed the vines to grow and spread upon a trellis near their surface. This was found to exercise a beneficial influence in the ripening of the fruit.

It is a very common thing with vine-dressers to express

their preference for leaving the shelly masses of our lime-stones upon the surface of the ground, instead of gathering and removing them. They are supposed to retain moisture in the soil as well as to radiate heat at night.]

The knowledge we possess of the unfavorable influence which a superabundance of moisture exercises on the vine, points out clearly enough the kind of sub-soil which is adapted to it. The substratum being of an impervious nature, water, by accumulating on its surface, would cause the roots of the vine to rot, or would keep near them an excess of moisture injurious to the quality of their product. Nevertheless, an impervious subsoil is more injurious to the vine in a temperate climate, and in a naturally moist atmosphere, than in a burning clime, where the vines frequently suffer from excessive drought.

In short, it is chiefly owing to this property, which the soil has, of receiving and retaining moisture, that we must attribute the principal differences in wines. This quantity, greater or smaller, quickens or slackens vegetation, which influences the transformation of the "*must*," and thus decides the relative proportions of all its component parts.

These observations have been confirmed by the examination of the vine regions in their aggregate. The wines from the hills of the West (Portugal, Médoc) are rich in tannin, and not so sweet as those from the East (Granada, Malaga, Xérès, Syracuse). Passing from south to north we also find the proportion of sugar decreasing as the moisture increases and the temperature falls. This is demonstrated by the successive examination of the wines of Languedoc, those of the banks of the Rhône, of Burgundy, and of the Rhine. We know likewise that wet years produce more acid, and less sugary, wines.

SITUATION.—A vineyard may be located in a valley, on an elevated plateau, or on a hill-side: let us examine whether all these positions are equally favorable.

Narrow vales are little adapted to vine-culture; the dampness of the atmosphere is too great; it prevents the ripening of the grapes, and the vines are more exposed than elsewhere to the spring frosts.

Neither are elevated plateaux, nor the crowns of high hills, more favorable: there, the air being too sharp, and always in motion, hardens the skin of the grapes, and they contain but a very small proportion of saccharine matter. Unsheltered plains produce very good wines; take, for instance, the vineyards of Médoc, those on the plains of Thassis (Drôme) or of Roussillon, of Crau, near Arles, of St. Nicholas de Bourgeuil, in Touraine etc., etc. Lastly, the hills of Burgundy, and those of a great number of other localities, celebrated for the quality of their wines, also prove how well adapted are inclined plains, or hill-sides, to the culture of the vine.

Upon the whole, in the northern portion of the belt which we have described as adapted to the vine, we must choose, *first*, large, level, open plains; then hills, and hillocks, or slight declivities, and, as we approach toward the southern portion of that belt, we must ascend toward the summits of high mountains, in order to remove the vine from the too scorching heat of the plains. The slopes of Vesuvius, the high hills of Madeira, the cloud-capped rocks of Teneriffe, and of the Cape, produce wines that are much esteemed, while the plains that are situated in their neighborhood, yield a liquor that is little sought after. To the north it is the reverse: the wines of exposed plains, or hillocks, are generally superior to those grown on the mountains.

[The subject of drainage and its necessity can not be too strongly urged upon vine-planters, especially those who select heavy lands. The majority of grapes require a porous and well drained soil, through which the superabundant moisture may readily percolate, and to which it will also return by capillarity in a period of drought; hence the importance of loams, or even sandy loams, for all cultivated lands, and hence the necessity for drainage in our heavy clays. For further argument in favor of drainage, and for instruction in the details of performing the operations, the reader is referred to the excellent manuals upon that subject which may now be obtained.

Surface drainage is very well in its way, but can not at all supply the place of thorough underdraining. The methods of applying surface drainage to the vineyard will be explained in another page.]

It will be equally well to avoid declivities that are too abrupt, for in such cases the cost of cultivation will be much greater. The plow can not be used there; the rain floods tear up the ground and wash down a portion of the soil, which has to be carried up again by hand. The transporting of manure, as well as the gathering of the grapes, is much more difficult.

[In our own country we have similar illustrations of the different situations that have been appropriated to grape culture. On the banks of the Ohio the first vineyards were all planted upon the abrupt hill sides, where it was necessary to perform every part of the labor by hand. From the preparation of the soil to the culture of the vines, and even manuring them, when that was done, nothing but human labor could be applied. Gradually the vineyards were extended upward to the exposed hill tops, and downward until they expanded over the level terraces of the river valleys. It was soon discovered that where the land was sufficiently level to admit of the use of the plow, the cultivation could be much more easily performed, and vines were much more extensively planted. Next came the observation that those on the tops of the hills, freely exposed to light and air, were more productive, and in every way preferable and more satisfactory in their results, being much more cheaply managed also.

Those on the gravelly and sandy river terraces, though easily tended, did not generally succeed, but planters on elevated plateaux of clayey soil were more successful with their vineyards.

In the northern portion of Ohio, on Lake Erie, flat lands and gentle slopes have always been selected, and they have been remarkably successful, in some cases, when but a few feet above the level of the lake, except in certain situations where a black, mucky soil was chosen, when the grape diseases soon made their appearance, and destroyed the crop. In that part of the country the soils vary, as above stated, but while heavy clay lands, rich in lime, are preferred, those of a more stony character, and gravelly drifts, with good natural drainage, have been found very successful, and some soils called sandy have yielded good results.

With the high price of labor in this country, it is absolutely necessary for us to select our sites with reference to performing the work of the vineyard as much as possible by the use of animals, with plows and cultivators. We must have access to our vineyards with the horse and wagon, to transport material to and from the soil, instead of depending upon human thews and shoulders, for "packing" the manure to the exhausted soil in baskets, or for transporting the abundant vintage from the vines to the press; horse-power must be applied, as cheaper than man-power, for which there will be found abundant need in the higher operations of the vineyard: therefore the abrupt declivities of our hill-sides will be abandoned for the plains and gentle slopes and hill-tops.]

It has been noticed that the neighborhood of rivers exercises a beneficial influence upon the products of the vine; certain it is that the most celebrated vineyards are almost all situated in the vicinity of large watercourses. Tokay wine is made from grapes grown on the Theiss; the celebrated wines of l'Hermitage, Côte-Rôtie, and Condrieu, are grown on the hills which border the Rhône. The Garonne flows not far from the best growths of the red and white wine of the gravelly districts extending from Langon to Bordeaux; the Gironde waters the far-famed vineyards of Margeaux, Latour and Laffite; the Dordogne is separated from those of Saint Emilion only by the alluvial plains stretched along its right bank. The Loire, the Marne and the Seine, see, as it were, nothing but vines spread over the whole extent of their course, and the famous ridge which traverses Burgundy overlooks a plain watered by the Saône. It is true that the no less celebrated vineyards of Champagne and the Côte-d'Or might be cited as exceptions. For this reason M. de Gasparin attributes the superior quality of all these growths to their location on hill-sides, and to their good exposure, rather than to the vicinity of water-courses.

[The influence exerted by rivers in favoring the products of the vine, as cited by the author, is probably not merely owing to the mere presence of water, for many of the streams are of moderate size. There are other concomitant circumstances which must exert a happy influence: near the streams, there are often terraces of warm and gravelly soils; the land is nearer the level of the sea, and may be sheltered by ranges of high mountains; on the sides of the valleys, advantage is often taken of favoring exposure to the more direct rays of the sun, and the surrounding hights may afford both reflected heat and shelter. But beside all this, the general level of the country, in a large portion of the grape region of northern Europe, lies at such an elevation as to be too cold for the successful cultivation of the vine; the mean temperature of the summer months is too low; while, in the favored spots just indicated, the requisite conditions for the vine are found. In this country, we have not generally the same differences of elevation between the rivers and the uplands, so as to make a marked change in the temperature, but, on the other hand, we have an obnoxious element arising from such situations adjacent to the streams. This is the occurrence of fogs, which are oftentimes disastrous to the welfare of the grape, when occurring at midsummer. These fogs, and an excessive rain-fall, alternating with periods when the atmosphere is very dry, are exceedingly injurious to the vine in the vicinity of some of our rivers.

The influence of the lakes, however, has proved to be exceedingly valuable, in so modifying the climate, both in winter and summer, as to enable us to cultivate the vine in latitudes which were formerly considered too high for it—as in northern Ohio, and all along the southern shore of Lake Erie, and portions of that of Lake Ontario, as well as in the vicinity of some of the lakes of New York State. The observations made upon Lake Erie will demonstrate this, and explain the phenomenon. In the spring, the waters are chilled by the supplies from the upper lakes, and thus retard vegetation until all danger of spring frosts has passed by. When the sap starts, at last, everything goes on rapidly, and without check. The mean temperature rises to a sufficient hight for the grape, and the accumulated warmth of the lake water modifies the temperature, so as to prevent autumnal frosts, and the season is prolonged in the same ratio that it was shortened in the spring, and the necessary length of time is furnished for the maturation of the fruit.

It has been demonstrated, for a series of years, that grapes will ripen in such situations, when favored by these influences, although they fail to reach maturity at inland situations much further south, as in the interior of Ohio.

For further details, and illustrations of the happy influence of our lakes, the reader is referred to essays and discussions, to be found in the Reports of the Societies above mentioned, which can be had of the Secretary, M. B. Bateham, Painesville, Ohio.

The following remarks upon this subject, are from an article on the "Climatology of American Grapes," by Jas. S. Lippincott, of New Jersey, which may be found in the Annual Report of the Department of Agriculture, at Washington, D. C., 1862, p. 206:

" The meliorating influence of our lakes is too marked to escape our attention. The peninsula of Michigan, northern Ohio, western New York, and western Vermont, show higher temperatures near the lake, and the abrupt curves of the isotherms, from the upper Mississippi valley to Lake Michigan, prove that altitude is not the cause of their melioration. The success attending fruit-growing in western New York, may be properly attributed to the influences of Lake Ontario and the minor lakes of that district. The spring frosts do not occur so late as at points further in the interior, and the expanse of melting ice retards vegetation until the season is so far advanced that it escapes injury therefrom.

" Throughout the month of May, the temperature of the water taken from about one foot beneath the surface, is but seven degrees above the freezing point. This is owing to the continued flow of waters from the melting ice of the upper lakes. It gradually rises to that of the atmosphere in the latter part of July, and above it in August. In September, it is nearly three degrees warmer, and in October, it retains the temperature of 53°, which is six degrees above that of the air on its southern shore. Its effect in warding off untimely frosts, is thus readily comprehended.

" The eastern shores of the lakes are much more safe than those on the west side. Altitudes make a great difference, and the best influence is not felt immediately upon the lake, but some miles distant, often upon higher ground.

" In the State of Ohio, ten miles inland from the shores of Lake Erie, the Catawba is unworthy of cultivation, and rarely ripens. On sandy soils, along the lake-shore, it generally matures, while, on the islands, on clayey limestone, it always ripens, and of a quality not uniformly met with elsewhere."]

EXPOSURE.—Writers on grape culture are very far from agreeing about the choice of exposure. Some advise a southern exposure exclusively; others think the north equally good; and, lastly, there are some who seem to think this a point of little importance, grounding their argument on the fact that if, on the one hand, a large number of celebrated vineyards are exposed to the south or east, several, not less renowned for the quality of their products are exposed to the north. Such are, in Champagne, those of the hills of Èpernay, Mailly, Chigny and Rilly; such are the most celebrated on the Rhine; several of those of Saumur and Angers; and, in the vicinity of Tours, the hills of Joné and St. Avertin, where excellent red wines are grown.   A certain portion of the vines of l'Hermitage are also exposed to the west.

What other conclusion can we arrive at, from these conflicting opinions, except that the best exposure can not be indicated with absolute certainty; that it must vary according to local circumstances, and be determined by the combined influences of latitude, elevation above the sea-level, as well as the nature of the soil and the frequency of white frosts in the locality?

The vine especially dreads a damp atmosphere, for such injures the quality of its grapes.   Therefore, as a general rule, exposures open to the influence of cold and damp winds from the north-west, the west and south-west, must be avoided.   In the northern portion of the climatic zone adapted to vine-culture, the southern, south-eastern and eastern exposures are preferable.   In the southern portion of that belt, the northern exposure may be added to the foregoing, provided the angle of inclination is not over 20 degrees.   This last exposure is even necessary in the warmest localities, in order to remove the vine from the action of too intense heat.

The elevation of the land above the level of the sea must also be taken into account in choosing an exposure; the higher the land, the more southern must be the exposure, especially in the northern portion of the zone adapted to the cultivation of the vine.   Where the soil will retain a great deal of moisture, the northern and eastern exposure, being generally dryer, must have the preference.   Lastly, the west must be chosen in localities where white frosts prevail, in order that the sun may not strike the shoots until after the frost has disappeared.

Thus we see how difficult it is to say what degree of success a vineyard planted on any particular spot will have, so much do certain causes, apparently unimportant, influence the result. Chaptal thinks that all soils in which the fig-tree, the soft-shelled almond and the peach-tree (ungrafted) will grow well and yield fine fruit, are adapted to the vine.

[The question of exposure is a new one to planters in this country, and hence the importance of observing the results of observation and experience in older lands. The suggestions in the text appear to be very sensible, and, guided by their home experience in the northern portion of the vine-growing region of Europe, our German vine-dressers selected southern slopes for their vineyards. It has seemed, however, that the exposure of the vines to the freely moving currents of air, was a more important element of success, in most cases, where these vineyards were situated on river hills, than the exposure to the sun on the southern slopes. As the vineyards extended, it often happened that other exposures were occupied, and it was soon observed that those which inclined to the north were equally successful. A well-founded prejudice, sustained by observation, exists against a bold eastern and south-eastern exposition, on account of the greater liability to frost, or rather the greater damage which is done by the frosts of spring, and even by the cold of winter, where the vines are exposed, while frozen, to the direct rays of a bright sunshine. It often happens that the shoots are destroyed in the open situation, whereas, if but partially shaded, even by one another and by the stakes and trellises, and by a different exposure, they may escape the damage, even where the freezing itself may have been equally severe. Hence, a western, or even a northern slope, is often preferred to one which lies more directly toward the rays of the rising sun.]

II.

PREPARATORY OPERATIONS.

THE location for the vineyard having been chosen, we proceed to a consideration of the preparatory labors for the vineyard.

FENCES.—It is to be regretted that most of our vineyards are without fences. They should all be inclosed; otherwise the following inconveniences may be the result:

1st. In countries still under the ban of the ordinances fixing the time for the gathering of the grapes, it is impossible to introduce in their cultivation certain much-needed improvements. For, what profit would there be, for instance, in introducing into one's vineyard a vine of more precocious growth, if the gathering of its fruit is to await the raising of the ordinance ban?— Neither will it be possible to derive benefit from operations having for their object the ventilation of the vines, so as to allow the grapes to remain longer on the stocks, without fear of the rot, and thus reach more perfect maturity. The grapes must be gathered before the proper time. And, lastly, if the vineyard is made up of different varieties of grapes, maturing at different periods, the ban will compel the gathering of the whole at the same time. Vineyards that are fenced in are free from all these inconveniencies.

2d. Fences protect the produce of the vineyard from the depredations of marauders and dogs.

But all kinds of fences are not equally adapted to vineyards. Evergreen hedges, planted on the level ground, often keep up a moisture which favors white frosts, or retards the ripening of the grapes; besides, the roots of these hedges injure the grapes, by exhausting the soil to a distance of from twenty to twenty-six feet. Stone fences are too expensive, unless on a small scale, or for the protection of very valuable crops. If suitable rock, or stones, be at hand, walls may be erected to protect the vineyards. Or, the vineyard may be surrounded with a ditch about five feet wide at the top, twenty inches at the bottom and three feet three inches in depth. The earth should be thrown on the outer edge, like a levee, or embankment. To prevent the soil from sliding back into the ditch, it will be necessary to sod the banks, and to plant the top with such

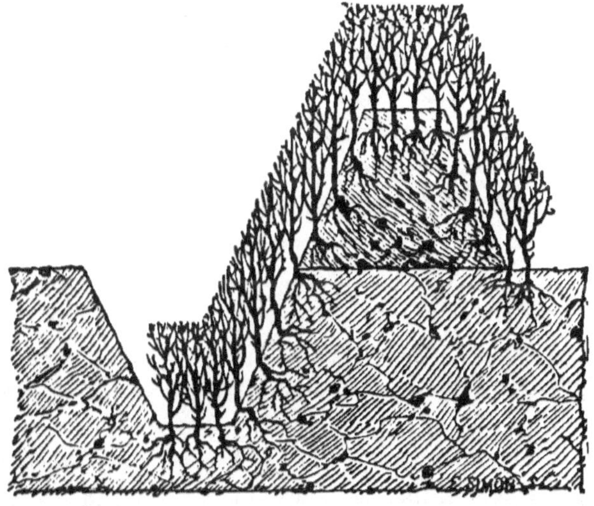

[FIG. 1.]

small shrubs as are best adapted to the climate and locality. These shrubs [Fig. 1] will strengthen the levee, and render the crossing of it more difficult.

[Americans can not realize that vast tracts of land in Europe are cultivated in common, with only a turning furrow, or a pathway, between the different proprietaries, and that all the country is open, even to the road-sides, in many places. We are so accustomed to see everything fenced in from intrusion, and have so long borne this burden of fencing, that we neither realize that it is more oppressive than all our other taxes, nor can we conceive how it strikes the Europeans, who look upon our fences as a great waste of lumber, and by no means as ornamental fringes to our farms.

Where timber or stone is plenty, and while labor is dear, we must have inclosures to restrain our cattle, or cultivated crops will be impossible. But we may feel encouraged at the progress we are making in this respect, and be happy to know, that in many of the States, laws have been made and enforced, which require that all cattle shall be restrained by their owners. The result of this is, or will be, the abolition of many of these burdensome and cumbrous appendages of the farm; the cattle will be confined to their appropriate grazing lands, or kept in stables and yards, and there fed by *soiling*, as it is called—carrying the feed to them all the year round—and our roads and lanes will no longer be the resort of lean kine and sharp-nosed swine, seeking an entrance into our gardens and cultivated fields, to commit depredations which can never be repaid by their owners; and causing a grievous moral wrong, by provoking the ill temper of the unfortunate proprietor, which no appraised damages can atone for nor alleviate.

We rejoice in our cattle law, and hope these *animals* may ever be restrained, that the fence burden may, in a great degree, be thus averted; but we do not expect to see choice vineyards and fruit gardens exposed to the depredations of wandering thieves, until they become personally interested in such treasures of their own; no common fences will bar their entrance, however, when they are disposed to trespass upon us: the watch-tower, as of old, must accompany the vineyard in the present state of society.

We may rejoice, too, that there is in this country no such thing as an "*ordinance ban*" to direct us when to commence our vintage, and to oblige us to gather our grapes at a certain date, whether they be early or late; the culture of the vine is here free as its tendrilled shoots, and every one may exercise his own judgment in selecting the period for the various operations he has to perform among his plants.]

ROADS.—It is very important that teams should be able to pass through all parts of a vineyard, especially when it is one of considerable extent. For this purpose it would be well, in planting the vines, to have roads conveniently laid out wherever the grades of the ground will allow it. This will render it easier to distribute by wagons, to all points of the vineyard, the manure, the soil etc., which may be needed in it, and it will cost much less than if done by means of packhorses and mules, or by hand, with baskets. The gathering of the grapes will also cost much less.

The principal roads of a large vineyard ought to be not less than fifteen feet wide, so as to allow teams to pass each other freely; they ought to be not less than fifty yards apart, and should run across, or at right angles with the rows of the vines; other roads, two yards wide, should cross the first at right angles, two hundred yards apart; by this means the soil or manure required in the vineyard may be carried in wagons close to the spot where needed, and unloaded in piles, whence it will be easily distributed at short distances, in wheel-barrows or baskets.   If the soil be a little clayey, it will then be equally necessary to make these roads by excavating; by this means they will carry off the surplus water always so injurious to vineyards.

[These directions, for the laying out of roads and pathways through the vineyard, are admirable, and something of the kind is practiced in all our large vineyards, though many are planted at such a width that a hand-cart, or a sled, something like a- "stone-boat," and pulled by a horse, may pass easily between the rows, to carry off the vintage; for few vine-dressers have yet done much in the way of hauling on soil or manure, though this may often be practiced with advantage, particularly on hill-sides, where the soil is washed away by the rains.   The surface drainage is very important, and should always be provided for; first, by laying out the rows in such a manner that the water may pass between them, toward either end, in a gradual flow; next, by providing proper conduits for its passage.   On abrupt slopes, or declivities, these may be across the rows, directly or obliquely, and it will be well to have them protected by masonry.   These conduits, or water-ways, are often made by setting long, thin stones on edge, as a curb, or by laying up two walls, at such distance apart as may be necessary to convey the water, and afterward, paving the bottom of the ditch between them. These water-courses are often used as the paths of the vineyard, and when very abrupt, they are sometimes paved like steps, for the convenience of the workmen.   As the reader will have observed, however, such steep declivities are not recommended for vineyard sites.

The author advises, in the concluding sentence, that in clayey land, the road-ways should be cut down so as to furnish a depressed water-course.   This method has been very nicely practiced by one of our most successful and intelligent vine-planters, and it is improved upon in a way that is worthy to be presented to the reader. Mr. Robert Buchanan,* of Cincinnati, O., provides shallow water-courses between all the "squares," or subdivisions of his vineyard; these are wide, and serve him also as roads. They are cheaply prepared with the plow, and the loose earth is distributed among the adjoining vines, or used in grading, so that there shall be a regular and easy fall with the road-way. In the first laying out of the vineyard, a proper grade for the roads was secured.

The crowning merit of these shallow ditch-roads, however, is, that they are laid down to grass, so as to prevent washing. They receive the surplus water that escapes from between the rows, and quickly convey it out of the vineyard. They give easy access to all parts of the ground; they act as turning rows in cultivating with the horse; they furnish an easy outlet for surplus surface water, without washing into gullies, and they admit the air freely to the vineyard; besides all this, they give a look of finish, at a very cheap rate.

The grass should be kept cut short during the season, and it may be fed to stock or thrown upon the soil as a mulch to the vines.]

III.

PREPARATION OF THE SOIL.

D RAINAGE.—One of the evils most to be feared for a vineyard is too much moisture in the soil. In such a condition the roots of the vine will rot, its life will be short, its produce limited, of inferior quality, and ripening slowly. If, therefore, it is intended to plant a vine-

---

*Author of a Treatise on Grape Culture.

4

yard in a soil of this nature, the first step is to drain
the land.   On the Lower Rhine district, near Saverne,
we have seen a vineyard located on an abrupt hill-side,
composed of argilo-silicious soil, resting on quite impervious clay.   In consequence of the stagnant moisture
arising from this bad condition of the soil, the vines
languished, produced little fruit, which was of inferior
quality and ripened with difficulty.   On this land, drains
have been made [A, Fig. 2] running with the slope, so
that each comes out at the base of the hill at B, on the
vertical cut formed at this point by the passage of a
vineyard road C.   The upper ends of the drains appeared on the surface of the land at D, on the horizontal plane situated above the slope.   This great

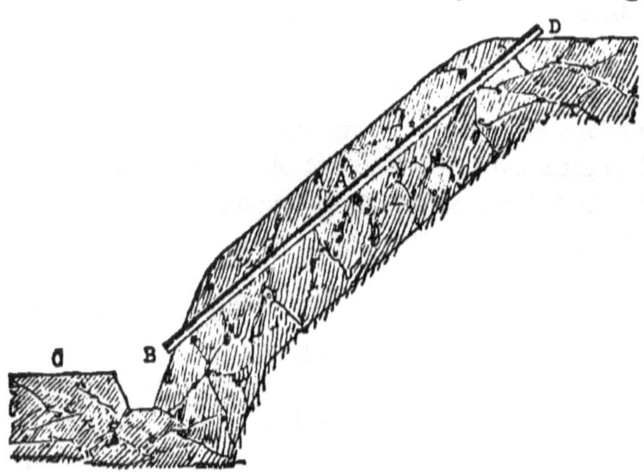

[FIG. 2.]

difference in the level of the two extremities of these
drains suggested the following observations: if, during
the heat of summer, a lighted candle is placed at each
extremity of one of these drains, the flame of the
lower candle will be carried, by the draft, into the

drain, while the flame of the candle at the upper end will frequently be extinguished by the force of the current escaping at this point. This abundant and rapid circulation of warm air below the surface of the soil, warms it while making it more salubrious. This vineyard at once became unusually healthy and vigorous, and its maturity was accelerated by two or three weeks. We think it unnecessary, here, to enter into the details of drainage. We refer our readers to special treatises on that subject ;* or, rather, we advise landholders having such work to do, to apply to the contractors of drainage, who are now to be found in every Department of France, and who, provided with special tools and skilled workmen, will do the drainage better and quicker, and at less cost, than if undertaken by the landholder himself.

[Too much importance can not be attributed to this subject of drainage, not merely as a means of escape for the surplus water of the soil, but also as affording access to the air, which will warm the roots by its direct influence, imparting its own temperature to the earth through which it passes. While alleviating the effects of a drought, by depositing its own moisture on the sides of the passages through which it flows, it also gives off the latent heat by which the water was kept in the state of vapor.

Our vine-planters are urged to drain their heavy, clayey lands, wherever it is possible, and the suggestion of Mr. Du Breuil is an excellent one, wherever professional drainers can

---

*A very practical work on "Drainage," by John H. Klippart, Cor. Sec'y of Ohio State Board of Agriculture, is published by Robert Clarke & Co., who have a new edition just ready.

The reader is also referred to the very practical work of Mr. George B. Waring, Superintendent of Drainage of Central Park, New York City.

be had, though in this country, the versatile genius of our people makes them feel competent to meet any emergency, and where no help can be obtained from without the farm or shop, men generally manage to succeed in whatever they undertake.

The inventive genius is also aroused in this direction, and we have already several labor-saving machines to aid in the work of ditching. Among these the mole-plows are found to work admirably, wherever the sub-soil is of a peculiarly adhesive character, so as not to disintegrate readily, and thus silt up the passages. Some lands that have been drained with these implements, for there are several devices of the kind, have continued for many years to reap the benefit of the drainage afforded, and the current of water continued to flow through them. As a mere outlet for the surplus water, the mole-plows are a success, but it is doubtful whether the other benefits of drainage can ever be so well furnished by any means as by the porous burnt-clay tile commonly used.

Messrs. Moon & Doan, of Wilmington, Ohio, have invented a machine to aid in opening the ditches, which, it is said, will lessen the expense by one half.

This apparatus was exhibited, in model, before the Lake Shore Grape Growers' Society, at their recent meeting at Cleveland. It consists of a strong frame-work, in which is suspended a wheel, armed with cutters on its periphery, that penetrate the soil as the wheel revolves, bringing up a portion of the soil, which is thrust out by a set of plungers, as they approach the summit. The dirt falls off to one side of the ditch. The frame is drawn along, and the wheel made to revolve, by a strong rope, that is wound upon a drum at the end of the ditch, by means of horses or oxen working on a lever.]*

---

*For further description of this excellent machine, and cut, see "Klippart's Land Drainage," p. 230.

BREAKING UP THE GROUND.—The vine, like all ligneous plants, requires for its proper devlopment a soil sufficiently pervious to the roots. The ground must, therefore, be broken up before planting, so as to bring it to that condition.

The depth to which the soil must be trenched will necessarily vary according to its looseness, and degree of dryness: a dry and warm soil must be dug deeper than a rich, substantial, and somewhat cold soil, because the root must penetrate deeper in the first than in the last.

It will also be evident, that soils of the same kind must be trenched deeper in a southern than in a northern latitude, because drought is more to be feared in the former than in the latter. In this respect it will be well to confine ourselves within the following limits: the dryest soils of northern regions ought to be trenched to a depth of eighteen inches, at least; in rich and somewhat cold soils, twelve inches will be enough. In the south, twenty-four inches will not be too much, in the first case, and fifteen inches in the last. The manner of performing this work depends on the nature of the soil.

But in all cases the following rules ought to be observed: 1st—the breaking up or trenching ought to be done several months before planting, so that the subsoil brought to the surface may have time to improve under the influence of atmospheric agents; 2nd—the subsoil must be replaced by surface soil, and *vice versa.* Some have, it is true, advised, in such cases, the loosening only, of the subsoil, without bringing it to the surface. This system, though adapted to herbaceous plants, the roots of which live at the surface of the ground, is little suited to the development of the vine, the absorbing organs of which at once penetrate to a greater depth, where, consequently, they need to find the nutritious elements of soils reversed by the plow.

✗ *Cultivated Lands accessible to the Plow.*—If the vineyard is to be laid out on cultivated lands, it will be well to sow it with a last crop of clover and sainfoin,* for the deep roots of these plants loosen the soil and improve it by their decay. If the breaking up is to be eighteen inches deep, two plows must be used in the same furrow; the first, an ordinary plow, which will penetrate about six inches deep; the second, of strong make, must be so constructed as to cut to a depth of twelve inches from the bottom of the furrow, and to carry this earth over that turned up by the first plow.

[FIG. 3.]

Bonnet's plow [Figures 3 and 4] performs this operation admirably, but it requires a team of six horses or oxen to reach this result. Thus plowed, the land must be left idle until the time for planting. The same mode of breaking up the ground to the depth of twelve inches is used, with this difference only, that

* *Hedysarum onobrichis.*

the first plow will turn up a layer of only four inches,
and the second one of eight inches.

When the breaking up is to be two feet, as is often
the case with the very dry lands of the south, the two
plows will be used to reach a depth of fifteen inches,
and the other nine inches will be obtained by men following the wake of the plow with spades, and throwing up the subsoil over that turned up by the last
plow. If a sufficient number of men are employed, so
as not to delay the teams, this work can be performed
pretty rapidly.

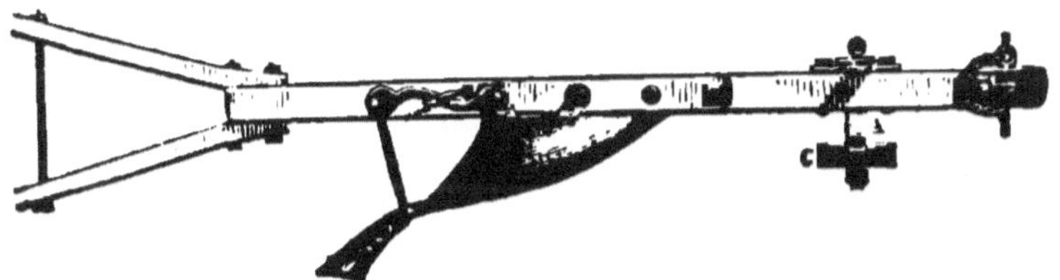

[Fig. 4.]

[The attention of the reader is directed to the beautiful
cuts of these implements, but they are not within our reach.
As we have, deservedly, a high reputation for the excellency,
and indeed, almost perfection, of our various agricultural implements—and as this has been accorded to us by intelligent
juries, at the great industrial expositions of Europe—we may,
perhaps, be justified in a few words of praise respecting some
American plows, with which our lands are very admirably
prepared for the planting of grape vines. These implements
can only be used, however, upon ground that is level, or
but moderately sloping, and which is not encumbered with
rocks, loose stones, stumps, or large roots, as when first re-
claimed from the forest; nor is such new land to be preferred
if that which has been long cleared can be had. If stumps

and bowlders exist, they must be removed by extra hands, as they are discovered by the plow.

Many farmers will prefer to use two plows, with two teams; the first one reverses the sod and surface soil; the second, made with a long and high mold-board, follows in the furrow, and throws out the next layer of earth, and piles it upon the furrow-lice cast by the first plow. In this manner, the two layers will be pretty well reversed and transposed; the deeper will be chiefly upon the surface. The second plow will require a strong team, to make it run six inches deep, and the two combined will loosen the earth to a depth of twelve to fourteen inches—seldom more. If desired, a subsoil-lifter plow may now be passed along the bottom of the deep furrow, and, with sufficient team, it may be made to loosen the soil or subsoil to the depth of six or eight inches more, completely filling the space with loosened material, and admitting the air to meliorate this compact layer of crude earth, which is often unfit to be placed upon the surface.

In this plan, the same ground is passed over three different times, first with a strong two-horse team, turning six or eight inches, next with a team of four horses or oxen, and lastly, with a powerful team of four or six oxen; for it is found that these patient creatures are best adapted to the heavy soil and obstructions that are often met with in the subsoils, particularly when they consist of tenacious clays. All the implements should be of the firmest construction, put together in the most substantial manner, made of the best material—steel, iron and wood—and kept duly sharpened.

The cost of such a force of men and teams, to say nothing of the wear and tear, will be considerable. The following estimate is based upon the prices paid for teams in this neighborhood :

Say one man and two horses,   -   -   - $3 25
     two men and four horses,   -   -   -   6 50
     two men and six oxen,   -   -   -   6 50

Total expense per diem,   -   -   -   - $16 25 .

At the close of the day, if all things have worked smoothly, and there have been no serious interruptions, the proprietor will find, perhaps, one half acre thoroughly plowed.

But we have an implement by which, with one team, we may perform the work of two plows. This is known as the "Double Michigan," and is really a trench-plow, though sometimes erroneously called a *subsoil.* This may be drawn, in light soils, by a team of three horses, or still better by four, or by three yoke of oxen. The object of increasing the power, in oxen, is to make up, by greater breadth of furrow, for the usual slowness of the cattle.

The " Double Michigan," or trench-plough, has one share and mold-board attached to the beam, in front of the other or larger one. The first reverses the sod, cutting to the depth of four or six inches, at the will of the workman ; the second, with its larger and longer mold-board, follows immediately behind the first, and takes the next layer, to the depth of eight or ten inches, and throws it over the first completely, and admirably disintegrates the soil. By this plough, a trench is opened to the depth of fifteen inches or more, according to the strength of the team and nature of the soil.

A favorite plan for the preparation of land for a vineyard, is to use the "Double Michigan" and the subsoil-lifter alternately, with the same team. Using oxen, there is no difficulty in making the change, going once around a land with the plow, and then, casting the chain hook into the ring of the lifter, all is ready to go around again and loosen the subsoil. A tilth is thus made to the depth of eighteen to twenty inches, or more, where the soil is not too heavy ; but in stiff clay and compact or tenacious subsoils, it is often dif-

ficult to make an average of eighteen inches, honestly meas-
ured, on the land-side, from the natural surface, for the plowed
soil will look much higher and measure deeper, at first.—
These teams and plows will pulverize one third of an acre
per diem.

This work will cost, say—

For two men and six oxen, per diem,   -   - $ 6 50
The same, three days, for one acre,   - -   19 50

It is very important in all these implements, to avoid friction, as much as possible, by having the joints well fitted, the
cutting edges sharp, and the mold-boards of the most perfect
pattern, and made of the best steel, highly wrought and pol-
ished.

The share of the lifter should be very slightly convex upward, it need not be more than two inches higher at the center than at the edges, and there should be a counter-sunk space
on the under side for the nuts that keep it attached to the
sheath and supporter. This attachment was formerly made by
riveting, but should be by tap and screws.

Some very good work has been done in this country upon
the plan suggested by Mr. Du Breuil, of having a gang of
hands with spades, to turn up, or simply to disintegrate the
third or lower layer of soil. This may be desirable when
there are stones to interrupt the subsoil plow, but the scarcity
of hands and the high price of labor, induce most of us to
prefer the oxen and a good steel subsoil-lifter.]

*Waste, Uncultivated or Swamp Lands, accessible to the
Plow.*—These lands must first be cleared of the un-
dergrowth which covers them and would impede the
work. The largest of this underwood, the roots of
which would stop the plow, must be grubbed up, and
may be turned over to the men in part payment of wages.
The lighter brush must be cut close to the ground, and
laid in lines parallel to the furrows; these lines must

be sufficiently near one another to be thrown into each successive furrow opened by the plow. The plows are then used as described above, to obtain the required depth, according to the nature of the soil and climate of the locality. As the furrows are opened to that depth, the brush placed alongside of each one is thrown into it; thus buried, it will soon be reduced to compost, and will furnish the vine with rich and lasting nourishment.

[In referring to swamp lands, Mr. Du Breuil has given no directions for the drainage which would be essential to them. Indeed, we should not think of planting grapes in such soils as we denominate swamp land, even if sufficiently dried by drainage; the peaty or mucky character of the soil would be a bar to its use for grapes, as we find that vines, so situated, will grow too much to wood, and seldom yield a paying crop of fruit, because they are most subject to attacks of disease.]

Steep, Hilly Lands, inaccessible to the Plow.—For the breaking up, or trenching of the lands just named, we have advised the use of the plow, because it is the cheapest process. But frequently it is advantageous to locate vineyards on hill-sides so abrupt that it is, unfortunately, impossible to use that implement. In such cases recourse must be had to manual labor to prepare the soil. In other respects, operations must be so performed as to produce the foregoing results; that is, the surface earth and brush must be placed at the bottom of the trench, if the lands have been uncultivated.

Breaking up in Strips or Ditches.—This mode of preparing the soil consists in opening a ditch of sixteen inches in width for each row of vines, and of a depth varying according to the circumstances indicated above. These ditches are separated by a strip of unworked land, broader or narrower, according to the distance of the rows from each other. The first ditch being dug, the plants are placed in it, and the soil taken from the new ditch serves to fill the first, and so on throughout the extent of the field.

Trenching in Squares or Pits.—In a straight line, little pits, about twenty-four inches square, are made, in each of which one layer or root is planted.

These two systems are much more economical than the immediate trenching of the entire surface, but they can only be used in fertile lands, which have been already cultivated; besides, in due time the untrenched spaces between the plants will have to be successively dug out, or otherwise the development of the vines will be checked, when their roots come in contact with the sides of the trenches or pits. We must add, in conclusion, that this partial and successive trenching will not be so well performed on lands already planted, as if performed, in the first instance, over the entire surface; from which we conclude that uniform trenching is better, without being expensive.

Lands Rocky near the Surface.—We have thus far supposed that the land to be prepared contained a layer of free soil, at least equal to the depth of the required trenching. Now, certain lands capable of producing very good wine, have a surface soil of five to six inches' depth, resting on lamellar or shelly rocks. In that case it will be necessary to loosen this superficial soil, either with the plow or by hand, according to the slope of the land. At the time of planting, a hole is made between the stones with an iron bar, large enough to admit a cutting to a sufficient depth.

Hill-sides covered with Rocks.—Certain lands which are exceedingly well adapted to vine-growing, especially as regards the quality of the product, are of difficult and expensive preparation. Such are abrupt declivities, covered more or less completely with rocks, that protrude above the surface.

It is impossible to adapt such surfaces to this cultivation, except by clearing them of rocks to a depth of sixteen or twenty inches. For that purpose crow-bars are used, and even blasting is resorted to. With these stones little walls are built along the side of the hill. This allows the construction of a series of benches, wider or narrower, according to the steepness of the hill. The surface of these benches, well trenched, is made level. Most of the vineyards on the Rhine, and some of those on the Rhône, are constructed in this manner.

[Most of our hill-side vineyards have been located upon such abrupt declivities as to preclude the use of the plow, and they were prepared for planting by human labor. The trenching was sometimes done with the spade, and sometimes with the grubbing hoe and the pick. In all cases, the object was to reduce the hill-side to a series of narrow levels, or slopes, generally called terraces, or benches. Where stone abounds in the soil, it is used for walls. On the river hills, the earth is chiefly composed of the detritus of the alternating shales and limestones of our silurian formation, known as the blue limestone; here there is plenty of material for making the walls. In digging the soil, the stones are thrown on top, or at once laid in regular lines along the side of the hill, and the soil thrown against the wall, so as to make the terrace approach to a level on the surface. The width of the benches, and the hight of the walls, will depend upon the steepness of the hill. It is a notable fact that the soil on the lower side of the walls is seldom dug so deeply as is desirable.

Sometimes these walls and benches are carried horizontally; sometimes they are made to incline a little toward one end, to give outlet to the water. Generally, the surface drainage is provided for, by making paved gutters at some point of the vineyard, toward which the ends of the benches incline on one or both. sides.

The cost of digging and walling these hill-sides, varies with the amount of stone and masonry, and will range from two hundred to as much as five hundred dollars per acre.

In appropriating a grassy slope to vineyard uses, where there is no stone for the construction of walls, the ground is often thrown into benches, or terraces, and the abrupt slopes are protected by sodding. This is either done by setting masses of earth with the grassy surface placed regularly on the lower line of the terrace, as the work progresses, so as to make a regular sod-bank, at once, or the earth is dug into shape and sodded with blue-grass afterward.

These sod-banks have quite a pretty effect in the landscape, and they answer a very good purpose in holding the soil in shape, if they have been properly constructed, but they do not furnish so good a drainage as the dry stone walls, and, being sloped, they occupy more space. There is another objection to sod-banks : they reduce the temperature by radiation at night ; and sometimes this reduction amounts to a frost, which would not have occurred, but for the grassy surface. This objection applies with equal force to the sodded roadways, recommended on a previous page, as a means of providing for the surface drainage.

The blue-grass must be cut by hand, and the first mowing should be done in the end of May.]

Vineyards recently Planted.—A vineyard, from which the old vines have recently been removed, may be immediately replanted, after being sufficiently cultivated, provided, at the same time, it has been well manured, so as to renew, in the lower strata of the soil, the nourishment which the deep roots of the old vine had exhausted.

If this expense of enriching the soil can not be incurred, it will be well, for some years, to devote this land to ordinary cultivation, by sowing it with forage plants, such as sainfoin and clover. These plants will, by degrees, renew the productiveness which the lower strata of the soil has lost.

[In this country, we have had little or no experience in replanting a piece of ground that had been devoted to vineyard, and which had become exhausted, or which had failed from neglect. But, upon general principles, such a course would not be recommended, until after a course of culture with farm crops, among which, clover should have a prominent place. This is only carrying out the idea of rotation of crops, to the vineyard, as to the other departments of agriculture.]

IV.

CHOICE OF VINES.

THE number of varieties of grapes cultivated for wine-making has gradually increased, by means of seedlings. Although the nomenclature of these varieties is not yet well established, they may be said to number at present, over twelve hundred. These different varieties are very far from possessing the same advantages for cultivation; they are not all adapted to the same climate, or the same kind of soil; they are especially far from yielding alike, either as to quality or quantity. From this springs the necessity of choosing from among them such as are best adapted to the climate, the soil of the locality where the vineyard is to be laid out, and the description of wine which it is intended to produce. This choice constitutes one of the most important operations of vine-culture. The following are the chief conditions which ought to influence it:

1st. That the vine ripen its fruit thoroughly in the climate for which it is intended.

2d. That it be adapted to the soil where it is to be cultivated, so as to develop itself with sufficient vigor, and that the quality of its product be not impaired.

3d. That its average product be as large as possible, and of good quality; that is to say, that its berries contain, in suitable proportions, the elements best adapted to the manufacture of fine wines. This double advantage will be the more valuable because it is seldom met with, for frequently the most productive varieties yield but poor grapes.

4th. That its period of leafing be backward in the spring, without delaying the ripening of its fruit, so that it may the more easily escape the injurious effects of spring frosts.

5th That it possess a sufficient degree of vigor to

resist, to a certain extent, the action of the frost, that its fruit may ripen in spite of the cold of autumn.

6th. That the strength and stiffness of its shoots need no support.

[With our limited experience in this country, we think we have learned enough to add another condition, as important as any above named, but which appears to have been strangely overlooked by the author.

Reference is made to the well-settled principle among pomologists, to insist upon the perfect hardiness and healthiness of the vine or plant, rather than to allow our judgment to be warped by the excellence of the fruit alone, without inquiring into the qualities of the plant.]

As regards the nomenclature, the characteristics, the period of maturity, the quantity and quality of the products of various vines, we still lack a complete work, in spite of the remarkable labors of Count Odart.— And, for this reason, the list which we give here comprises only the principal varieties cultivated in France. In this list we have preserved the nomenclature adopted by Count Odart, and have classified them on the plan proposed by Count Gasparin, based on the date of maturity, and the color of the grapes.

[Count André de Gasparin, here referred to, was the father of Count Agenor de Gasparin, whose work, called the "Uprising of a Great Nation," has made him dear to our countrymen, because it showed his deep sympathy with the American people in their recent struggle for the maintenance of the integrity of the nation. The glory of our free institutions was eloquently portrayed by Gasparin to his own countrymen, and secured from the masses of the French nation a hearty sympathy with the American people.]

FIRST PERIOD—*15th July in the South; 20th August at Paris.*

Almost all the grapes of this period are table grapes, yielding very inferior wine.

SECOND PERIOD—*25th August in the South; 7th October a: Paris.*

COLORED GRAPES.

Black " *Pinot.*"—Yields little, but most delicate wine ; its wood being very slender it must be staked.   (Burgundy.)

Reddish " *Pinot.*"—Table grape ; light wine ; fine aroma.

Moorish " *Pinot.*"—Very dark berry ; dark, inferior wine. (Dijon.)

" *Pulsart.*"—Pearl color ; leaves much indented ; large, thin pedicles ; bunches thin ; fine berries, easily picked when ripe ; very productive on level ground ; yielding a good wine, which keeps well ; requires to be trained high to be productive ; steep, clayey lands.   (Jura.)

" *Plant of the Dôle.*"—Of slow growth, but ripening early ; oblong, dark blue berries.   (Switzerland.)

Little "*Négran.*"—Yielding little, but of fine aroma.

" *Liverdun.*"—Large leaves, without down ; oblong berries ; yielding much wine, but not very alcoholic.   (Lorraine.)

" *Meunier.*"—Black grape ; leaves covered over with a white down ; very productive ; wine flat ; will not keep.

Black " *Franc.*"—Black, oblong berries ; light, pleasant wine ; adapted to light, calcareous soils.

WHITE AND GRAY GRAPES.

Gray "*Pinot.*"—Berries, dead leaf color ; very delicate ; light wine ; fine aroma.   (Sillery-Versenay.)

White " *Pinot.*"—Oblong berries—loose, with brown spot ; golden color ; fine wine ; yield small.   (Montrachet.)

Aligotuy.—Leaves large, and downy on the under side ; red wood ; fine skin ; liable to rot, but pretty good yielder.   (Pouilly.)

Sauvignin.—Round, sweet berries ; pretty good yielder.

Musquette.—Round, sparse berries ; amber color ; wood fawn-colored ; berries liable to rot ; requires long pruning.   (Gironde and Dordogne.)

Blanquette.—Under side of leaf somewhat downy ; berries rather oblong ; pleasant flavor ; large, full bunches, drying quickly on the stock.   (Aude and Dordogne.)

THIRD PERIOD—*1st September in the South; October 20th in latitude of Paris.*

BLACK OR RED GRAPES.

Plant of Pernant.—Leaves entire, of a yellowish green ; berries black, of moderate size ; hardy and prolific ; wine inferior in quality and aroma to that of the Black Pinot, but liked, because of its great productiveness. (Burgundy.)

Frizzled Pinot.—More productive than the other Pinots, but of inferior quality.

Black Muscat of Jura.

Merlot.—Leaves deeply indented; rough, downy, under side ; berries round, of a velvety black ; skin fine ; apt to rot in wet seasons ; very productive, and much liked.   (Bordelais.)

Sirah (little and great).—Leaves large and downy on the under side ; berries black and even, slightly elongated, purple eyes far apart ; very good wine.   (Hermitage.)

Deep-black "Dyer" (Oporto).—Productive ; berries close, black and round ; produces a reddish juice ; wines rich ; grown for coloring *"must."*

Big Gamais (large-headed Pinot).—Leaves downy on the under side ; leaf-stalk purple ; bunches numerous ; wine flat and acid.   (Burgundy.)

Little Gamais (black Gamais of Lyons).—Pretty productive ; yields a wine of good quality.   Mâconnais.)

Neyrau (big and little Moret).—Yields a dark-red wine, with a good bouquet.   (Allier and Puy de Dôme.)

WHITE GRAPES.

" Fendant."—Berries close, and remain green.   This kind is of red and pink varieties.   (Switzerland.)

White Morillon.—Leaves large, little indented ; berries not very close, quite round, not spotted brown ; sweet flavor and aroma ; good yielder. (Champagne.)

Semillon.—Leaves much indented, of a light green ; large bunches ; berries round and loose, light yellow ; hardy plant, eyes close together.   (Bordelais.)

Colomban.—Plant hardy and productive; grapes apt to rot; wine indifferent.

" Pascal " Vine.—Large leaves, downy underneath ; large bunches ; berries round, whitish green, with fine skin ; eyes close together ; good table grape.   (Bouches du Rhône.)

FOURTH PERIOD—*27th September in the South; do not mature in the latitude of Paris.*

The " Côt."—Very short jointed ; plant hardy; berries black, sparse, round; apt to rot ; wine of a fine color, of good body and flavor. (From the Lot to the Loire.)

Black Couché.—Leaves small ; little indented, downy underneath, yellowish on the upper side ; average bunches ; short stem ; berries long ; wine colored, alcoholic.

Simoreau.—Bunches long ;. stem red ; berries sparse, smoky taste ; very productive. (Lorraine.)

Carmenet.—Leaves thin, with fine pointed, smooth lobes ; bunches thin ; moderate sized berries, round and black ; stem and pedicles purple ; wood reddish ; wine fine and clear ; great bouquet; will keep ; yield pretty regular, but not large. (Bordelais.)

Black Serine.—Leaves slender, smooth and pointed ; one of the lobes smaller than the other ; bunches long ; berries oblong and scattering.— (Côtes du Rhône.)

Persaigne.—Good producer; dark, rough wine ; improves with age. (Lyonnais.)

Grolot.—Berries round ; table grape. (From the Loire to the Lot.)

Big Mérille.—Leaves little indented ; rough underneath ; fine bunches; berries round, black and close; very productive ; wine ordinary. (Garonne and Gironde.)

" Dyer" of the Jura.—The leaves, shoots and wood, are of a reddish tinge; grown for the same purpose as the " Dyer," already described.

Tanat.—Leaves rough on the upper side ; downy underneath, with edges turned in ; berries black, close and round, of moderate size, apt to rot at times ; wine colored, strong and agreeable. (Higher Pyrénées.)

Black Olivet.—Berries oblong ; smoke black ; rich pulp, crisp and sweet ; table grape.

Manosquin.—Leaves smooth and entire; fine bunches; berries black, large, slightly oblong; thick skin ; long wood; table wine ; adapted to transportation.

Black Ouillade.—Great yielder; berries large, oblong and black ; stem fine; wine of a beautiful color, and sweet, like cordial.

Milgranet.—Very productive. (Tarn.)

Savoyant.—Leaves of a fine green ; very downy underneath ; pretty well indented ; wood heavy ; very productive ; wine rough. (Switzerland.)

Black Muscat.—Very productive. (Vaucluse.)

Baclan.—Eyes far apart; dark green leaves; berries sparse; dark wine, of good quality; adapted to strong, clayey soil. (Jura.)

Trousseau.—Large, thick, round leaves, of a yellowish green; slightly downy underneath; berries black; strong wine, and will keep well; plant very hardy, productive, and requiring plenty of space; must be pruned long. The *little* Trousseau yields less, but is more certain. (Jura, Avalon.)

L'Enfariné.—Leaves longer than broad, sharp-pointed fringe, downy underneath, on the veins, bunches short; berries large and round, black, covered with a white bloom; very harsh; very productive; a tart wine, improving with age; trims very long.

WHITE GRAPES.

White Gouais.—Acid wine, without vinous flavor; will not keep; is very productive.

Green Savagnin.—Leaves round, dark green, downy underneath; leaf-stalks and veins red; long berries; skin thick, with greenish tinge. (Jura, Côte d'Or, Champagne.)

FIFTH PERIOD—*October 2d in the South; will not ripen in the latitude of Paris.*

COLORED GRAPES.

Aramon.—Very productive; wine clear, will keep well; easily affected by spring frosts, and liable to rot.

Agudet.—Bunches fine; berries oval; productive. (Tarn and Garonne.)

Carignan.—Berries round, black, apt to blight; yields largely in good soils; wine dark, of good quality. (Bouches du Rhône, Gard, Hérault, Aude.)

Tibouren.—Very productive when the blossoms do not blight; very early growth; berries very sweet; wine light colored, fine and delicate; light soil.

Black Terret.—Berries round, black; seldom blights, and yields little; dark colored wine, and good.

Mourastel.—Makes a great deal of wood, with short joints; berries large, crisp, sweet; never blights; strong, clayey soils; wine very dark, but flat.

Maulan.—Average leaves, yellowish green, shining, turned in; bunches fine; berries long, black, pretty large; early growth; often blights; is very productive.

Bouteillan.—Large bunches; large and small berries; of a reddish black; blights sometimes; wine light in color and body; very productive. (Lower Alps.)

Maldoux.—Very productive; wine flat and rough. (Jura.)

Grenache.—Leaves smooth on both sides; bunches fine; berries sparse, not very close, oblong, bluish black; joints short; suffers from spring frosts; wine very sweet; productive; strong ferruginous soils. (Gard, Hérault, Vaucluse.)

Mourvédre.—Leaves with purple veins; downy underneath; red wood, with purple eyes; berries round, of medium size, sky-blue, taste not very pleasant; thick skin; strong wine, which will bear transportation, and keep a long time; early bearer; does not blight. (Vaucluse.)

Black Spiran.—Berries black; bright red wine, good, and delicate; grown also as a table grape. There are gray and white varieties of this. (Gard, Hérault.)

Marocain.—Secondary leaves very much indented; large bunches, with large, sparse berries, hard, and covered with a white bloom; grown as a table grape. (Provence.)

WHITE GRAPES.

Picardan.—Light green grape, oval, somewhat firm, without being tough; very sweet; keeps well; wine smooth, will sparkle easily; not productive.

Calitor.—White berries, oval, not very soft; apt to rot; makes a good, dry wine, and yields largely after a few years.

Clairette.—Leaves very green on the upper side, and downy on the under side; bunches long; berries oblong, not crowded, firm, and sweet; keeps well; white wine, of good quality; very productive in virgin and fertile soils; somewhat apt to blight.

White Muscat.—Of all these grapes, this is the sweetest, and the one having the most aroma; very good for the table. (Lunel, Frontignan.)

SIXTH PERIOD—*10th October in the South; do not ripen in the latitude of Paris.*

Pique-Poule.—Close-jointed wood; berries oblong, close, reddish black; very good grape; fine, delicate, strong wine; not productive; must be close-trimmed. (La Nerthe.)

Terret-Bouret.—Light red, or gray berries, oval; large bunches, weighing as much as eight lbs.; hangs heavy; seldom blights; likes good soil, and will bear a good deal of manure; grown principally for brandy.

WHITE GRAPES.

Furmint.—Leaves nearly entire, slightly three-lobed, dark green; downy underneath; berries white, sparse, irregular; cylindrical bunches; very sweet; yields little; apt to blight; dries well without spoiling; very good wine.

SEVENTH PERIOD—*31st October in the South; do not mature in the latitude of Paris.*

COLORED GRAPES.

Danugue.—Large berries; reddish black; juicy; bunches very large; needs trellising; yields, in abundance, a weak, light colored wine; light soils.

Pocket Grape.—Trellis vine; very hardy, good grapes; berries red and round, the size of a hazel-nut, so hard that they may be carried in the pocket without mashing; not very sweet, and will keep a long time.

WHITE GRAPES.

Common Paunch.—Large bunches; berries long, firm, and large; good as table grapes, and keep well; white wines of good quality; strong, hardy vine, producing largely in good soils; needs training and little pruning.

Musked Paunch.—Berries very large, oblong, firm, and pointed at the end; sweeter than the foregoing; apt to blight; needs training and little pruning; good table grape, fresh or dried.

Spanish Paunch.—Large berries; round seeds; very sweet; fine skin.

Currant.—Berries very small, and without pulp; needs training and little pruning.

Gherkin.—Berries very large and curved, white; productive in good soils; needs training and little pruning.

White Olivette.—Berries olive shaped, but smaller; taste flat; keeps better than the others.

LIST OF AMERICAN GRAPES.

[The number of varieties of grapes that are now being introduced into cultivation, more or less generally, is becoming so extensive, that it is high time some one should undertake to reduce them to order, by adopting a system of classification.

This, however, will be a difficult task. Even the botanists, who observe the peculiar traits of the native vines, are not agreed as to the number of distinct species that exist within our borders. Our American authority, on such matters, is Dr. Asa Gray, who makes four species, the LABRUSCA, ÆSTIVALIS, CORDIFOLIA, and VULPINA, all of the genus *Vitis* proper. Besides these, he ranges two species under the section *Cissus*, as *V. indivisa*, and *V. bi-primata*, formerly called *Ampelopsis*, by Michaux, both beautiful ornamental vines.

Those grapes which are cultivated for their fruit, in this latitude, may, perhaps, all be referred to the first three of these species, though there are several varieties, the place of which it is very difficult to assign. They may be crosses, or simply variations from the normal type, or even hybrids of two distinct species; if so, they are, at least, fertile mules. Slight variations will constantly occur in our cultivated plants, which, as fruits, may be considered totally distinct, and which yet present no strong botanical characteristics to distinguish them from one or another species, and sometimes the specific characteristics themselves will be blended, so that we can not declare to which they belong. The present status of our knowledge hardly justifies an attempt to classify our cultivated varieties, by the species, and, desirable as some grouping would be, I hesitate attempting it, and shall content myself with an alphabetical list.

This has been compiled from various sources beside my own somewhat extended notes; among these I have been largely indebted to the list in the "American Horticultural Annual," including the school of vines left by the late N. Longworth. To avoid occupying too much space, the descriptions have been given in a very condensed form, merely to indicate the strong characters.

AMERICAN VARIETIES.

Adirondac.—New York. Dark, large, good; needs winter protection; not tested for wine.

Aiken.—Thought to be only a variety of Isabella, which it much resembles; berries round, large.

Albaiis.—Vine thrifty, hardy; bunch large; berry large, round, black; good.

Albino.—Pennsylvania. White; recommended in Missouri.

Allen's Hybrid.—Massachusetts. In favorable localities does well.

Alvey.—Southern. Bunch large; berry medium or less, black; fine flavor; promising for wine.

Anna.—New York. Poor grower; bunch rather small; berry large, amber yellow; very sweet.

Arkansas.—Vine vigorous, productive; berry small, black, resembling Norton; promises well for wine.

August Pioneer.—Black, early; not otherwise desirable; foxy.

Baldwin Lenoir.—Thrifty, hardy and healthy; very rich in sugar.

Black Hawk.—Pennsylvania, from Concord. Said to be earlier; very promising vine.

Black King.—Early; bunch small; berry medium; foxy.

Blackstone.—Early; black; poor and foxy.

Bland.—Virginia. An old variety of excellence, but not profitable; tender; bunch large, loose; berry large, purple, sweet.

Blood's Black.—Like Mary Ann; early; bunch compact; berry rather large, round, black; a market grape; vine hardy and productive.

Brackett's.—Late, large, and resembles the Union Village.

Brinklé.—Pennsylvania; Bunch large, compact; berry large, round, black, sweet.

Brown.—One of the Isabella style.

California Rosea.—Cincinnati. Thrifty and vigorous, productive; bunch large; berry large, red; very fine.

California White.—Originated with the above; bunch full, medium; berry large, yellow; very fine.

Canby's August, or *York Madeira.*—Early, black; good size.

Cape.—Much planted in the early vineyards; hardy, productive; berry round, black; pulp firm; has made a very good red wine.

Carpenter.—New York. Appears to be a foreign variety.

Cassaday.—Vigorous, but not free from mildew; bunch medium; berry full medium, white, sweet; foxy; makes a good white wine, says Hussman.

Catawba.—N. Carolina. This excellent variety is too well known to need a description; few sorts equal it in flavor and other good qualities. Its failure, from rot, has discouraged planters from increasing it, but no one should destroy a vineyard of this fine grape.

Charlotte.—Ohio. Very like Diana.

Charter Oak.—Connecticut. An enormous fox-grape, and nothing more.

Chillicothe.—Ohio. Bunch long, loose; berry medium, oval, dark purple

Christina.—Pennsylvania. Large, black, early; a fox-grape.

Clara.—Pennsylvania. Has a very foreign air; bunch long, loose; berry medium, light yellow; highly commended by Hussman, for amateurs only.

Clinton.—New York. Thrifty, hardy, productive; bunch medium, compact; berry medium, black, juicy. Makes a fair red wine.

Cloantha.—Kentucky. Black, like Isabella; earlier, and more foxy.

Concord.—Massachusetts. Well known, and everywhere successful; hardy and productive; yields a large quantity of wine—1000 gallons per acre, says Hussman. This has been called the grape for the million.

Corinh.—New Jersey. Hardy; bunch medium; berry small, oval, black or blue; good.

Corsican.—Ohio. Perfectly hardy; bunch large; berry small, round, red; very good.

Creveling.—Pennsylvania. Healthy; hardy; bunch loose, berry large, black; early; very good.

Cunningham.—Vigorous, healthy; bunch large; berry below medium, black, juicy, sweet; very good; promising.

Cuyahoga.—Ohio. A foreign look and behavior, as it is apt to mildew; when successful, very good, but late; berry greenish.

Cuyarano.—Bunch large; berry large; promising.

Cynthiana.—Arkansas. Hardy, healthy, productive; a rival of Norton, which it resembles; makes delicious wine.

Delaware.—New Jersey. Very famous; this delicious grape is subject to mildew in many places; has made excellent wine.

Delaware Seedling.—Ohio. Vine healthy; bunch short; berry full medium, dull red, rich, sweet, rather foxy; very early.

Detroit.—Michigan. Bunch medium; berry full medium, red, good; early.

Devereux.—Southern. Subject to mildew in Missouri; bunch very long, loose, shouldered; berry small, black, juicy, sweet.

Diana.—Massachusetts. Well known and highly appreciated; bunch compact; berry large, dull red, sweet.

Diana Hamburgh.—New York. "A hybrid of Black Hamburgh;" berry large, round, bluish purple.

Dorr's.—New York. Medium; early and red; "promising for wine."

Dracut Amber.—Massachusetts. Red, early, foxy; poor.

Early June.—Like Vitis cordifolia. Bunch large; berry large, dark, sweet, very early.

Early Lebanon.—Pennsylvania; bunch medium; berry medium, blue, very early; good for market.

Early York.—Is Canby's August, or York Madeira.

Elmira.—New York. "A luscious black grape,"—noticed in *Horticulturist*, November, 1866.

Elsinburgh.—New Jersey. Vigorous, hardy; bunch large, loose; berry small, black, juicy, sweet; very good.

Emily.—Pennsylvania. Bunch large, loose; berry rather small, pale red, sweet; not generally satisfactory.

Eva.—Pennsylvania. Little known; a Concord seedling.

Ewings.—Like Isabella.

Fancher.—Probably Saratoga.

Framingham.—Very like Hartford.

Franklin.—Like the Clinton.

Garrigues.—Like Isabella; early.

German Wine.—Is it York Madeira?

Golden Clinton.—Yellow; highly recommended by some.

Graham.—Pennsylvania. Black; sweet.

Guignard.—Vigorous, productive, not hardy; bunch compact; berry rather small, juicy, fine; brownish.

Hartford.—Connecticut. Exceedingly vigorous, hardy, productive; early; bunch large; berry large, black, pulpy, musky; for market.

Hattie.—Michigan. Like Catawba; early; good.

Herbemont.—Southern. Vigorous, productive, rather tender; bunch large, compact; berry rather small, brown, juicy, very fine; table and wine.

Herbemont Seedling.—Ohio. Like its parent; very good; promising for wine.

Hyde's Eliza.—Some think it York Madeira; black; early.

Iona.—New York. This celebrated grape is far in advance of most American varieties of the Labrusca type. Unfortuately, it has mildewed in many places. Bunch large; berry large, red, sweet and rich. The must weighs very heavy, as reported by M. Masson. Hence it is considered promising for wine.

Isabella.—An old variety, well known; not satisfactory for wines; not rich for table.

Isabella Seedling.—Ohio. An improvement on its parent, which it resembles.

Isabella Seedling.—New York. Said to be sweeter and earlier than its parent.

Israella.—New York. Bunch large; berries large, black; early, and hangs well.

Kingsessing.—Bunch long, loose ; berry medium, round, red, pulpy ; mildews.

Ives.—Ohio. Very thrifty, productive, and hardy ; bunch large ; berry large, black, pulpy, musky ; makes a very superior red wine.

Laura.—Ohio. Hardy, productive ; berry large, light green to pale red, sweet, foxy, little pulp.

Lenoir.—Southern. Vigorous ; resembles Herbemont ; black ; very good.

Lincoln.—Southern. Tender ; resembles Lenoir ; unproductive.

Little Ozark.—South-western. Bunch long, loose ; berry medium, black, juicy ; good for wine.

Logan.—Hardy ; bunch long, loose ; berry medium, oval, black ; no better than Isabella.

Long.—Southern. Berry medium, dark purple, sweet ; recommended for wine.

Longworth.—Ohio. Vigorous, healthy, productive ; shoots red ; bunch large, handsome ; berry rather small, black, juicy ; excellent.

Longworth's Monster.—Ohio. Exceedingly vigorous, healthy, productive ; bunch medium ; berry large, round, blue.

Lorain.—Ohio. Bunch medium ; berry large, amber yellow, sweet ; good.

Louisa.—Pennsylvania. Like Isabella, but earlier.

Louisiana.—Southern. Seems to be a foreign sort. Approved for wine, in Missouri.

' *Lydia.*—Ohio. Vigorous, healthy ; bunch medium ; berry large ; green to yellow ; sweet ; ripens early.

Lyman.—Healthy, vigorous, productive ; bunch large, handsome ; berry full medium, blue or black ; very good ; makes a fine red wine.

Macedonia.—Pennsylvania. A Concord seedling ; said to be early and white.

Maguire.—" Foxy and poor."

Manhattan.—New York. "An Isabella seedling ; bunch small ; berry sweet, tough, foxy."

Marion. Ohio. Vigorous, hardy, productive ; bunch large, handsome, close ; berry large, round, blue ; very good.

Marion Post.—Ohio. Too much like York Madeira. Not desirable.

Marique.—Ohio. Healthy, vigorous, very productive ; bunch full medium, compact ; berry oval, large, blue, spicy ; very good.

Martha.—Pennsylvania. A white Concord ; vigorous, healthy, and hardy ; bunch medium to large ; berry large, round, white, sweet ; very promising.

Mary Ann.—Too foxy to be desirable, except for early market; black.

Maxatawny.—Pennsylvania. Healthy, vigorous, hardy; rather late; white.

Mead's.—Massachusetts. Resembles Catawba, which some think it is.

Miles.—Pennsylvania. Hardy and healthy; early; black.

Miner's.—Pennsylvania. Wild, very vigorous, hardy; bunch medium; berry large, foxy, dull red; useful for wine.

Missouri.—Moderate grower; bunch large; berry small, very sweet; black.

Madeira.—New York. Seedling of Concord, which it resembles; black.

Mottled.—Ohio. Hardy, healthy, productive; bunch medium, compact; berry large, round, mottled red; a promising wine grape.

Mount Lebanon.—"Large and showy, but coarse and foxy."

Mustang.—Texas. Vigorous; bunch medium; berry full medium, black; acerb; not promising.

North America.—Healthy; bunch small; early; black; fair quality.

Northern Muscadine.—Vigorous, healthy, sometimes very productive; bunch medium; berry medium to large, round, dark, dull red; early; very foxy; poor; falls badly as it ripens.

North Carolina.—Bunch small, loose; berry medium, round, black; thought to be good for wine.

Norton.—Virginia. Vigorous, healthy, productive; bunch large, full; berry rather small, black, sweet, rich; very fine for wine.

Offer.—Bunch large; berry large, dark red, sweet, musky; not approved.

Ohio, or *Segar Box.*—Southern. Juicy; fine.

Ontario.—Very like Union Village.

Oporto.—New York. Exceedingly vigorous, hardy; bunch medium; berry medium, black, acid; poor; too much acid for good wine.

Pauline.—Southern. Resembles Lenoir somewhat; black.

Perkins.—Vigorous; bunch medium; berry large, light red, very foxy; approved by some for early market.

Pœschell's Mammoth.—Missouri. Healthy; berry large, red; late; not desirable.

Post Oak.—Texas. Foliage peculiarly lobed; fruit has not proved satisfactory.

Raäbe.—Pennsylvania. Berry full, medium, black, sweet.

Rachel.—Hardy; bunch medium; berry medium, white; early.

Rebecca.—New York. Mildews in some localities; never very robust; bunch medium; berry large, round, yellow; very good.

Red Shepherd.—Very vigorous; very foxy.

Rentz.—Ohio. Vigorous, healthy, productive; early; bunch rather large; berry full medium to large, round, black, pulpy, sweet, musky; makes very good light red wine.

Rogers' Hybrids.*—*No.* 1.—Vigorous; bunch large; berry very large, round, pale red, rather late; esteemed by some; said to improve in the west; foxy flavor, as are they all.

No. 2.—Late, large, black.

No. 3.—"Hardy and vigorous;" large; amber colored; quite early.

No. 4.—The most popular of the lot; may prove profitable for market; said to be healthy and vigorous; bunch handsome, rather large; berry large, black.

No. 9.—Foliage scanty; canes long jointed; early as Delaware; reddish, sweet. -

No. 15.—Vigorous, healthy, productive; bunch large; berry large, amber, rich, sweet, aromatic.

No. 19.—Resembles No. 4; not considered quite so good.

No. 22.—Resembles No. 15 in color and quality; more Diana flavor.

Nos. 41, 43, 44.—All black and large; better than No. 4, but not so large bunches.

Rulander.—Foreign; berry medium, black; valued as a wine grape in Missouri.

Sage.—Massachusetts. Vigorous; berry large; very foxy.

Sanbornton.—New Hampshire. One of the Isabella type; said to ripen where the Isabella will not.

Saratoga.—New York. Supposed to be the same as Fancher; very like Catawba; red, good.

Segar Box.—Same as Ohio; rather tender; vigorous; bunch large, rather loose; berry small, black, juicy; very good.

---

*These seedlings are reputed to be true hybrids, of the *Vitis vinifera*, on the *labrusca*, or wild fox-grape of New England. They were introduced at the meeting of the Lake Shore Grape Growers' Association, at Cleveland, Ohio, in October, 1866, when their merits were set forth by Hon. Marshal P. Wilder, who exhibited them. The above descriptions are condensed from the statements there made. There are said to be still others, some of which have merit. It must be confessed that if hybrids, they are far below the choice varieties of the European grapes that are their reputed parents; but, if only seedlings, from the miserable wild-fox grape, their mother, they evince a most wonderful tendency to improvement in that variety, that that would have transported Van Mons, had they occurred in his experience.

Shaker.—Is Union Village.

Shaker Seedling.—Resembles Union Village, but is earlier; black, large.

South Carolina.—Ohio. Vigorous; bunch large; berry small, black, juicy, spicy, very promising.

Schuylkill.—Same as Cape.

Taylor.—Kentucky. Very vigorous, rampant; not generally productive; bunch rather small; berry small, green, yellow, and rosy, juicy, good.

To Kalon.—Not vigorous; very like Isabella; bunch above medium; berry large, black, round, pretty good; by some highly esteemed.

Ulrey.—Indiana. Bunch medium; berry large, white, sweet, rich; "perfectly hardy."

Underhill.—New York. Vigorous, hardy; berry red, sweet; another fox.

Union Village.—Ohio. Very vigorous, healthy; not hardy when overgrown; bunch large; berry very large, blue; only an overgrown Isabella, to my taste; very attractive in the market.

Urbana.—A Concord seedling. Bunch medium; berry large, white; not very sweet; worthy of trial.

Venango.—Pennsylvania. Same as Miner's

Wachita.

Walter.—New York. " Hardy, productive; a cross between Delaware and Diana ;" bunch full medium ; berry medium, red ; very like Diana in many of its characters ; early.

Warren.—Is Herbemont.

Washington.—New York. Early, black.

White Catawba.—Ohio. Resembles Catawba, but inferior; bunch medium ; berry large, greenish, pulpy.

White Muscadine.

Wilmington.—Delaware. Vigorous ; berry medium, white.

Worthington.—Ohio. Vigorous, hardy ; bunch small ; berry medium, black, very acid, poor.

Yeddo.—Japan. Has not succeeded ; tender.

York Madeira. An improved fox, only ; valued for its earliness.

Young America.—Pennsylvania. A Concord seedling ; late.

Zane.—Ohio. Berry full medium, red ; not cultivated.

In most vineyards a long experience has pointed out what vines are the best adapted (considering the state of the soil, the location and exposure) to the production of the kind of wine desired. When, therefore, a vineyard is to be planted, the first thing to be ascertained will be the situation, the exposure, and the nature of the soil, and subsoil, of the land to be used; after which we must choose, in the neighborhood, those vines which, under the same conditions, have given the best results.

There are, however, a few general rules which may serve as guides in that particular.

1st. Consider whether quality of product is more profitable than quantity; for these two conditions can scarcely ever be united. It does not depend upon the cultivator to produce that bouquet—that smoothness which characterizes fine wines. Those qualities certainly depend partly on the climate, the nature of the vine, the character of the soil, and its exposure; but they are especially the results of certain local influences, which it has been impossible, so far, to determine in a very positive manner. Therefore, when a vineyard is to be planted in one of these favored localities, quantity must undoubtedly be sacrificed to quality; for, the high price which the product will command, may compensate for its smaller quantity; but, these desirable products excepted, it will be well to sacrifice quality to quantity; for, do what we may, the price will never be sufficiently high to compensate for the diminished yield. Nevertheless, it has been recently suggested, that the fine varieties should be everywhere substituted for the much more common, but, at the same time, much more productive ones. This is unfortunate, for it is evident that under no circumstances can one acre of Burgundy "Pinots," in their highest state of productiveness, yield the same quantity which the "Gamais" will yield, if planted on the same extent of land, and also in its highest state of productiveness. It is equally certain that the produce of the fine varieties acquires all its excellent qualities only under the influence of certain conditions of the soil, and its favorable exposure. This being admitted, let us suppose two acres of land, very richly manured, heavy, little subject to drought—one planted with "Gamais," the other planted to Burgundy "Pinots." The "Gamais" will yield 1056 gallons, which, at one dollar per gallon, is $1,056. The "Pinot," owing to the unfavorable state of the soil in which it is planted, will yield 264 gallons, of a quality below its proper standard, which, at two dollars fifty cents, will give $660. It is evident, therefore—the expense of cultivation being the same—that the advantage will be in favor of the "Gamais."

If, on the other hand, one acre of well drained land, of good depth, a little gravelly, situated on a hill-side, with a good exposure—in fact, situated in the conditions most favorable to the "Pinot"—is planted with "Gamais," that space will perhaps yield 422 gallons, which, at one dollar, will bring $422 ; whilst the same space, under the same conditions, and devoted to the "Pinot," will produce only 211 gallons, it is true, but it will sell at five dollars, and realize $1,055 for the entire crop. In that case, the advantage is in favor of the "Pinot."

Besides, supposing that fine wines could be produced anywhere, and that their greater value should compensate for their small yield, the production of fine wines, almost exclusively, would soon bring about the following unfortunate result, namely : that two-thirds, at least, of consumers, being unable to buy anything but common wines, producers of fine wines could no longer find a market. Therefore, it would not be advisable to be too positive as to the choice of vines, as regards quantity or quality. Quality, *exclusively*, must not be thought of, except in those favored localities where the high price of the product will compensate for the smallness of the yield; everywhere else quantity must have the preference.

2d. If wines of medium quality are to be obtained, the finer descriptions, generally very rich in alcohol, must be mixed with the more abundant but much weaker ones. It is thus that in the second class vineyards of Burgundy, the " Pinots," which produce a fine wine, but in small quantity, are mixed with the " Gamais," which is of inferior quality but produces largely. In the Gironde district, the " Verdal," the " Merlot," the big " Mérille," are mixed with the " Carmenet." On the banks of the Rhône the " Pique-Poule," yielding little, but excellent wine, is mixed with a small quantity of " Grenache," producing very strong wine, and with the " Terret," a large yielder of wine, but weak in alcoholic principle. The vine of l'Ermitage is composed exclusively of the " Big Sirah," which is very productive, but not so fine as the " Little Sirah," with which it is sometimes mixed.

3d. It is enough that ordinary wines contain a sufficient proportion of alcohol: that is, 0.08 at least; when weaker than that they are difficult of sale.— Therefore, the vines which will most readily give this result ought to be selected. Thus, as the " Gamais,"

in a good soil, will contain 0.0649 of alcohol, the " Pinot," which yields 0.1062, is mixed with it.

4th. If the wines are for distillation, preference must
be given to the most productive descriptions, and they
must be cultivated in rich soils. Weak wines will be
obtained, but their greater abundance will more than
compensate for their small yield of alcohol; besides,
this poverty will not be an obstacle to the sale of these
wines, since, in the process of prolonged distillation,
water has to be added to those wines which contain
over 0.10 of alcohol, and the buyer has to pay only for
the alcohol contained in the wine. What we have just
said is clearly proven by the following figures, which
we borrow from M. Bouchardet:

One acre of " Gamais," well cultivated, yields 1,689
gallons of wine, containing 0.048 of alcohol, or 216
gallons of alcohol per acre.

One acre of " Pinot," well cultivated, will yield
528 gallons of wine, containing 0.1062 of alcohol, or
56 gallons of alcohol per acre.

5th. Certain grapes produce wine which remains sweet
for the want of ferment; this defect may be obviated
by mixing with them such as produce *dry* wines. Thus,
a too large proportion of the " Grenache " often produces this result, in the South; if it has too little alcohol, the defect is corrected by increasing the number of
" Pique-Poule " plants, in the South, and of " Pinots "
in the North. If the wine contains much lees, and is
liable to sour, or turn to vinegar, those descriptions
which contain much tannin are mixed with it; such as
the Mourvèdre, in rich soils; the brown " Fourca " in
the dry soils of the South; the Merlot of the Gironde

in the West. In the South there are "*musts*" which ferment badly for want of a sufficient proportion of water; this inconvenience is remedied by planting a certain proportion of Aramons, or Terrets. This is the way to correct the defects of wine ; it is better than to add to the "*musts*" substances which assimilate themselves badly with that liquid, and which it is difficult to mix in the right proportions to all the elements which compose it.

6th. The degree of color to give to wine must also be attended to, in choosing the plants, for this exerts considerable influence on the sale of the wine. When they lack color, it is remedied, in the South, by planting the Tirtot, the Mourastel or the Carignan ; in the North the " Dyers" are employed.

7th. From the preceding positions, we conclude that in almost all vineyards several kinds of plants must be united ; but the number ought always to be very limited, and should comprise those only, the admixture of which will produce the results we have here pointed out. In any case, as the "*musts*" of the different kinds will have to be mixed in the same cask, the plants must be selected in such a way that they will all mature precisely at the same time. If it is sometimes proper to introduce varieties of different dates of maturity, it is when large vineyards are to be planted ; in such cases the different grapes are pressed separately. The planting is done in this way to counterbalance the risks which each variety runs from white frosts, rotting, etc. This also permits the harvesting of the crop to be done gradually, and to have always a sufficient number of laborers at hand. It is for this reason that in the large vineyards of Lower Languedoc, they plant one-third in " Aramons," which belong to the fourth period of maturity ; one-third in " Grenache," which belongs to the fifth period, and one-third in " Terret-bourret," which only ripens at the sixth period.

These are the chief causes which have determined the selections of the various grapes comprising our vineyards. These selections, sanctioned by long experience, are almost all founded upon common-sense principles, and for this reason, very frequently it is sufficient to imitate what has already been done in the locality to be planted. It is not that we absolutely condemn the introduction of new plants : numerous examples prove the advantage of sometimes introducing new varieties ; but these sorts of naturalizations ought to be attempted with great caution, as a failure might cause heavy loss.

As a general rule, the transfer of varieties from one country to another succeeds only where the climate, soil, and cultivation, of the country of which the plant is a native, perfectly resemble those of that into which it is to be introduced. And yet this rule is not without exception, for certain vineyards of the Northern and Middle districts have been improved by the introduction of vines originating in the South, and *vice versa:* the Northern varieties have given very good results in the South. Therefore, no positive rule can be laid down in this respect ; nevertheless, it will be well, when a new plant is to be introduced, to try it on a small scale, so as to observe how far, and in what manner, it has been affected by the new conditions to which it is exposed.

PLANTS PRODUCING THE BEST WINES.—Let us conclude the subject of plants by pointing out those which produce our best wines.

1st. *Burgundy.*—The best products of Burgundy are: For red wines—those of Romanée-Conti, Chambertin, Richbourg, Clos-Saint-Georges, Corton, Clos-de-Vougeot, Volnay, Pomard, Nuits.

These wines are produced chiefly from the black "Pinot."

For white wines—the best are from Montrachet, Meursault, Chablis, where the white "Pinot" is used.

2d. *Bordelais.*—The chief crops of this country are:

For red wines—those of Médoc, Château-Margeaux, Château-Lafitte, Château-Latour, Haut Brion, Saint Julien, Saint Estéphe, and in the gravelly districts of Bordeaux, those of Talence, Saint Émilion, near Libourne. These vineyards are composed, almost exclusively of the "Carmenet," "Malbeck," "Merlot," and "Verdot" plants.

For white wines—Château-Yquem (Sauterne), Coutet (Barsac) Château-Carbonnieux (Villeneuve d'Ornon). These wines are the produce of the "Semillion," the "Rochalin," and the "Blanquette."

3d. *Champagne.*—The products of Ay, Sillery, Èpernay, of Versenay, Pierry, Avise, Cramont, are the most celebrated of that country. The plants occupying the first rank here are particularly the "Gray Pinot," the "White Muscat," and "Black Muscat."

4th. *Banks of the Rhône.*—The products of Côte Rôtie and Condrieu are extensively composed of "Black Serine," and "White Vionnier."

5th. *Drôme.*—The red wine of l'Ermitage is produced by the " Big" and " Little Sirah ;" the plants of Marsanne and Roussane yield the white wine of l'Ermitage.

6th. *Hérault.*—The wines of Lunel and Frontignan, are produced by the " White Muscat," the " Picardan," and the plant of Calabria.

7th. *Upper Rhine.*—The Rhine wines, and particularly those of Johannisberg, are the products of the big and little " Riesling."

8th. *Eastern Pyrénées.*—The wines known as Alicante, Grenache, Collioure, are of the " Red Grenache," the " Alicante," and the " Grignane." The wine of Rivesaltes, is the product of the " White Muscat," " Alexandrian Muscat," and " St. Jacques Muscat."

9th. *Ardèche.*—The wine of St. Peray is from the " Big Roussette," and " Little Roussette."

10th. *Cher.* — The wine of Pouilly is from the " White Pinot."

11th. *Aude.*—The Blanquette of Limoux is produced from the " Blanquette."

12th *Lower Pyrénées.*—The red wines of Jurançon are from the following plants : " Pinène," " Mensec," " Menseing," and " Tannat." The white wines of Jurançon are from the " Réfiat," the " Menseing," the Claverie," the " Aulban" and the " Courtoisie."

13th. *Jura.*—The white wines of Château-Châlons, the yellow and spirituous wines of Arbois, known also under the name of the *straw wines*, are produced by the " Sauvagin," or wild plant.

[The importance of having a variety of grapes in cultivation, is very well argued by our author. Our list of hardy

American grapes is yet quite small, compared to the very numerous varieties which are cultivated in Europe ; which have probably all been derived from one and the same species, under cultivation, but have shown a wonderful disposition to sport into distinct varieties. With the different species of grapes in our country, their tendency to variation, and the great attention which has been bestowed upon them, with a view to the production of new varieties, by crossing and hybridizing, we already have quite a respectable assortment, and may expect, in a few years, to have very many more presented to the public.

Up to this time very little has been done in the way of commingling the products of different vines, by our wine-makers. Certain varieties, with very high aroma, have been suggested as valuable, to add to others that are deficient in character, and some few experiments have been made. Thus, the juice of the Diana, with its peculiar feline flavor, has been mixed with some grapes that were deficient or insipid, to dilute this character, and bring it within reasonable bounds. The highly musky juice of the Anna, has been mixed with the rich, but often rather tame, fluid produced by the Delaware, and the result was a most delicious product. These, and similar trials, have shown us that good results may follow from the judicious admixtures of some of our grapes, and no doubt future experiments will be attended with happy results.

Up to this time, our wine-makers have, very properly, taken a great deal of pains in attempting to produce pure wines from all of the grapes they were cultivating, keeping each separate and unmixed, so as to ascertain its peculiar character and merits ; but as the culture is extended, and the number of varieties is increased, we may very properly begin to experiment with this class of mixtures, which are perfectly legitimate, and are justified by the practice of the best wine-countries.

The same can not be said of the other class of admixtures: those of foreign ingredients of any kind, which may very properly be called *adulterations*, which will be considered in another place.]

V.

PROPAGATION OF THE VINE.

THE vine may be propagated from the seeds, from cuttings, by layers, and by grafting; let us consider under what circumstances the one or the other of these modes of reproduction must be preferred.

SEEDS.—Seeds can not be used, on a large scale, for planting a vineyard. For, although they may have been gathered from varieties of first-rate quality, and perfectly adapted to the locality, they will generally produce very inferior plants, and the seedling obtained will always be more or less removed from the parent stock, and approximate nearer to the wild state. But, as it has sometimes happened that seedlings have possessed superior qualities to the original stock, this mode of reproduction has been employed, to obtain new varieties still more worthy of cultivation. It is thus that our vineyards and trellises have been gradually improved by the excellent varieties which we now cultivate. This operation, practiced in gardens, or nurseries, is a very slow process, for it will sometimes be eight or ten years before the plants will bear, although it may, it is true, be hastened by laying down the young plants successively;

or, better still, by grafting some of their shoots on old plants.

[For the reasons presented by the author, propagation by seedlings, will never be practiced merely for the multiplication of plants; but the number of good varieties thus produced in this country, would make it appear that the tendency to run back to the wild characters was not so great with our vines as with those of the species *Vitis vinifera* of Europe. Nor are we obliged to wait so long a time for our vines to fruit, since many of our seedlings have given satisfactory evidence of their promising qualities, or otherwise, in the third year. In a collection of seedlings, a good many may be rejected the first or second season, if we allow ourselves to be guided by the appearance of the vine and its foliage, and an expert may be safe in depending upon these criteria.

The late Mr. N. Longworth, of Cincinnati, was a most indefatigable seed-planter, and he produced a great number of seedling grape-vines, some of which will yet make their mark. His seeds were taken almost at random, from any good grapes. He annually rejected great numbers of plants, which he thought were showing indications of wildness, that induced him to conclude they were worthless.

Mr. John Fiske Allen, and Mr. E. S. Rogers, of the vicinity of Boston; and Mr. Peter Raäbe, of Philadelphia, and others, have made systematic attempts to improve the native grape, by fertilizing with the pollen of choice foreign varieties. Their trials have been attended with more or less success, and many others have been encouraged to take up the subject of cross-fertilization, and to repeat these experiments. A doubt has existed in the minds of some of our most intelligent pomologists, whether all the results were really true hybrids, and this is based upon the observation that one set of plants was so decidedly foreign in appearance, while another set should show so little change in the characters of the native parent. This is a matter, however, which it is not proposed to discuss in this place.

One of the most reliable operators in this line of investigation, is the careful experimenter, and accurate observer, Geo. W. Campbell, of Delaware, Ohio; who is perfectly satisfied that he has succeeded in effecting veritable crosses between several varieties, and that he has even produced hybrids between the foreign and American species. Mr. Campbell has been so good as to communicate some ot the results ot his experiments to the public, with most interesting details, in papers to the *Ohio Pomological Society*, and in an elaborate article which may be found in the *Report of the Department of Agriculture*, at Washington, for the year 1862, p. 209, to which last the reader is particularly referred. In it the subject of hybridizing, cross-breeding, and selection of the seedlings, is pretty fully discussed.

Mr. Campbell does not give a very flattering or encouraging view of the prospects of any one who enters this field of investigation, when he says :—"that about ten years of further care and culture (after fertilizing the blossoms), will be required before determinate results are reached, and that the chances may be ten, or perhaps a hundred to one, that the product will be of no value. A good deal of enthusiasm, as well as a sanguine temperament, is necessary to enable the hybridizer to find much encouragement in his pursuit. He must be, emphatically, one who is willing

'To labor and to wait.' "

Up to this time the most of our leading kinds in cultivation are either natives, or accidental garden seedlings, which are the result of selection merely, and have not been produced by the application of scientific efforts bestowed upon the subject; so with most of our American seedling fruits, of all kinds.]

CUTTINGS.—Propagation from cuttings is, as regards

the vine, the simplest and most expeditious process; giving the best results, and is the one most in vogue.

The kind of cutting most generally used is that known under the name of "crossette" or "elbow-cutting." In some vineyards it is also known as "capon" or "hook."

The crossette is composed of one shoot, properly so called, [Fig. 5.] that is of the preceding spring's growth; it must have, at its base, a small portion of wood, of two years' growth, and be, altogether, about sixteen inches in length. The portion of old wood left at the end of the shoot forms a sort of hook, and from this has received the name of " crossette."— The base, or heel of the shoot, helps greatly to form the roots.

[FIG. 5.]

In the absence of crossettes, shoots, properly so called, are also used; that is, shoots without heels, but provided with an eye at each end. [Fig. 6.] These shoots take root as easily as the first, provided the section at the base is made in the middle of the thick part of the joint.

The two kinds of cuttings just spoken of, are put in nurseries, to make them take root, previous to permanent transplanting. Sometimes they are permanently planted, without

[FIG. 6.] this preliminary operation. We shall point out the precautions which they require, in this last case, when we treat of the setting out of the vineyard.— Let us now show the process of making a nursery for them.

Nursery for Raising Cuttings.—*Preparing the
" Crossettes."*—Crossettes are cut from late in the fall
until the end of February. In the northern latitudes
adapted to the vine, they must be put into the nursery
in March and April only, and in January and February
in the South. Until then the wood must be kept from
drying. It is well, besides, to hasten the development
of their roots. To this end the cuttings are treated as
follows : by means of a pruning-knife, the portion of
old wood which had been left only to prevent the heel
of the crossette from drying, especially when they are
for distant transportation, is cut away. The dry tendrils and grape stalks must also be removed. All the
cuttings are then made of one length—say about sixteen
inches. These crossettes are tied into small bundles,
which are then buried in the following manner : one or
more trenches are opened, of about fourteen inches
wide, and about as deep as the cuttings are long. The
bundles of cuttings are placed in these trenches, in an
upright position, but upside down. The earth is so
placed over them as to form a slanting or shelving bed
over each trench. This process, which we have seen
practiced by some vine-dressers on the " Aude," gives
this result : when about to be transplanted into the
nursery, these cuttings are taken up, when the heel of
each is found provided with a large, round swelling of
cellular tissue, which hastens the growth of the cuttings by one year.

[A similar method, but more carefully and judiciously managed, has been very successfully introduced, in this country,
and has been used by Mr. Wm. Patrick, of Terre Haute, Indiana. The details are given in the *American Annual of Horti-*

culture, a beautiful booklet, which has just been issued from the press of Orange Judd & Co., New York.

The point aimed at is the application of heat to the lower portion of the cuttings, to encourage the formation of the callus, whence the roots are to issue, while the buds that are to form the vine are kept cool and dormant, until the conditions are changed, at planting time, by reversing the cuttings. At this time young roots will have made their appearance.— The reader is referred to the article. See *"Annual"* and *Gardeners' Monthly.*

It is a very common plan to bury the cuttings as fast as they are made and tied up. They are generally set, butts down, in the trench opened for the purpose; fine earth is shaken over them, and filled in between the bundles, and the whole is covered from the weather. The bundles are often laid upon their sides, to avoid digging the trenches so deep. Those that go into the market, and these have amounted to millions, some years, are usually stowed in cellars, to keep them from the drying winds, but not covered with soil. They therefore sometimes become quite dry, and when received at the end of their journey, they should be plunged into water, for a short time, before being buried in the fresh soil, which is a necessary preparation for the planting.

There is a very common prejudice in favor of what are called heel-cuttings, or those that have a portion of the two-year old wood at their base, like those called by our author " crossettes," but we trim the old wood much shorter than he represents in the cut: these are also called " martelles," or hammer-cuttings, from the shape of the old wood. It is thought they root more freely, which is very probable because of the great number of eyes always clustered about the base of the annual shoot. Many of the varieties in cultivation strike so readily from cuttings, that any piece will grow as well as the lower portion; wood that is rather slender and close-jointed, succeeds better than such as is large, sappy, full of pith, and long-jointed, but, under all circumstances, the shoots used should have been well ripened, and firm. Some sorts are very difficult to grow from cuttings in the cold ground; these are propagated by layering, or the wood is turned over to the careful manipulation of those who propagate grape-vines by the aid of artificial heat and glass.]

To the same end, it is advisable to peel the cuttings for four inches from their base, so as to lay bare the inner bark. This operation is easily performed when the cuticle has been softened in water, or by the dampness of the ground. This removal of the skin hastens and facilitates the sprouting of the roots in the following proportions: if 200 cuttings of the same vine are planted in a straight line, and in the same conditions as to soil and moisture, and 100 of them are peeled, as we have just explained, and each one planted between two cuttings which have not been operated on, the following result will be obtained: while one-third of the unpeeled cuttings fail, the cuttings operated on will only fail four or five per cent., and will be more vigorous by half.

By laying the cuttings horizontally in the earth, or soaking them some time in water, somewhat analagous effects are obtained, by the softening of the cuticle, but these results are far from being as complete as in the two foregoing processes.

Nursery Planting.—The growth of cuttings must be hastened as much as possible, and, for this reason, in order to form a nursery, a rich, fertile soil, with a good exposure, must be selected. In the fall preceding the planting, it must be broken up and trenched to the depth of sixteen inches.   Just before being planted, it must be lightly plowed, so as to level the surface properly; a line is then stretched across one end of the vineyard, to mark out a trench twelve inches wide, and twelve inches deep.   One of the sides of the trench, against which the cuttings are to lean, must incline about forty-five degrees.   If the cuttings were placed vertically, they would have to be buried deeper, and their heels being too far from the surface of the ground, would not take root so well.   Cuttings leaning against this inclined plane, have one or two eyes above ground. If they are to remain one year in the nursery, they are planted four inches apart, on the line; if two years, eight inches apart.   The crossettes having thus been placed in this first trench, such manure as may be had— that is, old, loose manure, composted—is put into the trench, to the depth of six inches.   The line is then moved twelve inches from the first trench, if the plants are to remain one year in the nursery, and sixteen inches, if they are to remain two years; and another trench is then opened, similar and parallel to the first— the earth which is dug from it, serves to fill the first; this done, the earth is pressed down, with the foot, against the first lines of cuttings, so that, being in close contact with the earth to the whole extent planted, they may the more easily absorb the moisture from the ground.   The second row is then set like the first one, and so on, with all the rest.   It must be borne in mind that, if different vines are to be planted in a nursery, they will have to be grown separately, in order to prevent confusion at the time of setting out the young plants permanently in the vineyard.

When the nursery is to be of considerable extent, it will be well to divide it into beds four feet six inches, to six feet six inches in width, and separated from each other by alleys one foot six inches wide, running into roads about three feet wide, if the nursery is to be very extensive. The whole operation is finished by a light hoeing of the entire surface of the beds, in order to superficially loosen the soil trodden down by the feet.

Cultivation of the Nursery.—About the beginning of May, it will be well to hoe the soil a second time, and, if it be of a dry character, to cover the entire surface of the beds with a layer of straw, or dried leaves, or any such substance, to the depth of two inches, so as to prevent it from caking, under the action of the rain, to oppose the growth of hurtful plants, and, especially, to prevent the earth from drying up during the heats of summer. If the soil is a little clayey, a few hoeings during the season, will produce these results. These dressings may be done by hand, if the nursery is small; if one acre and a half, or more, it will be cheaper to harrow it. In this case, it will be unnecessary to have alleys, and the trenches must be made in the direction of the greatest length of the nursery. If this nursery be located in a southern latitude, it will not be sufficient to hoe and cover up the soil,—it will also be necessary to water it, to some extent, in the very hot weather.

The shoots must be allowed to grow freely during the first summer; all the pruning or cutting which could be done would only injure the roots.

In the fall, the young plants will appear as in *Figure* 7. These are called roots. They are sometimes permanently planted at this stage of their growth—in the South, for instance—when a vigorous plant is wanted, and a plantation is to be made in a rich and somewhat clayey soil. But it will be best, in most cases, to await until the second year. In that case, about pruning time, all the young plants are cut as at A [Fig. 7], and the small shoot, B, is so cut as to have but one eye at the base. Immediately after the trimming, the ground is lightly plowed, and, at the end of April, it is again covered with a new layer of straw, etc.

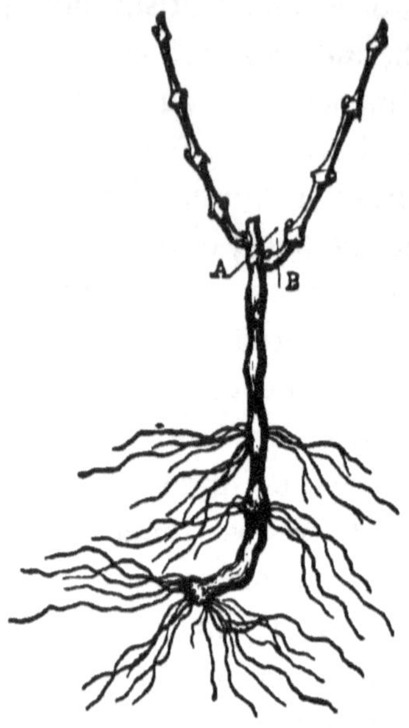

[FIG. 7.]—*One-year old Plant.*

It will be well, during the summer, to concentrate all the vigor of the young plant into one single shoot. For that purpose, as soon as the shoots have attained the length of eight inches, they must all be suppressed, except the finest one, the top of which must be pinched off, as soon as it has reached twenty-four inches in hight. About the beginning of August, the buds are again nipped, if necessary, to prevent confusion, and allow the shoots to be well strengthened by the action of the sun. *Figure* 8 shows the appearance of these two-year old plants in the fall.

Removal of the Plants from the Nursery.—Whatever length of time the cuttings may be left in the nursery, they ought to be taken up in such a way that none of their roots be mutilated, for these, being thick and fleshy, will not bear the least bruising, which afterward will cause them to rot completely. To avoid this danger, they must be taken up in this way : at one end of each of the beds, and cross-wise, open a continuous trench, a little deeper than the roots have gone down ; then undermine the earth, little by little, keeping the trench well cleared out all the time. In this way, all the plants may be taken up, without bruising a single root.

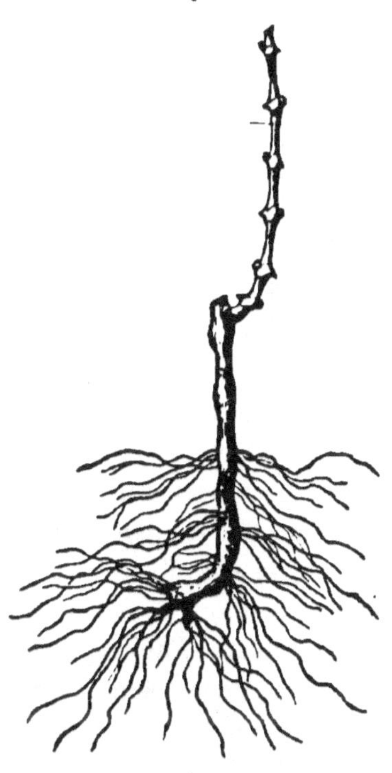

[FIG. 8.]—*Two-year old Plant.*

[Certain changes have been introduced into the system of growing cuttings and making plants, which should be noticed in this place. While some vine-planters prefer setting the cuttings at once in the vineyard, where they are to remain permanently, and thus avoid the labor of transplanting, and obviate the check to the plants incident to this operation, there are others who prefer to grow their vines in the nursery. All those parties at a distance who are to be supplied with plants, must have them grown one or two years in the nursery, and well rooted. Thus the production of grape plants has become a very important part of the business, and enormous quantities of vines are produced by the nurseryman, and sold to the vine-planter.

The nursery of long cuttings—such as were formerly used almost exclusively, was often made in this way. A mellow piece of loamy soil having been selected, either fallow, or, if in clover, so much the better, a trench was opened along one side, as recommended by Mr. Du Breuil. The garden line was stretched, and the bank of freshly dug earth was dressed to it, with the spade, and sloping to the bottom of the trench, which was made some fifteen to eighteen inches deep. -The cuttings were placed along this slope, about three inches apart, and so arranged that the top bud should barely reach the surface.

The spade was then taken, and a little earth from the undug land was cast upon the bases of the cuttings, and firmly trodden, so as to fix them in their places, without disturbing their upper points, however, which should always remain near the line. The digging then proceeded the whole length of the line, as in common preparation of the garden, and the fine soil thrown upon the cuttings, and pressed to them. When a strip of fifteen to eighteen inches width, was thus dug, the line was moved, and set at that distance from its first position, the earth graded to it, and another row planted.

When completed, the nursery was generally left without further care until the young shoots began to make their appearance, when the crust would require loosening, very carefully, with a weeding-fork or a rake-hoe. This process is one requiring great delicacy, because the shoots are very tender and brittle, and easily destroyed. In some soils which are apt to bake and form a hard crust, it is better, as the rows are planted, to raise a little ridge of soil over the points of the cuttings. This is done before moving the line, by using a fine garden-rake, or by putting on a small quantity of loose compost, or woods' earth, which has been prepared for the purpose, and which will not bake. Such material covers the cuttings, protects them from drying, encourages the starting of the buds, does not form a crust, and shows the cultivator just where to look for his young vines, and it is easily removed from the points of the shoots as they commence to push through it to the light and air.

Long and Short Cuttings.—The old rule for the length of cuttings was to make them a practical cubit's length, the measure being taken on the fore-arm and running to the end of the fingers. Where the wood was abundant, and the cuttings brought a low price, say of from one to, at most, three dollars per thousand, the vine-trimmer could afford to be generous, and it was found that in tying up the bundles of one hundred, this length was very convenient.

The objection to these long cuttings, particularly for nursery planting, and the production of vines for sale, was two-fold. The farmer had greater labor in planting, and also in digging them, and the purchaser had fewer roots than he desired; indeed, many of the yearling plants were little better than cuttings, by the time they reached their destination, as the slender roots were often withered and dried up, so as to be unfit for planting. Some cultivators divided their cuttings in the middle, making two of one, so that they were from eight to ten inches long, and had but three or four eyes to each. By careful treatment in the nursery, and by having the ground well selected, well cultivated, or well mulched, the success that attended these short-cuttings was remarkable, and highly satisfactory, both to the nurseryman and to the vine-planter, as the roots and tops were much longer and more vigorous. This shortening was pushed still further, until but two eyes were used; but these shorter cuttings only required a little care to guard against the effects of drouth. Some growers went even so far as to propagate from a single joint of wood, having the eye at the upper portion, and the lower end cut somewhat slanting, so as to remove the bark and a portion of the wood, and thus to encourage the formation of a larger callus, from which the roots are emitted. Beautiful and very well rooted plants, from such cuttings, were exhibited at the meeting of the Lake Shore Society, at Cleveland, O.

Single Eyes.—The plan almost universally employed by those who now devote themselves to the multiplication of the vine, is to use but a single eye or bud, depending upon artificial means for regulating the temperature, and other attendant circumstances, so as to make these as favorable as possible for the development of roots. For this purpose, bottom heat is used, and this is usually produced by a flow of heated water beneath the sand-bed in which the eyes are started. The idea is to induce the roots to grow in the warm, moist sand, while the cooler air above does not encourage the development of the buds, nor the expansion of the leaves, until after the formation of the roots. When the little plants are fairly under way, they are potted off into good soil, and put through a process of hardening, preparatory to setting them out in the nursery; or they are pushed, and, from time to time, shifted into larger pots, so as to produce the greatest amount of growth, by keeping the plants in the most favorable circumstances for their development. These will push out laterals, that are often removed, and used for the propagation of plants during the summer. Such are called softwood cuttings. Many plants are produced by setting the eyes in boxes, in which they are allowed to remain during the whole period of growth, and these are generally kept under shelter of the glass all summer, or they are hardened off, and exposed toward its close.

Most of the vines grow from single eyes, by starting them thus with bottom heat, and pointing them off, are set out in the open nursery ground so soon as they are prepared for this exposure by hardening, and when the season has so far advanced that the young plants will not receive a check by by the exposure. The ground should have been well prepared by thorough plowing, or by trenching and manuring; the line is stretched, the pots are carried out, and the planter turns them, ejecting the balls, which he sets with a trowel, in the loose earth, and presses it firmly about them. The line is moved a foot or fifteen inches, and another row is set. The plants are well watered once, and, in a day or two, the surface is loosened with the hoe, to overcome the effects of the tramping of the workmen, and then mulched.

In the fall, these plants are taken up much in the way recommended in the text, taking care to preserve the roots as perfect as possible; they are sorted, counted, tied in small bundles, and packed away in sand, moss, or damp saw-dust, and put into a cool cellar, until wanted for shipping or planting; or they may be heeled-in, out of doors, in a dry and sheltered situation, but the risk of loss, with additional labor requisite for the careful performance of this work, renders the cellar storage very preferable. Unfortunately, these little plants are often trimmed very short, for the sake of their wood, and this has been one of the objections to single eye plants, because they can not be set deeply in planting them out in their stations.

Objections to Single Eye Plants.—From some cause there has arisen a great prejudice against plants produced in the way that has just been alluded to. A great deal of nonsense has been uttered, and the process has been denounced as a "steam manufactory of vines;" the plants are said to have been forced unnaturally, and to have been "propagated to death," etc. Now it is not worth while to occupy space in repeating what every intelligent person, engaged in the cultivation of plants, should know: that it is no matter how the vine is produced, if it be well developed in leaf, shoots and roots. As has been well said by one of the most extensive vine-planters of our country, "give me a good plant, and I don't care a fig how you have produced it—by steam or otherwise." The good plant is what we should demand.

It must be confessed, however, that we do not always receive good plants, even when we have paid enormous prices for some of the new and fancy kinds; and it must be acknowledged that when these delicate, slender little things have been set out in the open ground of the vineyard, they have, too often, succumbed to the effects of the exposure. A question arises whether, in a majority of cases, the disasters we have suffered have not been incidental to the faulty character of the variety itself, rather than to the method of its propagation. Some kinds of grapes are much more subject to the attacks of mildew than others, and the little plants have not acquired sufficient force in their new stations to resist the malady.

The next question that arises is, whether we can honestly recommend the extensive planting of such varieties; and with these views some of our most reliable planters, and some of our most intelligent societies, have adopted the principle of not recommending any fruits for general cultivation that have not proved themselves *both hardy and healthy*, as well as productive of good fruit.]

LAYERING.—This operation consists in choosing one or more vigorous shoots, on the same stock, from which to make new plants. In March each one is laid down into the earth, to the length of about sixteen inches, and at a depth of five inches, the earth having first been well loosened and manured. The top of the shoot is cut so as to leave about two eyes out of the ground, and the end is fastened to a grape-stake. [Fig. 9.]

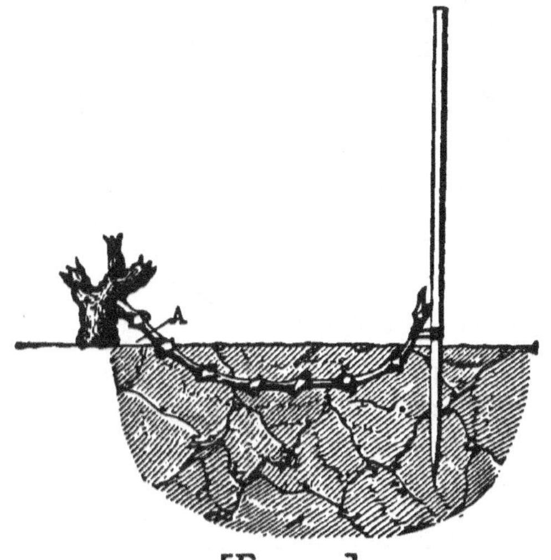

[FIG. 9.]

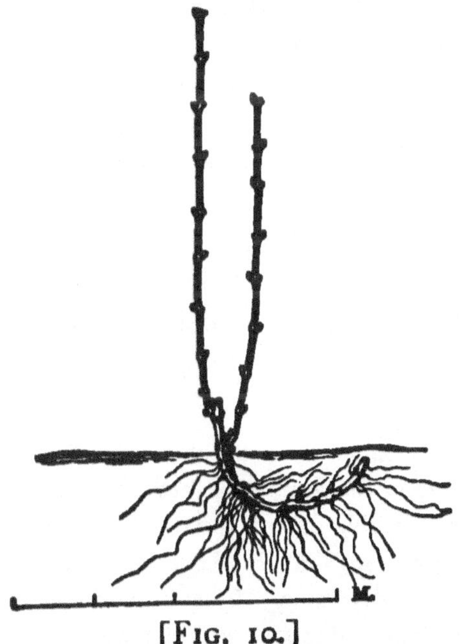

[FIG. 10.]

During the following summer the two reserved eyes shoot out, and, at the same time, each joint of the layer, covered by the soil, produces a whorl of roots. The year following, at planting time, this layer is weaned: that is, it is cut, as at A [Fig. 9] and then taken up with care, to be transplanted elsewhere.— These layers then appear as in *Figure* 10.

These roots, from layers, can not be used to make a vineyard ; their production is too costly, and it would, besides, be difficult to obtain a sufficient number of them.   A certain number of shoots, from the stocks of a neighboring vineyard might, it is true, be used, but experience has proved that this operation greatly weakens the stocks.   It will, therefore, be better to have recourse to rooted plants, or cuttings planted permanently, unless it is to replace a few missing vines.— Nevertheless, layering is customary in certain vineyards, either to replace missing stocks, or to renew the whole plantation ; but, in the latter case, it is not one shoot only, but the entire stock, which is laid down in the ground, in order to bring out, at convenient points, one or more shoots.   Besides, these layers remain permanently in their place.   This constitutes another operation, called vine-layering, and which we will examine when we come to the planting and keeping up of a vineyard.

[Here, as in some other practices, Americans think they can improve upon the European methods. Layering is practiced to a considerable extent, in established vineyards, for the sake of filling up gaps that may have been caused by the death of a plant, from any cause. The plan recommended by our author is generally adopted, only that we take care to select

a shoot that is long enough to reach to the next regular station, and we place it rather deeper than he advises. These
layers constitute the renewal of the vineyard by *provinage*.—
The plants, thus produced, will succeed much better than
strangers introduced into the soil that is already fully occupied by the roots of the old vines, among which the new
comer will stand a poor chance for its life. A good strong
layer, made from a fruitful branch, will often produce a moderate crop the first year, and make strong canes for the next
year's fruitage, besides establishing itself firmly on its own
roots, so as to bear a separation from the mother plant, which
should not be neglected.

An enthusiastic grape-grower in Illinois,* having observed
that young vineyards often escaped the rot, to which older
vines were very subject, proposed a plan of renewing the
vineyard by layering one-fourth part of it every year, and removing the oldest vines at the same time. The theory was
very plausible, but unfortunately we have observed this malady too often upon our newly layered plants, to have any
confidence in the proposed remedy.

As already observed, when speaking of propagation by cuttings, there are some varieties in cultivation that do not emit
roots readily, and therefore are not easily increased by that
method. These kinds are generalty multiplied by layering,
and we have adopted a method which proves very successful.
The long canes of the previous year's growth are trimmed of
their laterals, and the tendrils are removed; they are left as
long as the wood is well developed—sometimes ten or fifteen
feet. At the same time other canes are trimmed in the usual
way for the fruiting on stake or trellis. After the ground is
well prepared and put into fine tilth, in the spring, a shallow
trench, about three inches deep, is opened with the spade, and
into this the cane to be layered is introduced, and fastened

---

*Dr. Shrœder, of Bloomington, Illinois.

down with hooked pegs, which keep it firmly in its place.—
This is done just before the buds burst, but after the sap has
begun to flow freely into the canes. By this means the buds
all along the vine will have been excited, and in due time
they will break, and it is desirable to have them break evenly.
The soil near the layer is kept nicely cultivated, and as the
shoots grow, they are to be tied up to small stakes provided
for the purpose. The cultivation will bring some earth in
contact with the layer, and soon cover it ; but this is not
enough. Some good soil, or compost, is to be filled in against
the shoots, until the old cane is buried about six inches deep.
This furnishes a bed of fine soil for the young roots, which
will be very abundantly produced, not only from the parent
cane, but also from the lower joints of the young upright
shoots of the current year's growth.

Taking up and dividing, is to be done in the fall, so soon as
vegetation is entirely arrested. The soil is then in better
condition than in the spring, and the roots can be more perfectly removed than when the ground is wet and heavy, particularly in clayey lands. Great care is needed in taking up
the layers : a trench should be opened with the spade on one
side, then the earth is to be loosened with a fork, and the
fibers carefully preserved, and the whole branch, with its roots
undermined, until all be free. The cane is then cut off from
the parent vine, and divided, so that each shoot shall make a
separate plant. If all has been well, there may be almost as
many well rooted layer-plants as there were buds on the cane ;
but this is seldom, or never, the case. These new plants are
to be assorted and put away for the winter, either in the cellar, in sand or moss, or they may be heeled-in upon some
warm, dry spot out of doors.

These layer-plants are in great request among planters, and
they command an extra price, for though made up of young
wood, they are well furnished with roots, and are sure to

grow; while the shoots are often so well developed, and so long, that they admit of deeper planting than most of those grown from single eyes, and they will often bear fruit the first year of setting them out; this, however, is not desirable.

Some of the vine-planters of the lake shore will give double price for layer-plants, and will reject all others if these can be had at that rate. The effects upon the old vines are found to be very injurious, and good cultivators object to the practice on this score.]

GRAFTING.—This operation is sometimes performed in vineyards. It is generally practiced at certain points in the Departments of l'Hérault, Maine and Loire.— In the following cases, for instance: there are certain vines which, owing to their extreme vigor, do not bear a full crop before they are ten or twelve years old; such are the " Muscats," cultivated at Lunel and Frontignan. To hasten the maximum yield of these vines, any other descriptions are planted, provided they are very vigorous, and, when two or three years old, they are grafted. The result of this operation will be to reduce their vigor and increase their fruitfulness. Elsewhere, as in certain vineyards of Anjou, the plant adopted, owing to the nature of the soil, possesses insufficient vigor. A hardy variety is then planted, which adapts itself to that soil, and when the vines have attained sufficient size, they are grafted. In short, grafting will always prove an excellent operation when used to replace an inferior plant by a better one; provided, however, that the plants to be grafted are sufficiently hardy.

Grafting as practiced in l'Hérault, is simply the cleft graft placed upon the stock, below the surface of the soil. We prefer the way we have seen it performed by the vine-dressers of Anjou. It is as follows : in the beginning of January choose the scions that are to be grafted ; they ought to have a heel. Bury them in the same way we have indicated for the cuttings, and proceed to graft as soon as the vine begins to bleed. The stocks are then laid bare to the depth of twelve inches, and about twelve inches in width ; cut them on a long bevel, about six inches below the surface of the soil ; then make a vertical slit about one third the length of the upper part of this bevel. The slit may be kept open

[FIG. 11.]

with a small wooden wedge. [Fig. 11.] The shoot to be grafted is cut so as to have a length of about twelve inches. Notch or slit the plant between two joints, to

[FIG. 12.]

about the same extent as the slit in the bevel, and so as to cut one-fourth of its diameter. Cut away the bark between the two joints as long as the slit in the stock, and then make a slanting cut upward of about two inches in length. Hook the graft on the stock by forcing the splinter, or tongue, into the slit of the stock, in such a way that on one of the sides the bark may be in the same vertical plane. Bind the parts together with willow bark soaked in water, and cover them up with grafting wax. Lastly, fill up the cavity with the soil which has been dug out, so that the graft may have but one eye above ground. [Fig. 13.]

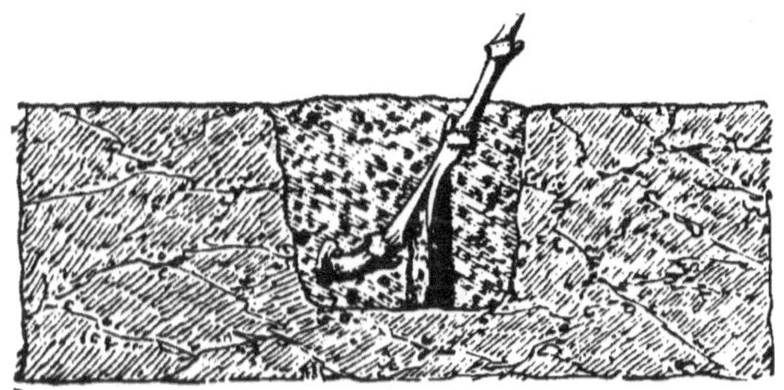

[FIG. 13.]—*Grafting.*

The top of the plant is fastened to a small stake. The union of the cutting with the stock soon takes place ; the bud of the graft shoots out, and a number of roots show themselves on the heel of it, so that it is both a graft and a cutting. From this comes the name of slit-grafted shoot, which we have given to that operation. [Fig. 13.]

The development of this early shoot is often so rapid, under the influence of this two-fold principle of vegetation, that it may bear fruit the first summer after the operation.

If the parent stock is somewhat large, two, instead of one graft, may be made—one on each side of the slit—provided the poorer one is cut away two years later, when the parent stock shall have been perfectly healed up.

[Grafting the vine has been practiced to a considerable extent in our country, but not for the object cited in the text. We graft simply to change an unprofitable vine to a good one, or for the sake of multiplying a new sort, and putting ourselves at once in possession of strong bearing wood of a new or desired variety. In this manner a worthless wild vine may be at once transformed into one that will be profitable with its heavy produce of desirable fruit; for such a stock will force out strong bearing canes for the next year; and, indeed, there will often be some fruit the first summer of grafting, if the scion have been selected from fruitful wood.

When the object is simply to multiply vines of any given variety, for home planting, or for sale, small, well rooted plants are often selected—yearlings or two-year olds. These may be grafted in the house, by the cleft or splice method, tied or waxed, and the vines can be planted in a nursery, or set at once in their permanent stations. I have had excellent success by using pieces of roots, taken from the wild vines that are to be found in an old, neglected fence-row. The underground stems, and the roots, were cut into lengths of ten to twelve inches, and cleft-grafted, tied, and planted at once.

The experience of the practice of this operation upon the vine has been exceedingly varied. Some have been perfectly successful, while others have been almost always unfortunate; and those who may have had all their grafts do well one year, have lost them all the next. Some advise grafting very early, and others prefer waiting until the development of the young leaves on the vine, keeping the scions back by preserving them in the ice-house.

Mr. Fuller, who claims to have been very successful in grafting the vine, recommends doing it in the autumn, or early winter. He excavates the earth, exposing the stock below the surface, and after grafting in the usual cleft method, he protects the graft from the action of the frost, by filling the earth about it, and then covering with an inverted flower-pot,

and throwing a mulch of straw, or leaves, over the whole.—
Under these circumstances, a moderate action among the cell
tissues results in the formation of a callus, and in a union with
the stock, so that at the opening of spring, when the cover-
ings are removed, the vine is prepared to grow at once.

A writer in the *Gardener's Monthly** has discovered the
mystery—or rather that there is no mystery at all about it.—
He says: "cut your scions in the fall, after they are fully ripe,
but before they are exposed to any hard freezing. Let the
wood be firm, not pithy, well matured, small and short-jointed.
These are packed in moss, or saw-dust, and kept in the cellar,
free from frost. They are cut in lengths of a foot, and tied
in small bundles."

"Have a short shoe-maker's knife to split the stocks, and a
sharp pen-knife to cut the graft; a small iron wedge to hold
open the stock when needed; a wooden mallet and a saw, and
you are equipped."

"*Time.*—He is most successful from the moment the frost
has left the ground until the vines bleed—February to April,
according to the season and locality. The stocks should be
strong—at least two years old; as soon as the frost has gone,
and the ground has settled, remove the earth from around the
vine, four inches deep; cut off the stock at a smooth place,
suitable for grafting, two or three inches below the surface.—
Graft as fast as cut, to avoid exposure to the air. The top
of the stock is cut smooth, and the bark is removed from the
side, as low as the graft is inserted, and split, or rather cut, by
placing the knife on the side and striking it gently with the
mallet, until you split the stock deep enough to insert the graft;
but do not split it through to the other side. Insert the
wedge to keep it open. Select the scion in proportion to the
stock, so that it shall be firm enough to withstand the pressure. Cut it long enough for the upper bud to be just above

---

*T. Stayman, Leavenworth, Kansas.

the surface; make it wedge-shaped; avoid wounding the pith; remove the bark from the part to be inserted; see that it fits the split correctly, and matches the stock exactly on either side; then withdraw the wedge, and if the work is properly done the graft will be held firmly in its place without tying; use no wax. Press the moist earth closely to the stock and graft, and fill up so as to have one bud above the surface."

If there be danger of frost, he recommends covering with straw, to prevent its heaving and lifting the graft. Afterward remove the covering, cultivate well; remove suckers, and tie up the young shoot as it grows.

Mr. Stayman concludes by saying that the conditions of success are good materials, grafting below the surface, within the period mentioned, and doing the work well.]

CHOICE OF PLANTS FOR PROPAGATION.—The choice of plants, of which to make cuttings, layers, or grafts, is a very important point. If taken at random, plants may be selected which have a tendency to degenerate. We have seen, on the stock of the black Pinot, a shoot, all the bunches of which were accidentally white. This shoot, if cut for propagation, would have continued to yield white grapes, and thus constituted a new variety, perhaps better, but more frequently worse, than the one it originated from. In order to avoid degeneracy, which is more common than is usually supposed, it would be well, when propagation is intended, to go over the vineyard during harvest time. Those plants which bear the earliest and most perfect bunches—which, in fact, possess in the highest degree those qualities which distinguish the varieties to be cultivated—are then marked, so as to be known again. Those are the plants of which to make cuttings, layers or grafts. By selecting in this manner, the variety chosen will soon be improved, by the gradual development of those qualities sought after.

[SPORTS.—A certain amount of variation is frequently observed among our plants of culture. These diversities are sometimes so remarkable as to attract attention, particularly when they relate to color, as in the instance above cited, where black was changed to white—a remarkable change, truly, and yet similar sports are not unfrequently observed in plants. Sometimes these sports, as they are called, occur in the foliage, in the habit of the plant, or in the fruit alone, and it is found that from the affected branches we may often propagate plants that may have similar qualities, and thus perpetuate the sub-variety. Our author calls it degeneration; it may also be improvement; it is simply *variation* from the original, normal type, and if we observe carefully and select judiciously, we may improve our fruits by taking advantage of these tendencies to variation in the product of the buds, just as well as by selecting superior seedlings, though, in the latter, variation is the rule and not the exception, as here; at least, such is the case in seedlings of most of our improved fruits of cultivation. In the case of seeds, too, there is a constant liability for them to have had a mixed parentage; and at our will, we may control the pedigree of the seeds produced, which is not the case with the product of buds. Here the close analogy which has been shown to exist between the seeds and the buds ceases.

The whole subject of *sports* is one of deep interest to the physiologist and scientific gardener, but practically, we may safely propagate any distinct variety, and expect to find all our plants like the parent.]

VI.

PLANTING OF A VINEYARD.

Arrangement of the Vines.—The three following plans are adopted, in the planting of a vineyard:

1st. *Mixed Planting.*—In all vineyards, the vines are, at first, planted in parallel lines, and the stocks at equal distances from one another. But in certain localities, the primitive plants are laid down without order, in all directions, so as to multiply them more, and to bring them nearer the required distance from each other; a confused planting is the result. This is the process adopted in the neighborhood of Paris, in Champagne, in Burgundy, the Jura, etc.

The following are the motives which have led to the adoption of this method: the expense of planting is smaller than if the number of vines required to plant the whole surface were at once procured. When the stocks are to be replaced, the places of missing plants can be filled up with the layers, without recourse to outside plants.

This method of replacing is more prompt in its results than a new planting. Lastly and especially, this layering, practiced each year on a considerable portion of the vineyard, renews the vigor of the plants, and increases the yield.

But, apart from the advantages we have just pointed out, irregular planting presents the following serious inconveniences: the tillage is performed with less rapidity, and is consequently more expensive than planting

in rows. Cultivation frequently bruises the underground stems resulting from this mode of propagating.
The transportation and distribution of the manure, and
the getting out of the trimmings, and of the crop, are
also much more expensive than in vineyards planted in
rows. In irregularly planted vineyards, the soil is not
so well warmed by the sun, the air circulates less freely,
and the plants shade one another more than in regularly
laid out lines.

2d. *Planting in Close Rows.*—By this method, the vineyard planted in rows preserves its shape, whatever may
be its age. These rows, being pretty close to one
another, occupy the entire extent of the ground in a
regular manner. We have just pointed out the advantages of these rows over the irregular planting. Thus,
all the labor of keeping the vineyard is less expensive,
even, than harvesting. The plants have more light,
more air, and the soil is better warmed by the sun.
Let us add, that for the same extent of ground, and the
same number of plants, these last will be less crowded,
when in rows, than when irregularly laid out. Lastly,
and not least, planting in rows allows the use of wires,
instead of stakes, thereby reducing, very materially, the
expense of keeping up a vineyard. For this reason, we
decidedly prefer that method.

3d. *Planting in Isolated Rows.*—In certain vine regions the vines are planted in isolated rows, separated
by spaces, varying from twenty to one hundred feet
apart, according to the localities—those spaces being devoted to other agricultural purposes. In the Bordelais,
these isolated rows are called "Joualles." It is hoped,
by that means, to draw from the soil as much produce

from the vegetables, as if the rows of vines did not exist, and, from these last to obtain a crop which costs almost nothing; but it is quite certain that the ground occupied by the vine can not profit other crops, and that the quantity of these last decreases in proportion to the number of rows of vines planted on the same surface. These solitary lines are also known to occupy proportionately more room than if just sufficient space for their proper growth were left between them. The tillage of these vines is less expeditious when they are isolated, than when they occupy the entire ground. Lastly, this tillage is often thwarted or delayed by the other crops planted in the vineyard. For this reason, we think this mode of cultivation offers but little advantage.

Space to be Left Between the Stocks.—This important question depends upon the following considerations :

1st. All varieties of vines do not develop themselves with the same vigor; therefore, the more vigorous the variety, the larger must be the space between them.

2d. All other things being equal, the vine grows more vigorously in the South than in the North; therefore, the warmer the climate, the larger must be the space between the vines.

3d. The vine is subject to greater evaporation in the South than in the North, from which, it follows that it requires a larger space in the South than in the North, from which to draw the moisture.

4th. The earlier the growth, the less vigorous the plant. An isolated plant blooms, and its fruits ripen, later than plants that are crowded together, and are less vigorous; the first ripe grapes are never gathered on the edges of the vineyard. The old, worn-out vines, and those planted in poor soils, mature earlier than those that are young and well manured. Now, in northern latitudes, the ripening of the grapes being imperfect, it will be well to reduce their vigor by crowding them more than in the South.

5th. Nevertheless, this crowding must not be overdone, otherwise the vigor of the plants would not suffice properly to nourish the grapes, which would then yield but an inferior wine. It must not, besides, be forgotten that light and air must circulate freely round all the plants, and that the soil must be warmed by the sun.

6th. In a word, while taking into account all the preceding conditions, such a space must be left between the plants that the tillage of the ground may be done by the plow, whenever the inclination of the surface will permit its use.

We have now only to point out the limits to be adopted under the preceding circumstances. Unfortunately no direct experiment has been made, to solve that important problem. Nevertheless, if we examine all that transpires on the subject, in the general practice of the different vine regions, it will be seen (by the following table) that this problem has everywhere been solved conformably to the circumstances just enumerated :

Amount of Space allowed between the Plants in the Principal Vine Regions.

LOCALITIES.	SPACES BETWEEN THE VINES.		NO. OF PLANTS TO THE ACRE.
	Ft.	Inch.	
Châteauneuf-Colurier (Vaucluse)..	6	6	1,000
Saint-Cécile (Vaucluse)............	5	9	1,299
Vauvert and Saint Gilles (Gard)...	5	1	1,606
Department of the Gers............	5	0	1,742
Department of l'Hérault............	5	0	1,742
Palus of Bordeaux.................	5	0	1,742
Médoc..	3	11	2,756
Haute-Garonne.	2	10	5,107
Beaujolais.	2	7	6,250
Touraine.........................	2	4	7,398
Côte d'Or.	2	1	9,120
Paris............................	2	0	9,983
Orléanais........................	1	11	11,102
Ain, Vosges......................	1	7	16,010
Épernay.........................	1	3	25,000
Moselle....	1	2	30,692

The above table shows that the mean distance between the plants in the South being eight feet, it decreases gradually as we advance North, where as many as 30,692 vines are planted to the acre, as is common in certain vineyards of Moselle. Are we to consider these distances, especially those adopted in the northern regions, as the best ? We do not think so ; we think that the excessive crowding of the plants has been carried too far, and that this system of planting now presents the following objections.

These plants shade one another mutually, and render insufficient the action of the air, and especially of the sun—influences so necessary to an abundant yield and fine quality of the product. This shade also prevents the soil from being warmed, and delays the ripening of the grapes. Moreover, the plants thus crowded, mutually starve one another, and they have frequently to be renewed by layering, which increases the expense and injures the quality of the product.—The tillage of the ground is more difficult and consequently more expensive. The staking also increases the expense considerably.

Lastly, we must add, that owing to the continual rise in the rate of wages, the plow must be substituted for manual labor wherever the lay of the land will permit its use; but the system of crowding the vines, adopted in the North, is an obstacle to this improvement.

On the other hand, too much space must not be left between the plants; for if, when planted much further apart, they each yield more and more abundantly, it may nevertheless so happen that the product will not be equal, in quantity, to that obtained from a larger number of plants. Besides, too large a space being left between the vines will so increase their growth, that the grapes will ripen badly in the North, and the wines will be of very inferior quality.

Let us, then, see how nearly we can reconcile these two extremes. The smallest space which will allow the easy working of the plow between the rows of plants is three and a half feet. We have, therefore, no change to suggest on that point, as to the vineyards of the South. But this is not the case with the northern and middle latitudes adapted to the vine. Nevertheless, by laying out the rows of plants, and the plants in the rows in a certain manner, which we shall point out fur-

I

ther on, an average space of at least twenty-six inches between the plants, would be enough to permit the working of the ground by the plow, thus making 10,000 plants to the acre. The change which we propose, as to space, would, therefore, only affect the vineyards of northern latitudes. Now, it is precisely in those latitudes that the crowding of the plants has been so overdone that the inconveniences arising therefrom begin to cause a reaction in the opposite direction. In the Côte-d'Or, and in Champagne, they have already tried planting further apart, and have obtained a yield as abundant, and of as good quality, as that of more crowded vineyards.

Upon the whole, therefore, we advise that an average space of at least twenty-six inches be left between the plants.

[We may compare ourselves to the South, rather than to the North, in respect to the distance between our vines. Our early plantations were made by Europeans from the northern grape regions, who set their vines very close together, some even three by three feet, on terraced vineyards worked by hand. The spaces were soon increased to four feet each way, and this was gradually widened to five and six, and even greater intervals. The vigor of many of our vines, and their enormous growth, as well as the comparative cheapness of land, and the absolute necessity of using the plow instead of the hoe; all these circumstances combined, have rendered it necessary for us to plant wider, and a very common distance now is six by eight feet, the wider space being between the rows. Some planters have even gone so far as to set their vines eight feet apart each way.

ARRANGEMENT OF ROWS OF PLANTS.—We have just advised planting in rows, and that an average space of at least twenty-six inches be left between the plants; but we must also point out the best way to lay them out relatively to each other. Indeed, several different plans might be adopted, in order to obtain that result.

In the South, where the plants are set far apart, they may be laid out in quincunxes, as in *Figure* 14, or in squares, of four only, as in *Figure* 15. In the quincunx, each plant occupies one of the angles of an equi-

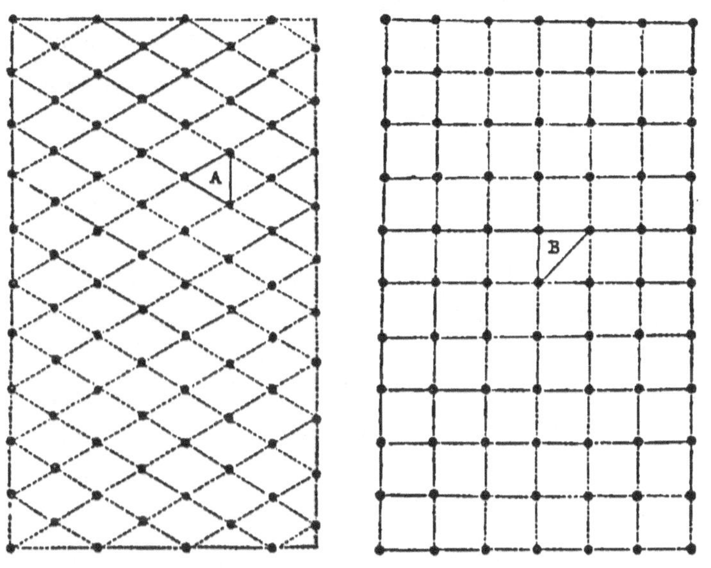

[FIG. 14.]—*Vines planted in quincunxes.*

[FIG. 15.]—*Vines planted in squares.*

lateral triangle [A, Fig. 14]; they are equally distant on all sides. The plow may be used in three different directions. In square planting, each plant occupies the angle of a right-angled triangle [B, Fig. 15]; they are not equi-distant on all sides, and the plow can only be used in two different directions. Lastly, the most important difference to be noticed between the two modes of planting is, that on two surfaces of one acre each—the one planted in quincunx, and the other in squares, and the plants the same distance apart in both cases—say, for instance, five feet—it will take 2,080 plants to the acre, planted in quincunx, while the same surface, planted in squares, will only take 1,742. For these reasons, we prefer the quincunx for wide planting.

As to the vineyards of the middle and northern regions, where the plants are much more crowded together, the quality and probably the quantity of the produce would suffer if the space necessary for the working of the plow were left between the plants. Our advice, therefore, is that the vineyards of the northern and middle regions be divided into two classes : those that are located on hill-sides that are too steep for the working of the plow, and those which can be so cultivated.

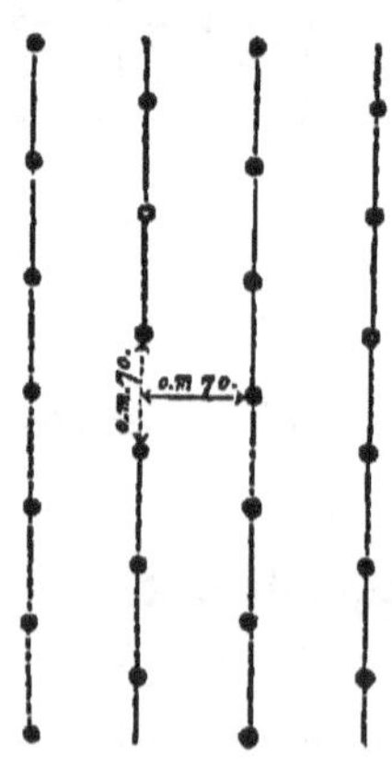

[FIG. 16.]—*Planting in Rows, on steep hill-sides.*

For the first, the lines must be laid out so as to leave between them the space generally allotted between the plants in that section of country, provided that this amounts to at least twenty-six inches. The same space must be left between them, setting out the plants of one line opposite the empty spaces on the next line. [Fig. 16.] In vineyards thus laid out, the work is done by hand.

This figure represents a regular quincunx.

For vineyards planted on lands which may be culti-vated with the plow, we advise the following combina-tion, which will allow of close planting, while, at the same time, it makes it possible to use the plow over the entire surface of the ground.

All the lines must be three and a quarter feet apart, and the spaces between the vines varied according to the requirements of the plants, the climate, and the soil.

Thus, for 5,200 plants to the acre, a space of 30 inches must be left between the plants on the lines.

For 6,000, - - - - - - 26 inches.
" 7,200, - - - - - 22 "
" 8,000, - - - - - - 20 "

If 10,000 plants are to be set, the following arrange-ment must be made: lay out the lines by twos and twos, with a space of three and a quarter feet between them [A, Fig. 17], and then reserve a space of twenty-four inches be-tween the close lines, B, with a space of twenty inches between the plants on the lines. But in this case, the large alleys, only, can be plowed, that is about two-thirds of the sur-face. A greater number of plants can not be cultivated with the plow.

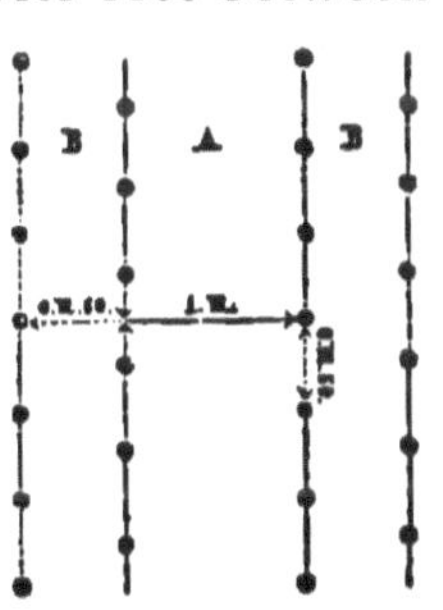

[FIG. 17.]—*Plant-ation of lands which can be cul-tivated with the plow.*

In what direction to lay out the Rows.—We know that the direct ac-tion of the sun on the entire vine and the soil which gives it nourishment, affects, in an important degree, the quality and quantity of its produce. It will be well, therefore, when the spaces between the plants are greater than the spaces between the lines, to lay them out, north and south, so that they will not shade each other at mid-day. Unfortunately, it is not always possible so to lay them out. The shape of the ground is frequently an obstacle. Suppose it to measure twenty to twenty-five feet wide, by six hundred and fifty or nine hundred and eighty feet long, as is often the case, and that this strip lies east and west, the lines can not then be laid out *across* so narrow a belt; the inclination of the soil and its exposure, also frequently prevent the execution of this plan. If an abrupt hill-side has a southern exposure, the vines can not be laid out in rows parallel to the declivity, except at the risk of soon having the soil torn up and washed down to the base of the hill by the heavy rains, in which case we should be compelled to carry it back. Therefore, the preceding directions must be followed as nearly as possible, at the same time taking into account such obstacles as may present themselves.

Last Preparation of the Soil.—We have advised the uniform breaking up of the entire surface of the ground destined for a vineyard. This work being done before winter, the soil will remain fallow until planting time. It is then lightly plowed to the depth of four or six inches, across the first plowing, and harrowed so as to level the surface soil and facilitate the planting.

Choice of Plants.—Under the head of propagation we have seen that either crossette-cuttings, or roots, may be used for planting a vineyard. We will now show how to choose between the two.

Planting roots is more expensive, especially if, as we have advised, two-year old plants are used. These plants must have been raised in the nursery, and the planting of them out permanently is more expensive than setting the crossettes, but their growth is more certain.

The crossettes cost less, as does also the permanent planting of them; but many of them, especially in dry soil, fail, necessitating the substitution of others, and thereby increase the expense, and injure the grand result.

[Many of our largest vineyards have been made by using cuttings instead of plants, and this practice would still prevail were it not for the extremely high price of cuttings of many of the varieties which are now being introduced into the vineyard. The cutting of four eyes can be made into four good plants, by the methods employed in their propagation; hence we can no longer afford to compete with the nurserymen, but can do better to purchase our vines than to set our own cuttings. This will not always continue to be the case, and when there is less demand for the wood we shall revert to the old plan, and the cheaper one, of placing the cutting at once into its permanent station in the vineyard, except in the case of those sorts which do not grow readily under this out-door treatment.

The advantage of planting the vineyard with cuttings consists in the greater cheapness of the stock, and the greater uniformity of the result, as well as in avoiding the check of the plants, incident to transplanting the vines, and disturbing the roots.

The cuttings should have been prepared by burying them in the soil, so that they may have formed a callus. The ground having been properly prepared and laid out, with a little stake at each point where it is designed to have a vine, a workman proceeds to make the necessary excavation. He opens a hole the width of the spade, and the length of the cutting, making it one spit deep. Fine, mellow soil is thrown slanting toward the top, at the stake-end. The planter then follows with his cuttings, in a bucket of puddle-water, to keep them from drying. At each station he takes two cuttings, and lays them so that their bases shall be separated the width of the excavation, but their tops approximate at the stick. Soft earth is thrown upon them, and tramped firmly with the foot, beginning at the base of the cutting. As he approaches the stick, the upper portion is bent into a vertical position at the stake, and pressed firmly into its place. This end of the hole is filled with mellow soil, and the head of the cutting is barely covered, but the further portion is only half filled up, the object being to secure the warming influence of the sun, to encourage the starting of the roots.

If both cuttings grow, one of them may be removed the next spring to fill a gap somewhere else, or the extra vine may be destroyed, by cutting it off below the surface with the pruning-knife, at any time.]

The conclusion arrived at from the preceding, therefore, is: that in rich and somewhat moist soils, where the crossettes easily take root, they are preferable, but for dry soils the roots are the best.

In some localities vine-dressers prefer, in all cases, cuttings to the rooted plants, maintaining that they are always more certain. This is owing, in most cases, to the roots of the plants being very much injured, either by being taken up from the nursery in an improper manner, or by their too long exposure to the air ; now, these roots, thus injured, soon rot in the ground, and the plants are then nothing but the fragments of old shoots, from which the new roots grow with much more difficulty than on the new wood of the cutting. We, therefore, maintain that the two-year old plants, carefully taken up from the nursery, and sheltered until planting time, will give better results than the crossettes or cuttings, in dry soil.

PLANTING.—*The proper Time.*—The best time for planting cuttings, or roots, differs in different climates.

In the northern and central parts of France the operation must be performed in the beginning of spring; if done before the winter there would be danger, on the one hand, of the terminal buds of the cuttings or roots which had not yet commenced growing, being killed by the frost; and, on the other, of the plants being injured by the excess of moisture contained in the ground during that season. In the South it is the reverse: the planting must be done before the winter, otherwise, if done in the spring, the hot weather of that season would suffice to kill the young plants before they had time to take root. Besides, it is known that vegetation, in that climate, is not entirely suspended during winter, so that when the spring comes, the young plants have already struck a few roots, which enable them more successfully to withstand the dry weather.

[The question of fall and spring planting is one which each must decide for himself. As above suggested, much will depend upon the climate—the soil has also much to do with our decision. Newly planted vines or trees, if set in light, dry soils, would do a good deal toward preparing themselves for growth, during mild weather in autumn and winter; but the same plants, set in wet, heavy, clayey soil, in the autumn, would be very apt to suffer from the effects of water freezing and thawing during the winter, and many would be killed.]

Distribution of the Different Varieties in the same Vineyard.—If anything is to be gained by planting several varieties in the same vineyard, it will always be well to keep them separate. It will be easier to give them the particular attention which each one requires, and the most hardy will not injure the weaker varieties. The gathering will also be easier, if the different varieties do not ripen at the same time.

If the ground to be planted is uneven, and the slopes have different exposures, the latest bearers must, if possible, be placed in the warmest exposure, in order that they may ripen better.

At what Depth to Plant.—The depth to which the cuttings or plants must be set ought to be such as will allow the air to act upon their roots, and, at the same time, such that they will get the proper quantity of moisture. It is evident, therefore, that this must depend chiefly on the climate and nature of the soil. In the burning clime of the South, or in light and dry soils, the vine must be planted deeply, to escape the excessive heat of summer. In the North, or in rich, damp soils, it must, on the contrary, be planted more shallow, so as to escape the great moisture, which, by causing it to grow too rapidly, would injure the ripening of its fruit, and diminish the quantity of its produce. For which reason, in the dry soils of the South, plant to the depth of twenty inches; in the rich soils of the same latitudes, twelve inches will be sufficient. In the northern and middle regions, plant at twelve inches if the land is dry, and at eight inches if it is rich and deep.

Laying out the Lines for Planting.—The various questions which precede having been answered, and the soil prepared in the manner indicated, the rows for planting must be marked out, and, for this purpose, any regular method of laying out may be selected. The following may be adopted—it is very easily executed, and gives good results:

We will suppose that the surface of the ground has been divided into a certain number of parallelograms, by roads previously cut, as directed above. Let us now suppose that *Figure* 18 is one of these parallelograms, and that the vineyard is to be laid out in rows parallel to its length, forty inches in width, and with a space of twenty inches between the plants on the lines. By means of a surveyor's chain

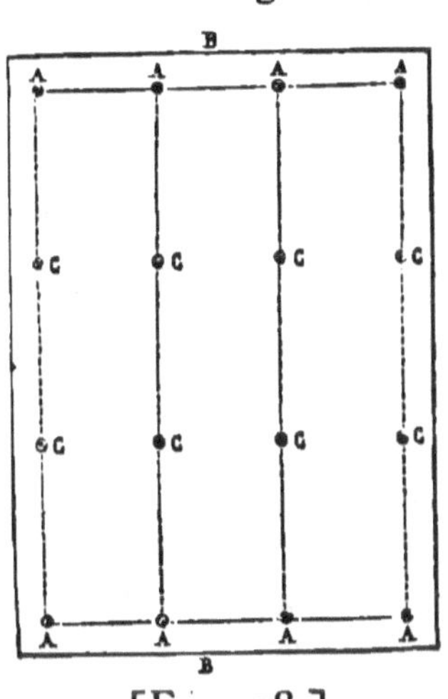

[FIG. 18.]

of sufficient length, the links of which are forty inches long, the end of each line A, is marked out with a stake on the two lines B, of the parallelogram. These stakes being fixed, two or three more in C, are marked out, according to the length of the lines. By means of these stakes and another chain, the place of each plant is then marked out. The links of this second chain must be twenty inches in length.

If the plan had to be laid out on a surface with an irregular boundary, the largest possible parallelogram would have to be drawn, and the lines then laid out as just described ; it will only be necessary to extend the lines to the boundary.

[The Yankee is again ahead in his calculations. This is the more readily accomplished in the wider planting he has adopted. With good sight-stakes, and a steady plow-team, he lays off the rows and digs the holes simultaneously, by plowing a deep furrow from end to end of the piece to be planted. Then, with a garden-line stretched across these furrows, and a measuring-rod of the proper length, he proceeds to set his pegs in the furrows, at the points where the line crosses them. Some will even do this by the measuring-rod and the eye alone, without the line, and make the stakes range both ways, with sufficient accuracy for all practical purposes.]

Planting.—The mode of planting depends upon whether cuttings or roots are to be planted.

Cuttings are most generally planted by means of the dibble, as follows: A man is provided with a dibble, having a cross-piece, or stirrup, on which the foot is

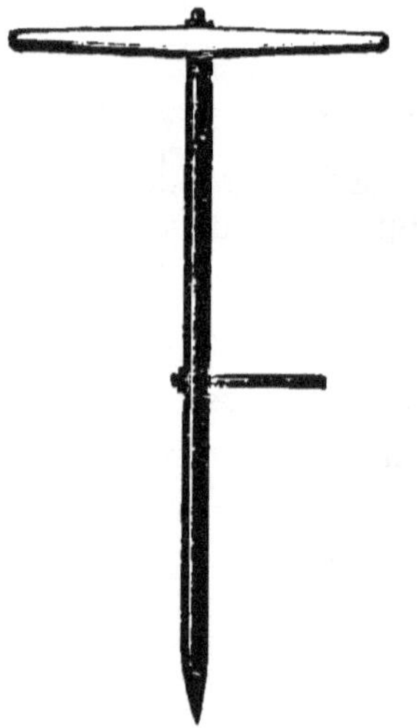

[FIG. 19.]—*Dibble, for Planting Vines.*

[FIG. 20.]—*Rammer, to ram down the earth and manure around the Cuttings.*

placed to drive the instrument into the ground, or to stop it at the required depth. Provided with this instrument, or any other like it, the workman drives it into the ground at each spot to be occupied by a plant, and to the required depth. As to the size of these holes, the poorer the soil the larger they must be.

Another workman, following the first, introduces into each hole a cutting, prepared in the manner described under the head of "Propagation."

Whatever may be the natural richness of the soil to be planted, it is always well to supply the cuttings or plants with a certain quantity of manure, when about to be planted permanently, in order to start them. This quantity may vary, according to the poverty or richness of the soil, from one to three quarts. For cuttings, the manure to be introduced into the hole made by the dibble ought to be composed of pulverizable and easily decomposed matter, such as old compost, horse-dung, poudrette, natural guano, ground oil-cakes, etc. These various substances must be mixed with a certain quantity of earth, and wood-ashes.

This manure being prepared, and distributed at different places along the roads where the rows terminate, a third workman follows and fills the holes with the manure which he carries, keeping each cutting in the center of the hole. By means of a sort of rammer, like the one represented by *Figure* 20, a fourth workman rams the manure well down. It is very important for the cutting to be in close contact with the soil, so that it may absorb its moisture. If there should still be an empty space, after this ramming, the same workman must fill it with the surrounding earth.

When the pulverizable manure of which we have just spoken can not be procured, liquid manures must be snbstituted, and poured into each hole after it has been filled with rich soil, but not rammed. These liquids (one quart to each cutting) may be composed of manure-water, excrements diluted with water, or of any organic matter that is rich in nitrogen, and easily dissolved in water.

Planting cuttings by means of the dibble, is, however, objectionable in clayey soils. The earth, solidly pressed by the dibble, at the sides of the holes, becomes an obstacle to the spreading of the young roots. In such a case it will be better to adopt the mode of planting out roots.

[I do not think the dibble is used in planting cuttings in any part of this country, and, indeed, it is to be hoped that it may not be, as it is an unphilosophical implement for the purpose. Nor would it be at all suitable in any of our so-called grape-lands, which are generally of stiff clay.]

In dry and warm soils, where cuttings do not succeed well, rooted plants are used in the following manner :

The manures required for the planting must first be distributed, here and there, along the roads bordering the rows of vineyards to be planted.

These manures must be composed, as much as possible, of equal parts of earth and dung. If the soil to be planted is clayey, then silicious, and especially calcareous earth must be used ; but clayey soils must be employed, if the land to be planted is silicious or calcareous. The mixture must be made some months in advance, by placing the layers of earth and dung in strata, in the form of compost. When about to be used, it must be thoroughly mixed.

Two-year old roots [Fig. 8] must be taken up from the nursery, with all the care indicated under the head of " Nursery," and then, to prevent them from being injured by the drying action of the air, proceed as follows : A thick mush of water, clay, and a considerable quantity of well compounded manure, such as horse and cow-dung, guano, excrement, oil-cakes, and other similar substances, is placed in a tub, by the side of the workman taking up the plants. Another tub is filled with dry wood-ashes. As the vines are dug, the workman dips four or five at a time, into the liquid manure, and sprinkles them with ashes. This sort of coating of the roots serves to protect them from the action of the air and sun, which are particularly injurious. It also stimulates their growth, and advances their development one year.

Thus prepared, they are immediately taken to the planting-ground, laid in small piles, and covered with straw. No more should be prepared than can be planted in one day.

A workman opens a little trench, about sixteen inches long, in the line of the row, twelve inches wide, and of the required depth, taking into account the nature of the soil and climate. The bottom of the trench must be an inclined plane, one extremity of which should reach the surface of the ground.

As the trenches are opened, a workman lays by the side of each from three to five quarts of the compost spoken of, and a child, following him, places a rooted plant in each hole. Another workman lifts the plant, spreads over the entire bottom of the trench one-half of the compost, lays down the plant, taking care to spread the roots well ; covers it with the balance of the compost, fills up the hole with the earth laid near it, and finishes by ramming the earth well, especially on the two sides of the trench. It is important, in this operation, that the greatest portion of the young shoot from the plant should be buried. It is on this young wood that the new roots are formed which are to hasten the development of the vines. This work ended, each trench will appear as in *Figure* 21.

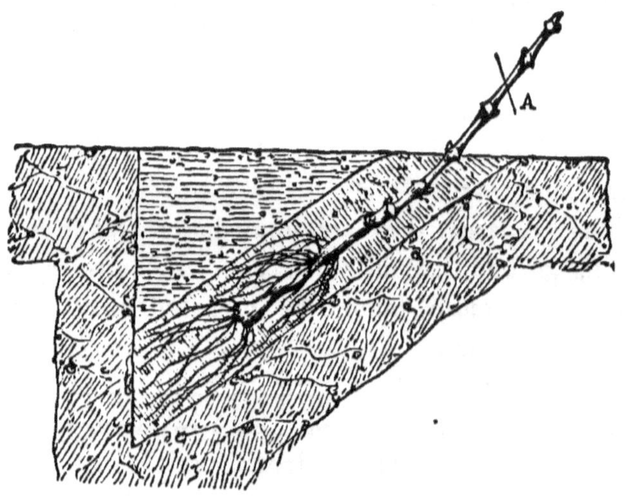

[Fig. 21.]—*Planting the Vine.*

In some localities the planting is done with the plow. The rows having been staked out, as above described, a furrow, sixteen inches wide, and of the required depth, is opened by two cuts of the plow. It is in these furrows that the cuttings are placed at the proper

distances, and with the same care as we have just described.

Whatever may have been said to the contrary, pretty
straight lines may be made with the plow, and the work
may be done more speedily than by opening a separate
hole for each plant.

Planting by Layering.—In those localities where the
vines are very crowded, as in Champagne, Burgundy,
and the neighborhood of Paris, only one-half or one-
third of the necessary vines are planted as cuttings, or as
roots, and then, when these have acquired sufficient
strength to put forth two fine shoots, they proceed as
follows :

Suppose the points A, in *Figure* 22, to represent
the places to be permanently
occupied by the plants, only the
points B, are first planted, and
when each of the vines has two
fine shoots, a trench is opened
during the winter, occupying the
entire triangular space, C, and
of the depth of twelve to sixteen inches, according to the
moisture of the ground ; a layer
of earth, mixed with manure, is
spread on the bottom of this
trench, and the two shoots are

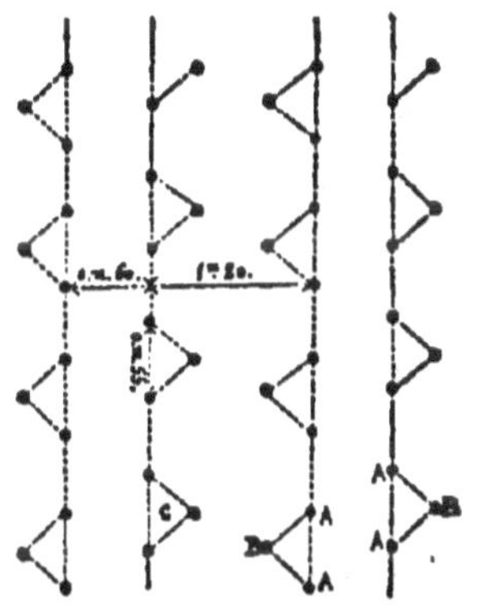

[FIG. 22.]—*Planting
by Layering.*

then laid down into it, giving them the direction of the
dotted lines, so that they may come out at the points
A. A small quantity of compost is placed over them,
and the trench is filled up with ordinary earth. This
trench, however, must not be entirely filled ; a space

of four to six inches ought to be left, so that the shoots, not being planted too deep, may take root more easily. The balance of the earth remains on the sides of the trench. It is only in the following year, when the ground is tilled, that it is leveled. If this first layering does not yield the required number of plants, a second one is made.

This mode of operating reduces the number of roots to be planted, by one-half to two-thirds, but we do not think the saving arising from it compensates for the inconveniences, for, undoubtedly, by this process, a larger quantity of wood is buried, and the numerous roots which shoot from this wood, being very close together, are much more liable to injure one another. By thus multiplying these underground stems, the chances of injuring them by the plow are also increased. Besides, the first saving soon disappears under the necessity of propagation—which is always an expensive operation. Lastly, if, on the one hand, there is a saving of plants, on the other there is a greater loss by postponing the maximum yield of the vines for two or three years. Therefore, our advice is, at once to plant as many cuttings or roots as are required for the whole vineyard.

OPERATIONS SUPPLEMENTAL TO PLANTING.—Immediately after planting the cuttings or roots, the extremity of the plant protruding from the earth, as at A, *Figure* 21, is cut with the pruning-knife, so as to leave but one or two eyes above ground.

In some countries, the cuttings, as soon as planted, are carefully covered up with the earth, and thus left until the beginning of July. While the wood is getting ready in the earth, and throwing out a few rootlets, the upper portion of it does not dry up, and the buds, when at last exposed to the air, soon develop themselves. This practice might be used with advantage in the dry soils of the south and middle of France.

All these operations once completed, a light dressing should be given to the entire surface of the soil, so as to loosen it wherever it has been trodden down by the workmen, and especially to level it well.

This young plantation requires no other care during the following summer than to be protected from drouth, and from being overrun with weeds. To this end, the ground is plowed or hoed a few times, to the depth of about two or three inches. The lighter the soil and the more southern the locality, the more frequent must be the plowings. We explain, further on, under the head of "Annual Cultivation of the Soil of Vineyards," the way to do this plowing.

Replanting.—No matter what may be the care bestowed on the planting of either cuttings or roots, there will, invariably, be some failures—say one per cent. on the roots, and two per cent. on the cuttings. Therefore, substitutes, consisting of roots only, must be provided as soon as possible,—that is to say, the following winter. For this purpose, a nursery must be made at the proper time, in order to have the roots ready at the time we have just named.

As for the planting of the substitutes, it is done as we have already explained.

[In planting a vineyard, whether with cuttings or with rooted vines, it is always desirable to set all the plants on a given side of the stakes; whether this be north or south, east or west, it is immaterial; but they should all be the same. This systematic order saves time, as it enables us always to look at once to the right place for the young vine, in all our operations among them in the vineyard, and thus we may often avoid injuring them with the hoe, or other implement, we may be using. So, also, in plowing across the rows, as we sometimes wish to do, while vines are young, we may know where to hold the plow or cultivator shallow, so as to avoid disturbing the main roots of the vine, which might otherwise be ruined by the plowshare cutting them off, or tearing them away, as has often occurred with careless workmen.]

VII.

PRUNING THE VINE.

OBJECT OF THE OPERATION.—If, after being planted, the development of the vine were left to itself, the long, spreading shoots would creep over the surface of the ground, which it would soon cover, in tangled confusion. The tillage of the soil would become impossible, and the branches, deprived of the sun, and in contact with the ground, would rot, and yield very poor fruit.

Besides, the fruit-bearing shoots, springing all the time from the young wood, and thus becoming more and more removed from the parent stock, would become less and less vigorous, and would soon end by producing nothing but poor and mean bunches.

The pruning of the vineyard must have, for its object, the giving of such a shape to the vines as will subject them completely to the action of the sun, facilitate the tillage of the ground, at all times and over all its surface, and prevent the fruit-bearing wood from being too far removed from the parent stock.

Let us first consider the best time of year for this work, and the best tools with which to perform it:

THE PROPER TIME FOR PRUNING THE VINE.—The rule to be followed in this respect, and which is as applicable to the grape-vine as to all other kinds of trees and shrubs subject to pruning, is this: prune as soon as possible before the rising of the sap, so that none may have escaped into the extremities of the stems which are to be removed, and thus be wasted. For, if this operation is delayed until the young shoots have grown three or four inches, those of them which are cut will have absorbed the sap, to the injury of those which are reserved, and if this mode of operating is repeated several years in succession, the plants will be gradually exhausted, whatever may have been said to the contrary. The pruning being done in the autumn, will allow more time in the spring for the numerous operations to be performed at that season. Besides, early pruning hastens the·development of the buds, and, all other things being otherwise equal, this early pruning is favorable to the early ripening of the crop.

Unfortunately, this very simple rule has to be modified more or less by the following circumstances:

1st. In the northern vine regions, the winters are, at at times, so severe that the effects of the heavy frosts are felt by the plants pruned in the autumn, and frequently all the reserved portions of the plants are killed.

2d. The result of early pruning, before winter, for instance, is, as we have just said, to develop the growth of the reserved shoots ten or fifteen days earlier than if pruned in the middle of March. The consequence of this is, that in localities exposed to late frosts, this early budding subjects the plants to their injurious influence.

From this, we conclude that pruning in January and February will be advantageous : 1st—in those localities where the winters are mild, and the late frosts are not of frequent occurrence ; 2d—for old vines, or for the less hardy varieties, whose strength will be preserved by forcing the sap to feed the reserved shoots exclusively. For certain varieties whose overgrowth is injurious to the quality and quantity of the product, for those localities where late 'frosts are to be feared, and the winters are severe, the pruning must be done in March, and to the 15th of April. We must say, in addition, that, whatever may be the time chosen, the wood must never be cut when frozen. At such times, pruning tears the wood, instead of cutting it, and the eye below each cut suffers very much.

[A very extended experience with the vine has induced some of our best cultivators to adopt fall pruning, which they pursue with very good effect. The cuttings are of greater value, and may either be planted at once, or at least they can be stored in suitable cellars and kept in better condition than if left upon the vine, exposed to the inclemency of the winter.

Those who bury their vines to protect them from frost, will find it a great advantage to have them trimmed first.

To avoid injury to the last eye on the canes, care should be taken to leave an inch or more of the internode beyond the outer bud; this is a good rule in all winter pruning. The author's remark with regard to cutting when the wood is frozen, deserves attention. Most of our vine-dressers practice trimming in any mild weather during the winter, whether in February or March; but after the sap has started, or is about to start, the vine will bleed profusely. This will sometimes occur in mild weather, after fall pruning, also.]

METHOD OF CUTTING THE SHOOTS AND LARGE STEMS.—The wood of the vine being spongy, and the sap very abundant, the shoots must be cut four or six inches above the last of the reserved eyes [Fig. 23]; for, as the wood dries up to the distance of a few lines below the cut, the last eye would frequently be destroyed, or would, at least, suffer very much, if the cut were made immediately above that eye.

[FIG. 23] —*Mode of Pruning.*

The cut must be made sloping, and on the side opposite to the eye, so that if the plant is in a vertical, or upright position, and the vine begins to bleed, the flow of the sap may not injure the eye.

The large stems must also be cut in the same manner, so that the wounds may heal up more easily. All stems that need removal, should be cut close to the stock, and all such as need to be shortened, must be cut close to the new shoots. Whenever any considerable scars are made on the vine, it will be well to cover them over with grafting wax. If this is not done, they heal up slowly—the wood is injured by the action of the air, and the life of the plant is shortened in consequence.

PRUNING INSTRUMENTS.—In the southern and south-western regions, where the wood of the vine is strong and vigorous, a sort of bill is used, the shape of which varies in different localities. *Figure* 24 represents the pruning bill of Médoc. It is about six inches long; its back is sufficiently blunt at B, to allow of its being touched without wounding, while the portion A, is sharp. In other places the bill is of the shape represented by *Figure* 25. It is about eight inches long, and is cutting at C and D. In the northern portions of the

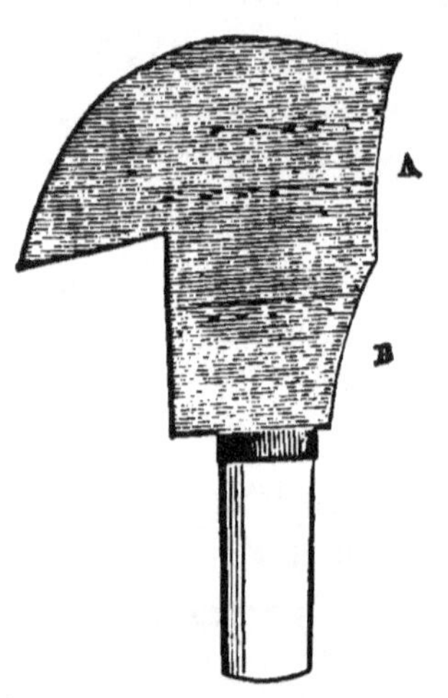

[FIG. 24.]—*Médoc Bill for Pruning Vines.*

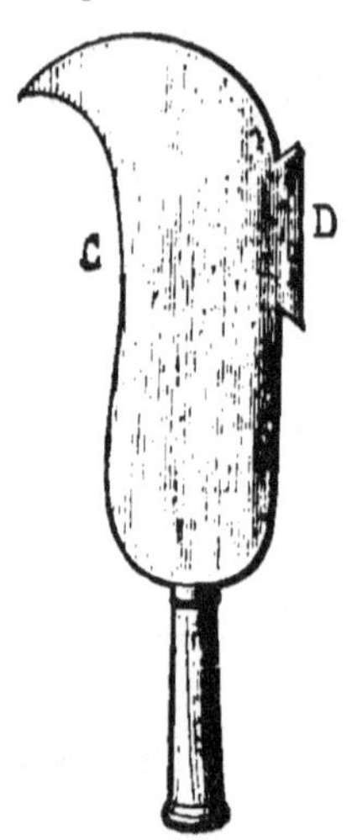

[FIG. 25.]—*Vine Pruning-Bill.*

vine regions, where the plants are smaller, the pruning-knife, *Figure* 26, is used. Nevertheless, for some years past, the substitution of the pruning-shears [Fig. 27], invented about a century ago, by the Marquis Bertrand de Molleville, has been attempted. The pruning-shears [Fig. 27] is composed of two limbs crossing each other near the forward part, one of which terminates in a rounded blade, while the extremity of the other forms a hook, with a thick projection, under which the blade slides. The two limbs are kept open by a spring.—

The size of this instrument must depend on the size of
the plants to be cut.

[FIG. 26.]—*Vine Prun-
ing-Knife.*

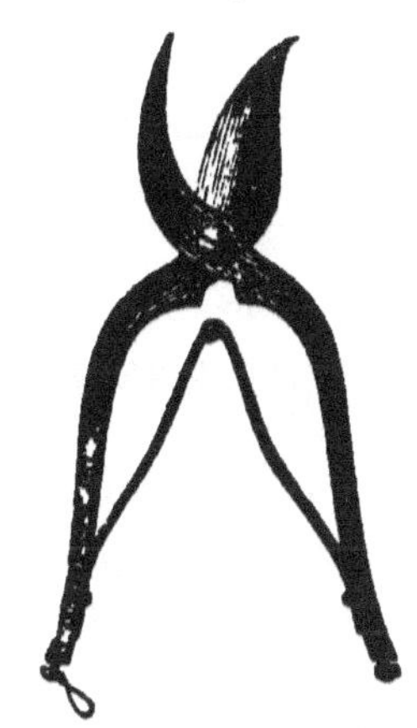

[FIG. 27.]—*Vine Prun-
ing-Shears.*

The numerous trials which have been made, for the
past thirty years, no longer leave any doubt as to
the advantage of the pruning-shears over the bill or
knife, for vine-pruning.   It can be used much more
rapidly, and with less fatigue to the laborer.   It is objected, it is true, that this instrument bruises the plants
somewhat, and that it does not make so neat a cut as
the bill or knife ; but if it is very sharp, and the blade
sufficiently curved—if, in a word, care is taken always
to have the dull blade, or hook, above,* this defect will
be scarcely perceptible, and will be largely compensated
by the rapidity with which the work is done.   Besides,
the bruising is of little consequence, since it is necessary, in all cases, to cut the stems from four-tenths to

---

*The hook is held above in pruning, that it may not crush the portions
left on the vine ; in making our cuttings with the shears, the implement is
held so that the hook shall press upon the portion that is rejected.

eight-tenths of an inch above the eye to be reserved, and the new pruning is done each year below the point operated on the year previous.

[The pruning-shears have come into almost universal use in this country, where any and all labor-saving implements are at a premium in public estimation. We use the grape-shears for making cuttings, and they are brought into play in all sorts of pruning, for all kinds of shrubbery, where the limbs to be severed are not too large—then the saw is needed, and it should always be at hand in trimming an old vineyard, where large, stumpy branches frequently need removing from the vine-stocks; often the whole stem must be taken away even to the ground, in order to make room for a new shoot from below. This is particularly the case in old vines trained to stakes in the bow system. Nor should the pruning-knife be neglected; the cut is certainly smoother and neater than that made by the shears.]

We have already seen that the object of pruning is either to give shape to the plant, or to insure a proper degree of fruitfulness. Let us examine these two operations separately, first ascertaining what is the best form to give to the plants:

WHAT FORMS TO GIVE TO THE VINES.—The forms given to vines, in vineyards, are very various. They are often justified by local causes, or by the peculiar growth of the varieties cultivated; but frequently this operation has been purely empirical. Let us, therefore, investigate the principles which ought to guide us in this matter.

Three things require our attention: the use of the parent stock, or frame-work of the plant; the dimensions of this frame; and its hight above the ground.

Use of the Parent Stock or Frame of the Plants.—The vine could easily be cultivated in the vineyard so as to obtain an abundant yield from it, without annually renewing the fruit-stems from the same stock. The only thing required for that purpose will be to layer, every year, the wood which produced the fruit-stems, so that the stock would be annually renewed. This is the ordinary method in most of the Champagne vineyards.—But experience has long since shown that this method, while it increases the vigor of the fruit-stems, has a very unfavorable influence on the quality of the grapes, and consequently, on the wine also. The sap must circulate slowly, and gradually, from the roots to the branches, so that it may the better ripen the fruit. The parent stock, being more or less knotty and crooked, intervening between the roots and fruit-stems, produces this result. The sap can circulate through it only at a certain speed, thereby assisting in the perfection, within the tissues of the fruit, of those elements which make good wines. It is for this reason that the older, the longer, and more crooked, the parent stock, the less vigorous are the shoots, and the better is the product.—The younger vines, on the contrary, yield inferior wine. This is easily seen in the first bunches of the young layers.

What I have just said is enough to show the use of the parent stock, but it must be added, however, that from this parent stock the shoot acquires a degree of development proportionate to its vigor, so as to assist its maturity.

Proper Dimensions of the Vine.—All varieties of grapes do not grow with the same vigor. The most vigorous require a pretty large frame in order to bear largely—such are the "Panses," and most of the varieties of the South.   If too much confined they produce a very large number of shoots, and leaves of prodigious size, but scarcely any fruit.   Other varieties must be much more reduced in size, as they will soon be exhausted ; such are the "Pinots," and many of the varieties of northern regions.   The size of the frame, therefore, must be in proportion to the vigor of the plant.

[These postulates of our author should be gladly received by the American reader, who will find great advantage from their application, as fundamental principles, in the treatment of some of our vigorous growers that are also unproductive in fruit, as is often the case with the Diana, Union Village, and some others, but especially with the Taylor ; by a proper mode of pruning, adapted to the extreme vigor of these varieties, there is no doubt their productiveness might be wonderfully increased.   Thus I have seen a combination of long training, and vigorous summer pruning, attended with an enormous crop of grapes, upon some vines of the Taylor and Oporto, and the bunches were unusually large.]

Hight of the Plants above Ground.—Experience has shown, in all vine regions, that the nearer the grapes are to the ground, without touching it, the earlier and more perfectly do they ripen their fruit.   This is owing to the reflection of the sun's rays, which, striking the soil, are thrown back upon the surrounding objects ; moreover, the soil having been warmed during the day, throws off this heat during the night, radiating caloric for the benefit of the nearest objects.   From this, we must conclude that the further we are removed from the South, the nearer the ground should our plants be.

This is, in fact, the general practice, as may be seen by comparing the vineyards of the southern, middle, and northern regions.

These principles being admitted, let us see what are the principal forms which have been adopted, and ascertain which are best adapted to the vine.

The various forms now used in the vineyards are all comprised in the three following :

[FIG. 28.]—*High-trained Vines.*]

1st. *High-trained Vines.*—This shape is a common one in Italy and Spain, in the southern portion of Dauphiny, in the Bigorre, and in Béarn, and can succeed in warm latitudes only. This mode consists in planting trees fourteen to sixteen feet in hight, in rows eighty to ninety feet apart, and the trees twenty-five feet from each other, on level land, and fifteen feet apart on the hills. For this purpose, the maple is used, the wild mulberry, the wild cherry, the plum-tree, and those of the hardier descriptions generally, and having few leaves. When these trees have taken root, two or three vine-plants, chosen from the most vigorous varieties, are placed at the foot of each tree.

They are trained, from year to year, round the tree to where it has been headed off. The principal limbs of these trees, reduced to five or six, and cut parallel to the rows, serve to support the vines, which form garlands from one tree to another. [Fig. 28.]

Sometimes, also, these vines are allowed to develop branches, which, shooting six or ten feet from the ground, are trained at right-angles with the row of trees, and supported on each side with stakes, so as to form continuous arbors. [Fig. 29.] At other times,

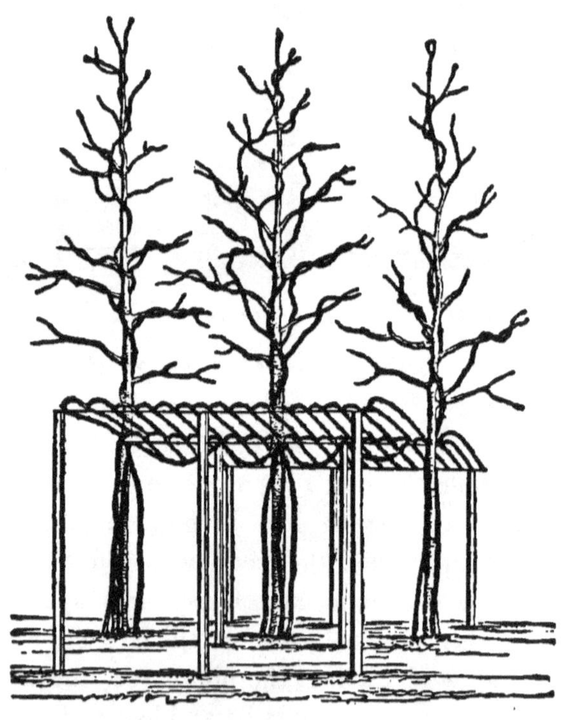

[FIG. 29.]—*High-trained Vines.*

the crown of the tree is cut in the shape of a round dish, on a stem of six to ten feet high, and supports the vines on its outward surface.

The yearly pruning tends to renew the young shoots which are to succeed each other in the bearing of the fruit; to suppress those which deviate from the proper direction, or cause confusion; and, lastly, to lop off those branches of the support-tree, which, by shading the vine, might retard its growth.

The objects of this mode of cultivation are the following: the necessity of allowing certain varieties to acquire a large growth, which otherwise would be small bearers; and especially the hope of drawing from the soil a double crop, by raising the vine-branches sufficiently high above ground.

Of all modes of cultivating the vine, there is none so picturesque or pleasing to the eye, but we must confess, wherever we have studied high-trained vines, in Béarn, in Dauphiny, we have invariably noticed the following facts: the grapes, being shaded by the leaves, ripen badly, and this defective ripening is retarded still more by the too great hight of the branches above the ground. It is for this reason that the wine produced by these vines is always very inferior, even in Italy. Besides this, the exhaustion of the soil by the roots of the trees, and the vines, as well as by the shade thrown over its surface, is such that other crops which are raised together with them, yield but poor results. Lastly, we have also observed that these high-trained vines are more liable to the *Oïdium* than low vines, and this is the more to be regretted, because it is more difficult to apply the sulphur to them, owing to their great hight, and the confusion of their branches. And it is owing to these facts, that high-trained vines have proved almost entirely barren for several years past.

In short, we think that if the strips of land occupied by these high-trained vines, were reduced to one single patch, and planted with an equal number of average-sized or low vines, a crop might be obtained which, by its quantity and quality, would yield a larger net cash profit than the one obtained from the high vines, and other crops raised with them. We, therefore, can not recommend this mode of cultivation.

[In this country, perhaps we have erred in attempting to dwarf and cramp our vigorous native grapes, by forcing them to keep within the narrow limits of our crowded vineyards. This has been obviated in the later plantings of grapes, which have greater space allowed to each vine; but we still trim severely, and think we find our advantage in this practice. The opposite plan of long pruning has been pertinaciously preached to us by certain theorists, who claim, among other advantages, that they would escape the rot and mildew, by avoiding the system of severe pruning, which they assume to be the leading cause of these disasters in our vineyards, overlooking the fact that some of the wild grapes, which reached the tops of our forest-trees, were affected with the same trouble. Our author informs us that the oïdium has destroyed the fruit of these high-trained vines in Italy.]

2d. *Average-sized Vines.*—In this group, the framework of the plants is of such a size that the fruit-bearing stems, each year, shoot out at a hight of from fifteen to forty inches from the ground. The frame of the plant must be developed proportionately to the vigor of the variety. This being the proper hight for vigorous vines and vines of moderate growth, is adapted to the southern regions and intermediate climates. In the North, if the grapes were too far removed from the ground, they would ripen badly. Vines of moderate growth are trained in various shapes. Let us examine the principal ones, and try to improve those which are inconvenient.

In Languedoc, Roussillon, Provence, where very vigorous varieties are generally grown, the plants have an upright stock, six to twelve inches high, which, at that hight, divides into three or five horns, or arms, six or twelve inches long, spreading like a cup, and measuring, at the top, about twenty inches in diameter. It is at the extremity of these horns that the fruit-bearing stems shoot each year, at a hight of from sixteen to twenty inches above ground. These vines are not provided with any support, but they are of such varieties as generally have pretty stiff stems. Nevertheless, if the plants are somewhat vigorous, the long shoots which they develop soon overspread the general surface of the ground. *Figure* 30 represents one of these stocks, fully grown, before pruning.

By giving this shape to the vines, we save the expense of staking, which is always great ; we also do away, to a considerable extent, with plowing, as the ground is soon overspread with the branches. Therefore, this mode of cultivation has the advantage of not being very expensive ; but, on the other hand, the bunches, being entirely covered up by the leaves, receive the influence of the sun in an insufficient degree, and the soil can not have the requisite tillage—both of which circumstances injure the quality of the wine.

Lastly, the plow, which it has been attempted to substitute for manual labor, in that region, can not easily

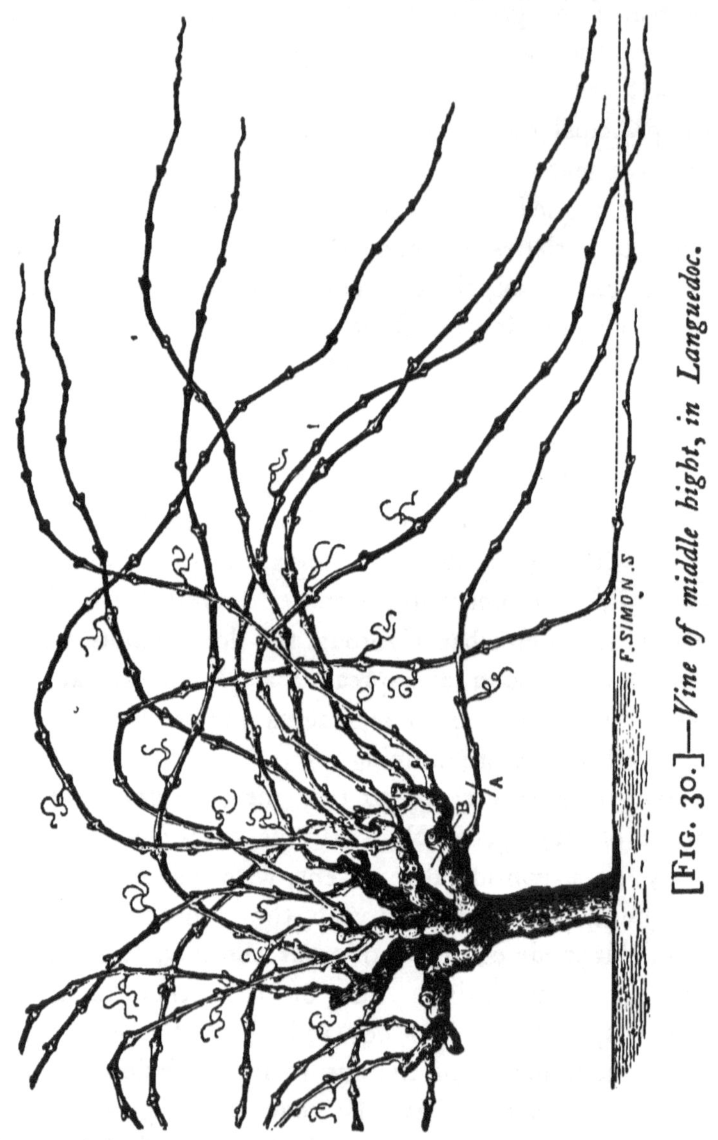

[FIG. 30.]—*Vine of middle hight, in Languedoc.*

be used, owing to the projection of the arms, or horns,

of these plants. But, in order to avoid these inconveniences, it would be necessary to substitute the form
of trellis, which we will point out further on.

But it is a question whether the increased value of
the produce arising from this modification, would compensate for the additional expense which would be in-

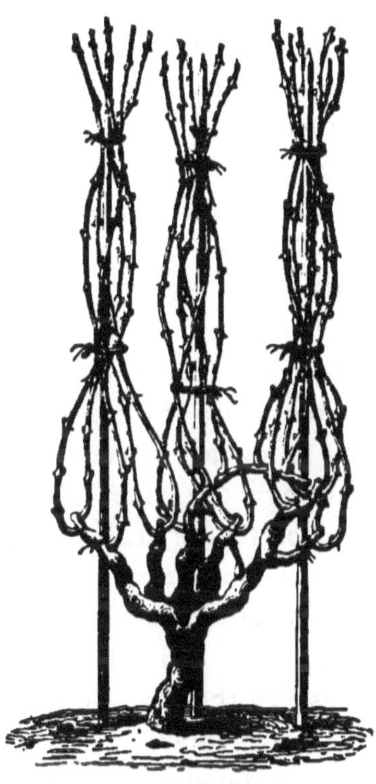

[FIG. 31.]—*Moderate-sized Vine, of the Marshes of
Bordeaux.*

curred. We therefore see nothing to change in this
shape, at least, for the varieties producing wines of low
price. But for those whose product is of more value,
such as the vineyards of Lunel, of Frontignan, of St.

George, of l'Ermitage, of Condrieux, of St. Péray, etc., it will be profitable to substitute the form which we shall describe further on, under the name of " Four-armed Trellis." The fruit, being more exposed to the sun, will be of better quality, and the tillage of the soil will, at all times, be more easy. In the marshy districts of Bordelais, and on the hills on the right bank of the Garonne, from Bordeaux to Blaye, where the vine grows rapidly, a similar shape is given to the vines, the stock, nevertheless, being a trifle higher and the arms a little longer, the shoots springing out at thirty or thirty-two inches above the ground. Lastly, and especially, these stocks are each supported by two or three stakes, as shown in *Figure* 31, illustrating one of these stalks before pruning. The much greater value of the product of these vineyards will compensate for the staking and the extra cultivation given to them. Nevertheless, the following objections may be made to this mode of planting : the bunches, being wrapped up in the shoots fastened to the stakes, do not receive the influence of the sun sufficiently ; the space occupied by each stock is unfavorable to the use of the plow where the form of the ground would otherwise permit its use. Last, and not least, is the extra cost and care of the grape-stakes, which it involves.

We therefore recommend the substitution of the shape represented in *Figure* 32, which is a full-grown stock before pruning.

By this arrangement, the fruit-stems feel the action of the sun on all sides, and the following year's shoots are better formed. Another advantage is that the frame

of the plant thus trellised is narrow, allowing the use of
of the plow at all times.

Lastly, this shape permits the substitution of wire for
grape-stakes, which is much less expensive, as will be
shown elsewhere.   Besides, each plant thus trellised,
will bear, at least as many fruit-stems as the old shape;
the same number of vines may be planted on a given
surface, and, consequently, the produce will at least be
equal in quantity, and certainly of better quality, than
on the former plan.

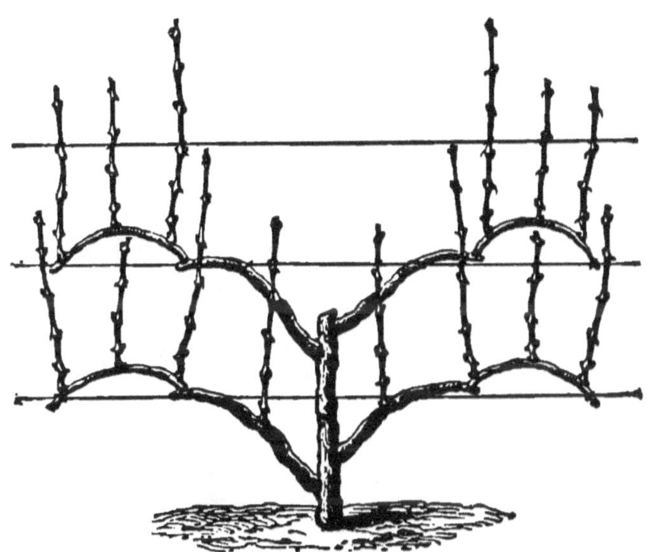

[FIG. 32.]—*Four-armed Trellis.*

In the rich vineyards of Médoc, the vines are shaped
as in *Figure* 33.   The trunk, rising perpendicularly to
a hight of four to six inches, divides into two branches,
depressed at an angle of 45 degrees, sixteen inches in
length, and producing the fruit-stems of each year on their

extremities. These two stems, arched upward, are fastened to a cross-stake, sixteen inches above ground.

[FIG. 33.]—*Middle-sized Vine of Médoc.*

This form seems to us to be a very advantageous one, at least for vines of vigorous growth. We would, nevertheless, advise the use of the cross-stake sixteen inches above the the first [Fig. 34], on which to fasten the shoots, instead of laying them down upon the lower rail, by which many of the bunches are deprived of the action of the sun, by being enveloped in the leaves.

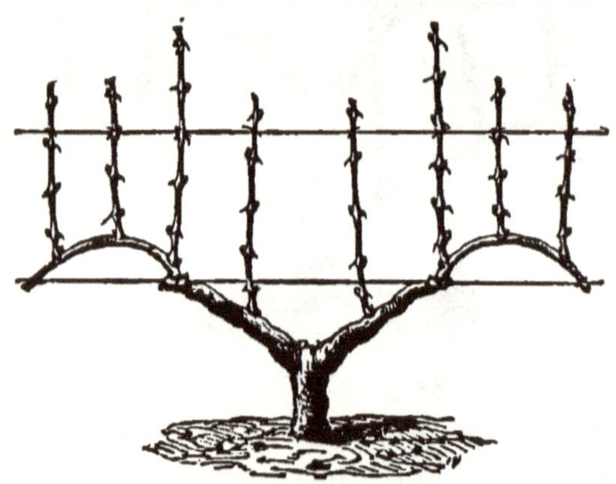

[FIG. 34.]—*Two-armed Trellis.*

The two branches dividing each plant ought always to be of the same size, otherwise the stronger one will soon exhaust the weaker. Now, if the relative care bestowed to maintain an equal growth of these two branches, in vines somewhat vigorous, is compensated by the possibility of extending the fruit-stems, it is not so with weak vines, whose yield must not be forced. We would, therefore, advise the suppression of one of the branches in the last named. By this means the vigor of the fruit-stems will be increased, to the benefit of the produce, and it may then be burdened, more or less, according to the vigor of the stock. *Figure* 35 represents one of these plants before pruning.

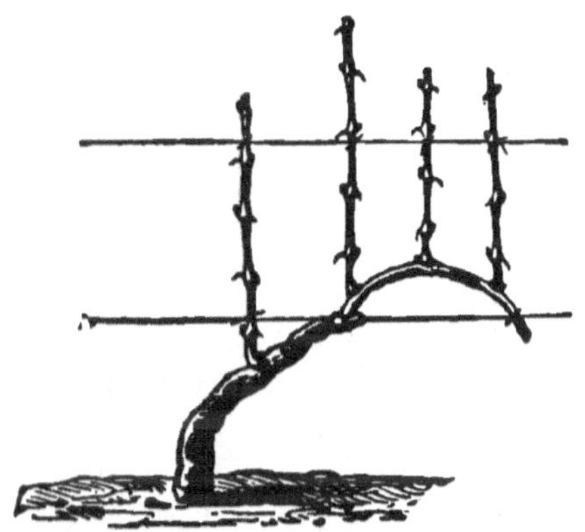

[Fig. 35.]—*One-armed Trellis.*

In certain localities, on the banks of the Rhône, may be seen a vine shaped like *Figure* 36, which also belongs to the medium-sized descriptions, and makes available those small patches of ground, here and there to be found between the bare rocks, on the steep hill-sides of burning climes. Vines thus shaped are termed *cones.* For this mode of cultivation, circular holes, six and one-half feet in diameter, and twenty-eight inches in depth, are opened ; young vines are planted, sixteen inches apart, and three inches inside the cavity. About the third year, a stake of some ten feet in length, is driven firmly into the ground, at the foot of eaeh plant, inclined toward the center. The stem of each plant as it grows, is fastened to these stakes. The fruit-stems shoot at sufficient distances on the entire length of these stocks.

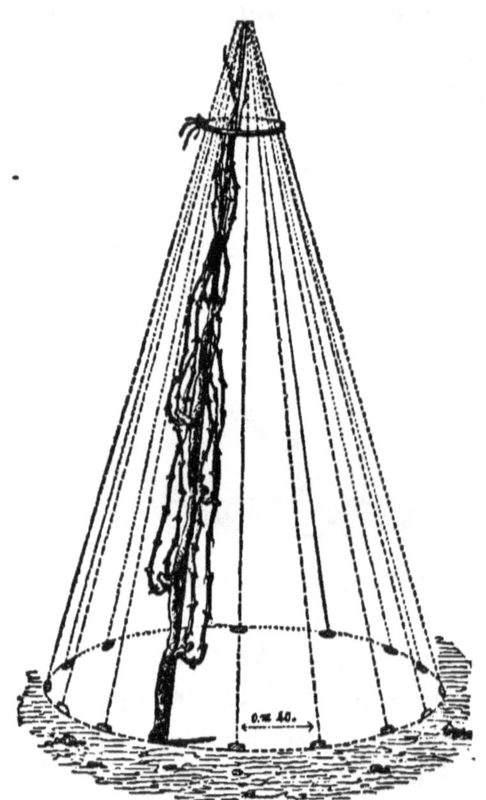

[FIG. 36.]---*Cone-shaped Vine on the Banks of the Rhône.*

Although the varieties cultivated in Burgundy are less hardy than most of those of Bordelais, the shape given to their vines places them in the medium-sized class.— In fact, the stock which supports the fruit-stem, rises to a hight of twelve to twenty-four inches, in a more or less inclined direction [Fig. 37]. Each vine is supported by a grape-stake.

It may be objected to this mode of training, for the less vigorous varieties, such as the "Pinots," that it keeps the grapes too far from the ground, thereby preventing them from properly ripening; also that by keeping this long stock in too upright a position, the sap, flowing all the time toward the top, prevents the shooting of the new stems on the old wood, and the shortening of the stock from time to time. The consequence is, that these stocks, by overgrowing, soon exhaust themselves, and have to be frequently

[FIG. 37.]—*Vine of the Côte d' Or.*

renewed by layering—a costly operation, and one always injurious to the quality of the wine.

We think that the form of *Figure* 35 is preferable. Besides, in the latter form, the wire may be substituted for the stake. This will reduce the expense, and allow the use of the plow over almost the entire surface of the ground.

For the more vigorous varieties in the same regions, such as the stronger descriptions of Gamais, which are

12

cultivated in rich soils, and generally undergo the same treatment, there is, besides, this other inconvenience: that, owing to the limited number of fruit-stems, it will not furnish so great a yield as might otherwise be had, and the bunches are badly shaded by being smothered in the leaves.   By treating these vines as in *Figure* 34, a number of shoots might be left on the fruit-stems, proportionate to the vigor of the stocks.

3d. *Low Vines.*—In low vines the shoots start from the stocks at eight inches, or less, from the ground.—This method is particularly adapted to the northern portions of the vine regions, where the less vigorous varieties are cultivated, and where the frames of the vines are but slightly developed.   The stocks are, besides, sufficiently close to each other to reduce their vigor, which, added to the close proximity of the bunches to the soil, favors their ripening.

In the vineyards in the vicinity of Paris, and at many similar points, as regards climate, the stocks are trained on the plan of *Figure* 38.   There, also, it will be profitable to substitute the form illustrated in *Figure* 35.   By this means, wires may be substituted for grape-stakes, and the plow for manual labor. In a word, the number of plants on an acre being reduced, without diminishing the yield, the bunches will be better warmed,

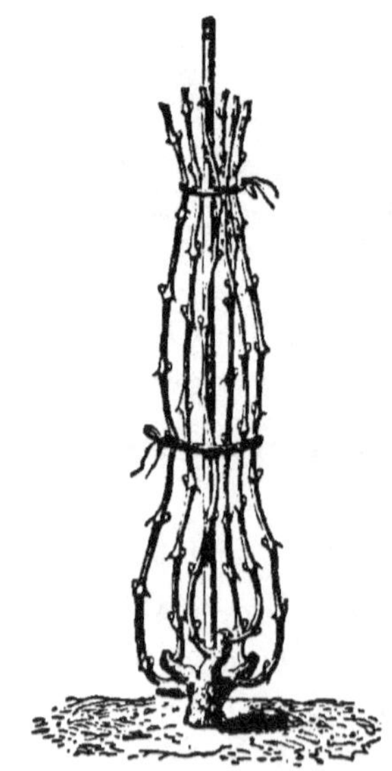

[FIG. 38.]—*Low Vine in the vicinity of Paris.*   by the sun, and the wine improved in quality.

In Champagne, the vines are not provided with stocks, owing to the yearly laying down of the plants; two fruit-stems shoot from the ground yearly, as is shown in *Figure* 39, and the stocks are planted irregularly, at less than sixteen inches from one another. We shall describe this mode of cultivation further on.

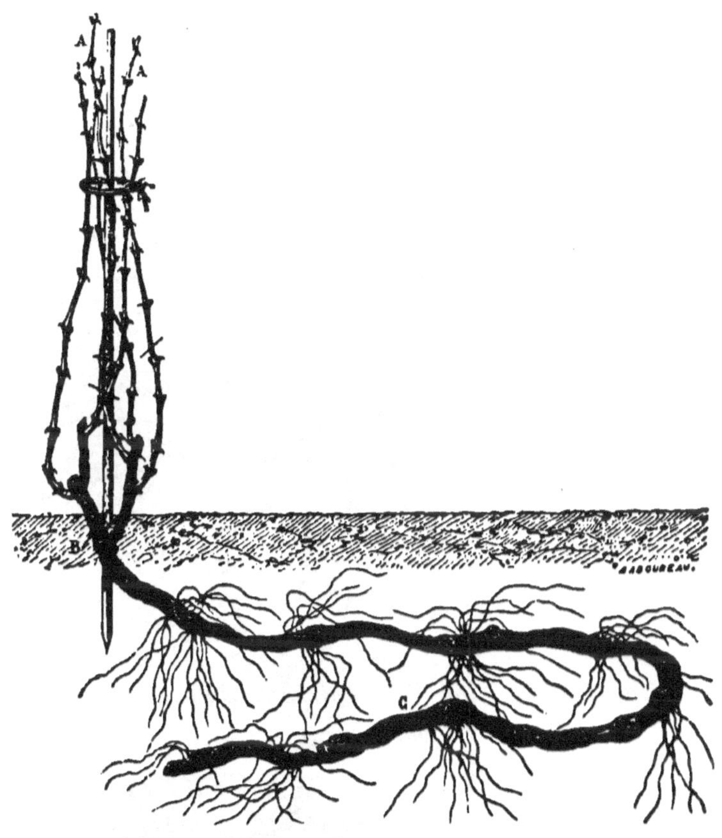

[FIG. 39.]—*Low Vine of Champagne.*

There will also be a marked advantage in substituting the form of *Figure* 35. The number of stocks will be reduced two-thirds; the yield will be the same, as experience has already proved in that country; wires will be substituted for grape-stakes; it will be possible to use the plow when the lay of the land will allow it; and the shoots and bunches being better exposed to the sun, will ripen more perfectly. Lastly, the fruit-stems, growing from a stock above ground, and of some age, will yield a wine of better quality.

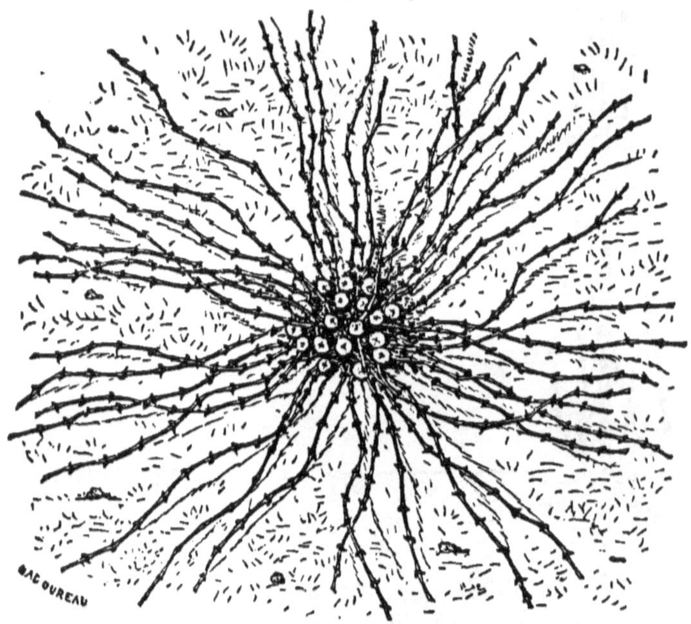

[Fig. 40.]—*Low Vine of l' Aunis, before Pruning—downward view.*

The vineyards of l' Aunis, in lower Charente, have another style of low vines. Here the vigorous sorts are cultivated; the vines are

[Fig. 41.]—*Low Vine of l' Aunis, after Pruning—side view.*

planted in very wide rows, from

four to six feet apart; the dressing is done by the plow, and the plants are not provided with any support. The frame is merely a sort of flat head, of five or ten inches in diameter, almost touching the ground [Figs. 40 and 41], and is the result of the very short and successive pruning of the numerous shoots which each year spring from and around this sort of stool. The long and vigorous annual shoots creep over and soon cover the entire space between the stocks.

This mode of cultivating has the following objections: the grapes, hanging upon the ground, rot in great numbers, and ripen badly, owing to being almost entirely excluded from the sun's rays. Secondly, the sulphuration which is, unfortunately, necessary in this region, can be very imperfectly performed. Thirdly, the stems, which overspread the ground, soon become an obstacle in the way of tillage, which is, therefore, insufficient.

We would recommend the substitution of those forms of stocks shown in *Figure* 32 or *Figure* 35, according to the vigor of the plants. The wires for the training of the vines will, undoubtedly, increase the expense, but this will be much more than compensated by the abundance and quality of the produce, resulting from the absence of rot, the more perfect ripening of the grapes, the possibility of performing efficient sulphuration, and, lastly, the more perfect tillage of the soil.

MODE OF PRUNING IN ORDER TO FORM THE STOCKS. —We have just compared the principal forms to which the vines are generally subjected in vineyards, and we have seen that most of them present certain objections which we have tried to remove, either by modifying those forms, or substituting others for them. Those we have recommended will answer under most of the circumstances in which vineyards are placed. We must now study the mode of pruning, by which these forms can be given to the plants.

We have carried the treatment of the vineyard to the end of the first summer after planting. Each of the young plants has from one to three rather slender shoots. They must all be removed except the stoutest, which is cut, leaving two eyes. At the end of this second year's growth, each plant is as represented in *Figure* 42. And now commences the pruning into shape.

[FIG. 42.]—*Young Two-year old Plant.*

[FIG. 43.]—*Young Three-year old Plant.*

Cup-shaped Vines of the South, without Stakes—[Fig. 30.]—The young vine being, at pruning time, as represented in *Figure* 42, the finer shoot, A, only, is reserved, and cut at B, leaving two eyes ; the following year, the two finest shoots obtained [Fig. 43], are also cut at A, leaving two eyes ; thus, at the end of the following year, we have four principal shoots [Fig. 44] to be converted into four arms, or horns. For the less vigorous varieties, this number of arms will be sufficient, and each of the four chosen shoots is cut in A, allowing it

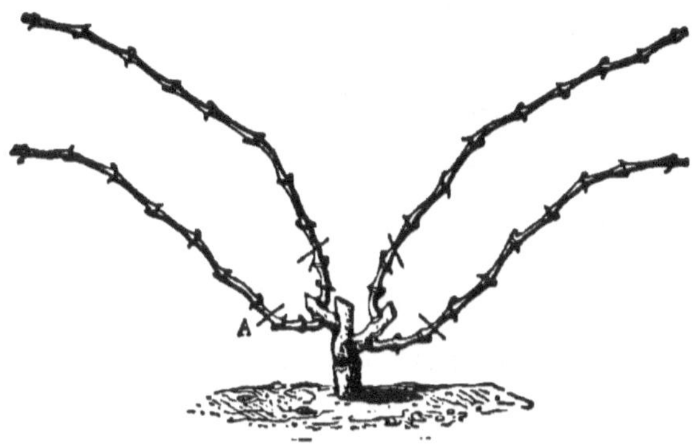

[FIG. 44.]—*Young Four-year old Plant.*

about eight inches in length. This pruning gives it, for the following year, the form of *Figure* 45. The stem A, only, is reserved on each arm, and it is cut in B, above the eye. The same operation is repeated each year. For

[FIG. 45.]—*Young Five-year old Plant.*

the more vigorous varieties, two of the original stems are made to fork [A, Fig. 46], so às to raise the number of arms to six. The fruit-stem, reserved each year at the end of each limb, must always be cut very short.

Nevertheless, those arms, or horns, grow a little every

[FIG. 46.]—*Young Six-Year old Vine.*

year.   When they begin to outgrow the proper limit,
the presence of a shoot [A, Fig. 30] on the old stock

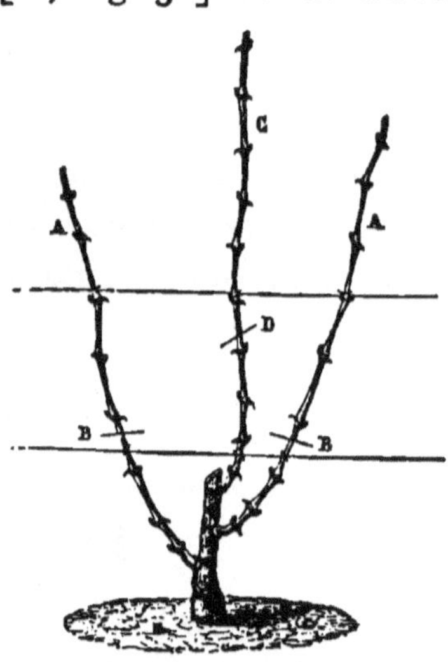

[FIG. 47.] — *Four-
armed Trellis, first
Pruning.*

[FIG. 48.]—*Four-armed Trellis,
second Pruning.*

is taken advantage of, to shorten the arms, which are
then cut at B, and the shoot, A, is cut as a fruit-stem.

The same process is adopted, in order to shorten any one of the arms which may have become more vigorous than the rest, and threatens to destroy the equilibrium of vegetation, which must be maintained among them.

Four-armed Trellis, for Vigorous Varieties, with Stakes —[Fig. 32.]—This shape is given in the following manner: the finest shoot, which is cut in A, above the third eye, is alone reserved on the two-year old plants. [Fig. 47.] The next year, the young plants have the shape of *Figure* 48. The two lateral shoots, A, are then cut at B, to the length of about twelve inches, and bent down on each side, so as to fasten them to the wire. The middle shoot, C, must then be cut at D, and about six inches below the second wire. This pruning will give, the following year, the shape of *Figure* 49. On each of the lower arms, the finest

[FIG. 49.]—*Four-armed Trellis, third Pruning.*

shoot, A, is preserved to the length of about twelve inches, bending it upon the lower wire, as shown by the two dotted lines, B. On the top of the plant, only the two shoots, C, are reserved, and are pruned to the length of about twelve inches, bent down, and their ends fastened to the upper wire.

Another year's growth gives the shape of *Figure* 50. The fruit-stem, A, of the previous year, is suppressed from each arm, and cut just above the finest shoot, B, and nearest the old wood. All the other shoots

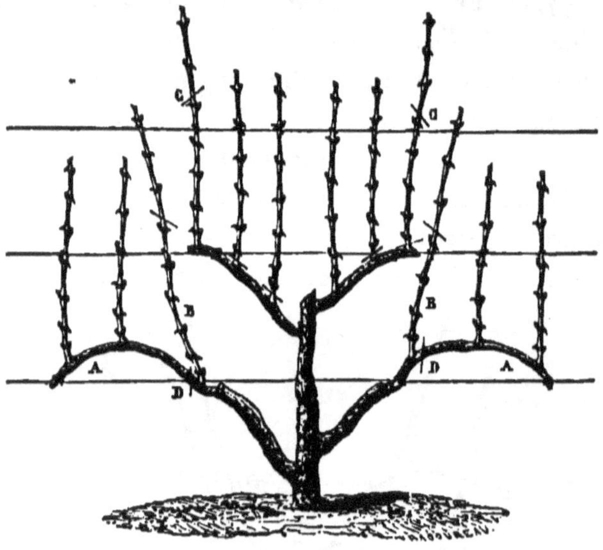

[FIG. 50.]—*Four-armed Trellis, fourth Pruning.*

are also cut away. The new fruit-stems are cut to about twelve inches, bent down and fastened to the wires, as in the previous years. As for the two upper arms, all their shoots are cut away, except the two end vines, C, which are cut to twelve inches in length, and bent down the same as the stems, A, of the year previous. The form is then complete.

There is nothing more to do each year than to prune it properly in the way I shall point out, under the head of "·Annual Pruning of the Fruit-Stems."

Whatever may be the mode of pruning these shoots, the arms, on the ends of which they are reserved, grow more or less each year. As soon as any one arm becomes longer than is convenient, it must at once be shortened, taking advantage, for that purpose, of a shoot [Fig. 32] on the old wood, previously reserved, to provide for this operation.

The curved form of these arms always favors the production of these reserved shoots. As it is also important to preserve an equal degree of vigor between these four arms, any one of them being too vigorous, might be shortened by the process just explained, or the fruit-stem pruned very short.

Trellis with two Arms, for Plants of Moderate Vigor— [Fig. 34.]—The shaping of these vines is done in the manner already described, with this difference : that the two inferior arms only, are necessary, as shown in our cut.

Trellis with a single Arm, for Vines that are not Vigorous—[Fig. 35.]—The formation of this single arm is obtained in precisely the same manner as those of which we have just spoken.

RESTORING BADLY PLANTED OR BADLY FORMED VINES.—The system of planting and shaping vines, which we have just described, can be applied, not only to new vineyards, but also to those already planted, and which it is desirable to remodel according to the system just explained. In that case, we must proceed in the following manner :

Pull up one row on the long side of the vineyard.
Draw a straight line in the place of the row which has
been taken up, and on it, drive stakes, to show the spot
to be occupied by each new plant. Choose, on each
stock of the next row, a number of shoots equal to the
number of plants which are to form the first row; then
cut off from these stocks all the arms, except those
bearing the selected shoots. This done, open a trench
at the foot of each plant to the depth of twelve or sixteen inches, according to the size of the stock to be
buried. This trench is carried to the first row, and to
each spot marked by the grape-stakes. The entire
stock, as well as the vigorous shoot which has been reserved, is then laid in the trench, and covered up again
with the earth. It will be well, also, to throw at the
bottom of each trench, and at the point where each
shoot springs from the ground, about two quarts of
manure, like that previously described for the planting.
The first row being completed, a second one is marked
out, and the plants of the third row serve to fill it up.
This operation is repeated until the opposite side is
reached, when the last row is filled up with new roots,
not less than two years old. The shoots projecting
from the ground must then be cut so as to leave them
three or four eyes.

This general layering is easily enough performed,
provided the stocks are not too large. It would be of
very difficult execution with the old stocks of the southern vineyards. When the stocks are of a proper size
the results are immediate. We have seen the operation
performed at the Count de la Loyère's, at Savigny,
near Beaune, with vines over twenty-five years old, and

which yielded, the very first summer, more abundantly than any of the best preceding years.

Nevertheless, there is danger that the general layering may injure, for several years, the quality of the produce of certain vineyards which, like the celebrated products of Burgundy, derive a part of their good qualities from the age of the stocks. The evil may be remedied in this way: in those celebrated vineyards, at least one-fifteenth of all the stocks are laid down yearly, choosing the stocks promiscuously. In order to make the change in question, it will be sufficient to lay down an entire row, in the usual proportions, and so on, progressively, beginning on one side of the vineyard.

ANNUAL PRUNING OF FRUIT-STEMS.—All we have said of pruning, until now, relates to the form of the stocks only; we shall now point out the care which the annual pruning of the fruit-stems requires. Let us first see on what principles this operation must be based.

Principles on which the Operation must be Based.—1st. The shoots alone produce blossoms on the vine [Fig. 51].

[FIG. 51.]—*Fruit-Stems.*

2d. The shoots growing out of the stems from the preceding year, are the only ones which produce grapes

[Fig. 51]. The shoots growing from the old wood, as sometimes happens, are invariably barren [Fig. 52].

[FIG. 52.]—*Vine-Shoot on the old Wood.*

3d. On a real fruit-stem [FIG. 53] the shoots are generally more fruitful as they grow further from the old wood; thus, the shoots growing out of the eyes A,

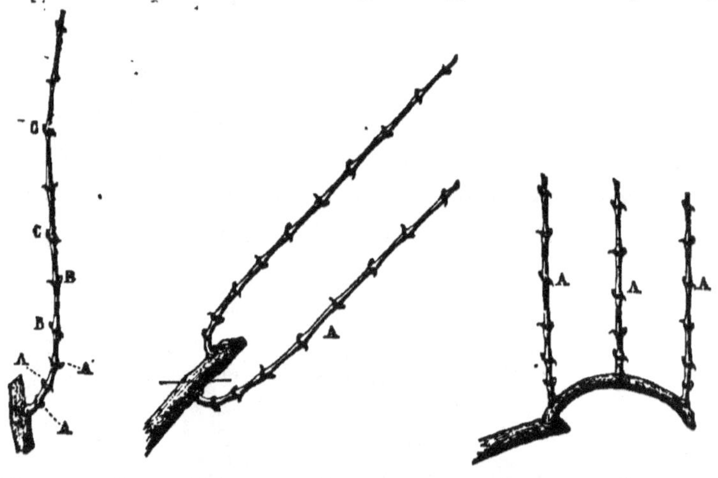

[FIG. 53.]   [FIG. 54.]   [FIG. 55.]

Pruning Fruit-Stems.

will be less productive than those of the eyes B, and those of the eyes C, will bear more than those of the eyes B.

However, the decrease in the fruitfulness of the

shoots on the same fruit-stem, from the top to the base, is more marked in some varieties than in others. It is in the most vigorous varieties that this decrease in fruitfulness is most marked, and it is for this reason that those varieties must be pruned longer than the others, as regards fruitfulness.

4th. Each plant can only nourish, properly, a certain number of bunches, proportionate to its vigor. If this number is exceeded, the quality of the wine suffers very materially.

5th, and Lastly. It will be well to adopt such a mode of pruning the fruit-stems, that each year the shoots

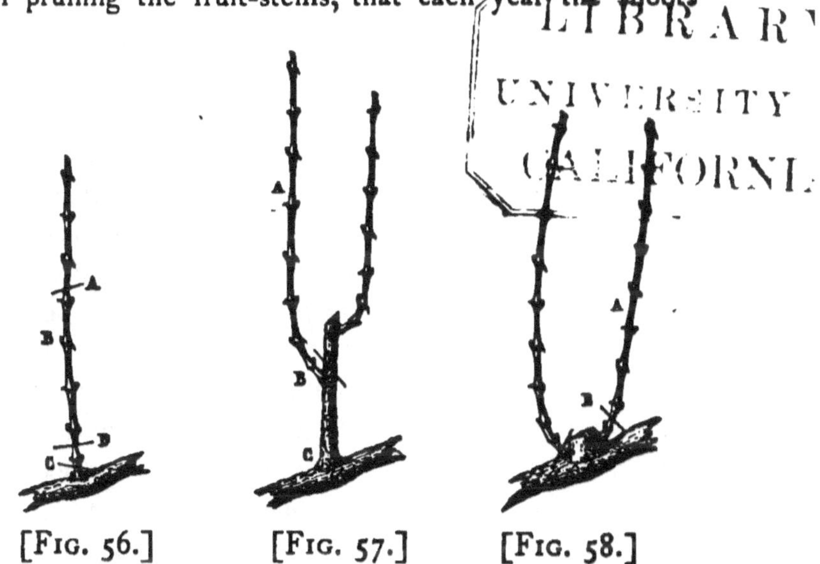

[FIG. 56.]   [FIG. 57.]   [FIG. 58.]

Pruning Fruit-Stems.

nearest the old wood (A, Fig. 54), may be reserved for a new fruit-stem. By this means, it will be easier to preserve the shape of the vine to a size proportionate to the soil from which it derives its nourishment; otherwise its growth will be seen to languish, and its yield diminish.

From the preceding facts the following rules may be established :

1st. The vine ought to be pruned in such a way as to produce, every year, a certain number of shoots, on the two-year old vine [A, Fig. 55].

2d. These shoots [B, Fig. 56] might be pruned very long with advantage, as regards the abundance of yield— at A, for instance. But this mode of operating would have the following disadvantages : all the eyes of this stem are not developed into shoots, for want of sufficient quantity of sap. The eyes A and B, alone, will be developed, and this plant, the following year, will have the appearance of *Figure* 57. The shoot A, will be reserved as a new fruit-stem, and the balance will be cut away. But the parent stock will thereby be lengthened by B C, and if the same process is used each year the parent stock will soon outgrow the proper limits, and become languid and unproductive. Besides, the bunches being too numerous, will yield nothing but an inferior wine. This inconvenience might be avoided by pruning the plant A [Fig. 56] at C, just above the eye nearest to the base. The next year's plant will be as in *Figure* 58. The shoot A, being also reserved, and cut at B, the parent-stock will thereby lengthen very little each year, but the shoots, growing so close to the old wood, yield few if any grapes. Here, then, is the practice which has resulted from the preceding observations.

All the weaker plants, whose shoots at the base are sufficiently vigorous, are cut at two eyes. [D, Fig. 56.]

The following year, the shoot A [Fig. 59], nearest the base is reserved.   For the very vigorous varieties, this pruning with two eyes would yield but a small quantity of grapes.   It will be necessary to reserve, each year, three buds at the base of the plant, and then, each year, reserve only the shoot nearest the old wood.   This operation is repeated each year, and by means of these two modes of pruning, a number of grapes proportionate to the vigor of the plant is produced, and the parent

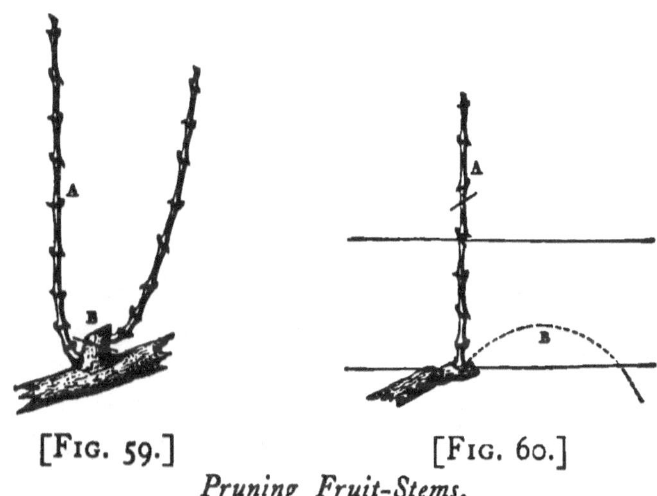

[Fig. 59.]   [Fig. 60.]

Pruning Fruit-Stems.

stock lengthens but slowly.   That portion which annually bears the fruit-stem is called *shoot-stump*, *spit*, etc., etc.—[in this country, the *spur*].

The following process appears to us better adapted to the less vigorous varieties than the preceding ones ; the fruit-stem, A [Fig. 60], is cut to twenty-four inches in length, and then bent down to the wire in the shape of dotted line, B.   This curve favors the growth of the buds, by retaining the sap to their profit.   As soon as the shoots have grown to such a length that the young grapes can be seen, a number of them must be rubbed out. Those nearest the base are reserved with one or two of those having the finest bunches. In the vine-yards of Médoc the same result is obtained, by cutting out the eyes from the shoot. We think, however, that the better way is to remove the *shoots*—the yield is then more certain.

The following year, the old fruit-stem is cut at A, [Fig. 61,] and the shoot, B, is cut and curved in the same way as the past year; and so on, every year. By this mode of pruning, the stock does not lengthen any more than by the preceding one, and we have the advantage of being able to choose the finest fruit-shoots, and to limit the number in proportion to the quantity of grapes they bear, and to the vigor of the plant.

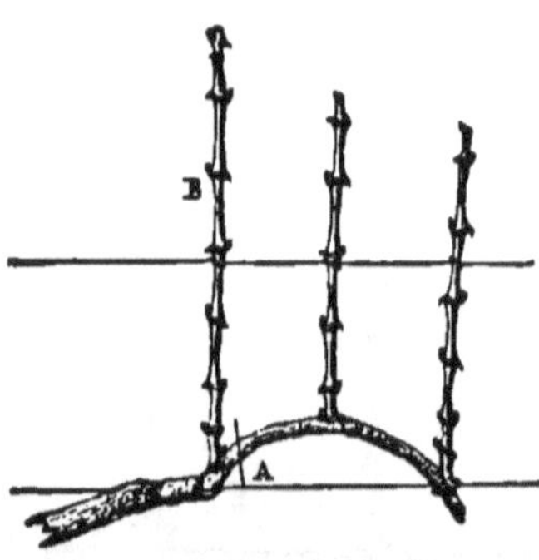

[FIG. 61.]—*Pruning of Fruit-stems.*

For varieties of moderate, or of great vigor, the fruit-stems are pruned in the same manner. The length of these shoots varies from ten to fifteen inches, according to the vigor of the variety. A certain number is re-served on each stock, according to its vigor. These long shoots are also curved, as shown in *Figure* 61.

The Foregoing Theory put in Practice.—We have but little to add to the preceding rules, for their application to the various forms of vines which we have recom-mended.

For the cup-shaped forms [Fig. 30], the arms, or horns being in sufficient number for the vigor of the plants, the fruit-stem on the extremity of each horn is pruned to three eyes. Nevertheless, for the most vigorous varieties which are pruned into this shape, and more especially for those, the eyes at the base of which are not very fruitful, one or two long curved shoots are left on the same or the adjoining arm.

Trellises with one, two, or four arms, according to the vigor of the plants, undergo the same treatment as shown in *Figures* 32, 34 and 35. The fruit-stems which are curved are cut longer or shorter, according to the usual growth of the variety under cultivation. This must also influence the number of fruit-stems reserved each year at budding-time.

VIII.

VARIOUS MODES OF SUPPORTING GRAPE-VINES.

NECESSITY OF THE OPERATION.—The vine is a shrub which nature has provided with tendrils, enabling it to keep itself from the ground, by creeping up the neighboring trees; it is not, therefore, intended to creep on the ground. If its long shoots are allowed to cover the earth, the quality and quantity of its product will soon diminish, especially when it is removed from the South. We know, in fact, that grapes require a certain degree of heat, in order to ripen. This heat they derive either from the direct rays of the sun, or by reflection from the surface of the ground, or by radiation during the night. Now, if the stems creep over, and cover all the surrounding earth, this last can not be warmed ; and the bunches enveloped by the leaves are shaded from the action of the sun. The stocks themselves, being partly shaded, are imperfectly developed, and yield but a small quantity of produce the following year. The buds, also, being loose, are frequently broken off during the summer, by the violence of the winds. And, lastly, most of the bunches in contact with the soil, rot in wet seasons, and exercise a very injurious effect on the quality of the wine. These various obstacles are removed as soon as the trunk and the shoots of the vine are so supported that the soil and the whole plant receive, in a sufficient degree, the action of the sun's rays.

In fact, the advantages of staking the vines are so evident in all vine regions, that in France, out of seventy-six districts which cultivate the vine, sixty make use of stakes. The sixteen districts which do not use the stakes, almost all belong to the southern region ; and there the only motive for not using them is that of economy, and the little value of the product of the vine. Besides, those varieties are chosen, the wood of which is sufficiently stiff to partially sustain itself. There is no doubt, however, that the quantity and quality of the produce would be materially improved, were those vines provided with stakes.

VARIOUS MODES OF SUPPORT.—Let us look into the various means employed to attain this end, and ascertain the one which gives the best results, with the least expense.

Self-supported Vines.—In order to avoid the expense

of supports, which is generally pretty heavy, Mr. Mira-
mont, a land-owner at Maurecort, near Pontoise, has
proposed to tie together the shoots of the plants nearest
one another, giving them the form of *Figure* 62.

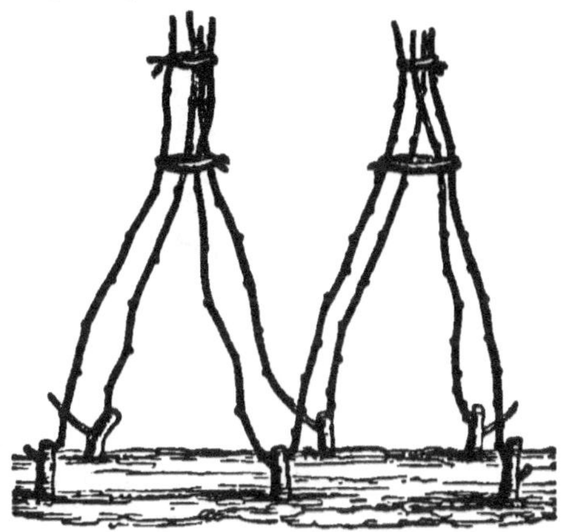

[FIG. 62.]—*Self-supporting Vines.*

These rows of pyramids are far enough apart to allow of their easy cultivation. This mode of training
vines always leaves the grapes partially shaded from
the sun ; besides, it is very probable that these pyramids
would soon be thrown down by the wind.

Vines Supported by Trees.—In certain southern regions—Italy, Bearn, Savoy, etc., etc., the annual expenditure for grape-stakes is saved by training the vines
to trees [Fig. 63]. We have already explained [page
127], how injurious this system is to the quality, and
even to the quantity of the produce, on a given surface.

Vines Trained to Grape-Stakes.—The support most
generally used consists of poles, of various lengths and
thickness, which are called grape-stakes.

These stakes may vary from three and one-half feet
to ten feet in length, according to the hight of the

vines, and eight-tenths of an inch to two inches in
thickness, according to their length.   They are of hard
wood, such as oak, chestnut, locust, etc.; or of white

[FIG. 63.]—*Vines Trained to a Tree.*

wood, such as willow, poplar, etc.   They are made
more durable by being burnt at one end, to the length
of sixteen inches, and the burnt part dipped immediately in hot tar.   For the past few years the system of
Boucherie has been much used in the preservation of
grape-stakes, particularly those made of white wood,
which are then almost as lasting as those made of hard
wood.   M. Baltet, nurseryman at Troyes, performs
this operation in the following manner:

Make a cemented cistern, of a depth proportionate
to the length of the stake.   Prepare, in this cistern, a
solution of sulphate of copper in cold water, in the proportion of one pound of sulphate of copper to six gallons of water.   This salt of copper, placed in small
baskets, on the surface of the water, gradually dissolves.
The stakes are cut while yet green.   Tie them up in

bundles, and immerse them entirely, for about a fort-night, in this liquid; then dry them in the shade, still tightly fastened together in bundles, to prevent them from warping. The solution must be renewed from time to time, that it may retain its strength. It is not necessary to bark the stakes.

In the Department of Maine-et-Loire, where slate quarries abound, this slate is cut in lengths of about four feet and six inches, and two to two and one-half inches in thickness, which are used as grape-stakes, and last indefinitely. The weight of each is from ten to twelve pounds.

Generally, but one stake is put to each vine (Fig. 38). Sometimes, as in certain vineyards in the valley of the Rhône, one single stake is made to serve for three vines. The shoots of the two plants nearest the one having the stake, are all fastened together to that stake, by means of a slip of willow. The three plants have then the appearance of a triangular pyramid.

Elsewhere, in the marshy district of Bordelais, and in the vineyards on the right bank of the Garonne, from Bordeaux to Blaye, two or three stakes are allowed to each stock (Fig. 31); the same in the Departments of Allier, and Puy-de-Dôme. But in the last named lo-cality the stakes, made almost entirely of white wood, and pretty pliable, are united together at the top by means of a tie.

On the rocky slopes of the Rhône, the stocks being planted in small groups, on such small patches of soil as will admit of cultivation, are trained on stakes about ten feet high, and fastened together at the top (Fig. 36).

The staking of newly planted vines takes place only

after they have taken root, and are about being pruned. The staking is done in the spring, immediately after the last winter-dressing of the soil. The stakes are all pointed, and driven into the earth to the depth of ten to twelve inches, according to the hight of the vine. The stakes are sometimes driven into the ground by means of a wooden mallet, but most generally by main strength, and bearing on them with the weight of the whole body. It is a tedious, expensive, and very laborious work for the laborer, to avoid which, and facilitate the work, several tools, such as stake-drivers, etc., have been invented.

The " driver," represented in *Figures* 64 and 65, was invented by M. Dugay, agricultural implement maker, at Argenteuil, near Paris. It consists of an iron rod A, provided with a handle B, at the top. In the middle of this rod there is a hook C, and at its lower extremity a sort of claw, the inside angles of which are cutting ; a stirrup E, projects on the op-

[FIG. 64.]—*Mode of using Dugay's Stake-Driver.*

posite side to this claw. The instrument is used thus:
The vine-dresser places the stake in the hook and the
claw, so that the last named is twelve inches above the
foot of the stake; he then places his right foot in the
stirrup, holds the stake with the left hand, and with his

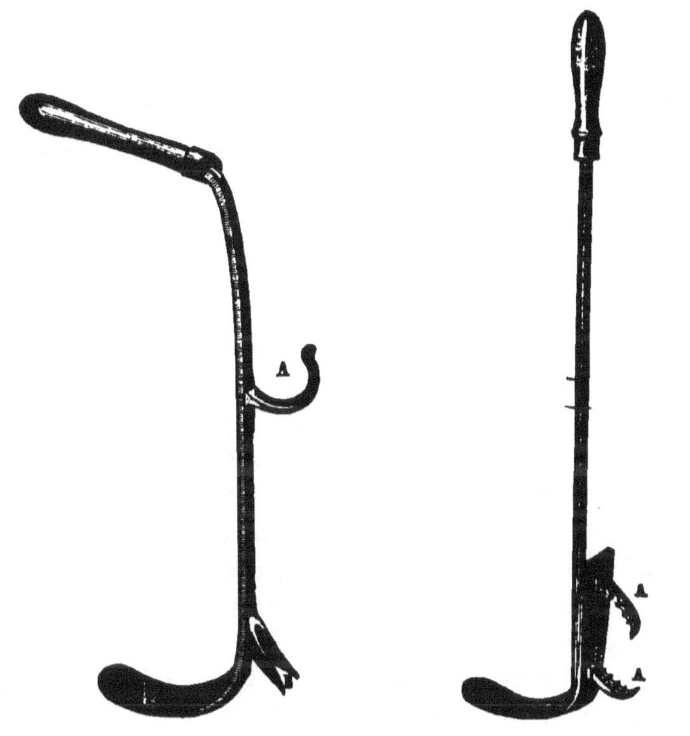

[FIG. 65.]—*Dugay's "Driver."*　　[FIG. 66.]—*Simon'*
　　　　　　　　　　　　　　　　　　"*Driver."*

right hand presses on the handle. In this manner he
bears down upon the stirrup with the weight of his
whole body, driving the stake to that point where the
claw is fixed. If the stake is not driven far enough, he
grasps it anew, and repeats the operation.

14

M. Simon, manufacturer of agricultural implements, at Savigny, near Beaune (Côte d'Or), has invented a stake-driver, which bears some analogy to the preceding. It consists of a vertical iron rod [Fig. 66], eighteen inches in length. This rod has, at its upper end, a wooden handle, five inches long, and at its base, two pieces of iron, A, having teeth like a saw, by means of which the stake is held fast. The lowest part is curved, forming a kind of stirrup about three inches long. The working of this instrument is the same as that of the preceding.

[Our vine-dressers would not like to depend upon setting their stakes by means of any such apparatus, nor would this kind of labor be at all attractive to them. They would greatly prefer the plan adopted by themselves, which consists in the use of a stout crow-bar thrust into the soft ground, as soon as it has settled from the frosts of winter. With this tool, they work holes for the stakes, which are duly pointed, and thrust into them as far as they will go; they are afterward driven home, with a wooden maul or beetle.

During some winters, the freezing and thawing of the surface causes the stakes to rise and become loose; in this case, it is necessary to drive them early in the spring. The workman generally carries a high stool, upon which to stand while using the maul to drive the stakes.]

In almost all regions where they are used, the stakes are removed from the ground every year before winter, and laid here and there in little heaps, kept up from the ground by cross-stakes, as shown in *Figure* 67. Elsewhere, in Champagne, for instance, these stakes are put up in stacks, as may be seen in *Figure* 68. This removal of the stakes is to prevent the buried ends from rotting during the winter. The pruning operations and winter dressings given to the ground are also more easily performed.

[FIG. 67.]—*Stakes Heaped Together after the Harvest.*

The expense consequent on the staking of the vines is undoubtedly the most considerable of all those involved in the cultivation of a vineyard.

[FIG. 68.]—*Stakes put up in Stacks.*

In Burgundy, and in the vicinity of Paris, the price of stakes, per thousand, is as follows:

White wood, per thousand $4 80
Wood prepared with sulphate of copper.. 6 20
Hard wood (oak).. 8 00

The mean duration of these stakes is as follows:

Stakes of white wood, 10 years, expense per year.........................$0 48
    "   sulphated wood, 15 years, expense per year..................... 0 40
    "   oak, 20 years, expense per year................................. 0 40

From this, it follows that whatever be the nature of the wood employed, the thousand stakes represent an annual expenditure of about $0.50. Now, in Burgundy, about 9,200 plants are set to the acre, and each plant must be provided with a stake.

We thus have 9,200 stakes to the acre, giving rise to an annual expenditure of..$3 68
To which add, for planting, taking up, and sharpening the stakes, for the same extent of surface... 1 92
Plus interest, at 5 per cent. on the cost of stakes, for the whole time of their duration, $42.75, which, divided by 15 years, their mean duration, gives, per year.. 2 85

    Total... $8 45

Therefore, staking the vines in Burgundy, costs $8.45, yearly, per acre.

In Champagne, this operation gives rise to the following expenditure:

The stakes, per thousand, cost:

In white wood, per thousand.. $8 00
In oak,   " 12 00

The mean duration of these stakes, is:

White wood, 10 years, cost per year.. $0 80
Oak, 15 years, cost per year... 0 80

In Champagne, as we have already stated, about

24,000 vines are planted to the acre, each provided with a stake.

These 24,000 vines give rise to an annual expenditure of............. $19 20
Planting, taking up, and sharpening the stakes......................... 2 80
Interest, at 5 per cent on the first cost of the stakes, while they
    last, $139.92—gives, per year.................................... 11 66
$33 66

The staking of vines in Champagne, therefore, costs about $33.66 per acre, yearly.

Finally, in the vineyards of the Bordelais districts, and of the hilly tract situated on the right bank of the Garonne, from Bordeaux to Blaye, the staking is not less expensive. The following is the average cost of the stakes, per thousand :

Pine, 7 feet 6 inches in length, barked.................................... $20 00
Pine, 7 feet 6 inches in length, not barked............................ 12 00
Chestnut, 7 feet 6 inches in length.. 30 00
Pine, 6 feet 6 inches in length, barked.................................... 16 00
Pine, 6 feet 6 inches in length, not barked............................ 10 00
Chestnut, 6 feet 6 inches in length.. 24 00

The average duration of these stakes is :

Pine, barked, 10 years, yearly cost.. $2 00
Pine, unbarked, 5 years, yearly cost...................................... 2 40
Chestnut, 15 years, yearly cost.. 2 00

In the region under notice, about 1,800 vines are planted to the acre, and each is provided with three stakes, on an average.

These 5,400 stakes give rise to a yearly expenditure of............... $10 80
The stakes remain in the ground until their ends are rotten ; we
    must, nevertheless, take into account the cost of replacing and
    sharpening the damaged stakes, which, put down at........... 65
Interest at 5 per cent. on the cost price of the stakes, while they
    last, $54—yearly cost for ten years.................................... 5 40
$16 85

Thus, the staking in this part of Bordelais costs about $16.80 per acre, yearly.

Vines Supported by Horizontal Laths.—In Médoc, as also in the Departments of the Doubs and Upper Saône, the vines are trellised on long laths, supported by stakes. In Médoc, the laths, which are about six feet six inches in length, are fixed sixteen inches above the ground, and maintained by stakes about twenty-four inches in length, and placed at intervals of five feet. [Fig. 33.] These laths are made of young pines, obtained from the clearing of waste lands generally covered with young saplings. As for the stakes, they are of locust, also cultivated in thick-set groves, in flinty soils, for the use of vine-dressers; they are also made of barked pine.

The annual expenditure arising from this mode of training the vine, may be stated thus:

One thousand stakes of barked pine	$2 00
One thousand laths of pine wood	3 00

The average duration of the stakes and laths, is:

The stakes, three years, per year	$0 66
The laths, two years, per year	1 50
7,200 stakes are required to the acre, costing, yearly,	4 75
And 1,800 laths, costing, yearly,	2 70
	7 45
These stakes and laths thus cost, per acre, yearly	$7 45
Replacing, sharpening, and binding the damaged stakes and laths	1 60
Interest, at 5 per cent. on the cost price of these stakes, per year, is	1 00
Total	$10 05

This mode of support, then, costs about ten dollars per acre, yearly. The different modes of staking we have just considered, have some serious drawbacks.

The amount of manual labor, already so inadequate to this branch of cultivation, is considerably increased by the staking and unstaking of the vines. The staking is a fatiguing operation for the laborers. Moreover, the laborers trample down the ground round each plant, and neutralize the effects of the first dressing. The stocks, or the principal roots of the plants, are often mangled by the stake driven at the foot of each; the hole made by the stake leaves, on its removal in the fall, an easy access to the winter frosts, which may affect the roots; the rough and splintered surface of the stakes, moreover, gives shelter to the eggs of certain insects injurious to the vine, and especially to those of its most dreaded foe, the *Pyralis*. These eggs are hatched in the spring, and passing from the stakes on to the buds, the larvæ there occasion incalculable mischief. Furthermore, the shoots are massed against these stakes, close around the bunches of grapes, and deprive them of the sun's action, which exerts so great an influence on the quality of the produce. The shoots, themselves, thus buried in the leaves, ripen their wood badly, and the produce suffers in quantity. Finally, staking gives rise to a yearly expenditure, amounting, on an average, to $14.50 per acre.

[The estimates of M. Du Breuil, appear too low, on the one hand, and too high, on the other. The price of his stakes appears high to us, and he assigns a greater durability to them than we should think such kinds of wood were entitled to. However, we have not tried the removal of these supports, every fall, for the sake of sheltering them from the exposure in winter. That may make a difference.

Our stakes are of locust, cedar, or oak, and cost, respectively :

Locust, 7 feet, per thosuand... $30 00
Cedar, 7 feet, per thousand... 50 00
Oak, 7 feet, per thousand... 20 00

DRESSING AND POINTING.

Locust and oak, per thousand $2 00
Cedar, per thousand 1 50

Our method of training, when stakes are used, is usually the bow and spur system—fruiting on the one, and producing new canes from the other. And we generally use but one stake to each vine. Some, however, have one stake for the fruit, and another for the canes.

A modification is suggested by the writer of " My Vineyard at Lakeview," which consists in having an additional rod, inclined from the base of one stake to the top of the next, where it is secured by a nail, or by an osier. This enables the vine-dresser to avoid crowding the vine on one stake, and obviates the use of the bow; but the author proposes to train the fruit-bearing branch to the upright stake, and to grow the young cane along the inclined one. In this, he is exactly wrong, for the inclination would favor the more even bearing of the branch, while the upright stake would be more suitable for the growth of the renewal cane from the spur.

Mr. John D. Clarke, Horticultural Manager of the Reform School, near Lancaster, Ohio, trained his vines to vertical stakes; but to equalize the flow of sap, and distribute the fruit evenly, instead of making the bow, he twisted the vine around the stake, in a coil, or spiral, and secured it firmly. He reports the plan very successful in its results.]

Training on Wire.—These serious drawbacks have long been recognized, and it has been sought to substitute other supports for those we have just spoken of.

M. de Macheco, land-owner at Brionde (Upper Loire), was one of the first to substitute wires. His method consists in setting on the rows of plants a line of permanent stakes, six feet high, and ten or twelve feet apart. These stakes have a wire of moderate thickness fastened at the top. A small stake driven in at the foot of each plant supports the shoots until, reaching the wire, they are there fastened, and trained in a horizontal direction. This system presents few advantages over the ordinary mode of training. It requires the use of stakes, and the shoots are attached to it in too confused a manner.

Later, in 1845, M. André Michaux, correspondent of the Institute, proposed a somewhat analagous system, which is as follows:

Posts made of hard wood, six feet in length, and from two to two and a quarter inches thick, are driven into the ground at the distance of sixteen feet from each other, along each row of plants. [Fig. 69.] The first and last are strengthened by means of braces, B.

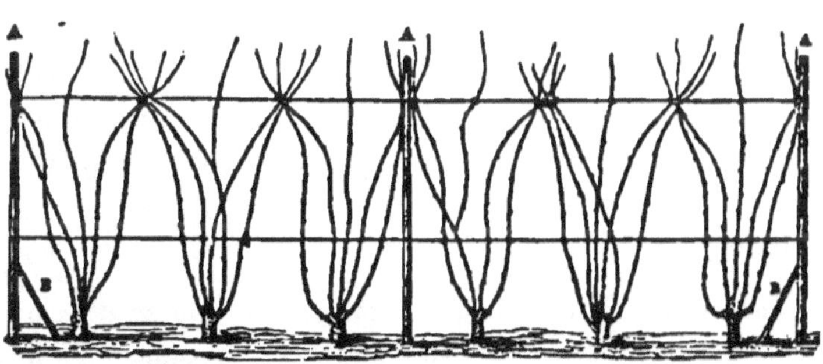

[Fig. 69.]—*Vines Supported by Michaux's System.*

Two wires are fixed to the stakes, by means of little hooks driven into their side. These wires are removed

15

at the end of the fall, every year, by rolling them on a sort of reel [Fig. 70], and they are replaced in the same manner, at the beginning of spring. When the time has arrived for fastening the shoots, they are, first of all, fixed on the lower wire, after it has been properly stretched, and then to the upper one ; on this second wire, the shoots of each plant are divided into two portions : one of these is tied, by a single string, to one-half the shoots of the right-hand plant, the other is similarly tied to one-half the shoots of the left-hand plant. This system of support allows of a great reduction in the number of stakes, and the shoots are so disposed as to receive the full action of the sun. But there is no means of tightening the wires, and the consequent necessity of removing and replacing them, every year, is expensive.

[FIG. 70.]—*Reel, for Winding up the Wires.*

[The French Government had so high an appreciation of this improvement and contribution to the advancement of the interests of the vine, that a beautiful gold medal was awarded to him for the invention. F. Andrew Michaux was the great historian of American trees, the author of *Sylva Americana.* While engaged, for many years, among the primitive forests of the Ohio valley, he formed some warm attachments for his botanical associates in this city, and, before his death, he presented this medal to the Cincinnati Horticultural Society, by whom it is preserved, as a high testimonial of their esteem of the distinguished donor.]

M. Collignon d' Ancy, of Metz, seems, to us, to have completely solved this question. Here is a description of the plan he recommends :

1st. At each extremity of the row of plants, a strong wooden post is placed [A, Fig. 71], four feet eight inches in length, and two inches square ; this is inclined outwardly, at an angle of forty-five degrees. Two holes are bored through these supports—one at ten and a half inches, and another at twenty-six and a half inches above the ground.

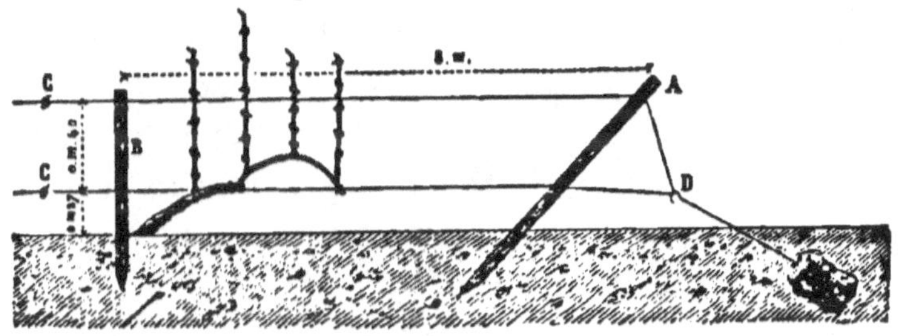

[FIG. 71.]—*System of Wire Supports.*

2d. At each extremity of the lines, and at thirty-two inches from the above mentioned supports, a hole is dug, twelve inches wide and sixteen inches in depth ; in this hole a block of stone is placed, about ten inches cube, surrounded by galvanized wire, doubled [E]. To this collar a galvanized connecting rod is fastened, one-half of the length of which should be under ground. The holes are then filled up, and the earth well beaten down.

3d. On each row, a series of stakes, B, are driven, perfectly in line with those at the extremities. These stakes, four feet six inches in length, and one and a half inches square, should rise twenty-eight inches above the ground. On one side of these posts two hooks are driven, the first, ten and one half inches above the ground, the second, sixteen inches above the first. To increase the duration of all these supports, it will be advisable to char and tar the part which is to be driven into the ground, or to saturate them with sulphate of copper.

4th. The end of a galvanized wire, No. 13, passes through one of the inclined supports, and is then fastened to the adjoining hook, D. This wire runs on to the other extremity of the line, hooking on the intermediate posts as it goes. Having been cut to the requisite length, a stretcher, C, is made to pass over it; it is then passed through the other inclined support, and fastened to the adjoining hook, and, finally, enclosed within the hooks, by hammering lightly on them. It is then stretched, by means of the stretcher, which is placed about the middle of it.

[FIG. 72.]—*Thiry's Stretcher.*

The second wire is placed in the same way, and so on for all the other rows of plants.

In order to stretch the wires, a great number of stretchers have been contrived. For vineyard purposes we recom-

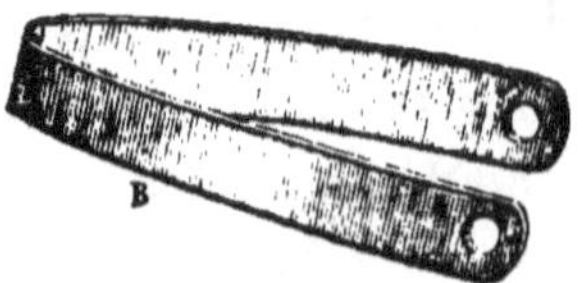

[FIG. 73.]—*Pincer.*

mend that recently invented by M. Thiry, and which is represented in *Figure* 72. It answers all the purposes required of it, and its price is extremely moderate—

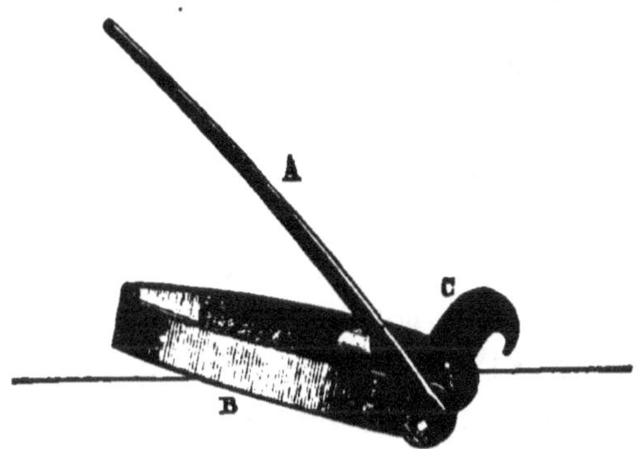

[FIG. 74.]—*Stretcher in Operation.*

two cents. This stretcher is used in the following manner: The wire being fixed at both extremities, and the stretcher made to slide about half way, the two square ends of the axle of the stretcher are introduced into the holes of the pincers, shown in *Figure* 73. This pincer, made of strong sheet-iron, and having hinges, costs only six cents.— *Figure* 74 shows the position of the pincers when fixed.

[FIG. 75.]—*Key.*

It is held firmly in this position with the left hand.— With the right hand the key [Fig. 75] is placed on the square end, A, of the axle of the stretcher, and a circular motion is given to the latter, until the wire is sufficiently stretched. The stop is made by means of one of the two hooked ends terminating the sides of the stretcher, C.

It will thus be seen that the system of M. Collignon may be adapted to vines of every locality. Some slight modifications applied to it would suffice for that purpose. Thus, for the vineyards nearest the North, the vicinity of Paris, Champagne, and the Moselle region, the wires may be arranged in the way indicated by M. Collignon. For the middle region, and the South, the first wire should be placed sixteen inches above the ground, and the second the same distance from the first [Fig. 34]. For vigorous vines, that are to be trained on four-arms [Fig. 32], three lines of wire should be employed, and there should be an equal distance of sixteen inches between them.

Let us now compare, as regards expense and results, this mode of training vines on wires, with that of staking. We have seen that the staking of the vineyards of Burgundy costs, yearly, $8.45 per acre. If we subject these vines to the mode of culture pointed out at page 100, and to the system of pruning shown in *Figures* 31 and 35, and then substitute the wire system for that of stakes, we shall have the following expenditure:

For a row of plants 325 feet in length,

A double line of galvanized wire, No. 13; 650 feet long, and weighing eleven pounds, at nine and one-tenth cents per pound... $1 00

Two end-posts, made of sulphated wood, at four cents each...... 0 08

Two stays, wire, and stone block, at six cents each.................... 0 12

Twelve intermediate stakes of sulphated wood, at two cents each, 0 24

Two stretchers, at two cents each... 0 04

Hooks... 0 02

Setting up... 0 06

In all.. $1 56

An area of one hectare (equal to two and five-elevenths acres), having a side of three hundred and twenty-five feet, and planted at the rate of 20,000 plants, laid out as shown at page 100, will admit of one hundred rows of plants. This number of rows multiplied by one hundred and fifty-six, gives a total expenditure of one hundred and fifty-six dollars per hectare, or sixty-two dollars and forty cents per acre, of which sixteen dollars will be for the stakes.

The duration of the wires may be reasonably laid down at forty years, or $46.40 divided by forty....................................	$1 16
The duration of the sulphated wood will be at least twenty-five years, or sixteen dollars divided by twenty-five.................	0 64
Interest, at five per cent, on the price of the stakes, while they last, will be twenty dollars, which, divided by twenty-five, gives, per year..	0 80
Interest, at five per cent., on the cost of the wires, while they last, equal to $92.80, which, divided by forty years, gives............	2 32
in all..	$4 92
The same surface, staked, costs................................	8 45
Difference..	$3 53

There is, therefore, by the use of wires, a yearly saving of three dollars and fifty-three cents.

It must be added that we have supposed the lines of wire to be three hundred and twenty-five feet in length (side of a hectare), but were these lines half as long again, the cost, as far as regards the stays, would be one half less, inasmuch as two only would be required, where four were needed in the former case.

We have seen that in the vineyards of Champagne, the annual cost of staking is about thirty-three dollars and sixty-six cents per acre. If the mode of culture and pruning shown at page 100, and *Figure* 35, be adopted, and if the wires be substituted for the stakes, these supports will give rise to the same annual expenditure as in Burgundy ; that is to say, to four dollars and ninety-two cents per acre. Now, this sum subtracted from thirty-three dollars and sixty-six cents, the cost of the staking system, shows the enormous saving of twenty-eight dollars and seventy-four cents per acre.

In the marshy districts, as well as the slopes of Borde-lais, the staking gives rise to a yearly expenditure of about $16.85 per acre.

If these vineyards be submitted to the mode of culture and pruning indicated at page 100, and *Figure* 32, and the wires be employed, the cost will amount to only $4 92

Add one-half that sum for the third line of wire required by these vines 2 46

In all.. 7 38

which gives a yearly saving of $9.47 per acre.

Lastly, the supports employed in Médoc, cost, yearly, $10.00 per acre. Substituting wires for the laths, and setting up a second line, as shown in *Figure* 34, the yearly expenditure would amount to only $4.92, which gives a yearly saving of $5.08 per acre.

To sum up : Wires, used instead of stakes, do away with the numerous drawbacks, already pointed out, as arising from the latter. Moreover, these wires allow us to realize a considerable saving—say, on an average, $12 per acre, annually. We, therefore, earnestly advise the adoption of this new method.

[The trellis, in different forms, has been considerably employed in this country. Some of the early vineyards were supplied by the German vine-dressers with a very cheap wooden trellis, consisting of poles tied, or nailed, to stakes—

these were quite low, and in some cases, the vines were allowed to cross from one row to another, so as to shade the ground completely; but generally the close pruning, adopted by the foreign vine-dressers, prevented such a result. Others were made higher, having three poles, or they were made of sawed lath, nailed to the posts; these last were more neat and more permanent. At length, the Americans introduced wire trellises for the vines, and in many parts of the country, nothing else is now used, in large vineyards. The wires are supported upon posts firmly set in the ground; these are generally placed twenty to twenty-five feet apart. The end-posts must be very firmly braced, by slanting timbers set into the ground. Sometimes, when a wagon-road is made across the rows, for convenience at the vintage, the posts on either side are made very high, and are not only braced, but are also coupled together overhead, by strong wires. When the posts are set at wide intervals, the wires may be supported between them by stakes driven into the ground at suitable distances. The size of the posts will depend upon the cost of material and its character for strength and durability; if squared, they should not be less than three by three inches. Locust posts, if from four to six inches in diameter, will last a long while.

To Mr. O. D. Ford, of East Cleveland, Ohio, I am indebted for the following estimates and data:

Number of vines per acre, at

8 by 10	544
8 by 8	729
6 by 6	1,210

Number of posts, per acre, at twenty feet apart:

10 by 8—231, costing	$23 10
8 by 8—297, costing	29 70
6 by 6—385, costing	38 50

No. 9 wire, running from nineteen to twenty feet per pound, will require, at:

10 by 8—per acre, 693 pounds, costing... $45 04
8 by 8—per acre, 911 pounds, costing.. 59 21
6 by 6—per acre, 1,151 pounds, costing... 74 81

The number of stakes, per acre, will be double the number of vines, and, at $33.00 per thousand, the expense, per acre, will be:

At 10 by 8, requires 1,088, costing.. $38 28
At 8 by 8, requires 1,458, costing... 50 13
At 6 by 6, requires 2,420, costing... 84 70

On the common plan of using but one stake, the cost of material will be diminished by one half.

There are different methods of fastening the wires to the posts. Some bore holes through which it is passed, but this is not recommended; others notch the supports with a wide-set saw, and lay the wires in the cleft, fastening them with small nails. Small staples are used by some, or a wrought-nail is driven in below the wire, and then the nail is bent upward and clinched. Mr. Morse, of Cleveland, drives cut-nails into the posts, and, as he applies the wire, he takes a turn on the nails at every post.

Mr. T. S. Hubbard, of Fredonia, New York, has his trellises fifteen rods long. His posts average three by three inches, and are seven feet long; they are set twenty-four feet apart. The end-posts are heavier, four by six, and well braced. He uses three wires, placing the first at from fourteen to eighteen inches above the ground; the second and third, eighteen inches, so that the top of the trellis shall be about four and a half feet high. He uses No. 11 wire, which costs eleven cents a pound, and the expense, when the rows are eight feet wide, is $50.00 per acre.

Dr. Spaulding, of St. Louis, Missouri, uses three wires of No. 9, and makes the trellis five feet high.

My friend, M. H. Lewis, of Sandusky, Ohio, where the wire trellises are used almost exclusively, has, very kindly, examined into this subject, and sends me the following estimates, which may be considered reliable:

"The rows are eight feet wide, and the posts twenty-four feet apart in the rows. The vines are generally set eight by eight feet. At these distances, two hundred and forty-five posts are required per acre. The estimates for wire are the net amount, and allowance must be made for slack, for joinings, and for attachment to the end-posts.

No. 9, runs $16\frac{1}{4}$ feet to the pound—982 pounds per acre, at $9\frac{1}{4}$c ... $93 27
No. 10, runs 20 feet to the pound—792 pounds per acre, at $10\frac{1}{2}$c.. 83 63
No. 11, runs 25 feet to the pound—634 pounds per acre, at $10\frac{1}{2}$c.. 66 57
No. 12, runs $33\frac{1}{3}$ feet to the pound—480 pounds per acre, at 11c.. 52 80

Telegraph wires, Nos. 9 and 10, may be had at 7 to $7\frac{1}{2}$ cents, and answer very well."

Heretofore, we have considered only the horizontal trellis, to which it has been objected that that the wires will sway with the wind; and, when stretched or broken, by a storm, or with the weight of fruit and foliage of the laden vine, the result is disastrous to the crop. Mr. Fuller gives a plan for a vertical wire trellis that will not be subject to such accidents. [See *Grape Culturist.*]

KNOX'S VERTICAL WOODEN TRELLIS.—A vertical wooden trellis has been used by Mr. J. Knox, of Pittsburg, Pennsylvania, with which he is very well satisfied, though I think it has some objections, as well as many advantages. His vines being planted six feet apart in the rows, a post is set every twelve feet. These stand six feet high; they are connected by strong boards, four inches wide, which are firmly nailed near the top of the posts, and at about one foot from the ground. Upon these rails, vertical strips are fastened every nine inches; they are made of inch-plank, sawed about an inch wide, and eight feet long; this makes the trellis nine feet high, which I consider too much, as it requires the use of a ladder for training, tieing, and trimming. A modification is now introduced, by using lath, similar to those prepared for the plasterers, except that they are made six feet long. This makes the trellis lighter, cheaper, and of a more convenient hight—seven feet. There is economy, also, in the smaller nails, as four-pennies may be substituted for six-pennies. The lumber for the lath should be well selected. An economical arrangement is also employed in making the posts, by using common hemlock scantling, three by four inches, spiked on to a short piece of locust or cedar, that is set in the ground.

The expense of this kind of trellis is estimated at $300 per acre, which appears sufficiently high; much will depend upon the relative cost of materials in different parts of the country.]

IX.

OPERATIONS OTHER THAN PRUNING.

Laying Down the Plants.—In the vineyards of Champagne, the vines, being irregularly planted, are so close that they mutually starve one another, and it becomes necessary, in order to maintain their fruitfulness, to submit them to the operation which, in that region, is called laying down. Every year, at the time of the winter plowing, each of the plants is laid bare on one side, and is then laid down into this small trench, so as to bury it to the depth of three or four inches, in order that the two finest shoots nearest to the base, A [Fig. 39], may be buried about two inches from where they spring. At the time of pruning, only these two shoots are preserved. The others are cut at B, while on the two shoots, A, only two eyes are reserved above ground. In this way the plant, in the following year, will be again composed of four or five shoots [Fig. 39]. The process of laying down is then renewed, and the pruning takes place on two shoots only. This operation is repeated yearly. If, as often happens, the ground be sloping, the laying down is managed so that the plants shall take the direction of the top of the slope. At the end of thirty years, through this annual laying down, each plant may have an underground layer,C, more than ten feet in length. All the plants being thus directed toward the summit of the ground, there must be confusion toward that point, while the base becomes bare, for which reason it is advisable, occasionally to replant at the base and thin out toward the top.

We have already shown the drawbacks arising from this confused planting, and from the too close proximity of the plants to one another. We have also drawn attention to the injurious effect arising from the absence of a parent stock, on the quality of the wine, and we have recommended the substitution of an oblique form, with a single arm, as in *Figure* 35. With this sort of form, the laying down of the stock is no longer required.

FASTENING OF THE PLANT, AND BENDING OF THE FRUIT-STEMS.—Immediately after the pruning it will be well to fasten the plants firmly to the wires. We should next endeavor to give the corresponding arms the same degree of inclination; otherwise the lower one would soon become less vigorous than the other.

It is also at this period that the fruit-stems should be tied. For, by the system of pruning we have recommended, it is important that we should be able to obtain, every year, a vigorous shoot, at the base of that which has borne fruit the preceding summer [B, Fig. 61]. The best means of obtaining this result is to bend the branch [A, Fig. 60], and cause it to take the position of the dotted line B [Fig. 60]. It would even be advisable to make the end of the shoot dip beneath the wire, so as to make it exceed the degree of depression indicated in *Figure* 60. The consequence then is, that the sap being prevented from following its natural direction, acts strongly at the base of the arm, and there develops a vigorous shoot. It will therefore, be understood that this bending of the fructifying stem should begin before the starting of vegetation, otherwise a portion of the sap will already have spent its action in the top of the shoot, and there would be less vigor at the base.

[Bending the bows, in the common mode of vineyard training, with stakes, is a very important affair, and an operation of some delicacy, requiring great care in its performance.— The object of using the bow is set forth by the author, in the preceding paragraph, where he speaks of bending the shoots when fastening them to the wires of the trellis.

But there is danger of performing this work too early in the season; the canes should be left until the sap has begun to flow, and the buds have become excited; otherwise, the object of attempting to equalize will be rendered nugatory, and the buds at the end will scarcely develop shoots, while those at the top of the arch may become, as they are always apt to do, the most vigorous, and even act as formidable rivals of those we desire to produce for next year's wood, from the spur. I prefer to wait until the buds are almost ready to burst, before bending the bows; but, in a large vineyard, it is difficult to accomplish the work in time, for the buds push very rapidly, and they are easily broken out, in handling the canes; therefore, it has been recommended to make the bows as rapidly as possible, securing the end to the stock, but not waiting to attach them to the stakes until they are all bent, when it is an easy matter to secure them in ·position without breaking off the young shoots.

In bending the bows, it will be found that the canes, which had been rather brittle and easily broken during the winter, become quite pliant, and somewhat tough, as they are filled with sap. Still, some care is requisite in bending them into the circular shape of the bows. Both hands are used: with one, sieze the cane near its extremity, and slightly twist it before bending, and, while supporting and aiding the flexure with the other hand, let the first be brought around gradually, until the end of the shoot comes to the stock, when it is secured to it by a willow tie.

The mode of using the osier, in this operation, is peculiar, and, though exceedingly simple, it is not easy to describe; suffice it to say, that the bending, or tieing if you please— though it is no tie—is done with the thicker end of the willow, and not with the smaller and more pliant portion, as a novice would expect. The security of this fastening depends upon the spring of the willow, which keeps the loop always upon the stretch. Vines that are well secured in the spring seldom fall away from the stake, even when laden with fruit, and exposed to storms. In the winter-trimming, we find the majority of these ties so little decayed or loosened, that it is necessary to cut them, as the first operation before touching the grape-vine with the knife or shears.

When we come to secure the bows to the stake, stouter willows are needed; the end is passed around the bow, and one or two turns are taken, twisting the thicker end about the smaller, before engaging the stake; this is to prevent its rubbing against the support. The vine is thus secured firmly enough to sustain its weight of foliage and fruit, throughout the summer. At the same time care is taken to have the plane of the bows correspond to the direction of the rows of stakes, otherwise they will project into the spaces, and offer obstructions to the movements of the horse in cultivating, and may be seriously injured by being caught in the single-tree.

In tieing the vines to the trellis, whether of wire or of wood, the same precaution will be necessary, to twist the willow upon itself, before fastening the vine to its place.]

The best ties that can be used to fasten the plants against the supports, are willow slips, for which reason it will be advisable to reserve, in the neighborhood of the vineyard, an area of land sufficient for the cultivation of the requisite quantity of willow. The soil for that purpose should be rich, fertile and rather cool. The willows may be planted quincunx fashion, at the distance of three feet apart. This land must be dressed twice a year—a plowing in winter, after the cutting of the willows, and a second plowing in summer.

[The willow chiefly applied to this purpose is that known as the golden or yellow, which our botanists tell us is but a variety of the *Salix Alba*, that has attracted so much attention, within a few years, in the west, as the White Willow. This is the tree which, in some parts of the country, has long been grown for making gun-powder charcoal.

The yellow willow may be planted along a ditch-bank, though water is not necessary for it. To produce good ties, the trees should be headed back to low pollards. They are cut every year, and the small laterals are taken off, tied up, and kept in a damp cellar until needed.

Another willow, which has been found very serviceable is the true osier, *Salix Viminalis*, the purple osier, cultivated for the basket-makers. These are cut in any mild weather during the winter. When the workmen are making the sheaves, the smaller twigs are allowed to fall out of the bundles, and these may then be gathered and stored in a damp cellar or cave, until wanted for tieing the grapes.

In this operation, the wand is first cast about the wire or stake, the larger end twisted around the smaller two or three times, or the two ends may be twisted together; the vine is then brought to its place, and the same thing is repeated.— There is no real tie made, but after the thick end has been thus twisted around the smaller, it is dextrously inclined toward the vine, which prevents it from untwisting itself. The whole operation is very rapidly performed by an expert, and it remains secure for a long time.]

RUBBING OUT AND PINCHING.—This operation consists in the removal of all the buds that are not required for the bearing of the present and the following year ; and it is also done for the preservation of the shape of the plant. It will be seen that the nipping of these buds will have the effect of giving to the bunches and the shoots retained, the benefit of all the sap which would otherwise have nourished, to no purpose, those which have been removed. We thus obtain a more abundant harvest, and finer shoots, for the following year. Hence it follows that there would be an advantage in nipping the buds as soon as possible, while they are but two or three inches in length. But this mode of operation would have a serious drawback : we should be liable to remove the grape-producing shoots, and to retain those which would yield none. This operation, therefore, should only take place when the young grapes have begun to be visible—that is to say, when the shoots have obtained a length of six to eight inches.

16

At the period we have named, the sap may change its direction, and concentrate its action on the shoots that have been retained, without any effort, or disturbance to the economy of the vine. The shoots assume a bolder development, and perform the functions of those which have been removed. But if the nipping is effected later, when, for instance, the shoots have attained the length of twenty-four to twenty-eight inches, the general vigor of the plant suffers, and although the shoots that have been preserved seem to increase, still a great quantity of sap has been uselessly absorbed, because the suppressed buds have been taken away before they have entirely developed the organs essential to the life of the plant—the new roots and the new alburnum.— Moreover, the abrupt change which takes place in the natural direction of the sap, at the very moment when its circulation was most brisk, causes a stoppage of veg- etation, which proves hurtful to all the tissues in course of formation. It is a long time before the sap directs itself toward the shoots which have been preserved, and they then grow less vigorously than if the nipping had been performed earlier.

Buds to be Suppressed.—The disbudding ought to be done from the early stage of the plant's growth; when they are first pruned, only the finest shoots on each should be allowed to remain. At the time of the sec- ond pruning [Fig. 47], there should be left on the re- served shoot, A, only two or three of the finest buds, according to the form to be given to the plant.

Later, when the frame is formed, no buds ought to be retained on the old wood, unless it be intended, as at A [Fig. 76], to furnish, by and by, the means of shortening the arms of the plant, when they shall have attained too great a length ; in which case the shoot resulting therefrom is every year pruned to one eye, until the time when the arm of the plant is cut immediately above this reserve. It is especially on the fruitstems that the nipping should be practiced. As we have above explained, these branches are allowed, every year, to grow to a length of about twelve inches ; they are then bent and fastened to the wire. When the shoots have reached a length of about eight inches, they appear as in *Figure* 76. The shoot B ought to be reserved, in all cases, in order to furnish a new fruit-stem

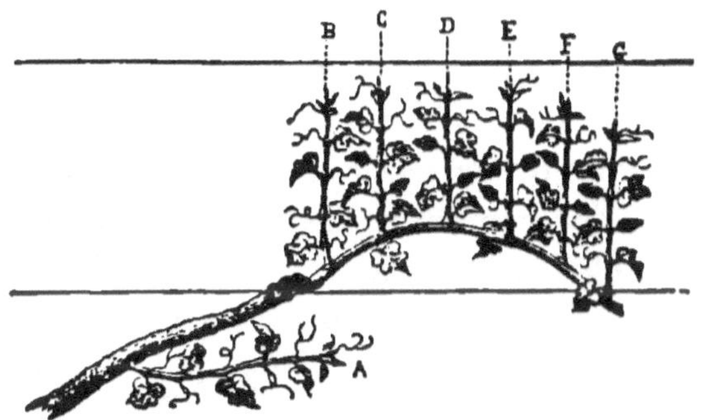

[FIG. 76.]—*Nipping the Buds.*

for the following year. We must then ascertain which of the remaining ones have the finest bunches, and preserve a number proportioned to the vigor of the plant. If there are not a sufficient number left we shall lose in the quantity of the yield ; if we leave too many, the berries will be smaller ; there will not be a perceptible increase in the quantity, while the wine will be inferior, and the plant exhausted. In this respect the following rule should be observed : for plants having little vigor— the " Pinots " of Burgundy, for instance—a single fruit-stem, C, should be left; the shoot D may be added if the plant is a little more vigorous. For plants of moderate vigor, three fruit-stems may be reserved, as C, D, E. Lastly, if the plants are very vigorous, three or four shoots may be kept, C, D, E, and F. If there are six shoots, as shown in *Figure* 76, the shoot D is always suppressed. If, as too often happens, one of the fruit-stems should yield shoots without grapes, while the opposite shoot has them, it would be proper to leave a number of shoots on the first equal to that which may be left on the second; otherwise, the barren arm, on which only the shoot B (for next year) has been left, would immediately become weaker than the other.

When, unfortunately, all the fruit-stems of a plant are devoid of grapes, it will still be well to preserve some shoots, besides the reserved ones, B; for if the disbudding be carried too far, it has the effect of weakening the plant, by depriving it of the organs necessary for the production of new tissues and roots.

NIPPING THE BUNCHES.—In some vineyards, and more especially in the Jura, where most of the plants produce very long bunches, the nipping of these is usual; that is to say, at the time we have mentioned as that for nipping the shoots, the points of the young bunches are nipped with the nail. This suppression always has the effect of making the berries become one-third larger, and ripen a fortnight earlier.

FASTENING THE SHOOTS.—This operation consists in fastening the shoots to the wires, when they have reached a certain size. This is a very important operation; its object is to have the bunches and shoots well exposed to the sun; to keep the bunches from touching the ground—the dampness of which would cause them to rot; to prevent the young shoots from being torn from the plants by high winds; and, finally, to allow of the summer cultivation of the soil.

The fastening should be done so soon as the shoots have exceeded by about six inches, the point at which they are to be fastened. They are then about twenty inches long. The operation must be executed so as to place the shoots side by side, in a vertical position, and so as not to confine the leaves in the fastening.

The ties most usually employed to fasten the shoots are wisps of rye-straw, cut twelve inches long, and softened in water; rushes, cut green, and dried in the shade; willow-bark softened in water, etc.

Of whatever kind the tie may be, it must make a complete turn around the wire before the shoot is fastened; otherwise the shoot might be cut by the tie.

PINCHING THE SHOOTS.—This operation consists in nipping the ends of the buds, when they have exceeded, by about twelve inches, the point at which they are fastened. This nipping is applied to the fruit-stems C, D, E, F, only. The shoots A, B, intended for the next year's pruning, must be excepted.

The object of nipping the buds is, to diminish the chances of the grapes blighting, and to favor their development. For the bunches, like the leaves, have the power to draw the sap from the roots. If the leaves are numerous on the shoot, their power of absorption exceeds that of the bunches, and they are apt to fail.— If the number of leaves is diminished by pinching, the power of absorption of the bunches is no longer interfered with, and they are more fully developed. Besides, by diminishing the vigor of the fruit-stems, we favor the growth of the shoots A, B, destined to form the plant the following year.

CLIPPING THE SHOOTS.—The shoots A, B [Fig. 76], which have not been pinched, grow all the more vigorously, from the fact that they derive a greater quantity of sap by the shortening of the fruit-stems. They might be left to grow indefinitely, at the risk of overrunning the ground, and interfering with the summer

culture to be given to it. It is, therefore, proper to clip them, when they have reached a length of about five feet, and to make this suppression sixteen inches above the wire highest from the shoot B. If we operate on very vigorous plants we may allow the shoot B to reach a length of five feet, and then lay it horizontally on the top wire.

The nipping applied to the fruit-stems, has almost always the effect of developing false shoots at the angle of the upper leaves [A, Fig. 77].—

[FIG. 77.] These false shoots acquire great vigor, and create confusion. It will be advisable to pinch them above the second leaf.

[This subject of summer pruning appears to be awakening a good deal of discussion among American Grape-Growers. The following Report appears in the May number of the *American Journal of Horticulture,* an excellent periodical, in which the cultivators of the vine will find much valuable information in the course of the year, upon this as well as upon many other branches of Horticulture and rural affairs:

"SUMMER PRUNING OF THE GRAPE.—At the winter meeting of the Lake-shore Grape-Growers' Association, at Cleveland, O., there were present some of the most intelligent men of the country, who are engaged in this interesting branch of cultivation. The discussions were directed to the practical questions which are constantly arising in a new line of business; and were of value to those present, as will appear in the report of the society, soon to be published.

"Among the topics discussed, one of the most important was that of *summer pruning*. Many of the members were loud in their denunciations of the practice, as it is often pursued in the vineyards, particularly where they are managed by European vine-dressers. Some went so far as to say that they preferred to let their vines go without any pruning at all, rather than to have them subjected to such a terrible "summer slaughtering" as was occasionally to be seen. They pleaded for the leaves, claiming that they were necessary to elaborate the sap, to perfect the crop of fruit, and to ripen the wood and the roots for the future healthiness of the plant.

"After a full expression of similar views by these tenderhearted vine-dressers, who adopted the motto " *Laissez faire*," in regard to summer treatment, a member, who has long had extensive opportunities for practice and observation, in the vineyard, stated that he should advise a middle course, consisting of judicious and systematic, but perhaps some would think *severe summer pruning*, as the best method of directing the sap into the proper channels, and of increasing the production of large leaves, good fruit, and healthy, vigorous shoots, where they were needed for the renewal of the vine. These results he preferred to the extremes that had been alluded to—the sacrificing of the growth and foliage, on the one hand, such as has been styled "summer slaughtering;" or, on the other extreme, allowing an indiscriminate and profuse production of shoots and leaves, that must interfere with the perfect development of the vine, and the proper ripening of the fruit.

" He claimed that by a proper performance of the different operations which make up the summer pruning of the vine, in our attempts to furnish a renewal of wood, suitable to produce the next crop, these several objects should be kept clearly in view :

"1st. That we should prune in such a way as to avoid that very common evil, the over-production of fruit.

"2d. That we should prune so as to provide for the largest development of the foliage, and for a renewal of the leaves upon the fruit-bearing branches.

"3d. That we should so direct the growth of the vine as to insure the production of vigorous, healthy canes, to bear the next year's crop.

"And, lastly. That we might, under certain circumstances, find it necessary to prune, or to *train*, in such a way as to check the growth by extension, and endeavor to develop the buds on the lower part of the canes that are to be appropriated to the production of the next crop. These topics were considered *seriatim*.

" The first operation of summer pruning is therefore a process for thinning the fruit, as well as for diminishing the number of shoots; but it does not follow that there will be any less wood produced ; on the contrary, it will be found, at the end of the season, that there is more available and useful wood, upon a vine that has had this important operation well carried out, than upon one which had been so neglected that all its shoots had been allowed to remain, and contend with one another to their mutual injury.

" This first process consists in what is called *rubbing out*. It should be performed early in the season of growth—*very early* —so soon as the young shoots have made their appearance, and have developed themselves sufficiently to show their little bunches of embryo fruit; this will be when the largest have grown five or six inches long. It is evident, that if delayed longer, there must be a greater loss to the vine.

" The vine-dresser removes the weaker shoots by rubbing them off with his thumb. When there are twins he should take away the weaker. Where the joints of the old wood are short, if the buds all break, the branches will be too close; in this case alternate shoots must be removed; or, even more than this, so as to leave the first branches not nearer than six inches—in many vines ten inches would be still better. If this work be well done, the after-labors of summer pruning will be very much lightened.

"This process of rubbing out is very useful for correcting the evils of insufficient winter pruning, as the surplus buds may be removed, and the amount of growth reduced to what the plant is capable of sustaining to advantage. A vine which may have been wholly neglected in the winter can still be thoroughly pruned, for all the practical purposes of pruning, by thus removing the surplus shoots—rubbing them out as they appear.

" Some vine-dressers depend upon this plan of reducing their crop, instead of severe winter pruning, which is the more direct method usually adopted. Sometimes, indeed, it may be advisable to trim the canes long, when there is apprehension that a portion of the buds have been winter-killed. Now if they still break regularly, the excess can thus be reduced to the proper standard. In some vineyards the whole summer pruning is done at once, by the systematic and severe removal of a large portion of the shoots, by rubbing them out, so as to thin the crop, which is afterward left to take care of itself.

" Certain insects are busily at work at the time of this rubbing out, doing a similar work by eating a portion of the buds; but we can not depend upon their judgment in the matter, and should kill the beautiful *Haltica chalybea* while we are disbudding our vines.

" The second division of the subject, or pruning to effect the greatest development of the foliage, and to produce new leaves during the season upon the fruit-bearing branches, is accomplished by systematic, judicious, and early pinching-in of the ends of the shoots. This operation should be done as soon as it is seen which are the best and strongest, and before the blossoming of the vine—so soon, indeed, as the bunches can be seen. It is often practiced at the same time as the rubbing out—at least on the strongest shoots. This pinching is a very simple matter. It is done with the thumbnail and the fore-finger; the point only should be removed —sometimes one leaf, sometimes two, or even three, are left beyond the outer cluster of grape-buds; but to produce the best effect, the former point is advised.

" It has been observed that an early and close pinching is always followed by a remarkable development of the thrift and size of the foliage; the leaves attain double the size of those on an unpinched shoot, and the aggregate of the evaporating surface presented by them will be greater than that of all the leaves that would have been produced by the shoot if left alone. But this is not all. At the base or axil of each of these enlarged leaves, the new buds will become very prominent, and will soon burst, and produce laterals. These are again pinched, at one or two leaves, and with the same effect, that of enlarging the foliage. We thus have a new crop of these valuable evaporating organs, or lungs, as they have been fancifully called, and at a season when it may be very desirable to the health of the plant that a supply of fresh foliage should be on hand, for the older leaves are often injured by storms, by insects, or by accident, and their renewal in this manner will be very opportune.

" This treatment is very different from the practice of many of the European vine-dressers, who attempt to manage the free American vine by subjecting it to extremely harsh measures. They break off the ends of the shoots at the last bunch, after they have made a considerable growth, and thus sacrifice a portion of the energy of the vine. They often defer this trimming until after the blossoming season, because of a prejudice that prevents any work being done among the vines during that delightfully fragrant period, when it is a joy to be in the vineyard almost equal to that experienced at the time of the vintage. Not satisfied with this sacrifice of growth, these tardy, but now energetic pruners tear out all the laterals that may appear, and thus, when provident arrangements have been made for renewing the foliage, they deprive the vine and its fruit of these valuable resources, and it is no wonder that, with all their efforts to expose their fruit to the burning rays of the sun, they often miserably fail in the desired result of well ripened fruit.

" This pinching can not all be done at once. As already observed, its best effects can only be obtained by commencing very early, when only a portion of the shoots will be sufficiently developed: these should be pinched. The backward shoots will rapidly advance, and in a few days these must be subjected to the same treatment; and very soon the laterals on the first will require pinching. In the course of the summer, other laterals will form, which will need shortening for the same purpose of developing the foliage ; but, toward the close of the season, they may be let alone.

" Thus it will be seen that the vine-pincher has no sinecure office, but that his attentions will be pretty constantly required during the season of growth.

" Third—Trimming to direct the growth of the canes. *Pinching* off the ends of some of the shoots is a very important part of summer pruning; but it is one which has been very much abused in practice, and still more so in the criticisms of those who theoretically condemn the practice. Before proceeding any farther, it is well for us to consider, that, in all pruning of vines, we must remember the necessity of keeping the plant in due shape as to its wood, and that we desire to have this properly distributed. We want the new growth, which goes to form the canes for the next year's fruitage, formed low down on the stock, and not at the ends, or higher parts of the vine, which would soon give us high, naked stocks, and bare, empty trellises, such as may everywhere be seen—striking witnesses of the ignorance of Nature's laws, as illustrated in the treatment of the vine.

" No intelligent cultivator need be told, that when a vine is tied up to a stake, or trained vertically upon a trellis, the terminal, or upper buds will break the most vigorously ; and if let alone, and allowed to grow upward, they will maintain their ascendancy throughout the season. This is often at the expense of those starting from a lower point, which were expected and desired to be the stronger, so as to produce the wood for the annual renewal of the vine. The same thing is true of vines trained upon the bow system, especially if the bending has been done too early in the season ; the object of the bow being to distribute the nourishment equally to the different parts of the vine. The bending should not be done till the sap has started toward the upper buds, and they have received an impulse. If they are then brought down to a lower position, they are subordinated ; and other buds at the upper bend become the highest, and thus produce the stronger shoots. In the mean time, those springing from the spur, for renewal-canes, can get the desired start ; and the pinching now to be described is intended to favor their growth. In trellis training, for the same reason, the canes should be allowed to hang loose, until after the starting of the sap, so that advantage may be taken of the condition of the leading buds, and we can subordinate those that are likely to receive too much nourishment.

"Do what we may, however, whether our vines be trained in one method or another, and despite all our forethought and care and management, the higher shoots will often become leaders, at the expense of those we are endeavoring to produce from the spur, upon the principle of renewing by canes from below, and thus keeping the vine in good shape. Here, then, the pinching becomes an agency of the greatest value to the vine-pruner; for, by the removal of the tips of these strong shoots, he may succeed in so directing the flow of sap as to develop the growth of those he desires to produce for the future crop, and which are suitably placed upon the vine.

"It may be objected, and we are all tired of hearing the objection, that we are contending against the natural efforts of the plant, which was only following its own instincts; and that, therefore, our attempts thus to thwart Nature were unwise and unphilosophical, and consequently wrong. But we may answer all such objections by telling them that we are treating the civilized vine in a civilized manner, and for the purposes of civilized man. The conditions of the problem are changed. One thing, however, remains the same in the wild and in the cultivated vine: in both cases, the fruit-branches spring from healthy and well matured shoots of last year's growth. In the native forest, the vines clamber over shrubs, and even upon the highest trees, where they can have free exposure to the air and light, and where God's creatures, called the inferior animals—for whom, in the bounty of His providence, they were produced—can enjoy the fruits of the vine, so lavishly furnished. Intelligent man, not wishing to rival these animals in climbing, and unable to fly with the birds, to gather the clusters, cultivates and improves the fruit for his own use, and trains the vines so that he may reach their luscious bunches. Of course, his treatment of the plants is not exactly according to Nature; and yet, the important facts and principles of the natural habits of the vine are ever borne in mind by the successful cultivator, who will take very good care not to set himself in opposition to them.

"We now come to the last subdivision of the subject—that of summer pruning and training, in order to check the too great extension, or the too late growth of the vine, and for the sake of developing the lower buds, along that part of the cane which will be called upon to produce the fruit-bearing branches. It may be that those who advocate this kind of shortening-in are right. Let us listen to the arguments advanced in its favor.

"The success of the renewal system, as is generally practiced, whether the vine be trained upon stakes or trellises, always depends upon the suitable development of the *renewal-canes*, or shoots that are provided for bearing the next crop. To this end, these shoots are encouraged in their growth; they are carefully tied up as they grow; and they are maintained in a vertical position, that they may continue to develop themselves. All laterals are removed as soon as they appear; and the tendrils are pinched off, at least so far as the cane is to be retained on the vine, at the winter pruning. At the same time, aspiring shoots in other parts of the vine, are subordinated, by pinching, as already indicated; or they are checked by their dependent position, caused by the weight of their fruit.

"With proper care, these canes will reach the top of the stakes or trellis; and, if strong, they will continue to grow, often for several feet, or even yards. What is now to be done with them? The Europeans we have among us advise to cut them off at this point. Intelligent American vine-dressers prefer to leave them, and carefully train them from stake to stake, or along the top of the trellis, and at last allow them to hang downward: they also let them produce as many laterals as their vigor may push out. These modes of treatment are diametrically opposite; and yet there may be good reasons for both. The American, knowing the great vigor of most of the vines he has to deal with, allows them to develop themselves, feeling confident that he would commit an injury by attempts to curb their rambling nature too abruptly. He has observed, that where cut off, or broken by a storm at the top of the stakes, the buds which contain the promise of the next year's vintage, are forced to break, and to produce very strong laterals, that blossom out of season: this, he apprehends, will be injurious to the next crop. On these strong canes, he has observed no difficulty arising from the want of development of the lower buds, upon which he confidently relies for his fruit the next year. On the contrary, the European, who has often come from the northern limit of grape-culture, in his own country, has been taught that in such a situation the plants of the sunny South will continue to grow too late in the season, and that, as a consequence, the buds may not be well developed, nor the wood thoroughly ripened, unless he artificially checks this late growth, by heading off the shoots at a certain hight. Under such circumstances, the practice is sound and philosophical; and it only needs judgment to indicate the proper period for performing the operation. It may be well for us to observe, among our grapes, whether some varieties may not be benefitted by a similar treatment, though it is evident that most kinds are seriously injured by it.

"In conclusion, upon this point it may be said, that, with our vigorous American vines, the canes should be cleared of laterals when quite young, and trained to the top of the support; then trained horizontally for a certain distance, and allowed to hang downward. Beyond the top of the stake or trellis, all the laterals should be allowed to grow unrestrained."

THINNING THE LEAVES.—In the middle and the north of the vine-growing region, the dampness of the soil and atmosphere being greater than in the south, the annual growth of the vine is prolonged, and this prolonged growth is often hurtful to the proper ripening of the grapes, which commences only from the moment that the growth of the vine has stopped. The bunches then contain all the elements necessary to their perfect ripening, and, no longer receiving any sap, they fully elaborate the fluids which they contain.

Thinning. the leaves, when practiced carefully, has the effect of stopping the vine's annual growth before the period at which it would otherwise have ceased, and so favors the ripening. This operation is, therefore, very necessary, especially in the north and middle of the wine-growing region, but it must be executed with judgment. If begun too soon, the thinning stops the development of the bunches; is prejudicial to the vigor of the plants and to the quality of the produce; and if performed to too great an extent at one time, it renders the bunches liable to be scorched by the sun.

This is the proper mode of proceeding: a first or preliminary thinning should take place when the grapes begin to appear transparent, and have reached their full size. Only a few leaves are then removed; those which protect the bunches from the direct action of the sun are retained. Fifteen or twenty days afterward, the work is completed,by removing a fresh quantity of leaves, allowing only one-third or one-half to remain, according as the plants are more or less vigorous, the climate more or less warm, or as the year has been more or less wet. Those which cover the bunches are then nipped off in preference to all others. While removing these leaves their stalks are left attached to the shoots, that the bud at that point may suffer less. This thinning has another effect, not less important, namely, that the maturity of the young wood is more complete, and has a great influence on the abundance of product for the next year.

[In this country no sane man would ever attempt to defoliate his vines the second time. The high sanction of authority, and European usage, might possibly induce an intelligent American vine-dresser—even one who had some knowledge of vegetable physiology—to experiment upon the effect of removing the leaves from his grape-vines, but the disastrous consequences which would be sure to follow such treatment would certainly deter him from ever making another attempt of the kind. Leaves are too important in the vegetable economy for us to sacrifice them, and the effect of their removal, in maturing the young wood, would not be satisfactory, but quite otherwise.]

Mild, overcast weather, rather moist than dry, should be chosen, in order that the shoots, flowers, or grapes laid bare, may not be suddenly exposed to the heat of the sun.

The different operations we have just spoken of—the rubbing out and pinching of the shoots, thinning of the leaves, etc.—are very rapidly executed by women.— The products of this sort of work—such as the shoots and leaves—compensate, in a great measure, for the ex-,pense. The vine-leaves, when dried, afford a very good winter fodder for cows, sheep, goats, and asses. At Mont-Dore, near Lyons, the vine-leaves, slightly fermented in cisterns, where they are soaked with a sufficient quantity of water, feed a very large number of goats, whose milk is used in the manufacture of the cheese of Mont-Dore.

All these labors are more or less practiced in most vineyards, especially those of the North. As for the vineyards of the South—in Languedoc, for instance—nothing, or next to nothing, is done during the growth of the vine ; and yet, the nipping and clipping of the shoots, and even the thinning of the leaves, performed a little before the vintage, would be as beneficial there as elsewhere.

[The southern vineyards to which reference is here made, are situated somewhat like our own, as to light and heat in midsummer ; and, from observations made here, upon the effect of summer pruning, with its defoliation, I can not help concluding that this advice of Mr. Du Breuil is of doubtful value. Certainly it can not be applied to our vines, with the prospect of any good results ; on the one hand, it is notorious that those vines which retain their foliage the latest—even until frost destroys it—always ripen their wood to the tips ; while, on the other hand, those that cast their leaves, from any cause, always have a considerable amount of immature wood, that dies in the winter. Of course the late and untimely efforts at growth, and the attempts made by the vine to restore the foliage that has been removed, by bad trimming, or by mildew, will not be likely to ripen perfectly, and such growths are almost sure to be killed in the winter.

It may be laid down as an axiom, that if the wood do not ripen perfectly, the fruit also, will be inferior, and often worthless.]

ANNUAL CULTIVATION OF THE SOIL.

THE soil which nourishes the vine, like all others on which crops are raised, requires to be exposed to the fertilizing action of atmospheric agents. It must also be preserved from the development, thereon, of weeds. Lastly, it is advisable to guard it, as much as possible, from the action of drought, during the summer. These various results are obtained by means of deep and light plowings. These two operations constitute the annual culture of the soil in vineyards.

PLOWINGS.—Two plowings are generally necessary for a well cultivated vine. One is performed in February or March, after the pruning and fastening of the shoots, when they are provided with supports. The second is effected at the end of spring, as soon as the shoots have reached a length of twenty to twenty-four inches.

The depth of these plowings ought to be such as not to reach the principal roots of the plants. Nevertheless, this depth must vary with the climate and nature of the soil. In the South, where the roots penetrate deeper, these plowings may reach the depth of six to eight inches. In the North, they should not exceed four or five inches.

At the time of the first plowing, we must contrive to lay bare the foot of the plants, by throwing the earth into the middle of the space between the two rows.—

It is owing to this mode of operation that the first cultivation is styled " plowing bare." Performed in this
way, the plowing has a double advantage : the soil being partially turned over, is more easily penetrated by
atmospheric agents ; next—and this is important—it
insures the destruction of the rootlets, which are strongly developed upon the plant near the surface of the
ground, under the influence of the moisture of the fall
and winter. Were these rootlets let alone, their active
functions would soon diminish the vitality of the deeper
ones, and they would languish. But the summer heat
soon destroys a large portion of the superficial roots,
or, at least, suspends their functions ; moreover, they
are often mangled by the action of implements ; the
consequence is that the plants suffer greatly ; for the
deep roots are no longer in a state effectively to replace
those of the surface. The laying bare of the foot of
the plants, which we have recommended, has precisely
the effect of destroying, year by year, these superficial
roots, and compelling the plants to live through their
deeper ones. It will occur to every one that this laying bare the roots is necessary everywhere, but that it
is all the more indispensable when the soil is exposed to
drought.

The second plowing, which is called " hilling," has
the effect of destroying the little ridges formed in the
space between the rows, and of leveling the ground by
filling up the furrows at the foot of the plants.

The greater or less quantity of moisture in the soil,
at the time of plowing, has a great influence on the
success of this operation. If the ground be very dry,
the work is more difficult and expensive ; if it be very

moist, and of a clayey character, it separates in large lumps, which soon dry, breaking up with difficulty, and leaving the surface in a bad condition for a long time. It is, therefore, advisable to hasten or postpone this operation for a few days, in order to seize the favorable moment when the soil, being neither too dry nor too moist, will be loosened and mellowed. Experience has also shown that before beginning the second plowing, it is as well to wait until the late frosts are no longer to be feared; for, a vine that has been recently worked freezes more easily than one around which the soil has not been stirred.

In some localities, the working of the soil in vineyards is not practiced in the manner we have just indicated. The plants are hilled-up at the first plowing, and the ground is afterward leveled at the second. As the foot of the plants can perfectly withstand the colds of winter, we think it better to uncover them at the first plowing, in order to reap the benefits arising from such a process as we have indicated above.

[It is a very common practice in our vineyards, to give them a thorough dressing very early in the season. On the hill-sides, this is done with the heavy two-pronged hoe, similar to the *bidens* of Virgil's Georgics, with which the ancient Romans probably worked their vineyards. In all grounds where the plow can be used, that implement is to be preferred to all others. If the vines have been laid by in the autumn, by throwing a furrow against them on both sides, the first operation is like that recommended by our author, and is performed by running the land-side of the plow close to the vines, which removes the earth thrown there in the autumn, and opens a furrow on each side that admits the warming influence of the sunshine. Where the vines are planted in squares, and trained to stakes, it is sometimes found desirable, at this working, to plow across the rows, and thus stir the soil between the plants, that was not touched by the plow or cultivator during the summer cultivation. Moreover, in our wide planting, two furrows to a space will not be sufficient to loosen all the soil, but three or four rounds, or more, will be required, beginning in the middle, and gathering a narrow land between two rows.

As to the time of the first plowing, in the spring, there is a diversity of opinions. Some advise its being done early, to admit the. air and sunshine to the soil, to warm it; while others recommend it being so done, because, they say, the vines will not start so early as on firm ground, and may thus escape the effects of a late forst. Some practical men postpone the plowing until the first weeds, such as the shepherd's-purse (*Capsella bursa pastoris*), and others of early habits, have grown up several inches, and are in blossom. Thus, quite a coating of green manure may be turned into the soil, for its inclioration, while the tardy vine-dresser has a good plea for his procrastination of the work.

The danger of frost is no doubt increased by plowing, as the soil is thus placed in a condition to radiate its warmth much more readily than when it was compact and level. It is well known that frosts—those of spring, particularly—are generally caused by the cooling of the surface, effected by the progress of radiation of the caloric, during clear nights, and, as well established, that this process is more rapid from a freshly plowed surface than from a compact stale furrow.]

Implements used in Working the Ground.—On steep slopes, the working of the ground can only be executed by means of hand-implements; the plow can not be used. The form of the tools employed in working the ground varies very much, according to the localities.

In rich soils, free from pebbles, hoes, like those shown in *Figures* 82, 83, and 84, are used, or else the spades, represented by *Figures* 80, and 81. In compact, or stony soils, the implements used are forked hoes, *Figure* 78, or triangular ones, such as *Figure* 79.

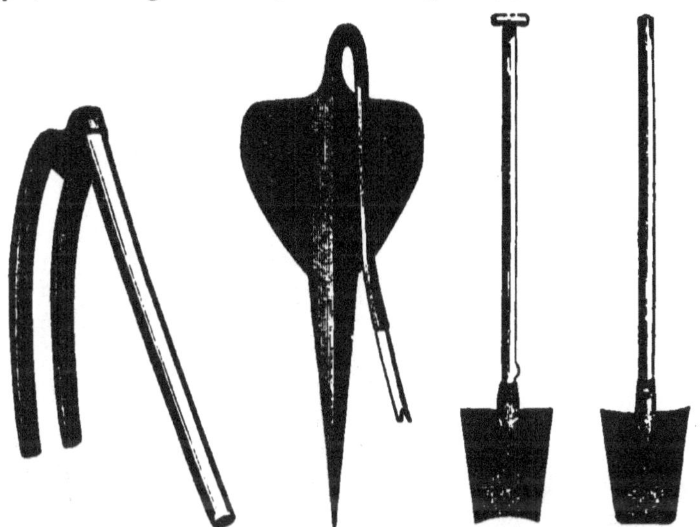

[FIG. 78.]—   [FIG. 79.]—   [FIG. 80.]   [FIG. 81.]
Forked Hoe.   *Triangular Hoe.*   *Spades.*

The cost of this hoeing, executed by hand, varies somewhat, according to the districts. In Champagne, only one hoeing is done, and that by means of the forked hoe. This work costs six dollars per acre.

In Burgundy, the ground is hoed twice. The first hoeing costs four dollars per acre ; the second costs three dollars, or seven dollars for the two. In the marshy district of Bordelais, and the hill-side from Bordeaux to Blaye, these hoeings are also executed by hand. The first costs five dollars per acre ; the second four dollars, or nine dollars for the two.

The working of the ground by hand is, undoubtedly, the best and most perfect, but it is much more expensive than that by the plow, and even on the supposition that the expense was the same, it would be advisable to substitute the plow, for the reason that the scarcity of hands is such that this mode of cultivation becomes impossible, even at the cost of the heaviest expenses,

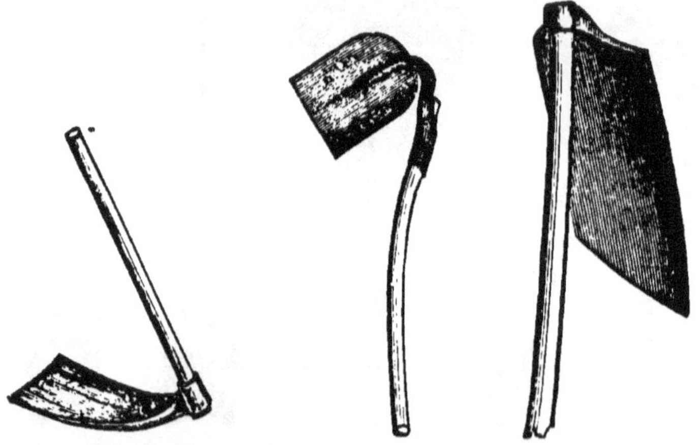

[FIG. 82.]—*Hoe.* [FIG. 83.]—*Hoe.* [FIG. 84.]—*Hoe.*

and also, because the work being done much quicker, it enables us to await the most favorable time for the operation. Unfortunately, the plow can not be used on steep slopes. Let us, therefore, consider the manner of using this implement, in vineyards where its working is not rendered impracticable by too steep a surface.

A space of at least three feet, between the rows of the plants, is necessary to allow the plow to be used with ease. Under the head of " Planting " we have pointed out the most favorable position to be given to the rows of plants, to facilitate the use of this implement.

For the vines of the South, planted at distances of four and one-half feet, and more, and pruned cup-shape, we have advised the planting in quincunxes, which allows the plow to be run in every direction, and will admit, on the same extent of surface, a greater number of vines than the planting in squares.

In vineyards where a space of from sixteen to thirty-six inches is left between the plants, the use of the plow would become impossible, unless there were a marked diminution of the number of plants per acre, and consequently a sacrifice of part of the vintage.— To obviate this difficulty, we have advised the setting of the rows three feet apart, at least, and the plants themselves close enough together to admit at least eight thousand to the acre. When it is wished to exceed this number, we have advised that a space of only twenty-four inches be left between the two rows, on each side of an alley, three feet in width [Fig. 17].— The plants being set at eighteen inches from each other, along the rows, ten thousand plants may be set to the acre, and yet two-thirds of the surface can be worked by the plow.

A plow intended for the culture of the vine should be so constructed as to fulfill the following conditions:

1st. That it cut a strip of ground at least sixteen inches wide.

2d. That it penetrate, if need be, to a depth of six inches.

3d. That it require only one horse to work it the whole day.

4th. That it be able to pass between two rows of

18

·plants, having a space between them of not more than
three feet.

The use of the plow, in vineyards, is not a new thing.
In the region of the South where the vines are set very
far apart, and where the produce—less sought after than
that of the North—had not the means of transit which
it now enjoys, there has long been an endeavor to diminish the cost of cultivation by the use of the plow.
For this purpose, the tool shown in *Figure* 85 has been

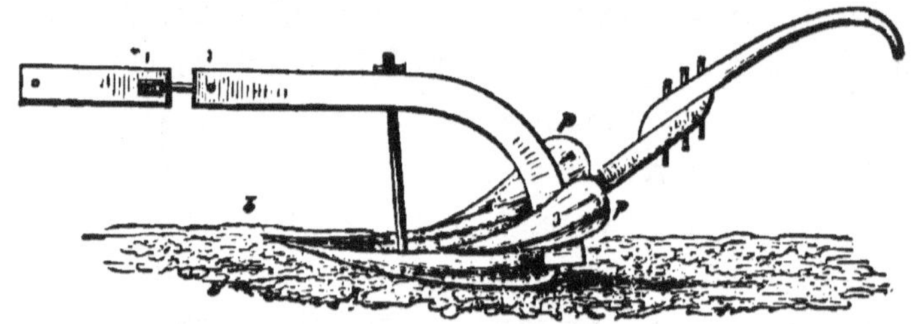

[FIG. 85.]—*Plow used in Provence.*

used.　It is nothing more than the implement introduced into Narbonne by the Romans.　This plow, having no mold-board, only displaces the soil without
turning it over ; it therefore does very poor work.

Nevertheless, this implement is still used, at least on
stony soils.　It is drawn by one good-sized horse,
hitched to it by means of a shaft or thill.

For vines of the same region, planted in deep ground,
plows with mold-boards are preferred.　This plow is
also hitched by means of a shaft.　This allows it to be
turned more easily in a small space, at the end of the
patch, and the horse is more easily handled.　*Figure* 86
represents one of these tools, constructed by M. Lacaze,
of Nîmes.　Nevertheless, a plow with a single handle

is generally preferred, as it is more easily lifted over the plants.

A land-owner in the neighborhood of Saumur, has invented the following vineyard plow, which also gives

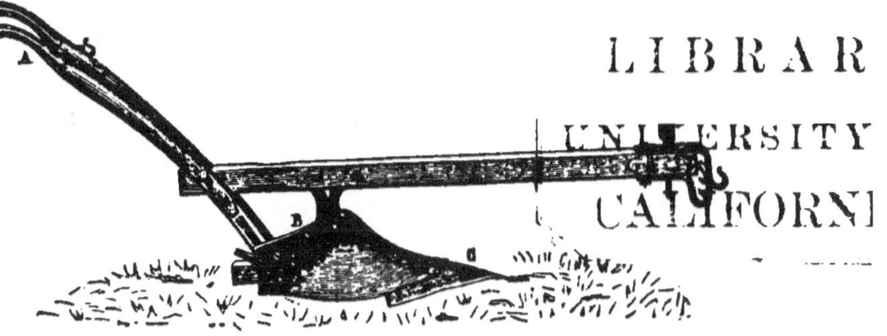

[FIG. 86.]—*Lacaze's Plow.*

very good results. It consists of a triangular plow-share [A, Fig. 87], ten inches long, and six and three-fourths inches wide at the base. The stock is twenty-six inches in length, beginning from the tip of the wing of the plow-share; it is lined with iron at the lower end. The mold-board, B, is curved; it is made of

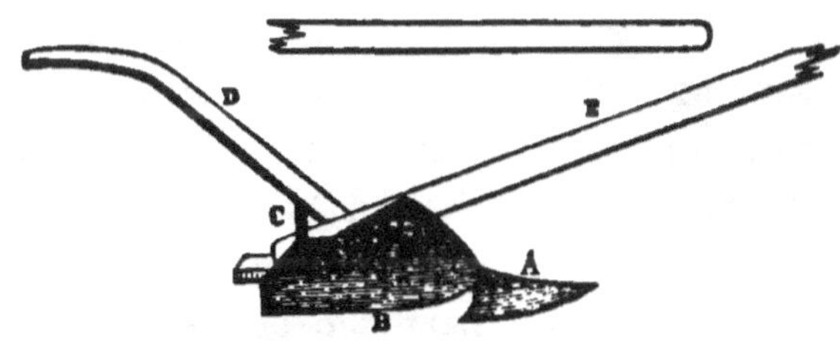

[FIG. 87.]—*Vine Plow.*

strong sheet-iron—is twenty-four inches long, and only ten inches high—is fixed to the rear stanchion by an iron rod, which keeps it opened five and one-half inches.　This stanchion, C, receives the extremity of the beam, in a mortise; its upper end fits into a conical handle, D, measuring about three-and-a-quarter feet from the point where it is dove-tailed into the thickness of the beam, to its extremity.　A second stanchion, placed twelve inches from the first, gives it the additional strength required.　The beam E, is not less than ten feet in length.　At twelve inches from its extremity it is rounded, and its diameter reduced to two and one-half inches.

The shafts F [Fig. 88], are kept together by two

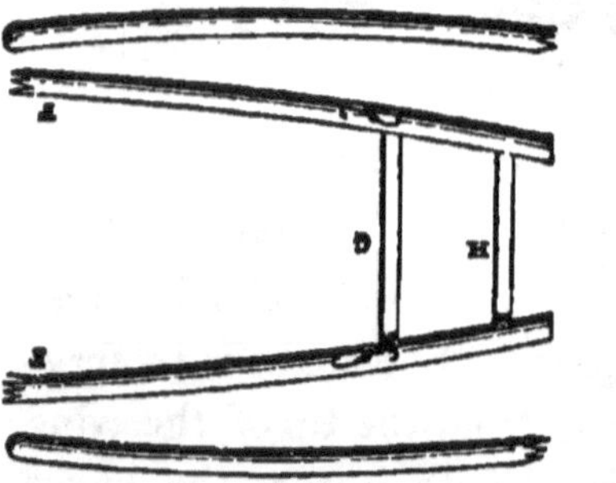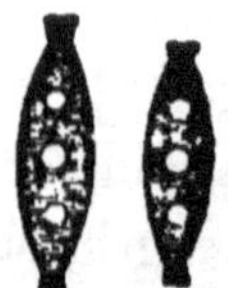

[FIG. 88.]—*Shafts.*　　[FIG. 89.]—*Cross-Pieces.*

cross-pieces [G, H, Figs. 88 and 89], each having three holes, corresponding with each other, and meant to receive the thin end of the pole, and secure it by means of a pin.　According as it is desired to hill-up, or lay bare the foot of the vine, in order that the horse may not be obliged to come too near the plants, the different holes—sometimes those on the right, and sometimes those on the left—are made use of.　Close to the cross-piece G, two hitching hooks are placed.

Drawn by a single horse, this plow, owing to its small dimensions, may be used between rows of plants only four feet three inches apart ; this plowing is so effectual that but little extra hand-work, with the hoe, is required. But it has the inconvenience of requiring a space between the rows of plants, which is found too great for the vineyards of the northern part of the vine-growing region.

M. de la Loyère, a large wine-grower at Savigny, near Beaune (Côte-d'-Or), has recently contrived a plow for vine lands, which we have seen in operation, and which gives him very satisfactory results [Fig. 90].

[FIG. 90.]— *La Loyère's Plow.*

Here is a brief description of it : It is a small plow, made entirely of iron, and having two shares, E.— These two shares, with their mold-boards, occupy, together, a width of sixteen inches, and, consequently, plow the same width. A wheel placed in front gives it steadiness. The holes in the vertical rod C, allow the clevis to be raised or lowered, and thus to regulate the depth of plowing ; a regulator D, at the extremity of the pole, also allows the plowing to come as near as possible to the line of plants. The two shares are movable, and may be substituted by a leveler, to lay

bare the roots of the plants, or a " hiller," to hill them
up.

M. de la Loyère hitches only one horse to this plow,
and the implement works perfectly between rows of
plants three and one-fourth feet apart.   The price of
this plow is eighteen dollars ; the extra " hiller," and
leveler cost eight dollars each.

M. de la Loyère plows two and one-half acres per
day, with his implement.   The day's work of the
horse and driver, being estimated at one dollar and forty
cents, makes an expenditure of two dollars and eighty
cents per day for the two winter plowings, or one dol-

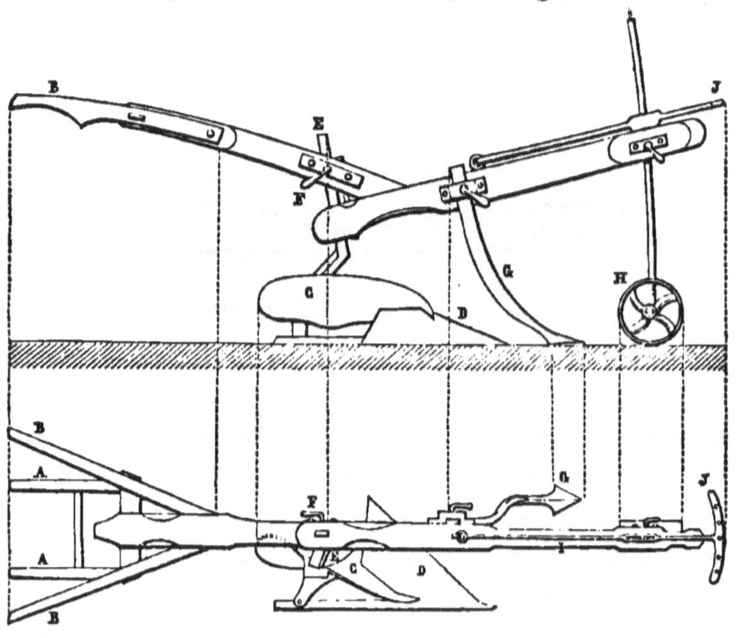

[FIG. 91.]—*Messager's Plow.*

lar and twelve cents per acre.   But to this must be added an expenditure of about one dollar and forty-four

cents per acre, for the working of the soil between the plants, by manual labor, thus making a total expenditure of two dollars and fifty-six cents per acre for the winter dressings.

M. Messager, a vine-grower at Chanvre, near Joigny (Yonne), has also invented a vine plow, of great simplicity, which we have seen performing with the greatest success, at the castle of the Vicomte de la Loyère, near Châlon-sur-Saône. Mr. Messager's plow [Fig. 91], is thus constructed:

The handles, A and B, are of wood. The latter fork outwardly, at their extremity, so as to protect the hands placed on the parts A, from friction against the iron wires; they are supported by the parts B. The mold-board C, and the share D, are fixed, by means of an iron rod E, which may be removed at will from the two mortises in which it is held by a pin, F. This rod has an elbow, so as to allow the share to be thrown to the right, and to approach as near as possible to the line of plants. The share works on a width of twelve inches; a cultivator-prong G, thrown to the left by means of an elbow, stands out four inches to the left of the share, so as to make the cut sixteen inches in breadth, and also to give some steadiness to the plow. A wheel, H, is placed in front, on an iron rod, slightly bent. This wheel, which may be raised or lowered, allows the depth of plowing to be varied at will. An iron rod, I, movable in a vertical direction, receives the draft-chain at its extremity, which is terminated by a regulator, J, that allows of plowing more or less near to the lines of plants.

Only one horse is hitched to this kind of plow, and

it works perfectly between rows three and one-fourth feet apart. Nevertheless, we think that the mould-board ought to be a little higher, for plowing six inches deep. This tool should be used for the first plowing—that of " bareing" the roots. It is made to pass along each side of the row of plants. As for the second plowing —that of " hilling-up "—it is done with the same implement, but by replacing the share and its mold-board, by a large double-share [Fig. 92]. This share

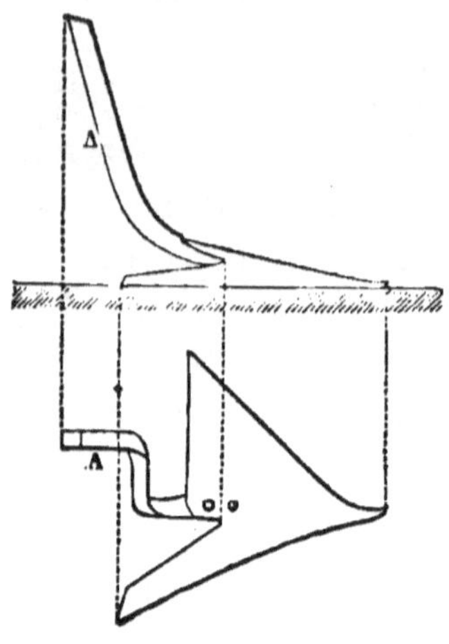

[FIG. 92.]—*Large Double Share, for Messager's Plow.* has, at its hinder part, a width of sixteen inches, and can throw up the soil to a depth of five inches. It is fixed to the beam by an iron rod, A, sufficiently elbowed to bear as much as possible on the right side of the plow. The cultivator-prong [G, Fig. 91] not being required for the action of this share, is laid aside. Two cuts of the plow, between the rows of plants, are sufficient to cover the roots again, and to level the ground perfectly. This work is also performed with one horse. The price of this plow, including the large share of which we have spoken, and a " hiller," which can be adapted to it, and which we shall mention again, further on, is twenty dollars.

M. Messager's plow can easily execute each of these two plowings, over a space of two and one-half acres per day, which will give the same expense as with the plow of the Comte de la Loyère. Nevertheless, the greater simplicity of the Messager plow, the possibility of having it repaired anywhere, and the more moderate price, seem to us to entitle it to the preference.

If these plowings were to be performed in vineyards where the rows are alternately twenty-four and forty inches apart [Fig. 17], as we have before explained, for the purpose of setting ten thousand plants to the acre, the cost would be rather more; for, the plow, in such a case, could only be used over two-thirds of the surface. The two plowings, to that extent, will cost seventy-five cents. To this we shall have to add the working by hand, over one-third of the acre, the cost of which, at six dollars and seventy-five cents per acre, will be two dollars and twenty-five cents, which will make a total expenditure of three dollars, instead of two dollars and fifty-six cents—the cost when the plow alone is employed.

[These implements show a great improvement upon the antiquated tools of the days of the Romans, but we are vain enough to think that the inventive genius of our countrymen has furnished us with much better machines than any of these which are so highly lauded by Mr. Du Breuil. The superiority of the American earth-workers, of various kinds, consists in their greater lightness, strength and finish, as well as their perfect adaptation to the particular office they are intended to perform, whether this be simply stirring the soil, or reversing it as in common plowing. For this latter purpose nothing can exceed the common bar-share plow, with a steel mold-board.

Though, when closely studied, and considered in a strictly mechanical sense, the turning-plow is a very unphilosophical

19

implement, on account of the loss of power by friction on the land-side, and on the sole, still it is justly claimed that a well made plow, with all the joints closely fitted up, is nearly perfect for its special purposes, and it has been correctly asserted that a high application of mathematics has been exercised in the production of the perfect model of this implement. The mold-board is a curved wedge, so constructed as to lift and reverse the soil in the most perfect manner, and at the same time to comminute it completely, if the soil be in a proper condition.

In looking at these figures, and descriptions, the intelligent reader will be surprised at the cumbrous clumsiness of the implements described, and so favorably spoken of. He will be particularly struck with the length of the beam—one of these being twelve feet long—for a one horse plow! The mode of attachment by shafts, instead of a short single-tree, will also strike the American farmer as useless. With our short beams, and a well broken animal, guided by a single line, and broken to the word, a good plowman can turn in the middle of the rows, if necessary, or wherever his horse or mule can get around; but of course this would require more space than the author assigns as his minimum distance between the rows that can be plowed; we plant our grapes at greater distances in this country.

A great triumph for American agricultural implements, of all kinds, is anticipated, at the approaching Exposition, at Paris, and it is confidently expected that the plows sent from this country will attract great attention, and accomplish a success in the approaching trials of these implements. The same may be predicted of the cultivators, of various kinds, and of all sorts of earth-workers, which the inventive passion of our people has furnished, for every kind of operation that is to be performed on the farm, in the vineyard, or in the garden.

Still we must not shut our eyes to the improvements of others, and Americans are not blind to their own interests, and are not slow to adopt what is really valuable ; so it cannot be doubted that many important suggestions will be made, by coming in contact with the display of the inventions and appliances of other countries, nor that those who visit Paris may bring back with them very much that will prove advantageous to their fellow-countrymen, in this, as in other departments of industry.

The arrangement of a guard in the handles of Mr. Messager's plow, affords a protection to the workman, the value of which will be appreciated by the vigneron and nurseryman. The regulation of the side-draft is better arranged by our lateral clevis, than by his changeable shafts.]

The first attempts which were made to substitute the plow for implements worked by hand, led, in some districts, and more especially in the South, to unfortunate results. The vine has been observed to fail. This has been noticed wherever the plow was substituted for hand-labor which had been executed too lightly. The principal roots of the plants, having, in consequence of such light workings, spread themselves out near the surface, the plow has mangled a great number of them. To avoid this misfortune, it will be advisable, with regard to vines formerly cultivated by hand, to make the plowings very shallow at first, and then to increase their depth, year by year, until they have reached a suitable depth. The plants will thus be compelled gradually to form new roots below that depth. This precaution will be the more necessary with the older vines.

Comparison between the Cost of Working by Hand and Working with the Plow.—We have already seen the cost of working by hand, and by the plow: we will now compare the two methods in regard to price.

The question being decided in favor of the plow, in almost all the vineyards of the South, we will now concern ourselves only with those districts where this mode of cultivation is not yet adopted.

In Champagne, only one dressing is performed, which costs six dollars per acre.

If the vines are planted in alleys, as we have explained above, and the Messager plow is substituted for hand implements, there will be a total expenditure of two dollars and fifty-six cents per acre, for the two plowings, and dressings by hand along the lines. This gives a difference of three dollars and forty-four cents per acre in favor of the plow.

In Burgundy, the price of the two dressings is six dollars and seventy-five cents per acre. With the plow it would cost two dollars and fifty-six cents: difference in favor of the plow, four dollars and twenty cents per acre.

In the moorlands (*palus*) of Bordelais, and on the hills on the right bank of the Garonne, below Bordeaux, the two dressings cost nine dollars per acre. If we employ the Messager plow, we shall have an expenditure of three dollars and twenty cents, owing to the greater depth of plowing. This gives us a difference of five dollars and eighty cents per acre.

The substitution of the plow for manual labor has the immense advantage of obviating the difficulty arising from the want of hands, and of diminishing the cost of cultivation in a considerable ratio.

It has been said that the plow is only advantageous

in large vineyards, as it is only in such large undertakings that the teams can be made use of in other work than that of plowing the vine lands. The objection seems well founded; nevertheless, we think that this mode of cultivation might be employed in small vineyards, by contractors, who could easily find employment for their teams, during the interval of the two dressings of the vine. It must also be taken into consideration that this work only requires one horse, and that the vine-grower will seldom be at a loss how to employ it in other work.

SECOND DRESSINGS.—These dressings are of a far more superficial kind than the two plowings already described. They do not exceed two inches in depth. Their object is chiefly to destroy hurtful weeds. They also prevent the soil from drying to any great depth, during the great heat of summer.

The number of these dressings must be in proportion to the rapidity with which the soil becomes covered with weeds. They should be more frequent in rather cool soils, in wet years, and in northern regions, than in dry soils, and hot years, or in the climate of the South. At least two of these dressings should be performed each year, in the course of summer. More frequently, only one dressing is given, either through motives of economy, or because, as in vines without props, the shoots, which spread out on every side, do not allow easy access through the vineyard.

The principal aim of these dressings being the removal of weeds, it follows that their performance is easier and more effectual during warm and dry weather, in order that these weeds, when rooted up by the implements, may perish more readily. Still, the operation must not be delayed until the soil has become hardened by the heat; the work would then be more difficult and expensive.

These dressings are done by means of a small hoe, with a light handle, and resembling, in its form, those shown in *Figures* 82 and 83.

The cost of this operation, per acre, is as follows, for the different regions mentioned:

In Champagne, the four following dressings are given:

1st. In May or June,..	$2 00
2d. In July..	2 80
3d. In the middle of September......................................	3 84
4th. In winter..	0 96
Total..	$9 60

In Burgundy, only one dressing is given, costing two dollars and eighty-eight cents per acre.

In the moorlands of Bordelais, and on the hills on the right side of the Garonne, above Bordeaux, it is most usual to give one dressing, which costs two dollars and sixty-four cents per acre.

[FIG. 93.]
*Triangular Plow-
Share.*

The advantages we have pointed out above, as arising from the substitution of the plow for manual labor, are the same for those lighter dressings as for deep plowing.

In the region of the South, where only one of these dressings can be given, use is made in some places, of a kind of plow, the share of which is replaced by a triangular blade [Fig. 93], the base of which has an expanse of about twenty inches; this contrivance allows the ground to be worked up to the foot of the plants.

The Comte de la Loyère, of Savigny, has also contrived a horse cultivator [Fig. 94], which works well, and does away with the necessity of employing hand implements for this kind of work.

[FIG. 94.]—*La Loyère's Horse Cultivator.*

It is made entirely of iron, and provided with five shares, F, and a coulter, D, placed in front. The space between the two side-pieces, to which the shares are fixed, can be widened, so as to vary the breadth of the surface over which it is wanted to operate. The greatest width is thirty-two inches. The wheel, fixed at the front of the beam, is used to vary the depth of the dressing; the vertical rod, C, allows this wheel to be raised or lowered.

M. de la Loyère puts only one horse to this implement, and can dress three and three-fourths acres per day, in a vineyard in which the rows are forty inches apart.

The price of this horse cultivator is twenty-six dollars.

This implement, drawn by one horse, sufficing to work an area of three and three-fourths acres per day, and the horse and man costing one dollar and forty cents per day, we have an expenditure of about thirty-five cents per acre for each dressing.

M. Messager has contrived a large plow-share [Fig. 92] to do the light dressings. Of this we have already spoken. It is fixed to his plow [Fig. 91] in the place of the share and mold-board intended for laying bare the roots. This implement, which is of great simplicity, is very effective, and only requires one horse. To work the space between two rows of plants, forty inches apart, it has to go over that space twice. From this it follows that two and one half acres may be thus dressed per day, making an expenditure of fifty-six cents per acre, for one dressing.

This expenditure is a little more than with the horse cultivator of la Loyère; nevertheless, the simplicity of M. Messager's implement, which we have seen at work, induces us to give it the preference. Moreover, the Comte de la Loyère's cultivator does not work very well on weedy ground.

The cost of the lighter dressing by the plow, of which we have just spoken, is applicable to vines cultivated in rows regularly laid out, forty inches apart. But, if the space between the rows is alternately twenty-four and forty inches, the cost of this operation will be greater; for the plow, in such cases, can only be employed over two-thirds of the area; the cost per acre, for each working, will then stand thus:

Working by the plow, over two-thirds of an acre....................... $0 38
Working by hand, over one-third of an acre, at two dollars and
　　eighty-eight cents per acre... 0 96

　　　　Total.. $1 34

Compartive Cost of Light-Dressing, by Hand and by the Plow.—These figures enable us to compare the light dressings done by hand, and those done by the plow.

In Champagne, the cultivation costs, altogether, nine dollars and sixty cents per acre.

The vine being planted in rows, forty inches apart, the use of the plow will give rise to an expenditure of fifty-six cents per acre, for each dressing, as we have shown above. This operation being repeated four times, we have a total expenditure of two dollars and twenty-four cents, instead of nine dollars and sixty cents, and this gives a difference of seven dollars and thirty-six cents.

In Burgundy, a single dressing is usual, and that costs two dollars and eighty-eight cents per acre. Performed by the plow, this work is done at a cost of fifty-six cents, which is a saving of two dollars and thirty-two cents per acre. This operation might be repeated a second time, and there would still remain a difference of one dollar and seventy-six cents per acre.

In the moorlands of Bordelais, and on the hills of the right bank of the Garonne, below Bordeaux, only one dressing is usual, which costs two dollars and sixty-four cents per acre. If executed by means of the horse cultivator, the cost will only be fifty-six cents, giving a difference of two dollars and eight cents per acre, and, if two dressings were done, instead of one, there would still be a saving of one dollar and fifty-two cents.

The dressings by the horse cultivator, therefore, greatly diminish the number of hands required, and allow of considerable saving in the expenditure.

[No one in this country will question the greater economy of using horse-power, and suitable cultivators ; and, as already stated, when discussing the selection of vineyard sites, the adaptation of the surface to the use of animals, becomes a question of prime importance in the choice of vine lands. Indeed, the abrupt hill-sides, that require manual labor, are now generally passed by, in favor of hill-tops, that may be tended with the plows, and, in many parts of the country extensive level lands are appropriated to vine planting.

The difference in expense is greatly in favor of horse-power; indeed, extensive vineyards would not be planted if they had to be cultivated by human labor. The whole expense is diminished more than one half, and as the cultivation is but one item of expense, and the manual labors are the same in both cases, the contrast between the expenditure by the hoe and by the plow, could it be presented to the reader, would be very much more striking.

The author suggests, very properly, that the introduction of the plow into old vineyards that had been cultivated by hand, should be very carefully managed, and that the culture should at first be very shallow, and gradually deepened. One of the serious practical difficulties and objections to the plow, consists in the danger of tearing off a shallow lateral root, of considerable size, which is often attended with a splitting upward of the vine-stock, for several inches, which is of course a great injury. This accident may happen with the most careful workman, and the most steady team, but is impossible to avoid it with a fast and spirited horse, to whom the slight resistance offered by the root is only a stimulus to greater efforts.

To obviate this difficulty, some vine-dressers advocate the practice introduced by the European vignerons, which they call cutting away the " dew-roots." It consists in removing the earth at the base of the vines, and cutting off all the roots that can be found within a few inches of the surface. The avowed object of this kind of root-pruning is very different, and is intended to force the vine to produce, and to depend upon deeper roots, which, it is claimed, are apt to decay and die when the superficial roots are encouraged.]

XI.

MANURES AND CHEMICAL APPLICATIONS FOR VINEYARDS.

MANURES, properly so-called, are more especially those substances which, applied to the soil, furnish the roots with the nutritive principles necessary for the development of plants. They consist, principally, of organic substances. The chemical applications, composed of mineral substances, have for their chief aim a more or less complete modification of the elementary composition of the soil, so as to render its physical or chemical properties more favorable to vegetation. Let us inquire into these two operations as applied to vineyards.

MANURES.—*Their Importance.*—The vine, like all other plants, in order to develop itself, requires, in the soil, the nutritive principles necessary for its growth. Almost all soils naturally contain a certain quantity of these elements. They are nitrogen, and certain saline substances derived from the atmosphere and rain-water. This natural richness of the soil, which is constantly renewed, suffices to insure to the vine a certain produce, as is proved by the vineyards of those localities in which the vine is never manured. Under these conditions, the product is about one hundred and thirty-seven gallons per acre.

Let us now examine whether this yield can be augmented by the application of manure, and whether the expense of this manure will be justified by the result.

According to M. de Gasparin, every pound of nitrogen, applied to vines in good condition, but which have never been manured, yields about fifteen gallons of wine. One thousand pounds of good farm-yard manure, containing four-tenths of nitrogen, will give four pounds, and, consequently, will yield sixty gallons of wine. Putting the cost of the one thousand pounds of manure at $0.90, and the sixty gallons of wine at $9.09, we see that the manure applied to the vine is largely repaid by the product, even supposing that, owing to unfavorable weather, only half the crop mentioned is obtained.

Are Manures Prejudicial to the Quality of the Wine?— This question has been a subject of much controversy, but we think that the parties to the discussion would have agreed much sooner, had both sides been less positive.

We now subjoin some facts which may throw light on this important question of vine culture. The sugary principle, the aroma which we like to find in all fruits, is the result of a special elaboration, within the cellular tissue of fruits, of those fluids that flow to them. It is under the influence of heat, and especially of a bright light, that this elaboration takes place.

If the tree, or shrub, possesses great vigor, from whatever cause that may arise, the sappy fluids will reach the cellular tissues of the fruit in such abundance that there will be no possibility of their being thoroughly prepared. The watery exhalation which takes place at the surface of the fruit, during its development, will be insufficient to rid it of its superabundant juice. The sugary and aromatic principles will be comparatively scanty, and the fruit of inferior quality. These facts are indisputable; they occur every day, under the eyes of agriculturists. The fruits of an old tree are—all other things being equal—much more luscious than those of a young tree growing vigorously. The fruit of a pear-tree, grafted on a free stock, is inferior to that nourished by the roots of the quince-tree.

Heat and light, as we have already said, play an important part in this question, by affecting the watery evaporation and the elaboration of the sappy juices flowing into the fruit. It is for this reason, that fruits gathered from trees trained against walls with a southern exposure, are better than those developed in a northern one. The grapes ripened under the climate of Paris are less sweet than those of the same descriptions grown under the southern sky.

Another consequence of excessive vigor, is the delay in the ripening of the fruits. For, the chemical reactions which take place in the tissues of fruits, and which influence their ripening, begin to take effect only from the moment the vegetation of the tree is nearly at a stand-still—that is to say, at that period when the sappy juices flow only in very small quantities into the tissues of the fruit. Now, the excessive vigor of trees has the effect of prolonging the vegetation, and, consequently, of retarding the ripening. It is owing to this influence, that, other things being equal, the fruits of trees having little vigor, always ripen sooner than on those of stronger vegetation. It is partly to diminish the vigor of the vines, and to check their development, that the growers of Thomery proceed with the *thinning of the leaves*—a process that ought to be more frequently adopted in vineyards of the North.

These injurious effects on the quality of the fruit, arising from the too great vigor of trees, are greater, in proportion as we recede from the South—that is to say, as light and heat are less intense.

All the preceding facts thus show that the vigor of the plants, to whatever cause it may be due, is hurtful to the quality of the product. Now, as manures have no other effect than that of increasing this vigor, it would seem reasonable to admit that the vineyard should be sustained by the natural richness of the soil, and that we should abstain from the application of all manures. We must, however, except the case in which, for want of sufficient nutriment, the soil may have become so poor, and the plant so languid, as to affect the quality of the product.

This would certainly be a rational conclusion, if, in this culture, *quality*, only, was looked for ; but *quantity* is also an object. Now, as we have seen above, the average yield of vines left to the natural richness of the soil is about one hundred and thirty-seven gallons per acre. If we are satisfied with this product in vineyards that, do what we may, can only yield inferior wines, sold at the rate of $0.22 per gallon, we shall have a gross product of $30.15 per acre, which will be quite inadequate to pay the expense of cultivation. In the celebrated growths, this yield would also be considered insufficient. For this reason, the quantity is increased, by means of manures, to about two hundred and thirty-two gallons the acre, in Médoc, and about one hundred and ninety gallons in the more celebrated growths of the hills of Burgundy. It is in the latter vines that the least manure is used, but the pomace of grapes, the fertile soils and the composts that are strewed over them, are, in reality, manures, whatever may be said to the contrary.

We must conclude, from the foregoing, that if manures exercise a hurtful influence on the quality of wine, the manuring of vineyards is, nevertheless, necessary for the sake of increase in quantity ; that this manuring should be abundant, in proportion as the high price of the product compensates for its scantiness ; and, lastly, that all other things being equal, manures may be the more freely used the more we advance toward the South.

[In the fertile soils of the West, that have been devoted to the planting of the vine, one of the difficulties that has attended this branch of culture has arisen from the excessive growth induced by this fertility, which, in some varieties, is attended with poor results in fruit. Hence, we have had little experience with manurial applications, and we are even advised to plant certain sorts on the poorest land.*   As a

---

* This is the case with the Diana, and some other strong-growing kinds.

general rule, any good soil, well prepared, is considered good enough for the vine. There are vineyards, however, that have been much benefitted by the applications of manures, and even very strong ones have been applied, without appearing to injure the quality of the product. Even in Missouri, it appears that some vignerons have applied manures with advantage. It is generally supposed that barn-yard manure should be composted before being spread. Chemical or artificial manures have been applied, with apparently good effect. Ashes, either directly applied to vines, or as an element of the composts, would appear to be an important application, unless the soil were unusually rich in potash.]

NATURE OF MANURES TO BE EMPLOYED.—According to M. de Gasparin, for every one hundred kilogrammes of grapes, we have the following constituents :

	NITROGEN.	POTASH.
64.50 kil. of wine containing	} 0.30	0.35 } 0.56
16.66 " of dry pomace 0.30		0.21
187.00 " of dry shoots........................... 0.50	} 2.84	0.17 } 0.35
123.42 " of dry leaves 2.34		0.18
Total 3.14		0.91

This analysis shows that nitrogen plays a very unimportant part in the fruitage of the vine, since one hundred pounds of grapes only contain 0.30 pounds of that substance. On the other hand, it is found in tolerably large quantities in the shoots, and especially in the leaves. With respect to the salts of potash, the reverse is the case : they are much more abundant in the grapes than in the branches and leaves. We must, therefore, come to the conclusion that nitrogenous manures favor the development of the wood, and that the salts of pot ash will powerfully contribute to the fruit-bearing.

Let us inquire what are the manures which best fulfill these conditions, respectively.

I. HIGHLY NITROGENOUS MANURES.—*Well Prepared Farm-yard Manure.*—This manure is certainly one of the best, for it introduces into the soil not only nitrogen, but also a considerable quantity of saline substances, necessary to the development and fructification of the vine. But this manure has the disadvantage of being too powerful, and of introducing into the must too large a quantity of mucilage and free acids, which are prejudicial to the quality of wines of celebrated vintages. Another objection made to it is, that its effect is not sufficiently sustained. And yet, if we except some celebrated vineyards of Burgundy, it is the manure most in use, wherever it can be procured. But this is often a matter of great difficulty; for the vineyard produces very little fodder for cattle. It would be well, if a sufficient extent of natural meadows, or else artificial ones, of long duration, could be connected with the vineyard. It is thus that this culture is carried on over a considerable part of Beaujolais. There, an extent of natural meadow nearly equal to that of the vineyard, is set apart for the production of manure.

The product of these meadows is consumed by cows. The manure yielded by these, their labor and milk, suffice to pay for their food, and the straw bought for litter. In the vineyards of Médoc, draught animals, which perform the work in the vineyard, also yield the manure, but, almost everywhere, the forage given them is bought. The waste lands, adjoining these vineyards, furnish the litter.

Night-Soil, Garbage, etc.—These substances, even

more than farm-yard manure, have the drawback of acting unfavorably on the quality of the wine. For this reason the employment of these manures must be avoided in those vineyards where the quality of the product is more an object than the quantity.

Broken Bones, Fragments of Horns, Wool-Waste.—These manures are likewise very rich in nitrogen, and they possess the following advantages over farm-yard manure: they are decomposed much more slowly; their effect, being far less sudden, lasts much longer; they very gradually yield their elements to the roots of the vine, and their action is prolonged over a period of from five to eight years.

Woolen rags are now very generally employed in Languedoc. Their use begins to be adopted in the South-West, also. We employ them ourselves, successfully.

Sea-Weeds.—The sea-weeds are employed as manures in some vineyards near the ocean, especially in l'Aunis. Although not so rich as farm-yard manure, these substances have a decided, but temporary, effect. They also impart a disagreeable flavor to the wine.

Composts.—These generally consist of alternate layers of dung and earth, piled up together. Some months after their first preparation, the composts are thoroughly mixed, and again allowed to rest for one or two months; they are then mixed again, as they are used. If the vineyard is situated on a dry and parched soil, composts which are of an argilo-silicious character are best; if the soil be clayey, those made with calcareous earths are preferred. To these composts are often added leaves, weeds, sods, etc. This kind of manure, being less rich than that of the farm-yard, is preferable for vineyards of celebrated growths, as it affects the quality of the wine in a less degree. It is often used in Champagne.

The Slimy-Mud of Rivers and Ponds, or the Sea.—These deposits are often very rich in organic matter, in a state of decomposition; but they contain acid properties which can only be made to disappear by exposing them to the air for a year, in a thin layer, on the surface of the ground. They may be employed sooner by mixing them, three months beforehand, with a certain quantity of the refuse lime from the kilns. We except sea-mud, however, which may be used immediately.

Herbaceous Plants.—When none of the foregoing manures can be procured, their place may be supplied by herbaceous plants, sowed in the soil of the vineyard. These plants are turned in by means of the plow, at the time when they are about to blossom. But, for this purpose, the vines must be in rows. In the South and South-West, the plants to be employed are the white lupin, in light soils, and the winter horse-bean in clayey lands. In the middle and north of the vine-growing region, recourse may be had to the winter-vetch and rye. This sowing should take place immediately after the first winter plowing.

In some vineyards, on the banks of the Rhône, it is usual to bury, in a fresh state, certain plants which grow abundantly in marshy places, such as reeds, Indian-grass, rushes, sedge, etc. These several vegetable manures are less rich than farm-yard manures, but they have the advantage of being much less expensive.

II. Manures Rich in Potash.—In general, the employment of substances more especially favoring the growth of the plants does not render unnecessary the use of nitrogenous manures. Otherwise, the plants becoming soon exhausted, would only put forth poor and meagre shoots.

Pomace.—This substance, which is very rich in salts of potash, as seen in the foregoing analysis, is in general use in vineyards, and yields excellent results.

Wood-Ashes.—These ashes, leached, or, better still, used in their natural state, give very good results, as is proved by certain growths of Volnay and Pomard. They may be procured in very large quantities in the neighborhood of moors, and waste and uncultivated lands, by removing the turf from the surface of the soil, and burning it on the spot. There have lately been discovered, in the very center of the city of Lons-le-Saulnier, and in the neighborhood of Poligny, immense deposits of ashes, left from the working of salt-pits, by the Romans. These ashes will prove a mine of wealth for the vineyards of the Jura.

Woody Plants.—All shrubs, especially those which retain their leaves, may be employed to manure the vine, after their young shoots have been trodden down by the horse's feet, or cart-wheels. Of this kind are the rock-roses, heaths, furze, box-wood, hedge-clippings, the juniper tree, young pines, and especially their twigs. These shrubs also contain a great deal of potash.

Quantity of Manure to be Employed.—It is difficult to state the precise quantity of manure which ought to be applied to the vineyard. That must depend, chiefly, upon the degree of vigor it is desired to impart to the plants. If the *quantity* of product is the main object aimed at, it is evident that a higher degree of manuring will be requisite than if *quality* is the principal end in view.

The elementary composition of the soil, its natural degree of moisture, and the climate, are so many circumstances affecting the action of the manure, and the quantity that ought to be used. We can, therefore, only give very general directions on this subject. Here are a few:

In the Department of the Gard, three hundred and twenty-four cwts. of manure, per acre, are applied to some vineyards, every four years, or eighty-one cwts. every year. It consists of sheep-manure, having about 0.67 per cent. of nitrogen. By means of this manure an average product of nine hundred and fifty gallons per acre is obtained.

In most of the vineyards of Beaujolais, two hundred and seventy cwts. of manure to the acre are applied every three years, and the result obtained is four hundred and seventy-five gallons to the acre.

In the moorland district of Bordeaux, about two hundred and forty-three cwts. of manure are used on the acre, every three years, or eighty-one cwts. a year, and the produce is an average of four hundred and seventy-five gallons.

In the Canton of Vaud (Switzerland), five hundred and eighty-five cwts. of manure, every three years, or one hundred and ninety-five cwts. every year, are applied to the acre. This enormous manuring gives an average product of one thousand two hundred and sixty gallons a year.

Lastly, in the vineyards of Languedoc, where woolen rags are used, that description of manure is spread, every five years, in the proportion of eighty-one cwts. to the acre, and the product is eight hundred and forty-four gallons.

The few examples that we have given show the fact that the abundance of the crop is in direct proportion to the quantity of manure; but it is highly probable that the quality of the produce is in an inverse ratio to the quantity of manure.

How to Apply the Manure.—We have already seen that among the manures adapted to the vine, those which contain much nitrogen favor the development of the wood, while those rich in salts of potash promote fruit-bearing. It is as well to examine whether these two kinds of manure should be employed together or separately?

We are of opinion that the formation of the woody structure, and roots of the plants, should be attended to as quickly as possible. With this end in view it will, therefore, be advisable to make free use of nitrogenized manures, shortly after planting. The use of the salts of potash, at this period, would be injurious, by causing premature crops, which would exhaust the young plants.

When the stocks are established, the two kinds of manure may be employed at the same time. These manures may be applied in two different ways: they may be placed at the foot of each plant, or spread in a straight line, at the bottom of a trench cut along the middle of the space dividing the rows of vines.

The distribution of the manures by p.acing them at the foot of each plant, is liable to serious objections, as each of them must be laid bare by means of hand labor, and this is a tedious and expensive work. Moreover, in order that the manures may exert all their power on the development of the plants, they must be placed within reach of the ends of the rootlets, which alone possess the power of absorption. Now, the roots of the vine being very long, and not branching out, the manures ought to be placed at a certain distance from the plants, and not at their foot. The process we have just described is, therefore, faulty. It tends, moreover, to the development of a great number of rootlets at the stems of the plants, and these are hurtful to the action of the principal roots, and are, besides, mangled, either by the action of tools, in working the soil, or damaged by drought. Nevertheless, it is difficult to employ any other method for vines planted in an irregular manner.

For vines planted in regular rows it will, therefore, be a great advantage to place the manure along the middle of the space, at a mean depth of six inches, in the North, and ten inches in the South. This operation should be performed, if possible, toward the end of the autumn; this manure will decompose during winter, and will furnish the roots with their nutritive elements, at the awakening of vegetation.

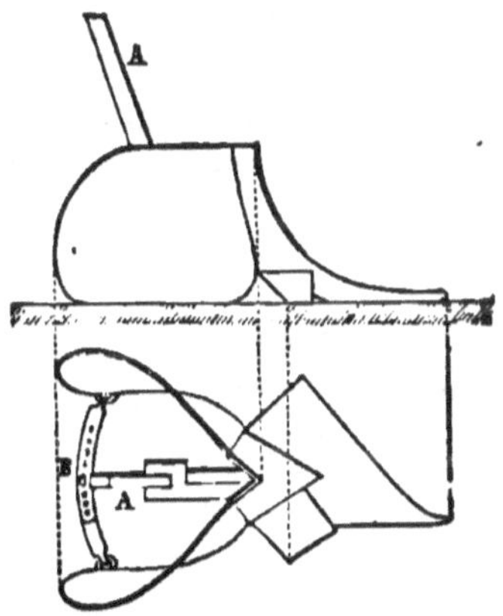

[FIG. 95.]—"*Hiller,*" *adapted to Messager Plow.*

The most economical way of putting this method into practice is to open a sufficiently deep trench, along the middle of each alley separating the rows of plants; this trench may be expeditiously opened by means of the "hiller" [Fig. 95], constructed by M. Messager, of Chanvre, and may be adapted to his plow, by means of the iron rod A. In order to cut such a furrow deep enough, by means of this "hiller," the two wings of the latter should be drawn toward each other as much as possible, by means of the rack B, so as to offer as little resistance as may be to the horse drawing the plow. M. Messager has given the right side of the share of this "hiller" a direction parallel to the line of draught, in order that the implement may be more easily maintained in the proper position. This "hiller" will open furrows over a surface of five acres a day.

When the manure is laid in these furrows, the latter are closed by means of a furrow on each side, with M. Messager's large share [Fig. 92]. In this way three and three-fourths acres may be manured in a day.

[TOP-DRESSING.—It has become a very common custom in this country, to apply the common manures upon the surface —top-dressing, as it is called. The apprehensions that were once felt about the wasting of the valuable portions, by such exposure, are not now considered well founded, since the wonderfully absorptive powers of the soil have been discovered by the investigations of chemists. There seems to be a peculiar affinity between earth and those volatile compounds, which, escaping from decomposing organic matters, give us an idea of their ammoniacal character by their odors. A very small amount escaping into the atmosphere will be perceived, but the greater portion is at once seized, and firmly held by the soil, until needed by the roots of the plants.]

MODIFYING AGENTS.—We have said that the part played by these agents consists chiefly in modifying the original composition of the soil, so that it may the more readily lend itself to the full action of manures, and to the profitable influence of atmospheric agents. The application of modifying agents, so useful for herbaceous plants, are no less so for those or a woody nature, and more particularly for the vine. The principal materials of this class are the following :

Chalks.—The prolonged cultivation of the vine, in clayey soils, results in developing acid principles hurtful to vegetation. The application of chalk modifies this acidity. Moreover, if the ground is rather stiff, chalk has the further effect of loosening the soil and making it more pervious to air and water.

Chalky marls are usually employed for this purpose. They should be friable just in proportion as the soil to be modified happens to be stiff and clayey. These marls should be used in the proportion of about sixty-six bushels to the acre. The application of marls is also very effective in flinty soils, but the proportion should only be twenty bushels to the acre.

The marl is spread over the ground at the beginning of winter. It breaks up under the influence of frosts. It is then spread out as evenly as possible, and finally buried, at the first winter plowing. This process may be repeated every twelve or fifteen years.

[The marls of some parts of our country are a material of great value to agriculture, and they are becoming more and more highly appreciated by the farmers. Those found in New Jersey and other places in the cretaceous formation, and known as the green-sand marls, are rich in potash, yielding from ten to fourteen and one-half per cent. of that material, and therefore must be valuable applications to the vineyard. Immense quantities of these marls are dug, and shipped to considerable distances, by water and by rail. The deposit is extensive in West Jersey.

In many places calcareous marls are found, that can not fail to prove useful, if applied as a top-dressing, or used in the preparation of composts.

Quicklime is a most valuable material to apply as a modifier of the soil, and it exerts the happiest effects. This material enters largely into the improved agriculture of many portions of our country; even on limestone soils, the application is found to be of great value, but upon those which are deficient in calcareous matter, it is of especial utility. The lime is carted into the field, and distributed in piles, where it is allowed to slake by exposure to the moisture of the atmosphere, which reduces it to a fine powder; it is then called air-slaked lime (chemically, a hydrate). This powder is spread evenly upon the surface, generally of grass land, and plowed in with a winter fallow. From fifty to two hundred bushels may be applied to the acre.

One of the most valuable applications of quicklime, is made by putting it into the compost heap, with any rough materials, such as chips, shavings, or brush, mingled with sods and the soil. These substances are rapidly reduced, under the influence of the lime, to a fine pulverulent mass, that makes excellent manure. Lime should never be added to nitrogenous matters, as it causes the elimination and escape of the valuable ammonia, that is thus lost.

To fix and retain this important nitrogenous material, another salt of lime is used—the sulphate, or plaster of Paris, gypsum—the action of which is to change the volatile carbonate of ammonia into the sulphate, while the lime becomes a carbonate; neither is volatile, and the ammonia is then said to be fixed. This salt is soluble; it can be taken up by grow-ing plants, and the elements distributed over their organization. The happy action of even small quantities of plaster of Paris upon vegetation is very surprising, and has not been satis-factorily explained, as the sulphate of lime is very insoluble in water; but as the soil has been shown to be largely sup-plied with ammoniacal salts, particularly the carbonate of that alkali, and as these substances are known to react upon one another, I have supposed that the result must be owing to these chemical interchanges.]

Gravelly Sands.—Gravelly sands may also be used for stiff clayey soils, but they do not yield such good results as the chalks. They must also be applied in greater quantities, that is to say, at the rate of fourteen hundred cubic feet to the acre.

Clayey Earths.—When the vineyard is situated on a parched, flinty, or chalky soil, the modification of it, by means of clayey soils will also be an excellent plan. But care must be taken not to use clays too stiff for that purpose, as they would not mix readily with the soil. They should be applied in the proportion of 1,400 cubic feet to the acre.

If these chalks, gravelly sands and clayey loams are saturated with nutritive principles, they will prove all the better. Of this kind, are the chalky muds of roads, sea-sands, clayey earths resulting from decomposed sods, but all these will then act both as manures and modi-fiers.

[The removal of mere earthy matter, as a modifier of the soils we have to cultivate, is attended with so great expense, that such a course of improvement will very seldom be re-sorted to with profit. Moving of earth is one of the most expensive operations to be performed upon the farm, and should never be undertaken where it is possible to avoid it; and yet, in the preparation of our composts, it will be very well to bear in mind the especial needs of the soils upon which they are to be spread, and to select clays, sands, or other modifying agents, as they may seem to be indicated by the character of the land. With our mobile population, and the comparatively small investment in the tenure of real estate, it is often better to move away from a bad soil to a better one, than to attempt any very expensive process for its melioration.]

XII.

MAINTENANCE AND RENEWAL OF THE PLANTS.

AT the age of from fifteen to forty years, according to the kind of plants, the method of pruning, and the more or less favorable circumstances of the locality, the vine crops begin to decrease, and this decrease, slight at first, becomes, at last, considerable. A vineyard that had produced two hundred gallons, with the same care and the same manures, will yield only from ninety-five to one hundred gallons, when the vines are thirty or forty years old. This state of things is not entirely owing to the exhaustion of the soil; it is chiefly produced by the crooked form of the wood of the vine. The principal branches become too much extended, and every year they are cut in such a way as to form a number of angles, in which the anastomoses of the vessels make a labyrinth through which the sap circulates with difficulty.

It is, therefore, advisable to begin renewing the plants when they present signs of exhaustion. The time to be selected for that purpose is indicated by the extent of decrease in the product; but this diminution may be allowed to go further, if we be inclined to sacrifice quantity to quality.

For, we know that quality increases in an inverse ratio to the degree of vigor in the plant. Therefore, to renew vineyards in which *quality* is chiefly sought after, we should wait until such time as the superior quality no longer compensates for the diminished product. On the other hand, in vineyards where *quantity* is the object, this renewal should take place as soon as the yield does not give a sufficient profit.

In a well laid-out and well-kept vineyard, where the different growths are cultivated separately, and in which each plant is situated on a uniform soil, the plants of each of these parts, being placed under the same conditions, will, at about the same time, present signs of exhaustion which will necessitate their renewal. This operation may thus be performed at one time over the whole extent of the vineyard. Nevertheless, individual plants may become languid, or disappear long before the rest, owing to some accident—such as the bad soil at the point where the roots happen to be, intense frosts, the presence of hurtful insects, diseases, the carelessness of work-people, etc. In such cases, recourse must be had to partial renewals. Besides, if the whole extent of the vineyard be renewed at one time, all the old plants are replaced by new ones, and this acts very unfavorably on the quality of celebrated growths. In such cases, also, it is better to renew portions of the surface, successively—beginning here and there, with the most exhausted plants, and continuing the process from year to year. The product of the old plants thus serves to conceal, in part, the inferior quality of wine yielded by the new ones. In Burgundy, about one-twentieth of all the plants is thus renewed every year.

From what precedes, it is seen that the renewal of the plants is oftener carried into effect in a progressive manner than effected all at once, over the whole sur-face. Be this as it may, the renewal of the plants may be effected by means of the four following operations:

PROVINAGE.—This operation consists in selecting the stock nearest the point where we wish to replace one or more vines by new plants. Care is taken that this stock be vigorous, and provided with two or three fine shoots. A trench is then dug, which, beginning at the foot of the stock, shall take the direction of the point or points to be occupied by the new plants. The width of this trench is about twenty inches, and its depth varies between twelve and sixteen inches, according as the soil is more or less exposed to drought. At the bottom of the trench, spread a layer of compost, about one-and-a-quarter inch in thickness, and the stock, trimmed so that the number of shoots shall be equal to that of the new plants needed, is then laid flat in the bottom of the ditch, and the shoots are placed in the direction of the points where the new plants are to be. One of these shoots [Fig. 96] should be brought back to the point occupied by the parent stock, in order to replace the latter. *Figure* 96 shows a stock thus laid down in a trench. This work accomplished, and the stock and shoots held in position by means of forks, the trench is half filled with compost; then, the shoots are cut, so as to leave only two eyes out of the ground. A stake is driven beside each of these shoots; the surplus earth is left around the trench, which is only filled up at the time of the first winter plowing next year. In this manner, the shoots, being less deeply buried, take root more easily.

The stock chosen for provinage should belong to the row on which the vacant space exists, and this in order

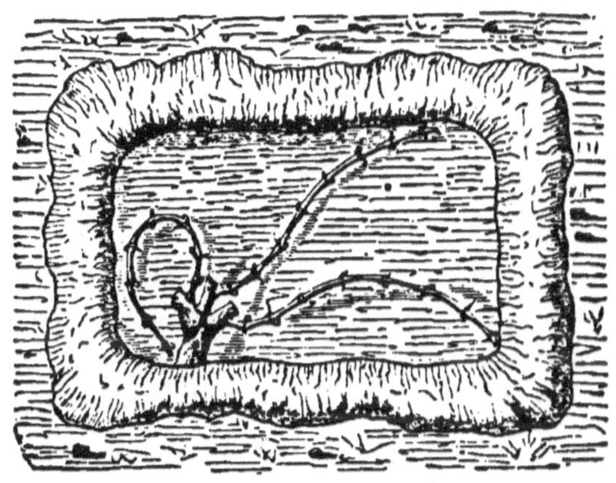

[FIG. 96.]—*Layered Plant.*

that a trench which would obstruct the action of the plow may not may not be left across the interval between the rows.

Layering is practiced late in the fall in dry soils, and in the spring in clayey ones. In the fall following the layering, and before the trenches are filled up, each of the young plants should be loosened a little, and such of their roots as are nearest to the surface should be cut away so as to encourage them to live through those which are deepest and least exposed to drought.

This method of renewal and of keeping up the vineyard, offers the following advantages : 1st. The vacant spaces are very quickly filled up without its being necessary to obtain rooted plants. 2d. A crop is obtained much quicker than from a new plant, for the propagated shoots often produce grapes the very first year, or, at the latest, the second year.

But, with these advantages, layering presents serious drawbacks. 1st. This operation is more expensive than the planting of young rooted vines, since a greater quantity of earth has to be moved. 2d. The propagated shoots laid down horizontally are less rooted than the young vines obtained by planting ; their roots strike less deeply into the earth ; they are more exposed to drought, and the plants obtained from them are less hardy, and do not live so long as those produced by rooted plants or cuttings. 3d. Finally, if this propagation is carried on for a certain length of time, the soil gets filled up with an inextricable net-work of roots, which are mutually hurtful, and working the ground can not be done without mangling these creeping and underground stocks, and diminishing the vigor of the plants.

LAYERING.—We have already described this operation, in speaking of the different modes of propagating the vine. It is also employed for the renewal of the plants. A long and vigorous shoot is chosen, growing near the foot of a stock, close to the empty space to be filled up, and on the same line. A trench is then cut, twelve to sixteen inches deep, according as the ground is more or less exposed to drought, and sixteen inches wide. This trench, which must be twenty-four to thirty-two inches long, extends from the stock to where the new plant is wanted to stand. The shoot is laid down, secured, and covered, as indicated in the article on "Provinage;" it is then cut, so as to leave two buds above the ground, and fastened to a stake. The trench is not completely filled up until the end of one year. The layer is weaned—that is to say, separated from the parent-stock, at A [Fig. 9], only after two or three years' growth.

The layering has all the advantages of the previous mode of propagation. It is to be preferred to it, when vigorous shoots are to be found conveniently situated for the operation, because it is more quickly done. The same objections are urged against this method of propagation, and it seriously exhausts the plant furnishing the layer.

CUTTING-DOWN.—This operation consists in cutting the stem of the parent-stock quite close to the ground, and renewing the wood by means of a vigorous shoot, chosen among those which always develop themselves after such treatment.

This cutting-down is variously performed in different localities. In Lorraine, advantage is taken of a shoot growing at the foot of the plant, and the stem is cut immediately above the point from which this shoot springs, which then serves to renew the plant.

In certain parts of Saintonge and l'Aunis, the foot of the parent-stock is slightly laid bare, and the latter is cut down an inch or so below the level of the ground. During the summer following the operation, a certain number of buds appear below the cut, and from these two or three of the most vigorous are preserved. The following winter, the most vigorous and lowest one is reserved. The stock is then covered over, so as to bury the base of the shoot which serves as a starting-point for the new plant. This latter mode of cutting-down, having the effect of causing the new stem to spring directly from the ground, is, in our opinion, preferable to the first. In any case, it will be advisable, at the time of this cutting-down, to give the ground a good plowing and copious manuring, so that the roots resulting from these renewals of the stems, may find the nourishing elements necessary for a vigorous development.

As to the value of this cutting-down operation, especially the last method, it is certainly to be preferred to provinage and layering, but it will be readily understood that it will only succeed when the plants have not reached the last stage of exhaustion.

PLANTING.—Of all the methods for the care and renewal of the vine, planting is certainly the easiest and most effective when the plant is in such a languishing state that the success of its removal becomes doubtful. In this manner plants are obtained whose roots are better distributed in the soil, and they strike deeper. For this reason, they are more hardy, and live longer. All the objections to provinage are also avoided. But this planting must be done with all the care recommended in our remarks on the establishment of vineyards. The renewal of the plants is executed here and there over the whole extent of surface, and it is necessary to use two-year old plants.

[It is found, in practice, that replanting an old vineyard with young vines, does not succeed nearly so well as replacing a dead or sickly vine by layering a healthy shoot from an adjacent plant. In planting, the new-comer finds the whole of the soil preöccupied by the roots of the other vines, which ramify through it, in every direction, and therefore the newly-planted vine has to struggle for existence, and seldom attains to a vigorous growth among its fellows, even when aided by the application of rich compost, or other good fertilizing treatment ; and scattered through the vineyard, as such plants necessarily are, they are apt to be overlooked. Whereas, the layers, if made with vigorous and healthy shoots, have the support of the parent-vine, to sustain them until they become fully established ; nor need they be severed from this connection until the second year, if there be reason to conclude that they have not sooner become sufficiently rooted.

Old vine-stocks are often renewed by cutting them off just beneath the surface, and allowing a sucker to take their place, but it is better to have this provided during the previous summer, by leaving a ground-shoot on such a vine. A whole year is thus gained, for these branches are not usually fertile until two years old.]

In the southern region, as a rule, they wait until the whole of the vineyard has become exhausted, and then the entire surface is renewed by means of a new planting, which is only done four or five years after the old stocks have been pulled up. During this interval, other crops are grown upon the soil. The old roots decay, and the inferior layers of the soil regain their richness, acquiring, by filtration, the nourishing elements they had lost.

This complete renewal, by planting, may also be applied with advantage to the vineyards of the North, when they have been much neglected, and the greater number of plants show signs of decay.

When the whole extent of a vineyard is thus removed, the cost of pulling up and digging, to extract
the large roots, is usually repaid by the wood of the

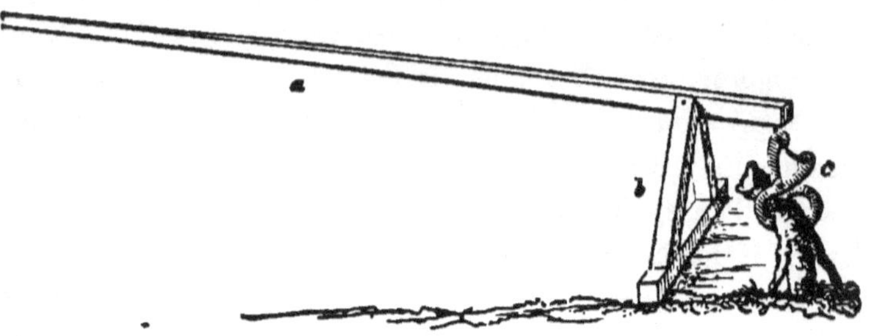

[FIG. 97.]—*Wrench.*

vine. Nevertheless, the work is abridged, and rendered
less expensive by using either the wrench, shown in

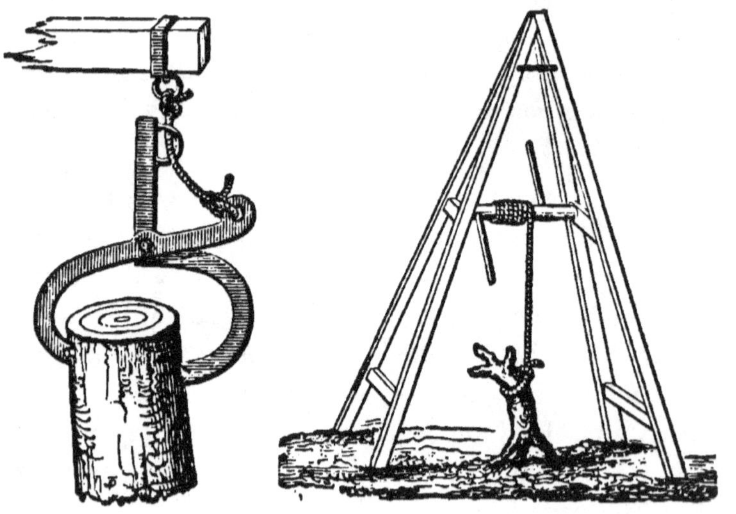

[FIG. 98.]—*Details
of Wrench.* [FIG. 99.]—*Crank.*

Figures 97 and 98, or the crank, employed in the vineyards of Saône-et-Loire [Fig. 99]. M. de Gasparin

recommends, for the same purpose, a sort of capstan, formed by a wooden axle on two cart-wheels. A rope is fastened to the head of the plant, and is then wound round the capstan, and the plant is pulled up, with all its roots. The work, by this means, costs one-half less than if done by hand.

[We have had little experience in tearing up old vineyards, and preparing them for replanting with grape-vines, and therefore can not cite the best practice; but, upon general principles, it may be said that the vines could as well be grubbed up, the ground plowed in the autumn, and exposed to a winter fallow, to be followed with green crops, such as corn or potatoes, well manured, and then allowed to lie in clover for a year or two before breaking up again, preparatory to replanting with the grape. Most of us would prefer taking a new piece of ground.]

XIII.

INCLEMENT WEATHER, DISEASES, HURT-FUL INSECTS.

A VINEYARD situated on soil, and in a climate adapted to the vine, and properly attended to, would certainly be one of the most productive kinds of farming, if a full crop could be obtained from it every year. Unfortunately, the same uncertainty attends the produce of the vine as that of other cultivated plants: inclement weather, diseases, and the presence of hurtful insects, but too often diminish its quantity, alter its quality, or sometimes destroy it altogether. Let us, then, see by what means we can fully counteract these evil influences.

INCLEMENT WEATHER.—The weather most injurious to the product of the vineyard, is, unusual cold, damp atmosphere, hail, and excessive heat.

1st. *Cold.*—A sudden fall of temperature has an injurious effect on the vine, according to its degree of intensity, and the time of year at which it occurs.

Early Frosts.—If a rather strong frost occurs in the fall, before the vintage, when the grapes are perfectly ripe, no harm happens to the plant, or crop; the quality of the wine is even improved. But, if the ripening is still imperfect, the grape withers, its ripening ceases, and it soon begins to rot. This accident can only be prevented by the use of mattings, or of the cloths of which we shall speak presently. These early frosts may also prove fatal to the young plants of the year, whose vegetation has begun late; their buds, which have not had time to mature sufficiently, are sometimes completely ruined, and the young plant does not grow again in the spring. Two-year old plants, carefully set out, will make a sufficiently early and vigorous growth, and this accident will be much less likely to occur.

Winter Frosts.—Although the vine is able to bear a considerable depression of temperature during the suspension of its vegetation, it sometimes happens that the severity of the winter frosts is such that the shoots are destroyed, and this effect may even extend to the old wood. There have been winters during which the plants in the vineyards of the middle and northern region were frozen to the very roots. Luckily, these accidents are very rare. It is impossible to foresee

them, and the expense of sheltering the plants against
them would not, in the greater number of cases, be repaid by the results obtained.

In those parts of southern Russia where vineyards
have been established—in the Crimea, and the neighborhood of Odessa—the winters are sufficiently severe
to render this accident one of frequent occurrence.
The plants are there protected from these intense frosts
by being buried every winter in a trench. Of course,
such immense labor can not be undertaken over large
extents of surface, except in countries where the price
of manual labor is very low.

In the vineyards of the Jura, which are often exposed
to this accident, the plants are often protected in this
manner: In November the young plants are laid down
and buried; as for the old plants, whose stems are too
large to be subjected to this operation, a shoot is kept at
the base, which is each year pruned to one eye. It is
this shoot which is buried, a little above its junction
with the stock. If the cold is sufficiently severe to
freeze the old wood, the base is still safe, where it is
buried. It is then cut off above this point, and the
shoot at the base serves to renew the stock. All the
plants are laid bare at the end of February.

Nevertheless, this is very hard work, and the roots
being often broken by the laying down process, the
plants suffer in consequence. For this reason, some
cultivators prefer the following plan: They think it is
enough to shelter the foot of the plant, on the south
side, by means of a stone, or handful of brushwood.
The snow is thus kept from melting in the sun. Now,
it is this partial thawing, which, occurring in February,

causes the plant, under the influence of the next night's cold, to freeze; this shelter prevents it.

[In many parts of the United States, it is necessary to bury the vines every winter, and those who pursue this plan, appear to think it a simple matter, not very expensive. It is known that a very slight amount of covering is all that is required to protect the vines from frost. Our author has happily hit the true idea, as we generally understand it, that successive thawing and freezing is what so hurts plants that are exposed to the rigors of winter. He accordingly recommends a slight shelter, such as a stone or a little brush, which wards off the sun's rays and prevents thawing. It is surprising how slight an amount of shelter is required; vines cut loose from the stakes and lying upon the ground, rarely suffer, but where there is a continuance of snow the protection is complete.

With young vines, there is little difficulty in bending down the canes and covering them with soil, but when the stock has grown old and stiff, and is large, it is a stubborn subject to deal with, and can not so readily be bent. It has been proposed to obviate this difficulty by adopting one of the following methods: either to plant the vine and train it, so that the stock shall be inclined to one side, or to branch its arms at a low point, very near the surface of the ground, and to train them in an inclined manner, so that, in either case, they may easily be brought to the surface, to receive their covering of soil for a winter protection.

The injurious effects of cold are sometimes quite severe—at others, very slight. In some cases, the wood appears green and perfect, while the buds are nearly all destroyed, so as to ruin the crop for that season.

Young vines—those recently planted—should always be covered with soil in the autumn of the first year's growth, particularly in the clayey, heavy soils, else the action of the frost may heave them out, and leave them on the surface, where the roots will be destroyed. It is possible, that in some very loose soils, the frost may destroy the roots of such young vines, without their being heaved and exposed, and the tops will have escaped, and may even push forth their leaves, to wither for want of support from these dead roots.

Such a result has frequently followed the fall planting of young vines, and the variety has then been condemned as tender; whereas, if they had been carefully protected until spring, and then set out and well tended, they would have become established in the soil, and enabled to resist the damaging effects of frost.]

When the frost has taken effect on the shoots of the vine, the crop for that year is lost; for, we know that the new shoots coming on the old wood, seldom, if ever, bear grapes. It even happens, at times, that a crop is not had until two years after such an accident. The only operation to be performed on the plants attacked by winter frosts consists in pruning and renewing them a little below the point where they have been frozen. The stock is then re-formed by means of the new shoots.

Spring Frosts.—The late frosts are the most usual foe, and the most to be feared, for the vineyards of the northern and middle region, when the frosts occur at the season of the budding of the vine—that is from the 15th of April to the 15th of May. The young shoots are then more or less affected, and the year's crop is destroyed. It is true that, sometimes, by the side of the shoot destroyed by frost, we see one or two new shoots with fruit-branches; but this only occurs when the shoots have been frozen on their first appearance, and have, as yet, absorbed only a very small quantity of sap.

22

Be this as it may, the crop thus obtained is far from equaling that which has been destroyed. Moreover, it often happens, if these late frosts are severe enough to destroy all the young shoots of a plant completely, that the vine grows no more, but withers. In this manner, one-tenth of all the plants in the vineyards of the Jura are destroyed annually.

These late frosts almost invariably proceed from radiation during the bright nights at the end of April and beginning of May. They are then called "white frosts." We know that all bodies on the surface of the earth possess a certain degree of heat peculiar to them. When the sky is clear at night, these bodies lose a part of their heat, in the shape of caloric rays, which rise into space. This radiation continuing, these bodies cool gradually, and the fall of temperature they undergo, is such, that the atmospheric vapor condenses on their surface. It is this first phenomenon which produces dew. If the cooling of these bodies goes on increasing, the dew covering them congeals, and gives rise to white frosts.

If the sky be cloudy, there is no dew, and, of course, no white frost, because the caloric rays, radiating from earthly bodies toward the sky, meet the clouds, and are sent back to the ground; there is an exchange of caloric rays between bodies on the earth and these clouds, but there is no decided cooling. The slightest obstacle interposed between woody or grassy plants, and the sky, would therefore suffice to preserve them from the action of white frosts.

As may be supposed, these white frosts are the more to be feared when the air is charged with moisture.

For this reason, frosts are more prevalent in the valleys than on the hills. On a vine-stock, the young shoots nearest the ground, and hence more exposed to cold, freeze more frequently than those at the top. A vineyard in which the soil has been quite recently stirred, freezes more easily than one in which the surface is hardened; for, in the former case, the evaporation of moisture is more abundant. Dew and white-frosts are not produced when the air is sufficiently in motion to carry away, by evaporation from the surface of bodies, the cold which is there produced by radiation.

[It is singular that after M. Du Breuil had given so distinct an explanation of the formation of dew and frost, which he very properly attributes to the effects of radiation, he should still be disposed to refer the evils of frost to moisture. And in the case of the freshly-plowed ground, to which reference is made on a previous page, our author attributes its freezing to the presence of increased moisture; whereas, it is the better surface of radiation, and its increased amount in the plowed ground, that causes the difficulty. The radiation being perfect, the cooling process will go on, whether the soil and air be wet or dry, but if the former be full of moisture, and its dew-point be low, the precipitation will be greater, and the dew or frost will be more apparent.

And so of the effects of a spring frost upon the lower part of a vine-stock being more disastrous than upon the higher shoots, the result is easily explained upon the common principles of physics. The radiation takes place from the surface, chiefly at the level of the ground, and the air is chilled only as it comes in contact with bodies thus cooled; the lower portion of the atmosphere must first have its temperature reduced, and the cooling of the next upper layer must take place very slowly, since the air is a non-conductor, and so the higher shoots on a grape-vine may escape when the lower ones will have suffered. The moisture of the air has nothing to do with the cooling and freezing ; indeed, theoretically, quite the contrary. The least motion in the air will prevent the occurrence of a frost, because, so soon as a layer of air, in contact with the radiating surface, is cooled, by giving up its heat to that chilled surface, it is borne away by the breeze, and mingled with the great mass of warmer air above it, and its place is occupied with a fresh supply of the warmer fluid. Every one knows the difference in the result of a still and windy night, even when the sky is perfectly clear, and the radiation is going on equally in both cases.

These views are confirmed by the venerable editor of the *Western Ruralist*, Lawrence Young, of Louisville, Kentucky, who has long been a successful fruit-grower, and a close observer of the influence of meteorological changes upon our crops, and of the mode in which they affect them.

In an article in the April number of that paper, when discussing the injury to the peach crop of the past winter, he says :

" The intense cold of our climate comes upon us in one of two ways, either by radiation, on still nights, or is brought to us in winds charged with the frigid temperature of the Rocky Mountains, generally moving in the wake of some rain cloud, and with the velocity of a gale, measuring sixty to ninety miles per hour. In the latter case, the driving force is so much greater than the power of gravity, that in passing over obstructions, such as hills, or dense forests, there is a volume of atmosphere on the lee side of such obstructions, below the cold wind, and undisturbed by it ; just as is often seen in a hurricane crossing a valley, the trees will be thrown right and left to the edge of the first hill, and the work of destruction will be renewed as soon as the hurricane crosses the valley, and reaches the opposite hill, but not a tree will be disturbed in the valley between. In cases when cold visits us in this way, the earth itself, and all the stratum of air lying between it and the rolling volume are warmer than the wind above. We know this because the thermometer rises as soon as the gale has stopped, but the highest points coming in immediate contact, lose more latent heat, and suffer most with cold.

"On the other hand, when intense cold is brought about by radiation, it is the crust of the earth, and low grounds which are coldest, and the air in contact with the earth parts with its heat, only by conduction, to restore in part that which the ground has lost by radiation. The hill-tops grow cold also, and rob the air above them of its heat; but, as the air on the hill-tops parts with its heat, it becomes heavier than the horizontal stratum of air pressing against it at the margin of the hill, and displacing the lighter air, it rolls down the hill-side, continually forming lakes or ponds of cold below, while warmer air takes its place upon the hills."]

It has also been observed that bodies in motion are less liable to freeze than those which are perfectly still. For this reason it is that the wine-growers of Auvergne, who preserve a long shoot on their plants for fructification, fasten it to the stakes only after the period of the late frosts. These long shoots, put in motion by the slightest breath of air, freeze less easily than those which are fastened immediately after the pruning.

The action of frosts is more pernicious to plants in proportion as the thawing is more sudden. It would seem that this sudden transition, from a frozen state to a higher temperature, makes a great impression on the tissues. It is for this reason that vineyards situated on hill-sides exposed to the rising sun, suffer more from frost than those exposed to the setting sun.

At all periods means have been sought to protect vineyards from the effects of the late frosts, and the aim of all the processes employed with this view has been to prevent the radiation of heat. Let us examine the principal ones.

The vine-dressers of Champagne, who drive in as many as twenty-four thousand stakes per acre, attribute to these stakes a certain preservative action against white frosts. It may, indeed, be the fact that these stakes, being so close together, oppose radiation to a certain extent. They may also act in delaying the thaw, by the shade they cast. We must, however, acknowledge that this means is very inadequate. Nevertheless, it is with this end in view that the vine-dressers of Champagne hasten to set up the stakes before the late frosts occur. Attempts have also been made to cover the vineyard with a cloud of smoke, which, producing the same effects as natural clouds, might prevent radiation. The process is this: At the period when late frosts begin to be apprehended, there are placed around each piece of vineyard, which must not exceed twenty-five acres in extent, heaps of bad litter, bad hay, brushwood, dried leaves, dandelion roots, etc., which are kept rather damp, and placed at distances of about sixty-five feet apart. This being done, account is taken of the weather. If the wind blows from any direction between north-west and south-east, and the sky be clear, frost is to be apprehended. In this case, early in the morning, before day-light, fire is set to the heaps of brushwood accumulated on that side of the vineyard whence the wind blows. There soon rises a thick smoke, which, being conveyed by the current of air, extends horizontally all over the vineyard. This smoke produces the effect of a cloud, and prevents white frost by opposing radiation. In vineyards exposed to the rising sun it will be advisable to keep up this smoke till about ten o'clock A. M., so as to delay the action of the sun on those plants which may have been attacked. It has been said that white frosts occur only under the influence of a perfect stillness of the atmosphere, and that, under these circumstances, the smoke, rising vertically, is unable to prevent them. This objection is true in theory, but it has been exaggerated. It is very seldom, indeed, that the currents of air are insufficient to lay a column of smoke. Be this as it may, we know that this process has given very good results in some vineyards, and even, in Auvergne, in saving the crops of large apple orchards. Besides, this method costs but a trifle, and only requires a little attention during the period of white frosts.

[This smoking plan is quite feasible, and has been practiced with the happiest results in this country, for the object here recommended. The peach crop sometimes suffers from a late frost, after the blossoms have set, and the fruit has begun to swell, but while the leaves are still too small to afford any protection to the tender germs. Under such circumstances, a sufficient volume of smoke to the windward has saved the whole crop from destruction.

A fog rising opportunely, has acted in a similar manner, by arresting the radiation, and also by preventing the access of the sun's rays.]

Some land-owners in Burgundy and Touraine have been benefitted by the use of another process, which is as follows. It consists in putting together the vine-twigs arising from the pruning, so as to make so many little bundles, tied together with a vine-slip. These bundles, about sixteen inches long, and having a diameter of about eight inches, are fastened horizontally above each plant, by making them cross each stake.

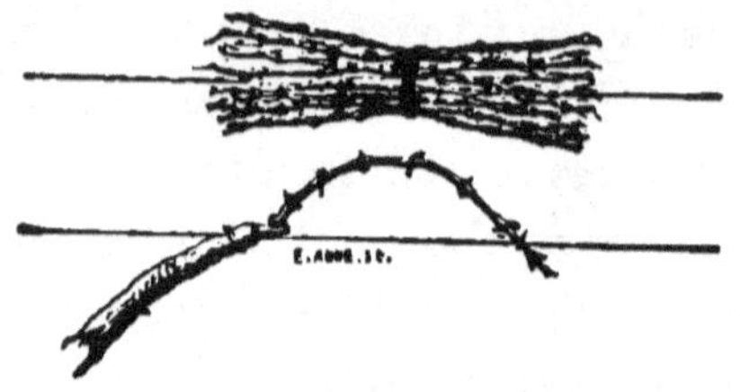

[FIG. 100.]—*Shelter made by Vine-Twigs.*

This process, which is not more expensive than the first, also gives very good results, by almost entirely preventing the effects of radiation.

For vines submitted to the process of pruning we have recommended, it will be sufficient to fasten the bundle of twigs by means of a single tie, on the wire above each of the fruit-stems, as shown in *Figure* 100; or we may, with advantage, use bundles of brushwood of any kind, such as heather, fern-leaves, etc., and these will weigh less on the vines.

Mr. George Perrier, a wine-grower of Ay (Marne), has contrived a plan analogous to the preceding, but which we consider preferable. Twigs of the broom-plant are put together in the shape of a fan, and fixed to the end of a stick, the length of which may vary according to need [Fig. 101]. This

[FIG. 101.]
Shelter made of the Broom-Plant.

is stuck into the ground, so that the fan may take a slanting direction, such as will shelter the plant from the rising sun. These little fans, manufactured during winter, cost little, and will last six years. One of Mr. George Perrier's workmen can set up about eight thousand of them in a day.

For vines subjected to the method of pruning we have recommended, these shelters may be placed as in *Figure* 102. The wooden handle is notched at A, so that the wire may be let into the notch, and the fan is fastened to the top wire by means of a willow-slip.

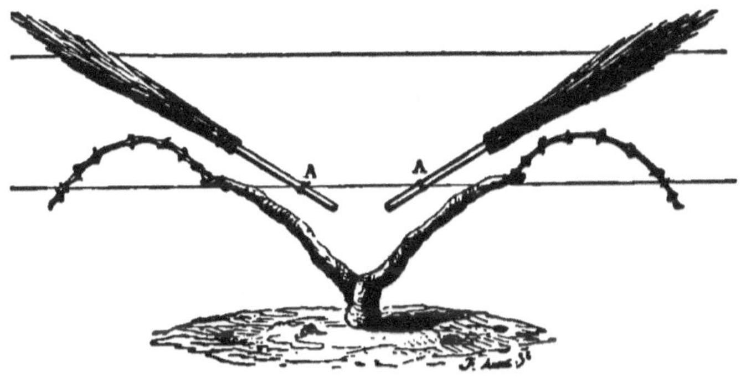

[FIG. 102.]

The shelters we have just spoken of may generally suffice to protect vineyards from white frosts—that is to say, from a fall of temperature not exceeding two degrees below zero (centigrade—about twenty-eight degrees Fahrenheit). Unfortuately, the cold sometimes exceeds this limit, reaching to three or four degrees below zero (twenty-five degrees Fahrenheit). This fall of temperature is no longer due to night radiations, but arises from currents of air which reach us from the cold regions of the north and north-east. It is not only bodies near the earth that cool down, but all the mass of the atmosphere is subjected to this fall of temperature.

The winter frosts, which occur late, do not act in the same way as the white frosts, and, contrary to what happens in the case of the latter, vines situated at elevated points suffer more than those placed in the sheltered valleys. Exposures to the west, north, and east, are more affected than those to the south.

The causes producing the late winter frosts being

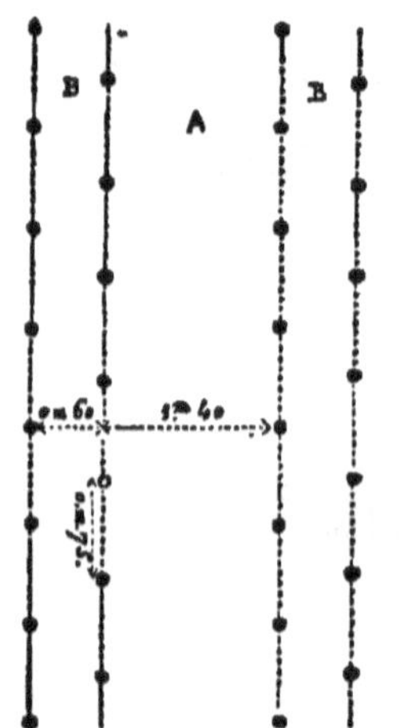

[FIG. 103.] — *Plantation adapted for Matting, at the rate of 5,200 Vines to the Acre.*

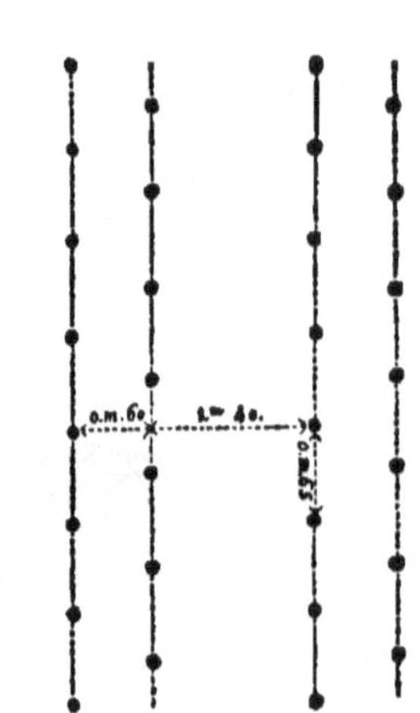

[FIG. 104.] — *Plantation adapted for Matting, at the rate of 6,000 Vines to the Acre.*

different from those giving rise to white frosts, the means employed to obviate them should be different. For this purpose, we must have recourse to more effective, and, unfortunately, more expensive shelters.

Doctor Jules Guyot is the first who has thought of adapting to vineyards, the mats employed in gardens for the protection of fruit-trees. He has described his method in a book full of useful instructions on vine-culture and wine-making. The method of matting which he recommends leaving, as we think, something to be desired, in the way of solidity and application to our different wine-growing regions, we have thought better to modify it in the following manner.

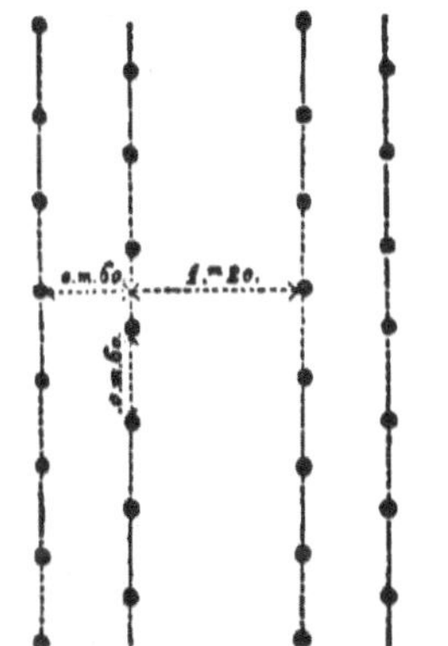

[FIG. 105.] — *Plantation adapted for Matting, at the rate of 7,200 Vines to the Acre.*

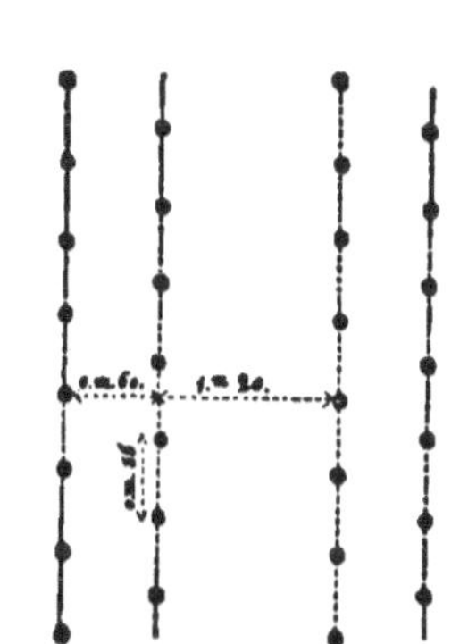

[FIG. 106.] — *Plantation adapted for Matting, at the rate of 8,000 Vines to the Acre.*

For this purpose, it will be necessary to make a change in the mode of planting we formerly recommended. Thus, instead of placing all the rows of plants at an equal distance from each other, it will be requisite to leave a space, first, of twenty-four inches between the rows, and then another varying from three feet four inches to four feet six inches, according to the number of vines to be planted on each acre. The space between the plants themselves, along the rows, will have to vary from twenty to thirty inches, according to the number per acre. To exemplify this, we give the following table :

NO. PLANTS TO THE ACRE.	WIDTH OF THE SMALL ALLEYS [B, FIG. 103.]	WIDTH OF THE LARGER ALLEYS [A, FIG. 103.]	DISTANCES BETWEEN VINES ALONG THE ROWS.
5,200	24 inches.	4 ft. 6 in.	2 ft. 6 in. [Fig. 103]
6,000	24 inches.	4 ft. 6 in.	2 ft. 2 in. [Fig. 104]
7,200	24 inches.	4 ft. 0 in.	2 ft. 0 in. [Fig. 105]
8,000	24 inches.	4 ft. 0 in.	1 ft. 10 in. [Fig. 106]
10,000	24 inches.	3 ft. 4 in.	1 ft. 8 in. [Fig. 107]

The consequence of this change in the manner of planting, will be a slight increase in the annual expense for the cultivation of the ground, since the plow can, in that case, be used only along the larger alleys—that is to say, over two-thirds of the surface of the ground, at least.

The plants submitted to the mode of pruning shown in *Figures* 32, 34, and 35, are fastened on two or three horizontal wires, according to the hight to be given to the plants.   These wires will be fastened and supported by the contrivance shown in *Figure* 71.

When the matting is to be applied to the vines, it will be requisite to place one of the two upper wires four inches lower than the other. That one should be made the lower one, which is nearest the quarter whence blow the prevailing winds of the particular region. Thus, *Figure* 107, showing a cross-section of a double row of plants, and the prevailing winds blowing as indicated at by the arrow at A, the wire, B, and its supports, are placed four inches lower than the wire, C. The effect of this will be that the mats, stretched upon the two wires, will offer less resistance to the wind, and that the rain falling on them will run off without penetrating them. The wires being thus placed, it is necessary,

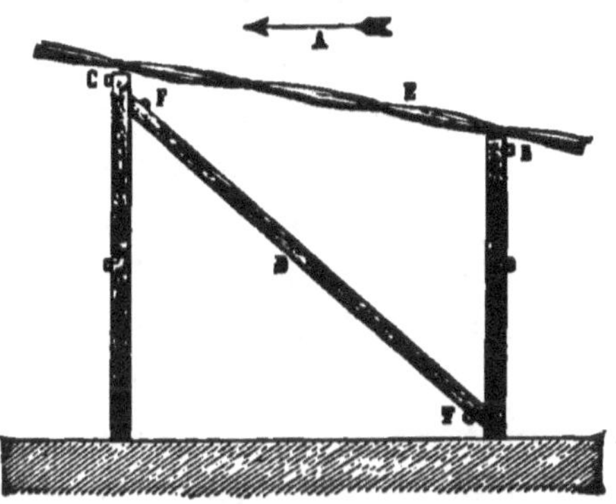

[FIG. 107.]—*Supports for Plants arranged for receiving Mats.*

in order to make the supports firmer, to connect them by means of a cross-piece of sulphated wood, D, laid obliquely from one support to the other. This cross-piece, which must be removed at the same time as the mats, to allow the plow free working-room, is fixed thus : the two ends cut on a bevel [Fig. 107, *a*], are fastened by the two screws, F. These cross-pieces rest alternately on the top of the longer and shorter supports. Thus, in *Figure* 107, the cross-piece rests on the top of the higher support, while for the two adjoining supports, the cross-piece will rest on the top of the smaller ones, and so on, all along the line, alternating.

[FIG. 107, *a*.]—*Cross-Pieces, for Supports.*

The supports being thus set, a mat, E, is placed above them.   These mats [Fig. 108], being thirty-two inches wide, overlap each of the two lines of wire by four inches, as they are twenty-four inches apart.   The mats are made of rye-straw, kept together by means of four strands of twine.   The straw and twine are preserved from rot by being immersed in a bath of sulphate of copper [Page 158].   The length of these mats is sixty-five feet, and they last about ten years.

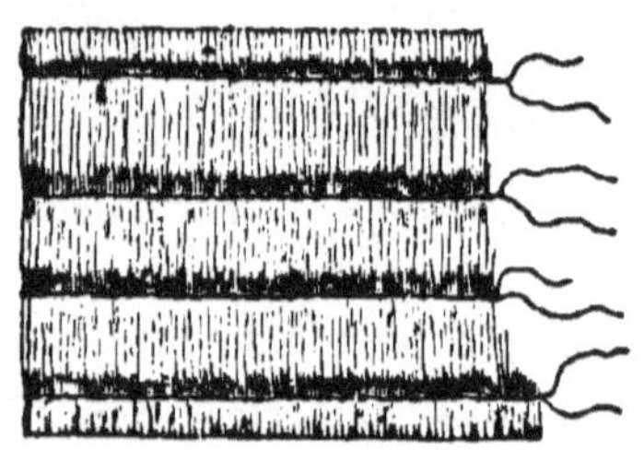

[FIG. 108.]—*Mat for Vine-yards.*

The rows of plants, at alternate distances of twenty-four and forty inches apart, we shall have, over a surface of one acre, the side of which is two hundred and eight feet, seventy-eight rows of plants, two hundred and eight feet in length.   As the mats shelter two rows at once, there will be required eight thousand one hundred and twelve feet of matting to the acre.

For the manufacture of these mats Dr. Jules Guyot has contrived a machine [Fig. 109], which, as may be seen, is but a weaver's loom, adapted to that purpose. M. Guyot has yielded the right of working this machine to M. Dorlèans, who follows this business at a manufactory, situated 37, Rue du Landy, Clichy (Seine). The mats manufactured there are too expensive to be used in vineyards, but if manufactured on the spot, by the vine-growers, they are much cheaper.   M. Dorlèans rents out machines for making mats, and gives all the instructions necessary for that purpose, but he reserves to himself the right of two centimes per lineal metre (forty inches)—that is to say, about eight dollars per acre of vines thus sheltered—less than a cent a rod.

[FIG. 109.]—*Dr. Guyot's Loom.*

The placing of these mats must be done as follows: In fine weather, and as soon as late frosts begin to be feared, say in April, the rolled mats [Fig. 110], are

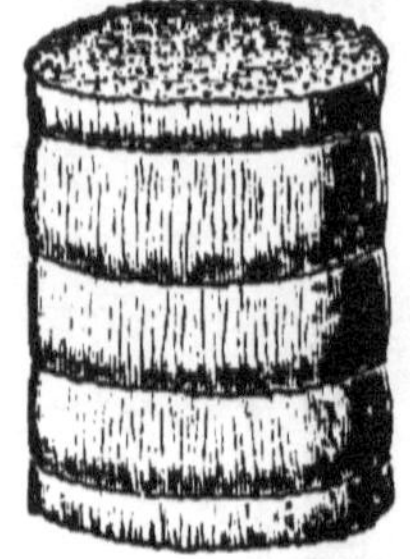

placed in the roads where the rows of plants terminate; two workmen then unroll one of these mats, along the wide alley separating the double line of plants, and, lifting it up, spread it out. Two other workmen, proceeding along each line, fasten this mat to the wires, by means of wil-

[FIG. 110.]   low-slips placed at distances of six
Mat Rolled up.   and one-half feet. They proceed thus until the mats are spread and fastened.

These mats should remain until such time as the berries begin to be formed. They are not at all in the way of the needful operations, such as nipping, clipping, and fastening the shoots, applying sulphur, etc. When they are to be removed, cloudy weather is chosen, so that the plants may not suffer too much by the change, taking care, also, that the mats are quite dry. First, the ties fastening them to the wires are cut, then two workmen take hold of the ends of a mat, place it on the ground, and roll it up; the mats are then put under shelter. This process of matting, including the removal and storing, requires about six days' work per acre.

During cold and wet years, in which the continued rains of the fall prevent the ripening of the grapes, as we shall explain further on, it will be very beneficial to mat the vines again, at the beginning of September, to protect the grapes from the influence of the rains. These shelters should then be left until harvest. Of course, this second operation must be performed in the same manner as the first.

The necessity of storing up these mats during the time they are not in use, requires that light sheds should be set up, here and there through the vineyards, to serve that purpose. A mat sixty-five feet long, and thirty-two inches wide, has a diameter of twenty-four inches. There must be about one hundred and fifty feet of this matting to fill up a cubic yard. Therefore, the eight thousand one hundred and twelve feet of matting required to cover an acre, being divided by one hundred and fifty, we see that to shelter the mats of a single acre, requires a shed of the capacity of about fifty-four cubic yards—that is to say, having a surface of twenty square yards, and a hight of eight feet.

Further on we give the yearly cost of matting per acre, and point out the circumstances under which its use will be profitable.

Summer Colds.—It is not necessary that the thermometer should fall below the freezing point, for the growing vine to suffer from cold. A marked fall of temperature, though insufficient to produce frost, often brings about results quite as bad as frost itself.

If the temperature falls for a few days at the moment of the first development of the bunches, there will be a suspension in the circulation of the sap, and in the growth of the vine. The elementary buds which the bunches bear will miscarry for want of nourishing juices; the pedicles bearing these young buds stretch out, and the bunch is transformed into a tendril. Vine-dressers, in such cases, say that the bunches have "run" (blighted).

[We have become convinced, by long observation, that these sudden depressions of temperature are often disastrous in their effects upon our vines, by favoring the dreaded mildew, which destroys the fruit and foliage of some of our favorite varieties. For the purpose of avoiding this disaster, Mr. W. Saunders, the intelligent manager of the propagating gardens at Washington, D. C., long ago suggested a plan for sheltering the vine trellis.* It had often been noticed that vines which were trained against buildings, and sheltered by the wide projecting eaves of the roof, escaped the mildew and rot, when all others suffered from this casualty. Mr. Saunders improved upon this hint by capping his vine trellises with a couple of boards, making a narrow roof above the vines.

This shelter has been found abundantly satisfactory. Such a covering must act favorably, by arresting, to a considerable extent, the cooling by radiation, and may thus prevent the effects of a spring frost also ; but it is considered a certain preventive of the mildew. The observations and experiments of Mr. Saunders have been verified by many others, in different parts of the country.

The expense of this mode of protecting a vineyard is considerable. At the usual distance between the rows, eight feet, there will be five thousand eight hundred and thirty-two feet of trellis per acre ; this will require two boards, of a foot width, to make the roof, or eleven thousand six hundred and sixty-four feet of lumber, which, in its thinnest, cheapest, and least finished condition, at twenty dollars per thousand, must cost two hundred and thirty-three dollars. Besides this, the supports, nails, and labor of setting them up.

An ingenious patent has been taken out by a man in Illinois, for a movable protector, arranged with jointed posts in the trellis, so that the whole apparatus can be let down in the winter—posts, wires, vines, roof, and all—as a winter protection. Common use precludes any one from patenting Saunders' plan, which he has given freely to the world, and its

---

*See Patent Office Report for 1861 ; page 495.

combination with hinged posts, though making a very pretty plaything in the model, would probably be anything else in its practical application in the vineyard, and would be attended with an expense which the inventor wisely keeps in the background; besides, its liability to get out of order would render it impracticable. Otherwise, its efficiency, both summer and winter, as a protection against mildew, and frost can not be gainsayed. Will it pay?]

A little later, when the branches are in bloom, the same fall in temperature may destroy the crop. Vegetation being suspended at the very moment when the plant has most need of all its vital energy to carry it through fructification, the young ovaries receive that influence but imperfectly, and the berries prove abortive. This is also called "running" (blighting).

Many means have been tried, to prevent running. The annular incision [Fig. 111] recommended by Colonel Bouchote, of Metz, diminishes this hurtful influence to a certain extent. It is performed by removing a ring of bark at the time of blooming, at A, immediately below the joint bearing the bunch. This incision, which should not be wider than two-tenths of an inch, is very easily performed, by means of the sapchecker [Fig. 112]. Unfortunately, this is too minute an operation to be performed economically over large surfaces, and has, moreover, been observed to have a deleterious influence on the quality of the wine.

[It is a common practice among those who attempt to prepare choice show fruits for the exhibitions, to pursue a somewhat similar course. They ring the bark below certain specimens, knowing that they will thereby be greatly enlarged, and rendered very attractive. It is one of the tricks of exhibitors. Sometimes it is effected by strangulating the circulation, by twisting a piece of wire around the twig, and was, no doubt, discovered by the accidental strangulation produced naturally by the clasping of a tendril. Like all other tricks, however, it brings its own punishment; for, it is found that, though very attractive, from their unusual development, the grapes are deficient in flavor and richness, and their value depreciates as soon as the interdict, " Hands off," is removed.]

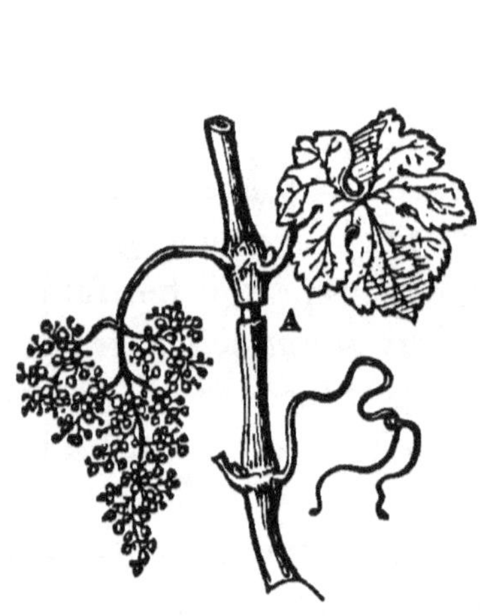

[FIG. 111.]—*Annular Incision of the Vine.*

[FIG. 112.]—*Sap-Checker.*

M. Troubat, of Bordeaux, has recently taken out a patent for a process having the same object, and which consists in cutting the shoots immediately above the highest bunch, and doing so as soon as the bunches appear. This process, which yields good results, has already been tried long ago, and at different times. It has been given up, on account of the delay it occasions to the ripening, and also on account of the abundance of false shoots that are developed at the foot of the principal shoots, and which endanger the crop of the following year.

[This matter has been very fully discussed, under the head of "Summer Pruning," in the editorial notes of a previous page. It is essentially the plan proposed and practiced by Mr. George Husman, of Missouri, and verified by many others. But, as already stated, it is done for a very different purpose—the development of enlarged leaves, and the successive crops of these valuable organs, and, through them, for the improvement of the fruit.

No delay in the ripening of the berries has been observed to follow the practice ; nor, am I aware that any difficulty has arisen from the development of the false shoots mentioned by our author, to interfere with the crop of the next season. Laterals will often be forced out, on the bearing branches, and so much the better, as we thus obtain new foliage to support the economy of the vine, through the season.]

Since the employment of sulphur to prevent oïdium (of which we shall speak, presently), it has been proved that the application of this substance to the vine, and to most other plants, has the effect of stimulating vegetation in a very high degree, and also that the sulphur, applied at the moment the bunches begin to be formed, prevents the running (blighting).

But the most efficacious means of preventing the effect of these colds, is the matting we have described, or the cloths we shall mention further on, and which are left standing until the grapes begin to be formed.

2d. *Damp Atmosphere.*—When the dampness of the

atmosphere exceeds the limits of its beneficial action, it may become very prejudicial to vineyards.

Abundant and continuous rains, falling while the vines are in bloom, are injurious to fructification, by cooling the atmosphere and suspending the vegetation of the plants.

[Another result of continued rains, during the period of inflorescence, appears to have escaped the attention of the careful observer who has prepared this manual. I refer to the injurious effect produced when they occur too profusely at this critical period—the washing away of the pollen-grains. This has been observed repeatedly, with different kinds of fiuit, and has sometimes resulted most unfortunately. Only last year, many of the vineyards in Northern Ohio were seriously injured by this cause.]

If these rains, which are frequent in summer, become almost continuous in September and October, the damage is quite as great. The vegetation of the vine then lasts too long, and the ripening begins too late. The grapes being watery, ripen very imperfectly, and rot before they are completely matured. The result of these circumstances is the production of very inferior wines, as was the case in 1860, in all the vineyards of the northern and middle regions.

[In our delightful climate of bright sunshine, we do not often have reason to complain of injuries from such a cause, and yet they do sometimes occur, and the excess of rain-fall during the summer months is known to have as serious an effect upon the fruit as a diminution of the mean temperature of the same season. This matter has been very fully set forth by Mr. James S. Lippincott, to whose essays on this subject, the reader is referred.* The sad influence of unusual rains upon the crop of 1865, in the grape region of Lake Erie, is well remembered by dealers in table-grapes, for which that section of country has become famous. The fruit would not keep as usual, but very quickly became moldy in the boxes, and was unsalable.

After a dry season, and as the vintage approaches, an occasional shower will appear to swell the grapes, and does, no doubt, cause their enlargement, but it is generally conceded that while the bulk of wine may thus be considerably increased, its quality will be impoverished in the same ratio. Dry weather is much more desirable, even at an expense of a few gallons per acre, which is more than compensated by the greater richness of the product.]

The thinning of the leaves, of which we have already spoken, and, more especially, the mats and cloths, are again the only means of preventing the injurious effects of too abundant rains at the beginning of summer and in the fall. For the last, it will be advisable to replace the shelters toward the end of August, and to leave them until harvest, as we have explained above.

Cost of Matting.—As we have shown, the use of matting may exert great influence on the vineyard, since it allows us to protect the latter from late frosts. Unfortunately it is a very expensive process, and applicable with advantage only to those vines whose produce has a certain value. The following is our estimate of the cost of this process for each acre, per year.

One hundred yards of matting, thirty-two inches wide, with straw and twine, cost:

---

* Report Agricultural Department, Washington, D. C., for 1862; p. 194.

Four hundred and five pounds rye-straw, at six dollars and thirty cents per one thousand pounds..	$2	55
Four and one-half pounds of twine, at eight cents per pound......	0	36
A man's and child's day's work..	0	80
Preserving with sulphate of copper....................................	2	00
Rent of Machine for this length of mat...............................	0	37
Total...	$6	08
Interest of capital, at five per cent.................................	0	30
Grand total..	$6	38

We have already seen that it requires about eight thousand one hundred feet of matting to shelter one acre, which, at six dollars and thirty-eight cents the one hundred yards, would give a preliminary expense of one hundred and seventy-two dollars. As these mats will last ten years, the annual expense, per acre, will be seventeen dollars and twenty cents for the mats alone.

But we must also take into account the building of sheds, in which to store these mats; and, lastly, the manual labor for placing and removing them. We have already said that the mats necessary for each acre require a shed of fifty-four cubic yards' capacity. This shed will cost about twenty-six dollars, with interest at five per cent. Its duration will be about twenty years, and this gives an annual expenditure of one dollar and thirty cents per acre, each year, for the sheds.

Supposing these mats to be laid down and removed twice each year, as we have already advised, this will necessitate twenty-four days' labor, at fifty cents, or twelve dollars and sixty cents per acre, including interest on capital, at five per cent.

We must also reckon, in this expenditure, the increase of cost for yearly cultivation, arising from the particular mode of laying-out the vineyard. This increase will be about forty-eight cents for the two winter plowings, and one dollar and sixty cents for the summer plowings.

The yearly cost of matting, per acre, will then be:

Mats.	$17 20
Sheds for storing the mats	1 30
Manual labor	12 60
Increase of cost for cultivation of soil	2 08
Total	$33 18

This is certainly a heavy expenditure, but capital so invested will often give very handsome profits. Nevertheless, let us inquire what are the descriptions of vineyards in which the use of matting will be really useful.

In the Côte-d'Or region, good vineyards of "Pinots" yield an average crop of one hundred and fifty-eight gallons per acre, which, at one dollar and twenty cents the gallon, gives one hundred and eighty-nine dollars and sixty cents. Losses arising from frost and blight are set down at the value of two crops and a half in ten years, or four hundred and seventy-two dollars—that is to say, forty-seven dollars and twenty cents a year. The matting only costing about thirty-three dollars, there would be, in using it, a saving of fourteen dollars and twenty cents per acre, yearly.

In the same region, the Gamais, when well cultivated, will yield, on an average, six hundred and thirty-three gallons to the acre, which, at twenty-three cents, would make one hundred and forty-five dollars and sixty cents. Failures of two and a half crops in ten years, make a loss of thirty-six dollars and forty cents a year. The matting would, in that case, give a yearly saving of only three dollars and forty cents per acre, for Gamais grapes, yielding the gross cash product we have mentioned.

In Champagne (Épernay, Ay) the crop amounts to about one hundred and fifty-eight gallons per acre, and the average selling price is sixty cents per gallon, or about ninety-four dollars and eighty cents for the whole product. In that region, the losses through frosts and blight are set down at the value of three crops in ten years, which makes a yearly loss of twenty-eight dollars and forty cents per acre. In that case, unfortunately, the use of mats would not be profitable.

The vineyards of Médoc give about two hundred and thirty-three gallons to the acre, and the selling price varies, according to the quality, from seventy cents to two dollars per gallon, or an average of one dollar and thirty-five cents, which makes three hundred and fourteen dollars for the gross product, per acre. The loss arising from frosts and blight is estimated at the value of one and a half crops in ten years, making a yearly loss of forty-seven dollars and ten cents per acre. Matting would therefore give, in this case, a saving of fourteen dollars and ten cents per acre.

Lastly, in the less celebrated vineyards of the moorlands, and on the hills of Bordelais, on the right bank of the Garonne, between Bordeaux and Blaye, the average crop is five hundred and and twenty-eight gallons to the acre, having a value of about one hundred and sixty dollars. The losses arising from frosts and blight are equivalent to three crops in ten years, or to forty-eight dollars yearly, per acre. Matting, in that region, would therefore give a yearly saving of sixteen dollars.

The foregoing examples will be sufficient to point out the importance of matting, and show under what circumstances that operation may be made profitable.

The use of mats to shelter the vineyard from inclement weather, presents one drawback, however—the weight of these shelters when wet, or covered with snow. This weight strains heavily on the wires supporting it. We think the objection might be avoided by substituting for the mats cloths, such as described below, in which case there would be no occasion to modify the system of planting, as is required when mats are used. The cloths should be such as are manufactured in Picardy, from the stalk of the thistle, and which are similar to those employed in the papering of apartments. Their texture, however, should be closer, and they should have a width of forty-eight inches. The wires which are to support them ought to be arranged in the same way as for mats. In order that they may be easily stretched on the wires, they should have

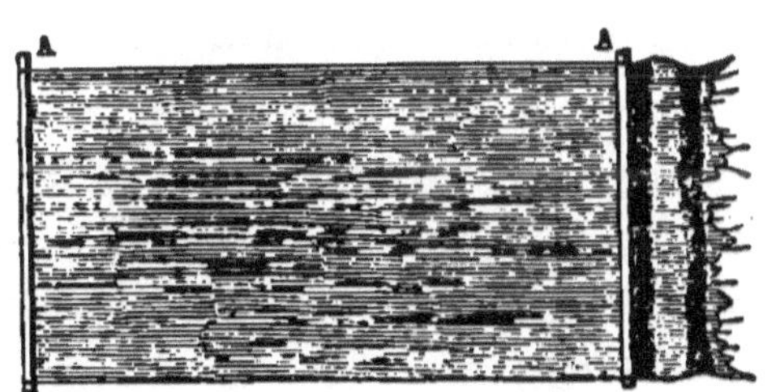

[FIG. 113.]—*Cloths for Sheltering the Vine.*

a length of about one hundred and sixty feet, and

should be provided with wooden cross-pieces. The latter, made of pine wood, and cut by steam, will be eight-tenths of an inch wide, four-tenths of an inch thick, and four feet two inches long. They must be fastened across the cloths at each end, in a seam made for the purpose, and placed along the whole length, at the distance of six feet apart [A, Fig. 113]. After these cloths have been manufactured, it will be as well to steep them in a bath of sulphate of copper, so as to make them more durable.

These cloths, with a close texture, may now be had at five and one-half cents the lineal yard. Their cost may be ascertained in the following manner, for a length of one hundred yards.

For a length of one hundred yards there will really be required one hundred and two yards, on account of the fold to receive the cross-pieces, which, at five and one-half cents per yard is...... $5 60
Fifty cross-pieces, at one-fifth of a cent each........................... o 10
Fastening the cross-pieces on the cloth................................. o 20
Steeping in sulphate of copper.. o 40

Total.. $6 30
Interest of capital, at five per cent................................. o 30

Grand total.. $6 60

All the rows of plants being forty inches apart, there will be required 2,200 yards of cloth, which, at $6.60 the 100 yards, would give rise to a preliminary expense of $145.20. The duration of these sulphated cloths will be about fifteen years, which gives a yearly cost of $9.70 per acre, for the cloths alone.

The sheds intended for the storage of these cloths may be diminished by three-fourths, for the same surface of ground—that is, may contain thirteen and a half cubic yards, instead of fifty-four. They will consequently cost only about $6.50, with interest at five per cent. As they last about twenty years, this will be $0.32 yearly, per acre.

The process of laying down and removing these cloths will be the same as for the mats, and they are to be fastened on the wires in the same way. They should also be laid down and removed twice every year, but as these cloths are more easily transported than the mats, there will be needed only twenty days' labor, instead of twenty-four, which, at $0.50 per day, will give an expenditure of $10.50 per acre, including interest at five per cent.

The use of these cloths will therefore give rise to the following yearly expenditure per acre:

Cloths	$ 9 70
Sheds, for storing the cloths	0 32
Manual labor	10 50
Total	$20 52

From what precedes, we see that the use of cloths as shelters, instead of mats, would be a saving of $13.50 per acre, yearly, at the same time giving results quite as satisfactory. Moreover, the drawback arising from the weight of the mats when they are wet, or covered with snow, would be avoided. Lastly, the much more moderate cost of this system of shelter would make its use practicable in vineyards where the use of mats would yield no profit—the vineyards of Champagne, for instance. For these reasons, we think that cloths might be profitably substituted for mats.

3d. *Hail.*—This scourge is all the more to be dreaded, as it can neither be prevented, nor its effect remedied. A few moments suffice for a locality to be completely ravaged, so great is the violence and rapidity of its action. Fortunately, it acts, generally, within quite narrow limits. But there are certain localities, which, owing to the situation of mountains in their neighborhood, are much oftener ravaged than others. When hail strikes a vineyard, not only is the actual crop lost, but even that of the following year is endangered, for the buds are so mangled that they can only produce weak and barren wood for the following year's crop. Nevertheless, if this misfortune happens to a vineyard in the beginning of June, we may still hope for a tolerable crop the following year, provided effectual means are at once employed. In this connection we can not do better than quote here the answer we addressed, in 1861, to the Departmental Administration of the Aude, by whom we had been requested to state what was best to be done for the vineyards of that region which had just been smitten with hail :

" If I have properly understood your letter, the vines of the districts ravaged by hail, now consist of stocks bearing the year's shoots, but the latter completely deprived of leaves and berries, and mangled on one side by hail-stones.

" This year's crop is lost : the point now is to save that of next year. This can only be done, provided healthy and vigorous wood is obtained for next winter.

" If the vines be left in their present state, the little sap that will be drawn into the leafless and mangled vines will cause a few weak and sickly shoots to be developed anew, and the stocks, becoming languid, will be a long time ailing, if they do not die altogether.

"The health of these vines can only be restored by the immediate development of new and vigorous shoots. If, to this end, the mangled shoots be pruned so as to keep on them five or six buds, the sap will cause them all to *develop*, but that sap being insufficient for all of them, they will only produce shoots too weak to be productive, and this want of vigor will cause the stocks to languish.

"It is, therefore, advisable to concentrate all the action of the sap on a smaller number of eyes, and, to that end, to prune immediately, as is done at the winter pruning, with this difference: that we must now prune down only to one eye, instead of two. In fact, only one single shoot is requisite at the winter pruning.

"Proceeding thus, all the sap will be concentrated on a small number of eyes, which will give rise to vigorous shoots. The latter will renew the organs requisite for the maintenance of the annual growth of the plants, which organs had suffered from the destruction of the leaves. The season is not yet so far advanced, but that these new shoots will have time to mature, and we may hope for a tolerable crop next year.

"In addition to this operation, it will be as well, immediately after the pruning, to give the soil a slight dressing, to assist vegetation by preventing drought. It will also be necessary, to prevent oïdium from attacking these young sprouts, by applying sulphur as soon as they shall have reached a length of about eight inches. This latter operation, being indispensable for keeping off that disease which acts more violently at the end of summer than at the beginning, will also have the effect of greatly increasing the vigor of these new shoots.

"Such is the process which appears most rational to me, and which I should not hesitate to employ if I had vines mangled by hail, like those of which you speak. It is, no doubt, a pity that the means I indicate involve fresh expenditures, but I think the loss would be still greater if nothing were done, for the stocks would at least be condemned to barrenness for several years."

If hail struck a vineyard at too advanced a period for us to entertain a hope of seeing the new shoots mature themselves sufficiently before winter, we should have to give up the idea of this short pruning. In that case it would be proper to reduce the length of the shoots only one half. Some new shoots will be obtained, intended to keep up vegetation in the stocks until the end of the season. At the winter pruning, the original shoots being better organized than in the former case, since they have been struck later, will be pruned as usual. It will, however, be requisite to prune a little shorter, for the plants will necessarily be less vigorous.

4th. *Heat of the Sun.*—The heat of the sun may prove hurtful to the products of the vine under the following circumstances: In the burning summers of the southern, and even the middle region, when the grapes are laid bare by a premature fall of leaves, the bunches thus suddenly exposed, and struck directly by a burning sun, are often scorched, and they dry up more or less completely. Bunches struck directly by the sun, at a very early stage, recover more readily from this accident, the cuticle of the berries having gradually become used to that influence. Nevertheless, when the ground is much parched by drought, and the vine no longer finds, in the soil, the moisture necessary to repair the losses it experiences, through evaporation, the bunches we have just spoken of may also be scorched.

[Sunscald is a trouble we do not dread, notwithstanding the great heat of the solar ray in our climate. By judicious summer pruning, and the avoidance of the defoliation practiced in Europe, and with healthy, vigorous vines, that do not mildew, and cast their leaves, we rarely sustain any loss from sunscald. This trouble will follow bad summer pruning, by which the foliage is too freely removed, and will follow the terrible defoliation of the vines caused by mildew, when this occurs early in the season, and it may happen when the vines have been broken down by a storm, or by the parting of the ties with which they were fastened to the stake or trellis. The first and the last are within our control; we may learn to do our summer pruning more judiciously, and we may be on the alert, promptly to restore the fallen vines, and be careful, when raising it, and securing it to its place, so to arrange the foliage as to cover every bunch from the sun. We can not so well manage to prevent the defoliations produced by the mildew, though judicious and persistent sulphuration promises to be effective. In this treatment our author appears to have great confidence, as will appear in those pages where he discusses the subject. Some cultivators have arrived at the conclusion that it is useless to plant such varieties as are subject to the malady, and they confine their attentions exclusively to the culture of those that appear perfectly healthy and hardy. This is a good practice, certainly; but, unfortunately, some of our very best table-grapes are those most subject to the malady; we have them, and are unwilling to give them up.]

To prevent this accident, the thinning of leaves, in the first place, must be practiced with moderation only during very hot years, and when the season is already well advanced, so that the sun has lost part of its power. Besides this, lighter plowings must be executed, to prevent the ground from drying up too much.

[The closing remark of this section, in which the author advises "lighter plowings—to prevent the ground from drying up," is so opposed to the established axioms of our agriculture, that it should not be allowed to pass without a word of explanation. Had he insisted upon more plowing than usual, under the circumstances indicated, he might have been pardoned for recommending lightly stirring the surface; and this would be sound advice, to plow frequently, even shallow, rather than not to plow, as all experience will show that such treatment will tend to retain the moisture of the soil. Late in the season, however, it is not desirable to stimulate growth, nor to retain moisture in the soil, and most vine-dressers would then lay aside the use of the plow, unless it became necessary for subduing the weeds.

One of our most successful and intelligent cultivators of the vine, M. Werk, Esq., was so impressed with the importance of keeping his vineyards dry, that he took pains in cultivating the ground, during the early part of the season, to make the spaces between the rows into shallow gutters, to carry off all the rain that might fall upon them, and for the rest of the season he used shallow scraping with the hoe, simply to keep down the weeds, and to make the surface as hard and smooth as possible.]

DISEASES.—The vine is subject to various diseases, of which the following are the principal.

Jaundice.—This disease is characterized by the change of color in the leaves, which pass from green to yellow.

This yellow color is owing to a want of tone in the cellular tissue of the leaves, which want of tone suspends their functions, and prevents the formation of chlorophyle, a green matter which imparts its color to the tissues, under the influence of light.   The cause of this want of tone in the cellular tissue always proceeds from a diseased state of the roots.   It is for this reason that jaundice makes its appearance when the roots are in contact with stagnant dampness, which causes them to rot, and when they are attacked by the larvæ of certain insects.   To combat this evil, then, we must remove its causes.

Red Leaves.—This second malady bears a certain analogy to the preceding one.   Nevertheless, it differs from it, in the color of the leaves, which assume a more or less deep red tint, as early as the month of July, and

[FIG. 114.]—*Leaves Attacked by Leprosy.*

finally drop off.   This change, which is almost always

fatal to the plant, is also due to the bad state of the roots.

Blight.—This affection presents the following characteristics : the leaves, the young shoots, and even the berries, assume a greyish tint, owing to the cuticle of these parts splitting, and drying up. The growth is completely arrested, and the berries split instead of ripening. Vine-dressers refer this alteration either to the cold rains of summer, following warm weather, or to a too abundant crop the year preceding. This disease is made to disappear by fully manuring the plants affected, and making them barren for one year.

Oïdium, or White Leprosy.—Of all the diseases attacking the vine this is certainly the most to be feared.

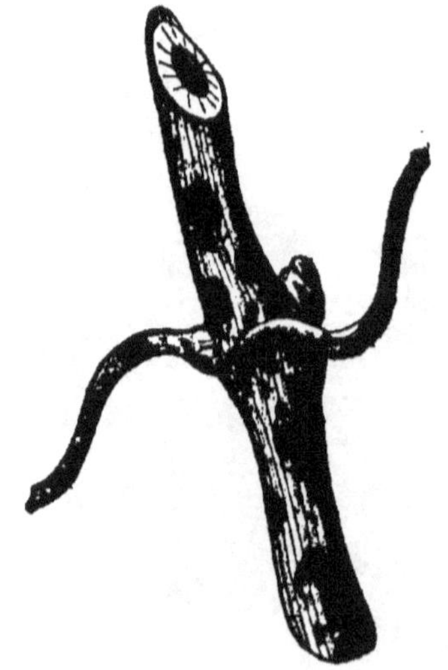

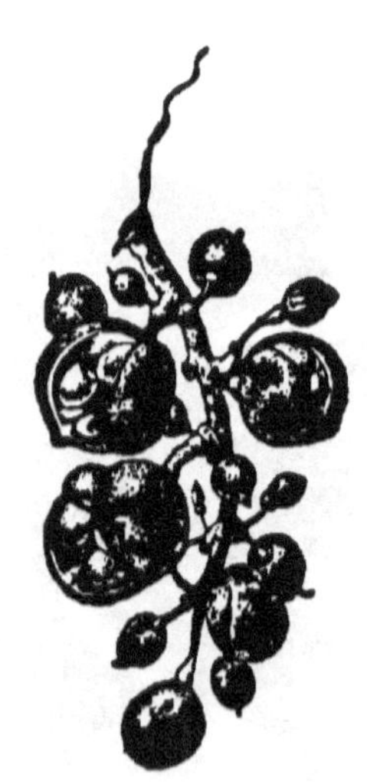

[FIG. 115.]—*Vine At-
tacked by Leprosy.*   [FIG. 116.]—*Fruit Attacked by Leprosy.*

This affection presents itself under the form of an efflorescence of a greyish white, first on the leaves

[Fig. 114], and the young shoots [Fig. 115], whose development it suspends, then on the berries themselves, whose growth it arrests. The cuticle of the berries hardens and assumes a tawny color; these berries split [Fig. 116], acquire a bitter taste, and rot before ripening. The leaves and shoots attacked are covered with brown spots, the leaves drop off, and, if the disease be severe, the shoots themselves are disorganized to their very base, so that not only is the crop of that season lost, but also that of the following year, and if the plants be subjected to this scourge for two or three years in succession, they soon perish.

It was in 1845 that oïdium was first observed on the vine in England, by Mr. Tucker, a gardener at Margate. Since 1849, this disease has shown itself at several points in the neighborhood of Paris; first on vines in hot-houses, then on garden trellises, and finally on vineyard plants. It has now, unfortunately, invaded all parts of our territory, acting more intensely in proportion as the vines are situated in a hotter climate, or have a warmer exposure. It seems to attack all varieties alike, but it acts with greater force on the most vigorous. [!]

Opinions are very much divided as to the cause of this serious affection of the vine. Some attribute it entirely to that white efflorescence which has been recognized as a little parasitical mushroom of the genus *oïdium* of the numerous family of the *mucedinæ*, and to which the specific name "Tuckeri" has been given. Others look upon the presence of this mushroom (which is not called in question) as the result of the disease, and they think it brought about by certain microscopic insects. Finally, others again attribute it to atmospheric influences analagous to those causing the potato rot. Thus, the cause of the disease remaining still undetermined, it has been difficult to find its remedy. Numerous means have been employed to combat it since its invasion of France in 1849. We shall only speak of the three following processes, which, alone, have yielded satisfactory results. The first consists in the employment of flower of sulphur, sprinkled over all the green parts when they are wet. This process, originally employed by Mr. Kile, an English horticulturist of Leyton, was first tried in France in 1849, by M. Marie, a physician of Ecouen.

All the vine-growers of Thomery employed it on a large scale in 1851. They obtained very good results therefrom, but objected that it caused the sulphur to adhere to the grapes, so as to damage the sale. Moreover the necessity of employing water, rendered this process somewhat unadapted to vineyards.

The second means is that recommended in 1852, by M. Grison, head gardener of the kitchen-garden hothouses at Versailles. It consists in the employment of hydrosulphate of lime, prepared as follows : One pound of flower of sulphur, and an equal volume of newly-slaked lime, are well mixed together. This mixture, placed in a cast-iron vessel containing five and three-quarter pints of water, is boiled for ten minutes. The liquid is first allowed to clear itself, and is then decanted. This liquid is a solution of the hyrosulphate of lime, and is kept in a closed vessel, to use as occasion requires ; it is then diluted with one hundred times its volume of water, and all the green parts of the vine are wetted with it. This mode of operating, employed in 1852 by a great number of wine-growers at Thomery, yielded results much less satisfactory than flower of sulphur.

During the winter of 1852–53, M. Rose-Charmeux, a vine-growing land-owner of Thomery (Seine-et-Marne) was warming vines under glass, by means of a hot-water apparatus. The idea occurred to him of spreading a trail of flower of sulphur along the copper pipes of his apparatus. The heat of boiling water was sufficient to create a sulphurous emanation, which completely prevented the appearance of oïdium. Made sanguine by this discovery, he determined during the summer of 1863 to submit all his open-air trellises to the action of dry sulphur, and he advised the growers in the vicinity to do the same. That year, almost all the trellises of Thomery were subjected to dry sulphuration, and the crop was unaffected.

The excellent effects of this process have been admitted by an official commission, appointed, on our representations, by the Minister of Agriculture, and the report of that commission, inserted in the *Moniteur*, confirms the claim which M. Rose-Charmeux has to the gratitude of all vine-growers, as the inventor of the only truly practicable and efficacious means of combating this terrible scourge. The indications furnished in that report have served as a starting point for all sulphur operations now applied to our vineyards and trellises.

M. Laforgue, a vine-proprietor of Béziers, was the first to apply it on a large scale. Messrs. Marès, of Montpellier, and Vial, of Béziers, by their writings, have powerfully contributed to the adoption of this method in all the regions of the South.

We now give the main precautions which sulphuration requires to produce its beneficial effects. The sulphur must be uniformly sprinkled, and well distributed, on all the green parts—shoots, leaves, and bunches. M. Charmeux perceived, and it has since been proved, that the action of sulphur is all the greater, as it is applied at the first appearance of the disease, and even before, for it is especially a preventive measure. For this reason, it is as well to make a first application of sulphur when the shoots have barely a length of six inches, a second one on the unfolding of the flowers, and a third when the grapes have attained to a third of their size. If an abundant rain should occur shortly after one of these applications, it would have to be immediately repeated. For this purpose, fine still weather should be chosen, so that the sulphur may not be blown off by the wind. The two first applications of sulphur are made over the whole plant; the third may be directed to the bunches only.

Certain plants in a vineyard—and always the same, be it observed—are first attacked by this disease, and may serve as a sort of index to point out the proper time for each application of sulphur. These plants are generally such as are most shaded.

Since the application of sulphur has become almost an universal operation, the consequence has been an enormous consumption of this material, then a marked increase in its price, and finally its adulteration. It is therefore important that consumers should beware of being cheated on making their purchases. It was at first supposed that sublimated sulphur, or flower of sulphur, ought to be exclusively used for this operation, but M. Laforgue has discovered that common sulphur, well ground, produced the same effects with the same volume; of course, as the latter is much cheaper, it should be preferred.

It has also recently been recommended that certain foreign matters be mixed with the sulphur, such as plaster of Paris and other substances, and this with a view of lessening the expense. But the results obtained by these means are not sufficiently conclusive for us to recommend them. .

[Mr. John E. Mottier, a distinguished and successful vine-dresser, for many years resident of the neighborhood of Cincinnati, used air-slaked lime in combination with sulphur. To a portion of his vines he applied the lime alone, and, as he thought, with equally good effect.

Some persons have claimed that even the fine dust from the roads would be productive of the same results in checking the mildew; but, unfortunately, the disease has been observed in some situations where the grape-vines are constantly covered with this material.]

When sulphur began to be employed, means were sought for sprinkling it as quickly and as economically as possible. With this object, two kinds of instruments have been employed. First—bellows, whereof M. Gontier, a grower of early produce at Montrouge, near Paris, was the first to contrive one for that purpose. This bellows was afterward improved by M. Gaffé, of Fontainebleau, following the suggestions of the growers of Thomery.

We subjoin a description of this instrument. It consists

first, of an ordinary bellows [A, Fig. 117], to which
is adapted the apparatus meant to hold the sulphur.
This is made of tin; consists of an oval box, B, fixed
to the end of the nozzle of the bellows, and having
three openings. The first [C, Fig. 118] admits the air

[FIG. 117.]—*Gaffë's Bellows, for Sulphurating Vines attacked by Oïdium.*

expelled by the bellows; the second, D, allows the sulphur to be introduced into the box, and is closed with a
cork stopper, E; the third, I, allows the air which has
entered the box to escape, taking a certain quantity of
sulphur, F, with it. The box is divided inside by two

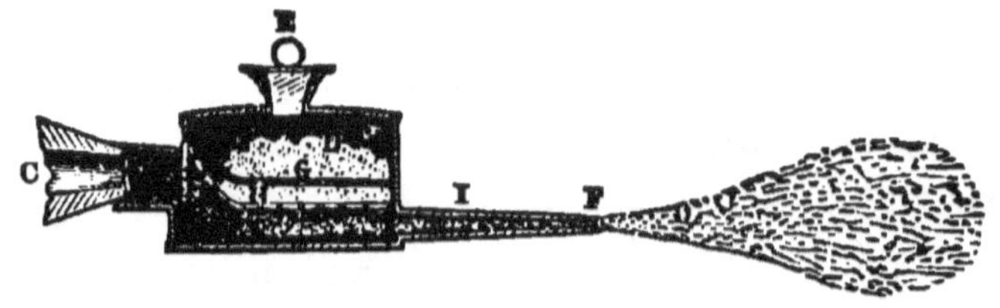

[FIG. 118.]—*Vertical Section of the Preceding Figure.*

horizontal open partitions. The first one, G, is composed of seven iron wires, stretched at distances of
four-tenths of an inch from each other, lengthwise in
the box. The second, H, is a copper cloth, stretched at
four-tenths of an inch below the first partition, and the

meshes of which have a width of about four one-hundredths of an inch.

It will now be seen that if sulphur is introduced into the box D [Fig. 118], and the bellows be made to act, the current of air driven through the nozzle, C, will follow the direction, H I, and meeting the sulphur running

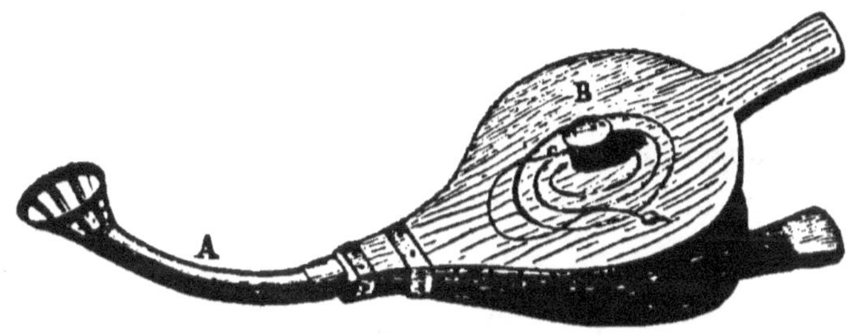

FIG. 119.]—*La Vergne's Bellows.*

through the two partitions, will carry it along, and make it appear at F, in the form of a little cloud, the impalpable particles of which will deposit themselves in a thin but sufficient layer, on surrounding surfaces.

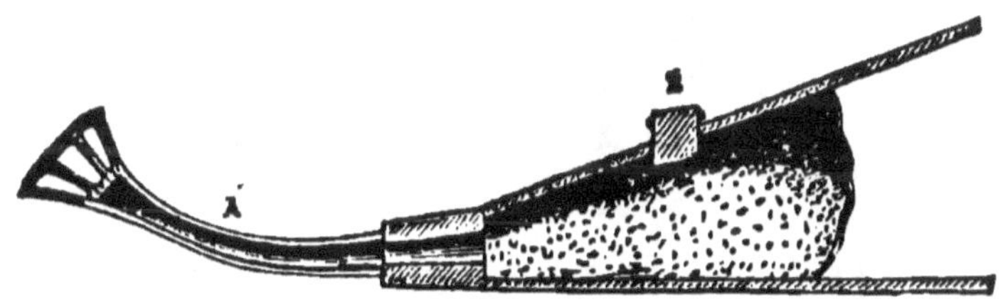

[FIG. 120.]—*Section of La Vergne's Bellows.*

It has been objected to this instrument that it does not work quickly enough, and furthermore, that the weight of sulphur being placed at the front part soon fatigues the operator. For which reason it is now nearly superseded by M. Vergne's bellows, constructed at Bordeaux.

The dimension of this bellows [Figs. 119 and 120], are those of ordinary ones. The top and bottom are made of poplar wood, and terminate in a nozzle, two and three-fourths inches long, the interior of which spreads from the inside outwardly. There is no iron work of any kind, either inside or out. The side-leather is fastened to the top and bottom by small common iron nails. A hole, one and one-half inch in diameter, is made in the top, and is kept closed with a cork stopper, B. There is no valve, the air coming in and going out at the opening of the nozzle.

[FIG. 121.]—*La Vergne's Sulphur Bag.*

The nozzle, A, is regularly curved, and has a diameter of one and one-fourth inch; it is fastened to the end of the bellows by means of two hooks, placed at the side. A copper cloth, with meshes eight one-hundredths of an inch apart, is placed in front. The sulphur is introduced into the bellows through the hole B, near the top. The weight of sulphur being near the operator's hands, the instrument is not so fatiguing. The workmen who are entrusted with this operation carry with them a small stock of sulphur—from five to six pounds—in a linen bag, fastened in front of them. This bag [Fig. 121] is thirteen inches wide at the bottom, only eight at the top, and eleven inches high. It is provided at one of its lower angles with a conical tin nozzle, C, closed by a cork stopper, and intended to introduce the sulphur into the bellows. The peculiar construction of the nozzle of this bellows allows the jet of sulphur to be sprinkled with ease in all directions —up and down, and from side to side. The cost of this instrument, at Bordeaux, is fifty or seventy cents, with the bag.

Other apparatus have been constructed on the same principles. But it is objected to them, as well as to M. de la Vergne's bellows, that the sulphur comes in contact with the leather of the bellows, which very soon destroys it. A manufacturer of Béziers has succeeded in overcoming this objection, while retaining the advantages of M. de la Vergne's bellows.

[The distinguished vine-grower, G. W. Campbell, of Delaware, Ohio, has produced an implement for the purpose of dusting his vines, that has some advantages, and may easily be made by any one who desires to use the sulphur, or other dry pulverulent substances, as a remedy against mildew.

Mr. Campbell writes that he can not give the expense of this bellows, because he made it himself, and kept no account of the cost of materials, nor of the time spent in its construction. He says he finds it very convenient and effective, and that he can throw a cloud of sulphur and quicklime through a trellis nearly as fast as he can naturally walk. He sends some drawings, which will make the matter clear.

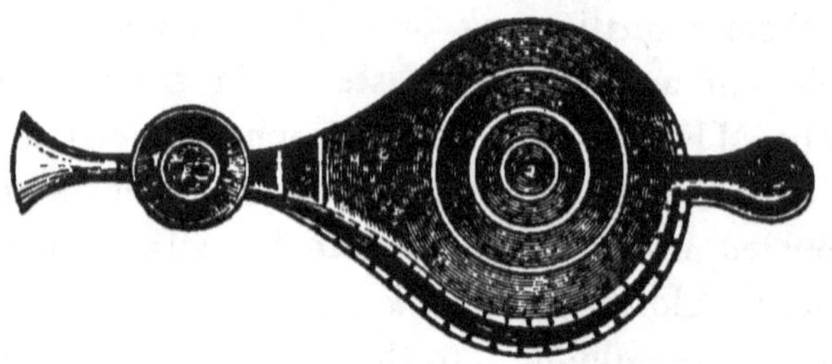

[FIG. 122.]—*G. W. Campbell's Bellows.*

A, reservoir for sulphur, made of tin, soldered upon the pipe *b*, which is also of tin, and made somewhat like the nose of a watering-pot, but left open, and flattened at the end, leaving a wide space for the escape of sulphur; *d*, a small

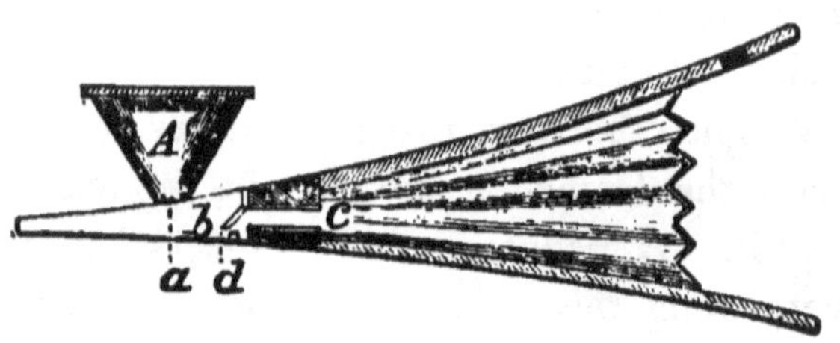

[FIG. 123.]—*Section of the Preceding Figure.*

leathern valve, opening into the pipe from the hole *c*, which closes when air is drawn into the bellows, preventing the admission of sulphur into the air-chamber; *a*, small holes in the bottom of the reservoir—by closing a part with pegs the quantity of sulphur can be regulated.]

The two following contrivances have also been made for the application of sulphur. The first is a sort of dredging-box [Fig. 124], invented by M. Laforgue, of Béziers. It consists of a tin cylinder, of a rather conical shape, and eight inches in hight. The base, B,

which is three and one half inches wide, is slightly convex, and pierced with a great number of small holes.
A lid, A, two inches in diameter, allows the sulphur to
be introduced at the upper part. Inside, a little above
the bottom, some crossed wires, C [Fig. 125], serve to
pulverize the lumps of sulphur. The objection to this
dredging-box is that it does not reduce the sulphur suf-

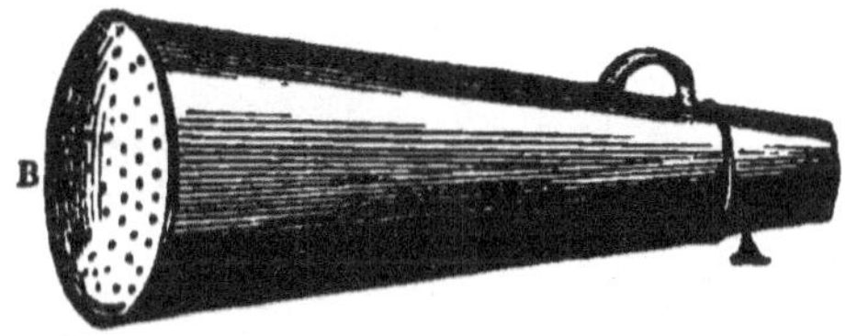

[FIG. 124.]—*Laforgue's Dredging-Box.*

ficiently fine when scattering it, thus necessitating more
material for the same surface, and it does not send out
the sulphur with so much force as the bellows, so as to
sprinkle the plants all over. M. Laforgue has improved
his instrument by diminishing the size of the holes, and
it has since worked well.

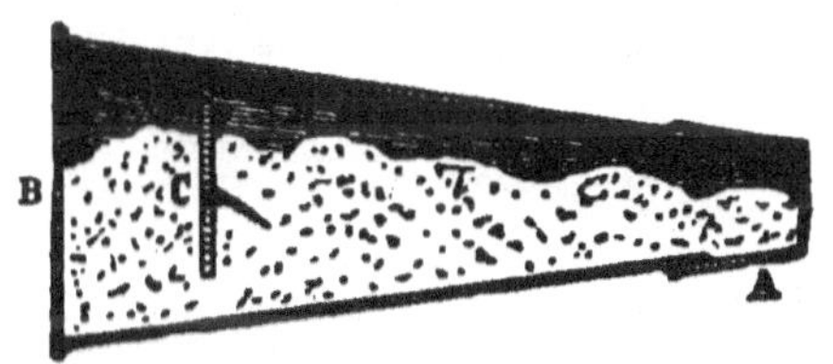

[FIG. 125.]—*Section of Preceding Figure.*

Messrs. Ouin and Franc have tried to improve M.
Laforgue's dredging-box, by adding a woolen tuft, A
[Fig. 124], attached to the bottom, B [Fig. 125], also
pierced with a number of holes. The sulphur is thus

more finely·sprinkled, but the instrument can only be
used after the evaporation of the dew, which, otherwise, would soon saturate the tuft and render it unser-
viceable.

We do not think that either of these instruments
should be preferred to the other, in all cases.   Thus,

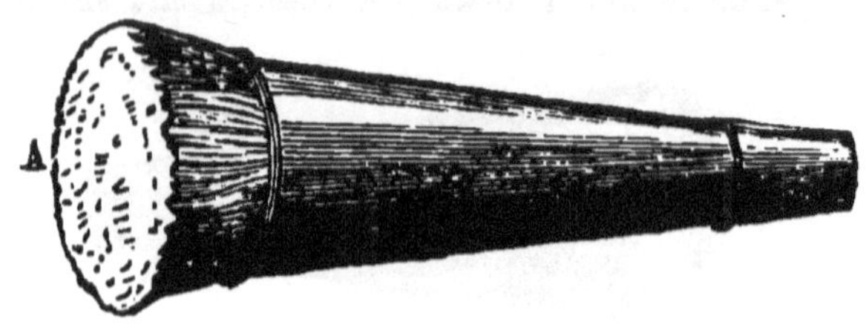

[FIG. 126.]—*Messrs. Ouin and Franc's Dredging-Box,
with Tuft.*

for the first two applications of sulphur, which are made
over the entire plant, bellows should be preferred.   But,
for the third operation, which is only applied to the
bunches, M. Laforgue's dredging-box seems to be bet-

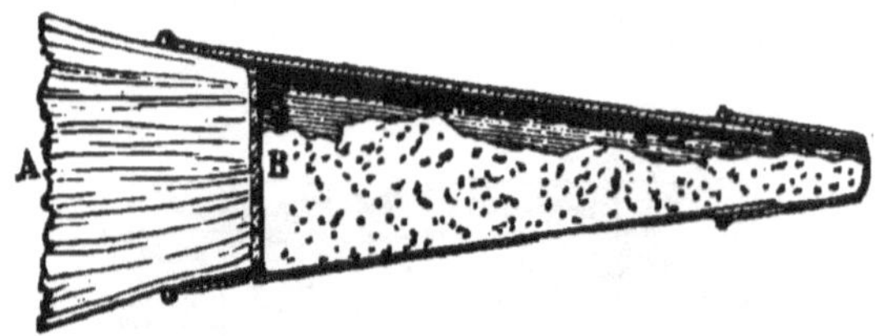

[FIG. 127.]—*Section of Preceding Figure.*

ter adapted.   This instrument is held in the right hand,
while, with the left, those bunches are laid bare to
which sulphur is to be applied.

One more question remains to be considered, with
regard to this important operation—and that is the expense it gives rise to, per acre of vineyard.

The quantity of flower of sulphur to be employed to the acre is, on an average, twenty-seven pounds for the first application, and fifty-four pounds for each of the other two—in all, one hundred and thirty-five pounds, which, at two and a quarter cents a pound, make three dollars.

To distribute the sulphur, requires twelve women's working days, at twenty-two cents, or, altogether, $5.64 per acre.

Of course the cost of this operation varies according to the price of sulphur and manual labor, and also depends upon what kind of weather follows the application—a rain-storm compelling the work to be begun anew. Lastly, that cost will depend upon the mode of pruning the vines—the creeping vines of Languedoc requiring more time, and calling for more sulphur than those of Médoc.

HURTFUL INSECTS.—*The Vine-Beetle* [Fig. 128].— This little beetle, known to vine-growers under the name of " devil," " scribbler," etc., has its elytra of a brownish-red, and the remainder of its body black ; it is to be found on vines from the month of July. This insect, in gnawing the leaves, makes on them those linear impressions that have been compared to written characters [Fig. 127]. When it is present in large numbers, it also attacks the grapes, and dries them up. It is when in the larval stage that this beetle is especially injurious.

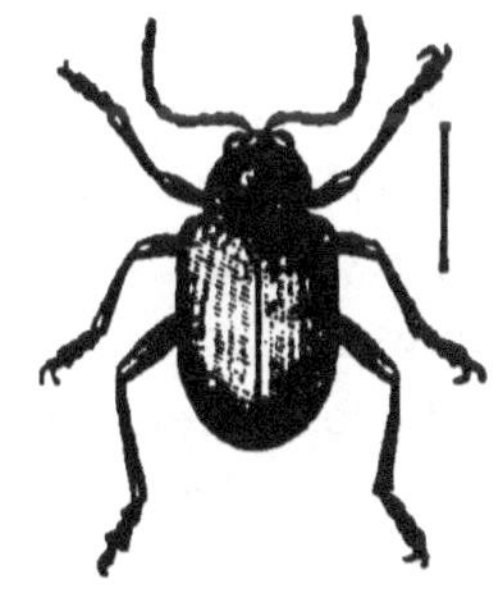

[FIG. 128.]
Vine-Beetle.

It presents itself in the shape of a little elongated worm,

first whitish, and afterward assuming a brown color.
This larva spends the winter in the ground, and gnaws
the roots of the vine; in the spring it devours the
shoots and young leaves.

M. Paul has lately conceived the following plan to
destroy this beetle. Grind oil-cakes in an oil-mill;
spread them over the ground in the proportion of 1,080

[FIG. 129.] — *Leaf attacked by the Vine - Beetle and
its Larvæ.*

pounds to the acre, and plow them in immediately.
These oil-cakes must not have been heated beyond
eighty degrees, and are made as dry as possible, otherwise the essential oil of mustard, which has the property of destroying the insects, will have disappeared.
The operation, repeated every three years, completely
destroys the larvæ of this beetle, which live in the
ground.

Spider-Shaped Beetle [Fig. 130].—The elytra of this beetle are green or blue. It attacks, indifferently, the leaves and young shoots, and, like the insect first described, it lets itself drop to the ground, as if dead, at the approach of a hand about to seize it. The female lays her eggs in the leaves, which she rolls up [Fig. 131], and which may thus be easily recognized, and taken off to burn.

[FIG. 130.]—*Spider-Shaped Beetle.*

[FIG. 132.]—*Blue-Beetle of Dunal.*

[FIG. 131.]—*Vine-Leaf rolled up by the Spider-Shaped Beetle.*

Blue Beetle of Dunal [Fig. 132].—This small beetle appears about the end of April, and fastens on the young shoots and the bunches, the stalks of which it eats. It pairs about the end of May; a fortnight later, lays its eggs on the underside of the leaves, and in the last days of June, the larva is hatched—a small worm, that eats the leaves.

No means of destroying these last two insects have, as yet, been found, except hunting them continually. When they are fully developed, a kind of very wide-mouthed tin funnel, ending in a bag, is made use of. The funnel is fitted to the foot of the plant; the stems are then shaken, and all the insects fall into the bag. This work should be performed early in the morning. As for the larvæ, they are disposed of by removing all the leaves that are rolled up, and burning them.

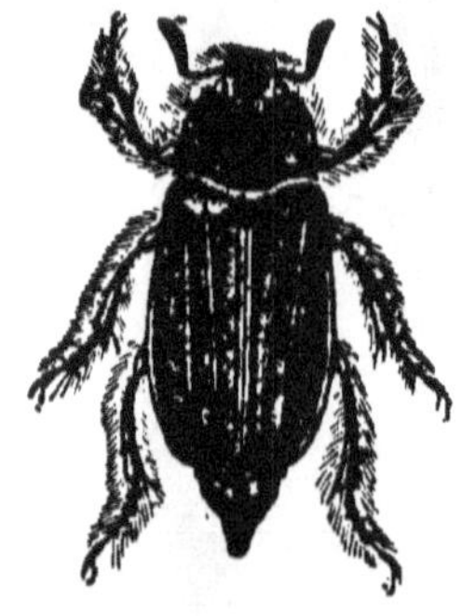

[FIG. 133.]— *Common May-Beetle.*

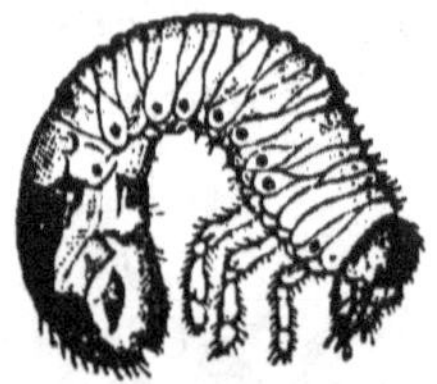

[FIG. 134.]—*Larva of the Common May-Beetle.*

Common May-Beetle [Fig. 133].—This insect is very destructive. The larvæ [Fig. 134] are especially feared, as they destroy the roots. They are known to wine-growers by the name of *White Worm, Turk,* etc. There is no other means of preventing the multiplication of this insect, than by destroying it, either in its larval stage, or when fully developed. The larvæ should therefore be destroyed, when brought to the surface by the plow. As these remain in the ground for three years, a periodical killing is all that will be required. The beetles, also, should be collected and destroyed. They may be shaken from the trees early in the morning in the early spring.

Some animals wage unremitting war against May-beetles: such are the bat, the rook, the owl, and the screech-owl,* all of which devour the fully developed insect, and the mole, which feeds on the larvæ. It will, therefore, be advisable not to destroy these animals in localities infested by May-beetles.

The Vine-Pyralis, also known to vine-dressers by the name of vine-worm. This is, beyond doubt, the insect causing most ravages in vineyards; it appears twice a year in the shape of a larva, or worm, and is first seen at blossoming time. At this period, its larva [Fig. 135] devours the leaves and young bunches, which it wraps up in numerous silky threads. It is next seen in the fall, between the berries, which it also covers with silky threads. The larvæ pass the winter in silky cocoons, placed under old ragged bark, or in the slits of old stakes. In April or May, they are transformed into little butterflies, of a yellowish white [Fig. 136]. These butterflies lay their eggs in July, on the silky tissue enveloping the grapes.

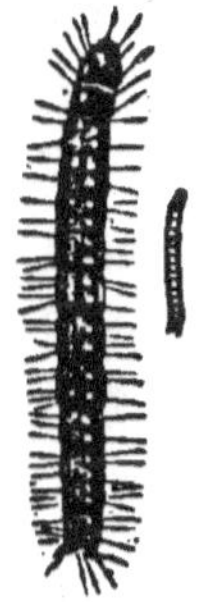

[FIG. 135.]— *Larva of the Vine-Pyralis.*

The three following plans have been proposed for the destruction of this mischievous insect: 1st, the careful removal and burning of all the bunches inclosed in silky threads, as well as of the rolled-up

[FIG. 136.]—*Butterfly of the Pyralis.*

---

* In this country the skunk eats the beetle, and the crow and blackbird consume the larvæ of our May-beetles.

leaves; passing the grape-stakes through an oven, during the winter, so as to destroy the eggs or larvæ that might be adhering to them, and the removal of old bark and of the moss covering the stem of the plant. These operations will certainly have a very good effect, but they are incomplete, and always leave on the stem some eggs, or larvæ, which, owing to the two generations they produce annually, soon infest the vineyard anew. 2d. The plan of scalding the plants with boiling water, has been tried with success. This operation, suggested by M. Raclet, of Romanèche, is employed in some vineyards, and particularly in Beaujolais, where, by its means, the pyralis, that had made great ravages during several years has been got rid of. The process is as follows :

Immediately after the pruning, and before vegetation has set in, when there is neither frost, wind, nor rain, a workman, provided with a tin pot, holding one quart, and having a long, tapering spout [Fig. 137], pours boiling water over the old wood of the plant, so so as to wet all the surface of each stem. Care must be taken to avoid wetting the young shoots with this water, as it would destroy them. This scalding suffices to kill the larvæ and eggs deposited in the cavities of the bark. We borrow from the *Journal of Practical Agriculture*, the cut of the boiler intended to heat the water [Fig. 138]. This apparatus consists of a chimney, or heating cylinder, F F, rising from the fireplace E, and forming the interior walls of the boiler. The exterior walls of the vessel, A, B, C, are twelve and three-quarter inches in diameter at C, and ten inches in diameter at A. The fire-place curved, and

spreading out fourteen and a half inches at C, rises
thirty-two inches, to B. D
is the funnel for filling the
vessel; G, the steam-valve;
II, two stop-cocks, for boiling water; HH, two hooks,
through which two stakes
are slipped, to carry the apparatus; J is the fire-grate.
The grate and hooks are of

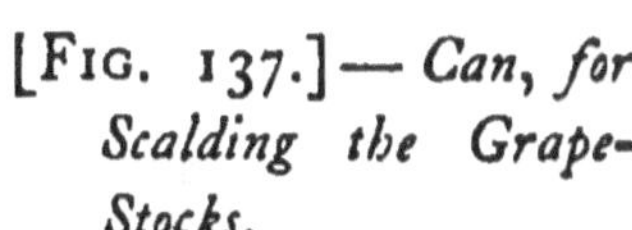

[FIG. 137.]— *Can, for
Scalding the Grape-
Stocks.*

iron; all the rest is made of copper. This apparatus
is heated with coke.
Every quart of boil-
ing water taken out
is replaced by its
equivalent of cold
water. The water
does not cease boil-
ing, and keeps four
men at work. Two
thousand vines can
be scalded in a day.

This mode of op-
erating gives very
good results, but, in
order that the suc-
cess may be entire,
the stakes must also
be scalded, or passed
through an oven.

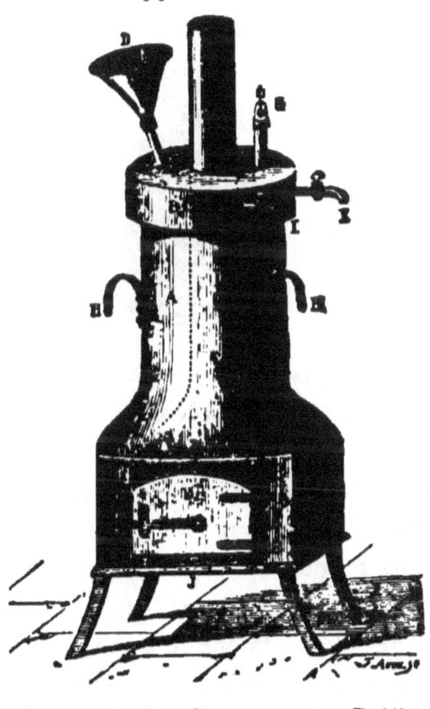

[FIG. 138.]—*Furnace, for Boiling
Water in the Vineyard.*

3d. M. George
Perrier, a wine-grower at Ay (Marne), has employed

sulphurous acid with great success, for the destruction of the pyralis. This is his process:

For Stakes.—These being stacked up here and there in the vineyard, during winter, as shown in *Figure* 68, he covers each with a kind of wooden bell [Fig. 139], having two iron handles. Before placing this bell over the stakes, a vessel full of sulphur is placed close beside them, on the ground; fire is applied to it, and the bell is put over all, care being taken to keep a little earth round the base of the bell, to prevent the admission of external air. The fire continues to burn until the air is exhausted of its oxygen, and this produces sulphurous acid gas, which kills off the larvæ and eggs lodged in the seams of the stakes. In the space of about two hours, the desired effect is produced, and the bell may be removed and placed on another stack.

[FIG. 139.]—*Wooden Bell, for Sulphurating the Stakes.*

For the Plants.—M. Perrier begins immediately after the pruning, before the stakes are placed, and before there is any sign that vegetation has commenced. It is also proper to begin before laying down the plants—an operation usual in Champagne—as described on page 180. Were this not done, the eggs and larvæ of the pyralis might be buried, which would not hinder them from being developed. When the time for operating has arrived, a piece of tile, on which is laid a sulphurated wick, is placed at the foot of each vine; the match is lighted, and each plant is covered with an iron bell [Fig. 140], which must be perfectly air-tight, and of sufficient dimensions to inclose the plants, without crowding them. These bells are slightly pressed into the ground, to prevent the entrance of air at the bottom. The effect is then the same as that produced on the stakes. In order that the operation may go on rapidly enough, it would be advisable to have about one hundred of these small bells, so that when the last has been laid down, sufficient time may have elapsed—say two hours—since the

[FIG. 140.]—
Iron Bell, for Sulphurating the Plants.

placing of the first, which should then be transferred to another plant, and so on with the rest, throughout the extent of the vineyard. Of course, the dimensions of these bells must necessarily vary with that of the plants, and the length of sulphurated wick to be used should proportioned to the size of the bells. It will always be better to put too much than too little. M. George Perrier estimates the cost of this process, both for stakes and plants, at $14.40 per acre. But it must not be forgotten that in that part of Champagne there are 24,000 plants to the acre. It is true that these plants are reduced to very small dimensions, as we have shown, further back.

[We have an insect in the United States, which is very similar to the May-beetle of Europe, and called by the same popular names, but by the entomologists it is named the *Lachnosterna fusca.* It appears, in the winged state, early in May and is often quite injurious to many of our cultivated fruits, but I do not know that it has been found to damage the vine. The larva is the common white grub, and as it remains a long while in the ground in this form, and is quite a voracious feeder, it is often very destructive ; though I am not aware of its ever having been detected eating the roots of the grape-vine, its appetite for similar vegetation renders it an unwelcome visitant. The remedies and the natural enemies are similar to those given by the author.

Pelidnota punctata, is the name of a much larger beetle, which feeds upon the grape-leaves in midsummer, and consumes considerable quantities of the foliage. I have not learned its history in the larval condition, but suppose the grub may also prefer to feed upon the vine, and if so, it will destroy the roots.

The perfect insect is to be found in the day-time, among the leaves, where it may easily be caught, and should be destroyed. It may be known by its large size; the wing-covers are shining, of a dull yellow, marked by three black dots on the outer side of each, and one on each side of the thorax.

The Rose-Beetle (*Macrodactylus subspinosa*) is often very injurious to the grape-vine, sometimes destroying the crop by cutting off the bunches, as well as eating the foliage in May and June.

In its perfect state, this insect is exceedingly voracious to many of our cultivated plants. Though each individual be quite small—about half an inch long—their immense numbers cause serious destruction of vegetation, and they continue to feed for about a month. The rose-beetle is .33 of an inch long, is of a dull, rather pale buff yellow. The claws are large and black. Their eggs are deposited in the ground, where they hatch in about twenty days, and the grubs feed upon roots, until fall, when they descend into the ground to hybernate, and emerge the next season as beetles.

The Rose-Chaffer has many natural enemies among predaceous insects, but we must depend upon human agencies for their destruction; hopeless as the task may appear, they must be gathered and destroyed by hand if we would save our crops where they abound. They are sluggish, and easily caught, when they may be destroyed by throwing into hot water. The appearance of this insect is often quite local, being abundant in one neighborhood, and rarely seen in others.

The *Haltica chalybea*, or Grape-vine Flea-Beetle, is a very annoying insect in some vineyards. Though quite small, being only 0.16 of an inch in length, it is voracious, and eats into the buds and young shoots as they swell and begin to push. This beetle is oval, shiny, deep greenish-blue, or deep green, or purple. The name "chalybea," is intended to describe this varying, steel-blue color.

The insect spends the winter in the ground near the foot of the vine, feeding upon the roots. This beetle is referred to in vol. II, page 60, of the *Practical Entomologist,* which every vine-dresser should read; and in vol. I, page 40, is a description by J. Kirkpatrick, of Cleveland, Ohio, in which neighborhood the haltica is quite troublesome. With regard to the larval condition of these insects, he says, that "the eggs are laid upon the leaves in May; when hatched, they feed upon the upper surface. They soon arrive at their full growth, when they are about three-eighths of an inch long, light-brown, with eight rows of black spots above, those of the two dorsal being confluent; head and feet black; antennæ very short; on each of the spots on the back there is a single hair, and from the breathing apertures, two. * * * When in motion, it brings its body up with a jerk. About the first of June, it enters the ground, and changes to a pupa, emerging from it in about fourteen days, as a perfect insect. There are several broods in the season. * * * * *

It is difficult to capture the perfect insects, although much may be done during cool weather, by careful hand-picking.

The larvæ are rather tenacious of life. When not numerous, the most certain method of shortening their days, is to pick off the infested leaves, and to burn them ; but this can not be done when they are very numerous. I would recommend syringing with lime, or very strong soap-suds—whale-oil soap is the best. Dusting newly air-slaked lime on the leaves, when dry, will probably have a good effect."

In the lake-shore vine-region, of Ohio, a curculio—species unknown—has been found, affecting the shoots of the current year's growth. The egg is deposited at some time during the summer. A mark similar to that found upon the plum is seen on the bark of an internode; on cutting open the wood, a small worm is found, unless it has changed to the beetle, when it escapes through a small, round hole. My attention was directed to this insect by Charles Carpenter, of Kelley's Island, who may be called the pioneer grape-grower of that favored region.

The grub being yet a study for entomologists, and comparatively little known, I have not been able to identify this species. It will probably be spread, by transporting cuttings and vines.

The common curculio, *Conotrachelus nenuphar* (Herbert), is accused of depositing its eggs in the grape, as in other smooth-skinned fruits. This is doubted by many observers ; and, forsooth, the little Turk has sins enough to answer for without having this laid to his charge.

In the next order—the *Orthoptera*—we find the tree crickets, some of which deposit their eggs in the vine shoots that are marked with a roughish raised line between the joints ; if cut or broken, the fibers will be found pierced and torn to the pith, and a double row of yellowish eggs may be seen. These insects were formerly supposed to be vegetable feeders, but from an article in the *Practical Entomologist* for February, 1867, it appears that one species, at least, may prove to be a valuable friend to the grape-grower, as it is stated that the favorite food of the tree-cricket, *Œcanthus niveus*, was aphides, particularly those from the pear and the grape. This, the Editor well observes, is an important fact. The observer, by the by, is a lady, living in Port Byron, Ill. Her first observations of this insect eating the aphides, are recorded in Vol. I, p. 126, of the same periodical.

The order *Hemiptera*, the true bugs, furnishes us a vast number of injurious insects. Here we find the scale insects, or bark-lice, and the aphides, or plant-lice.

Of the former subdivision, Dr. Fitch mentions a bark-louse found on grape-vines, in June; believed to be the *Lecanium vitis*, of Linnæus. It is hemispherical and brown. A cottony substance was extruded from beneath the shell until July, when minute insects crept out, and scattered over the bark, upon which they fixed themselves.

It is believed that this insect is not very common; I have not seen it myself, but it should be watched for and destroyed before it can increase.

The history of the *Aphides*, and their wonderful procreative powers should be familiar to every one who has to do with vegetation, since almost every kind of leafy plant has one or more species, peculiar to itself. The insects, individually, are very small, but their numbers are almost beyond calculation. They live by suction only, and draw the vital fluids from the plants, which suffer exceedingly from their attacks. Fortunately, these creatures have insect enemies that keep them in check. Among these are the Aphis-Lions, or larvæ of the Golden-eyed and Lace-wing flies, belonging to the order *Neuroptera*, and the Coccinelidæ, or Lady-birds, belonging to the Beetles, *Coleoptera*.

The grape has its peculiar Aphis, called *Aphis vitis* (?) which is described by Mr. Glover, in the Patent Office Report for 1854, p. 79. It is found on the ends of young shoots, during the summer. The insects are black. Another vine-leaf aphis—called *Pemphigus viti folia*, by Dr. Fitch—causes an excrescence to appear on the upper sides of the leaves of some kinds of grape.

In the same order, we find one of the most numerous and troublesome enemies of the grape-vine. It is that which is commonly but erroneously called the Thrips—which belongs to another group. This insect, which is familiar to every vine-dresser, is the *Tettigonia (Erythroneura) vitis*, of Harris, described and exemplified before the Cincinnati Horticultural Society, as such, in 1865, by the appropriate committee, who begged that it should no longer be called "Thrips," nor Thrip.

The instructive and amusing, as well as learned editor of the *Practical Entomologist*, has given a thorough exposition of these insects, in the February number of this year (1867), to which the reader is referred. His illustrations are distinct, and enable any one to identify the insect. The editor, Mr. B. D. Walsh, mentions seven distinct species, that feed upon the grape-vine, in North America.

These creatures are so numerous by September, that when the leaves are disturbed, and they fly and leap out into the air, it seems filled with little specks, for they are quite small. They appear to affect certain varieties of grape more than others. Some of those with thin foliage have their leaves almost entirely destroyed by them, while those with thick, substantial leaves, somewhat pubescent on the underside, will entirely escape their ravages, though growing close beside them in the same vineyard. Concord and Hartford will escape, while the Delaware and Clinton suffer.

The next order of insects is a very large one, embracing a great many that are destructive to the vine. The single species mentioned by M. Du Breuil, as the Pyralis, I have not been able to identify, from the limited number of books at my command. It may be introduced into our own country one of these days, and require the expensive and tedious treatment recommended in the text; but, in the meantime, we have insect foes enough of our own, among the Lepidoptera alone, to occupy us in their study and destruction—for, with all insects, it is highly important that we study their habits and become familiar with their ways, in order that we may successfully combat them.   Nor should we ever forget that we have hosts of friends among these creatures, in the cannibal tribes that preserve the balance of power in the great scheme of creation of this world.

This order—the *Lepidoptera*—embraces the butterflies, sphinges, and moths, with their caterpillars; some of each of these divisions are injurious.   The moths are most destructive and numerous.   A few of the most troublesome, only, will be mentioned.

The Fall Web-Worm (*Hyphantria textor*), is nearly omniverous, and is often found enveloping a branch of the vine with its ugly silken web, while the gregarious worms are feeding upon the leaves.   The remedy is to break these off, and destroy them, and it is satisfactory to know that we may kill from two to three hundred of these caterpillars at one operation.   The eggs are deposited on the underside of a leaf, but do not attract attention.   Soon afterward, the watchful eye of the vine-dresser may observe two leaves, attached together by silken webs.   Within this shelter, the young worms are feeding, and may easily be destroyed by the thumb and finger, if taken in time.   They grow to about an inch in length, when they are clothed with whitish hairs; the head and feet are black, and they have a blackish stripe along the back, and another beneath.   The perfect moth is white, 1.25 to 1.35 inch in width.   (Vide *Harris' Report*, p. 358.)

The Tortrices, or Leaf-Rollers, are a family of moths, the pupæ of some of which are quite troublesome in the vineyard. The moths are generally small, prettily marked, and fly only in the evening.   Prominent among these, in our Western vineyards is the *Desmia maculalis,* or Spotted-Winged Sable, better known to the vine-dresser as the Leaf-Folder. This beautiful little moth scatters her eggs—which hatch upon the leaves—into a very active, slender, green worm.

This caterpillar secretes itself, by rolling a leaf upon itself, so as to make a tube of about half an inch diameter, in which it feeds. This fold of the leaf is retained securely by strong bands of beautiful white silk.

These insects begin to appear in June, and continue, throughout the season, to disfigure our vines. They form the pupæ within these rolled leaves. They can best be attacked while in the larval condition, but great dexteriy is required to secure these active little caterpillars, which will quickly escape at either end of the pipe in which they live. They are smooth and shiny, of a pale-green, and move by wriggling to the open end of their shelter, when they drop to the ground and escape, so that many of the rolled leaves will appear empty. Some of the warblers are very fond of these caterpillars.

Pterophorus perisceidactylus, or the Gartered Grape-Vine Plume, is described by Dr. Fitch, in the "New York Agricultural Transactions," and in his "Report," p. 139. He says it is a pale-green worm, half an inch long, which feeds upon the foliage of the grape-vine, after fastening several together with silken threads, so as to form a hollow ball.

The *Obis Myron,* described as the *Chœrocampa Pampinatrix* by Harris, and often called the Vine-Dresser, is quite troublesome in some vineyards. It eats the leaves, and cuts off the bunches of grapes.

The moth emerges from the ground in June, and lays her eggs upon the leaves. The caterpillar is a pale-green, freckled with pale-yellow dots; it becomes a pale, dusky olive when fully grown, and is 2.25 inches in length.

The *Procris Americana,* or the American Forester, is found to be quite troublesome on some vines. The worm is small, and feeds in groups of twenty or more, keeping closely side by side. At first they leave a skeleton of the leaf, but as they grow larger, they consume all but the largest veins. They are yellowish, semi-transparent, and at full size are .60 inch long. The perfect insect is a small moth blue-black, with a bright orange neck.

The *Alypia octo-maculata*, or the Eight-Spotted Forrester, is a light blue caterpillar, 1.25 inch long. In July the worms leave the vine, and spin their cocoons on the ground; the moth is black, its shanks orange; each of the fore-wings has large, yellow spots, the hind-wings have white ones. The width of the insect is 1 to 1.50 inch. It appears in May.

Among the *Sphinges* there are some that attack the vine, and as they are large and voracious, their depredations are to be dreaded. The *Philampelus satellita*, and the *P. Achemon*, literally the vine-lovers, the Satellite and Achemon Sphinges, are large, green worms, that feed upon the vine. They may be found after midsummer, before they descend into the ground to become pupæ. These caterpillars were very abundant in New York last summer (1866).

A tribe of sphinges is called the ÆGERIANS, from the well-known peach-tree borer, *Ægeria exitiosa*. If this is dreaded by the orchardist, how much more its larger cousin, which infests the grape-vine. The *Ægeria polistæformis* is mentioned by Mr. Glover, in the Patent Office Report for 1854, p. 80.

It is said to be very troublesome in North Carolina, attacking all vines except the Scuppernong variety. This insect has attracted very little notice among our western vine-dressers, because, as it works under cover, it has escaped observation, but it is feared that it will increase, and become a serious enemy. Some specimens of the caterpillar, and the vines it had consumed, were brought to the Cincinnati Horticultural Society by Mr. McWilliams, in 1865, when the natural history of the insect was investigated, and reported on.

The eggs are laid near the base of the vine stock, and,

when hatched, the larvæ bore into the bark and wood, descending into the roots, and consuming the substance so that the vine sickens and dies, or breaks off. The full grown worms measure from an inch to an inch and three-quarters in length; they are thick-bodied and whitish. They form a pod or chrysalis similar to that of the peach-tree borer, and from this comes the perfect moth, which is of a dark brown color, tinged with orange, and banded with bright yellow on the edge of the second ring of the body. The fore-wings are dusky, and the hind ones transparent.

The only remedy known is constant inspection of the vines, and an examination of their roots when there is any appearance of disease, and to destroy the worms when found.

Of the *Hymenoptera*, there are some insects that seriously attack the fruit of the vine. Wasps, hornets, and bees, are all of them accused of taking a part in this, and certain gall-flies, breed upon the foliage of some varieties of the grape, producing unpleasant excrescences upon the leaves.

, A new enemy to the vine is described by Samuel H. Scudder, in the March number of the *American Journal of Horticulture*, page 154. It appears to be a genuine white ant, and is said to devour the substance of the roots, excavating the woody fibers, and sometimes leaving only the shell; of course this must be very injurious to the plants. Whether this insect be native, or have been introduced, is not set forth by the writer, but he has adopted the name *Termes flavipes* (of Köllar), who supposed it to have been introduced into Germany from Brazil. He considers it the same insect described by Mr. Haldeman as the *Termes frontalis*. Mr. Scudder says that the head is large, and the body pale or whitish, by which it may be distinguished from our common ants.

In the proceedings of the Cincinnati Horticultural Society, there has been quite a discussion as to the ravages committed

by the bees, and a paper was prepared by Mr. George Graham, the President, in which was embodied all that is known
as to the injuries committed by that insect. From this it appears that after the hornets and wasps had punctured the skin,
the bees followed and abstracted the fluids, leaving only the
dry husk. Certain it is that a prejudice prevails among our
vine-dressers against this useful and industrious insect, and
many declare war upon the bees.

There is a slug, the larvæ of the *Selandria vitis*, which is
found upon the leaves of the grape-vine in July. They feed
in companies of a dozen or more, eating the upper surface,
and injuring the foliage. At present, these insects are not
numerous in our vineyards, but they may increase, and then
will deface the foliage as badly as their congeners do the
orchards of cherry and pear-trees.

Various remedies have been suggested, such as dusting with
lime and other dry and acrid substances, and syringing with
soap-suds and petroleum, as recommended, by Mr. Parkman,
for the rose-slug. To a gallon of soft-soap, he adds two-
thirds of a pint of petroleum, mixing thoroughly ; he then
dissolves this mixture in half a barrel of water, and applies
with a syringe. But after all, it will be best to exercise
watchful care and observation of the first approaches of this
and all other insects that are injurious, and then a little per-
severing labor, in the way of hand-picking, will enable us to
keep them in check.

In making up these remarks upon the insect depredators of
the vineyard, I have had recourse to various authors, but have
chiefly extracted from my own compilation, the chapter on
"Insects," in the volume of *American Pomology*,* just published,
where credit is given to the different authorities. Many of
the statements have been personally verified by myself, and

* American Pomology :—The Apple. Orange Judd & Co., New York.

that compendium has been revised by my kind friend, E. T. Cresson, of Philadelphia, an eminent entomologist.

It is hoped that this very condensed account of these pests may serve as a guide to direct the vine-dresser to investigate, and to study the habits of these very interesting creatures, so as to enable him more successfully to combat them.

Every one should study the insects for himself, and become acquainted with their wonderful ways. The student will be delighted with their curious instincts, and he will soon see abundant evidence of the design of the Creator in this department of His universe. The beautiful checks and balances that make up the harmonies of nature, will soon attract his attention, and he will be delighted to find that among insects, despised though they be, there are many that are constantly working in aid of man, and doing more, by checking the increase of those that are injurious, than he, with all his boasted powers, could effect.

And now, before leaving this branch of the subject, let your friend urge upon every one of the readers of these pages, to subscribe to the monthly publication so often referred to— the *Practical Entomologist.**]

Slugs, Snails.—Besides insects we must also mention snails, as they do considerable damage by devouring the young shoots in the spring, so as not to leave a single one. At this period they cover the stakes, and the stems of the plants; it is advisable then, to have them collected by women and children. In some localities a certain price is agreed upon for each measure of slugs collected. It has struck us that the sulphur process, employed to prevent oïdium, tended, in a great measure, to do away with the slugs.

---

* E. T. Cresson, Philadelphia. Fifty cents a year. One Dollar for the two years, from the beginning.

XIV.

VINTAGE.

GRAPE-GATHERING terminates the series of annual operations involved in the culture of the vineyard. The first question, then, to be settled, is the degree of ripeness the crop ought to have.

DEGREE OF RIPENESS OF THE GRAPES.—It is always an advantage, the quality of the wine being the chief object, to allow the grapes to attain their highest degree of ripeness. This condition is indicated by the combination of the following signs:

1. The ends of the stems turn from green to brown.

2. The bunch hangs down.

3. The berry loses all its toughness; its pellicle becomes thin and transparent.

4. The berries come off with ease.

5. The juice of the grape is pleasant, sweet, thick, and sticky.

6. The seeds are free from any glutinous substance.

All other things being equal, however, dark grapes offer these signs sooner than white ones.

There are circumstances owing to which the grape-gathering should precede these signs; on the other hand, there are others which require that it should follow at a long interval.

Thus, in several localities in the north of France, the grape seldom reaches the degree of ripeness we have just indicated; nevertheless, the crop must be gathered, otherwise it will rot through the wet fall weather. In such localities the gathering should be done when it is seen that the grapes no longer derive benefit from the stock. Grapes intended for the manufacture of sparkling wines should also be gathered before they fully ripen. The same holds good for the white grapes of the South, intended for the manufacture of dry wines.

On the contrary, very alcoholic wines may be obtained by allowing the grapes to remain a long while on the plant. It is thus that at Rivesaltes, and in the isles of Candia and Cyprus, the grape is allowed to shrivel before it is cut. The same is done with regard to the alcoholic wines of Spain. Those of Arbois and Château-Chalon in Franche-Comté are obtained from grapes which are not gathered till December. At Condrieux the vintage takes place in November. On the hill-sides of Saumur the white grapes are not cut until their pellicle shows some sign of decay.

[A very common error, often committed in this country, is the premature harvesting of the crop. Grapes should never be gathered until perfectly ripe, if it be possible to avoid it. Up to that period there are changes going on within the economy of the fruit that tend greatly to its improvement; these consist in the transformation of the elements into sugar; this is attended by the diminution of the acids, particularly those which are injurious to the wine. The more complete ripening of the grape also results in the evaporation of a portion of the watery fluids. The amount of wine produced to the acre may be diminished, but a corresponding improvement in the quality will be observed.]

Formerly, the vintage time was everywhere fixed by ordinances. That custom has been preserved in most districts, but it has lately been abolished in some, as affecting the liberty of the individual without any real benefit to the country. These vintage ordinances take away every excuse for robbery, but they have great drawbacks, especially in districts where the vine is cultivated on a small scale. The red growths, for instance, ripen sooner than the white; young and vigorous vines, and vines recently manured, ripen later than old vines, and such as grow in poor soils. Grapes of the same kind will often be seen rotting in the low grounds when they are not yet ripe on the hill-sides. It is thus impossible to satisfy all demands, and it is sometimes difficult to silence some great private interests in the presence of the less eloquent ones of the mass of small growers.

When the vintage time has arrived, a succession of fine days must be taken advantage of, and the work should not be begun until after the sun has evaporated the dew. The bunches have then lost their superabundant moisture, and the wine will be of superior quality.

In vineyards where the quality of the wine is an especial object, the vintage is made at two or three different times. At the first operation, the finest and ripest bunches are collected, and from these a first-class wine is obtained; another gathering gives a wine of second quality, and lastly, the inferior bunches are collected, and yield a wine of third quality.

RECEPTACLES EMPLOYED IN MAKING THE VINTAGE.—There are two kinds of receptacles required in collecting and transporting the vintage.

1st. *Vintagers' Baskets and Buckets.*—These receptacles

vary greatly in form, according to localities, but they should not hold more than fifteen quarts, that the vintagers may easily carry them from vine to vine, and they must be perfectly water-tight, so that the juice of the

[FIG. 141.]—*Vintage-Basket of Bordelais.*

[FIG. 142.]—*Vintage Tub of Bordelais.*

riper grapes may not be lost.   In the district of Bordeaux, these baskets are made of wood, and have one of the two shapes shown in *Figures* 141 and 142.

[FIG. 143.]—*Vintage Tub of Bordelais.*

[FIG. 144.]—*Side view of Dorser, used in the Vineyards of the Jura.*

2d. *Tubs, Dorsers, Etc.*—These names are given to another kind of receptacle, intended to receive the grapes from the baskets, to be then taken directly to the wine-press.   The shape of these also varies

according to localities; they should be water-tight, like
the baskets. They should all have the same capacity,
so that the quantity of the crop may at once be ascertained from the number of tubs brought into the wine-
press. If the distance between the vineyard and the
wine-press is trifling, these tubs are borne on the head,
in which case they hold twenty-five quarts, and have
the shape shown in *Figure* 143. At times, they have
the shape of a dorser of the same capacity. This dorser, which has two arm-straps [Figures 144 and 145],
has a cushion, which prevents the bearer being bruised

[FIG. 145.] — *Front
view of Dorser used
in the Jura.*

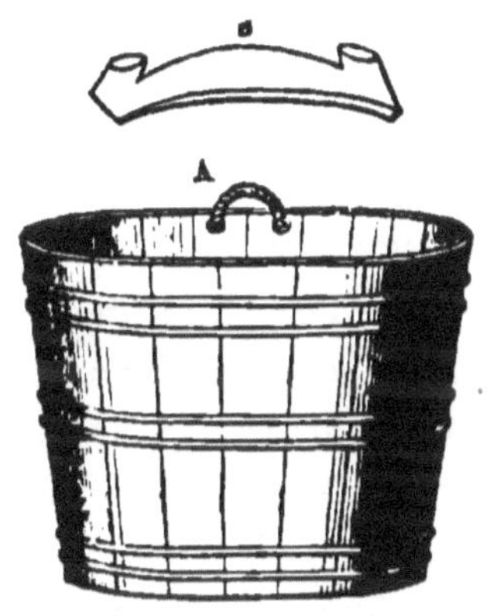

[FIG. 146.] — *Large Tub,
drawn by Horse, for the
Carriage of Grapes.*

by the pressure of the vessel. When the distance from
the vineyard to the wine-press is too great, and the
vineyard is intersected by roads, rendering that mode of
transportation feasible, the grapes are transferred by
means of horses. The capacity of the dorsers is then
fifty quarts, and they have an oval form [Fig. 146]

Two tubs are fastened to a horse's back, by means of the saddle, B, and the handle, A.

Finally, if the distance from the vineyard to the wine-press is very great—say from three-quarters to one and a half mile—it will be advantageous to employ some vehicle, provided it can pass freely over the roads in the vineyard. On this vehicle should be placed tubs holding twenty-six gallons, each, and having an oval form, to allow of their being packed closely in the vehicle, and two handles, so that they may be easily loaded and unloaded.

These different receptacles are inspected with care; some days before the vintage; they are coopered, and then they are soaked, so as to become perfectly water-tight.

Vintagers.—Four squads of workmen are requisite for the grape-gathering.

1st. *Cutters.*—This is the most numerous squad, and the one intrusted with the least fatiguing work, that of removing the grapes from the vines. For this reason, women, children, and old men are employed on it. Each cutter should be provided with a vintager's basket and a pruning-knife, or shears, to cut the grapes. The shears are preferable, as, in cutting the bunch, one is less liable to break off and lose the berries. When the cutters begin work, each places himself at one end of a line of plants in regular succession, and proceeds to the other extremity; from thence they begin on another series of lines, nearest to the last, and work in the opposite direction. The number of cutters should be such that the produce of one day's gathering may suffice for one *pressing*, that being the only way to obtain a uniform fermentation. A squad of twenty cutters can gather about 1,056 gallons of grapes per day; there may be more, if the grapes are abundant, and less, of course, if the same quantity of produce is spread over a larger surface.

2d. *Basket-Carriers.*—These bring empty baskets to the cutters, and empty the full ones into the tubs. It is also their duty to see that the cutters leave no bunches behind, and that all the berries which may have fallen to the ground be carefully picked up. One basket-carrier can wait upon five cutters.

3d. *Porters, or Tub-Carriers.*—The task of these workmen is to carry the tubs on their heads or backs, to the wine-press, and bring them back empty; or they drive the horses or vehicle, if the distance be great. We can not lay down positively what should be the number of these porters—that must depend upon the distance to be gone over—so that the cutters and basket-carriers may not have to wait their return.

4th. *Superintendents of Vintage.*—The duty of these is to superintend the entire work; to see that the cutters may not have to wait for empty baskets, and that the basket-carriers may always have porters ready to attend to them. One superintendent may attend to twenty cutters and four basket-carriers.

Picking and Cleaning the Grapes.—The cutters, as they fill their baskets, should take care that along with the grapes they allow no foreign substances, such as leaves, shoots, etc., to enter into the baskets. These things, if introduced into the vat, always hurt the quality of the wine. In districts where the utmost care is bestowed on the process of wine-making, sorting

and cleaning the grapes must be attended to. Such
bunches, or portions of bunches as are not sufficiently
ripe, or are affected in any way, by rot, scorching, etc.,
are put aside. This picking may be done in three different ways : sometimes the cutters are intrusted with
the duty, in which case they are provided with scissors,
which serve, also, for cutting the grapes. They throw
into a basket, set for that purpose between two cutters,
the refuse we have just spoken of, which is afterward
consigned to a tub, also set apart for that purpose.
Sometimes this picking is done by a woman, at the
time when the baskets are emptied into the tubs. Lastly, this work is often done at the wine-press, as the tubs
are brought in, and just before the grapes are crushed.
There the work can be done more completely, and conveniently. The refuse of these pickings often serves
for making wine-cider for the vine-dressers.

XV.

DIFFERENT MODES OF WORKING A VINEYARD.

A VINEYARD may be worked by means of the
three different methods applicable to all landed
property, that is to say, *renting, letting out on shares,* and
working by the proprietor himself.

RENTING.—Renting is undoubtedly the way of obtaining the revenue of a vineyard with the least care
and trouble to the owner. Nevertheless, it would be a
great mistake to suppose that this species of contract
releases the owner from the care of overlooking his

vineyard. The fact is, the farmer and the proprietor have opposite interests ; the first wishes to draw from the soil all that can possibly be obtained from it, even at the expense of the stock of the vineyard, so that he leaves it depreciated in value. The owner, on the other hand, not only wishes to see his property remain unaltered, but rather enhanced in value.

The terms of the contract must be so arranged as to reconcile these rival interests, and the proprietor's active superintendence is needed, to see that they are fulfilled ; but do what he may, the owner is the party whose interests most usually suffer. The difficulties of renting become much more serious with large vineyards. First, this particular culture, to be really profitable, requires a very large working capital. Frosts, the rot, the bad quality of the produce arising from deficient ripeness, oïdium, hurtful insects, hail, etc., are, from their frequent recurrence, so many causes of this being an uncertain crop. A good and abundant crop scarcely occurs once in four years, sufficient to pay the cost of cultivation which must have been carried on during the years of failure. These circumstances compel the farmer to demand a long lease, as otherwise he would run the risk of not making up for bad years by a sufficient number of good crops. But these long leases are with difficulty consented to by the proprietors, who are thereby hindered, for a long series of years, from freely disposing of their lands. Finally, supposing one to be willing to lease out his property for so long a period, and supposing him to have found a farmer having a capital adequate to the undertaking, there will still remain the difficulty of protecting the vineyard from the rapacity of the farmer during the latter years of his lease. By cutting down the necessary expenses of cultivation, and forcing the produce of the plants beyond bounds, the farmer may leave the vineyard in such a state that several years will be required to restore it to its original healthy condition, and even, in some cases, require it to be renewed by an entirely new planting. These abuses, it is true, the owner may try to prevent by the clauses of the lease, but the details of this particular culture are even less easily regulated than those of other branches of agriculture, so that such clauses would, in most cases, prove of no force, and their rigid execution would give rise to contests which would be perpetually renewed between the owner and the farmer. In short, the drawbacks we have just pointed out, as attending the system of renting vineyards, are so serious that this method of working them is seldom resorted to.

LETTING OUT ON SHARES.—This system of working is a species of partnership between the owner of the vineyerd, and the person cultivating it. The owner furnishes the land, and a greater or less number of the cattle, implements, seeds, etc. The lessee furnishes his labor and the balance of cattle, implements, etc., requisite in the working of the vineyard. For the rest, the proportion in which the owner and the lessee contribute the cattle, implements, etc., is very variable, according to the locality. There are certain poor districts in which the lessee only furnishes his labor. The product of the working is then divided between the owner and the cultivator, in proportion to the contributions of each.

Although the working of vineyards on shares is not very common, it is yet more in use than renting. But it has also its objections. In the first place, the owner has not full liberty to apply those modes of cultivation he may deem advisable to introduce into his vineyard ; he must obtain the consent of his lessee, who, on his side, may apprehend that his interests will suffer through such innovations. This consent is all the more necessary if, as usually happens, these innovations demand an increased expenditure, and the owner wishes to levy on the products the interest of the capital employed. Again, when through any of the accidents we have enumerated, the crop of the vineyard is destroyed, during one, or several consecutive years, and the lessee has not managed to create a reserve fund for himself, the owner is obliged to make him advances of money which he has often great difficulty in recovering. This mode of working, moreover, has one of the drawbacks we have indicated as attending that of renting, when the farmer's lease is about to expire. It is the lessee's interest to extract from the vineyard the greatest amount of product possible, and that without regard to the duration of the plants ; and so, some time before the expiration of the contract binding him to the proprietor, he may so prune the plants as to increase their yield, but, at the same time, cause their complete exhaustion. Lastly, this system requires the frequent presence of the owner, who ought constantly to overlook the work, and see that it is properly executed, and who, at all events, should be present at the gathering, in order to divide the produce.

WORKING OF THE VINEYARD BY THE PROPRIETOR.—
The working of the vineyard by the proprietor, is, un-
questionably, the most rational proceeding, when he has
the information necessary for the proper direction of such
culture, and possesses the capital requisite for the advances it demands. He is at full liberty to adopt the
innovations he may think really beneficial, and he avoids
all the drawbacks attendant on the two modes of working described above. But his presence is now more
than ever necessary to superintend the execution of all
the labor; for, as he is the only person to derive a profit
from this culture, no one has a direct interest to help
him in its judicious management. Now, this is a task
which many proprietors will hesitate to undertake. It
entails upon them the necessity of living almost entirely in the country, with their families, and of giving
up, in a great measure, those social relations to which
they have been accustomed. Nevertheless, the management of a vineyard is far less complicated than that
of any other kind of farming on a large scale. The
chief improvements of which the vineyard is susceptible
having been made under the owner's eye, and the order
and mode of executing the annual operations having
been properly settled, the owner's presence will be less
necessary. He may employ a steward, who can direct
the work, and who may receive the owner's instructions
relative to any especial operations. It is in this manner that the greater number of the large vineyards of
Bordeaux, Burgundy, Champagne, and Languedoc, are
administered.

Work Done by the Piece or Day.—As to the manner
of having the work in vineyards performed, it may be

either by the piece or by the day. These two systems have advantages and disadvantages, as in other agricultural labors. Work by the piece proceeds more rapidly, but its execution is often faulty; work by the day is generally better done, but it proceeds more slowly. It will be advisable to have recourse to these two systems, and applying them to the work best adapted to each. Thus, all operations which can be easily directed, such as plowing the land, carriage, distribution, and application of manures, should be done by the piece. But all operations directly applied to the plants, such as pruning, sulphurating, fastening, nipping, and harvesting, should be done by the day. It will, however, be advisable, in either case, to ascertain beforehand, by a preliminary trial, the quantity of work which can be done in one day, so as to enable the proprietor to give the jobbers no more than their due, and to direct the industry of the day-laborers.

THE END.

A NEW EDITION

OF

The Principles and Practice

OF

LAND DRAINAGE;

Embracing a brief History of Underdraining:
A detailed examination of its Operation and Advantages;
A description of various kinds of Drains, with
Practical Directions for their Construction;
The Manufacture of Drain Tile, etc.

ILLUSTRATED BY NEARLY 100 ENGRAVINGS.

By JOHN H. KLIPPART,

Author of the "Wheat Plant;" Corresponding Secretary of the Ohio State
Board of Agriculture, etc.

2nd Edition.   1 Vol. 12mo., Cloth, Price, $1.75.

Within the last few years the subject of Drainage has been
thoroughly studied, and its importance and advantages practically demonstrated by the Agriculturists of Europe, and particularly of Great Britain; while in this country it has received but little attention from farmers generally; so little,
indeed, that when occasionally intelligent men undertake the
thorough drainage of their farms, they usually get credit from
their do-as-my-father-did neighbors, of burying their money
with their tiles.   The resulting improved appearance of their
farms, and the increased quantity and superior quality of their

crops, however, soon convince even the least observant of the profit of burying money in this way. No doubt much money may be and has been expended fruitlessly in ill applied drainage. The subject must be understood, both in theory and application, before any of the great practical results which have been attained, can be secured by every one who undertakes the drainage of his farm. The purpose of this work is to supply that information, in a plain, practical way, easily understood by any intelligent farmer. It tells him the properties of his soil, and how it is affected by drainage; what kind of land needs drainage, when and why it will pay. Some of the advantages of underdraining are summed up and thoroughly explained under the following heads:

1. It removes stagnant waters from the surface.
2. It removes surplus waters from under the surface.
3. It lengthens the working season.
4. It deepens the soil.
5. It warms the undersoil.
6. It equalizes the temperature of the soil during the season of growth.
7. It carries down soluble substances to the roots of the plants.
8. It prevents "freezing out," "heaving out," or "winter killing."
9. It prevents injury from drouth.
10. It improves the quantity and quality of crop; it increases the effect of manures.
11. It prevents rust in wheat and rot in potatoes.

These advantages are not suppositions, but are proved by the actual experience of intelligent men, which is given in detail.

In the second part of the book are given practical directions for the location, cutting, and laying of the various kinds of drains, according to the position and quality of the land;

modes of preventing and removing obstructions in drains; descriptions of the tools, the various improved plows, and other inventions used in the operations; and of the several kinds of tile, their respective advantages, and minute directions for their manufacture, including the selection and working of the materials, molding, drying and baking of the tile, etc., etc.

The whole is illustrated with nearly a hundred engravings of sections of drains, tile, implements, etc.

The work is thorough and comprehensive, and supplies the farmer with all the information which he must possess before he can intelligently and profitably commence operations. It ought to be in the hands of every farmer in the country.

It is handsomely printed and well bound in cloth.

NOTICES OF THE WORK.

From the North-Western Farmer, Indianapolis.

In answer to a query from a subscriber, on the subject of drainage, the editor says:

"Underdraining is a pet theme with us. We advise our subscribers to get a copy of John H. Klippart's work on Land-Drainage, which is undoubtedly the most comprehensive and reliable work, on the subject extant. The Publishers, Robert Clarke & Co., of Cincinnati, have just issued a new and improved edition of the book, which anticipates and answers every question our subscriber has, or can well raise, on the subject of drainage, and no farmer can well afford to be without a copy."

From the Boston Cultivator.

" This is a very comprehensive work, in regard to the history and advantages of drainage, and will be found highly useful to most of our farmers. We recommend this book as worthy the attention of all farmers, who are interested in the subject of land-drainage."